SARASWATI

SARASWATI

GURNAIK JOHAL

First published in Great Britain in 2025 by Serpent's Tail,
an imprint of PROFILE BOOKS LTD
29 Cloth Fair
London
EC1A 7JQ

www.serpentstail.com

Copyright © Gurnaik Johal, 2025

1 3 5 7 9 10 8 6 4 2

Typeset in Tramuntana Text by MacGuru Ltd

Printed and bound in Great Britain by
CPI Group (UK) Ltd, Croydon CR0 4YY

The moral right of the author has been asserted.

A CIP catalogue record for this book is available from the British Library.

We make every effort to make sure our products are safe for the purpose for which they are
intended. For more information check our website or contact Authorised Rep Compliance Ltd.,
Ground Floor, 71 Lower Baggot Street, Dublin, D02 P593, Ireland, www.arccompliance.com

HARDBACK ISBN 978 1 78816 948 6
TRADE PAPERBACK ISBN 978 1 80522 581 2
eISBN 978 1 78283 921 7

Contents

——

SUTLEJ

A pond equals ten wells, a reservoir equals ten ponds, while a son equals ten reservoirs, and a tree equals ten sons.

Matsya Purana, 154:512

October

There was water in the dead well. It might have been a trick of the light, Satnam thought, or his eyes – his contact lenses in the suitcase Air India had lost – or maybe he was seeing things, still a little light-headed from the drive, from the hours of conditioned air in the rented hybrid, driving up to the Sutlej and back to the farm, his parents looking out at the passing view, noting how things had changed, how nothing was the same, and Satnam nodding along, the emptied urn snug between his knees, warm. But here it was, water: a reflection. He looked down at himself looking up.

He'd asked his bibi about the well the last time he was in Punjab, when he was a child. It had been dry for as long as she could remember, she'd said, his dad translating. The farms around Hakra relied on electric pumps to survive, which were lengthened every few years to reach the ever-receding groundwater – perfect, plastic roots. Still, on some evenings, Bibi would walk to the dead well at the corner of her square plot, and that summer Satnam would follow. She would light the candles sheltered in a small makeshift shrine on one side of the well, and then a cigarette, which she didn't smoke. Satnam would watch it burn out like incense, trying to guess the exact moment the lengthening ash would fall. When Bibi was done thinking, she'd flick the butt into the opening, one more piece of confetti. His parents had explained that the shrine was a samadhi: 'Tradition,' his mum said; 'Superstition,' his dad. It was about honouring ancestors, they agreed, remembering the dead.

Satnam leant over the edge of the well and felt something move within him, like the bubble in a spirit level. His left ear was yet to pop from the flight, his body caught between varying pressures. A bead of sweat dropped from his lip into the dark, the sun eclipsed on the surface by his shadowy face. Featureless, he could have been any number of people before him, reaching for water.

He picked up the bucket, which he remembered using as a basketball hoop when playing with Pala, whose family lived in the annex. Back then, he hadn't realised that it was Pala's family who did the work on the farm. He'd believed that it was all Bibi.

The candles of the samadhi were still in their place, along with a lighter. Satnam lit one of the wicks and lowered the bucket. Pala had bet that he could throw Satnam's orange bouncy ball so hard into the well that it would come back. Satnam had stood ready to catch. It must still be down there, the ball, he thought, outlasting them all. He pulled the frayed rope across the ragged brick lip as the bucket made contact. There was a satisfying weight to it as he lifted it up. The water was cold, clear. He'd been told to test bottle caps, avoid ice cubes – 'You're not made like us,' his dad had said – but he drank from the bucket anyway, washing his face, feeling human again.

The droplets that fell from his short hair darkened the dirt in spots which were gone when he looked down again. At last, there was the sense of some movement in the air, and a soft breeze cut across the golden crop, lifting the acrid scent of pesticides with a sound like the hissing of mustard seeds blooming in oil. According to Bibi's will, this farm and the house at the edge of it were now his.

All his. He had no siblings, and his father's sister had long fallen out with her mother. But why not leave it to his parents? He figured it might have something to do with his recent work at VertiCrop and his interest in growing food when he was young. He'd kept Bibi's vegetable patch going in Wolverhampton after she'd moved back to Punjab, would wordlessly show her the tomato vines and chillies on Face-Time and she'd say her one English phrase – 'Good luck' – which Satnam understood to mean 'great', 'well done' or 'goodbye', depending on tone.

It had been years since Bibi's small plot had turned any form of profit. The Hakra farm once grew mustard and gram, but Pala, its sole worker, had long given in to the increased demand for rice, shipping in water by the truckload once the monsoon began, forming artificial paddies on the arid land, the weight of the water across the state causing the ground to depress over the exhausted aquifer. The seasons didn't mean what they used to, the old borders eroding between summer and winter. Bibi had joked that the only seasons she now knew were rice and wheat.

Anyone with sense had sold, his father said; developers were circling. Villages like this, which had seemed so distant from anything when Satnam was a child, were being steadily consumed by aimless sprawl: you could Swiggy a Burger King here now, order manure on Flipkart. As the world changed around her, Bibi was marooned by her stubbornness. She would never sell. She wouldn't even buy the tractor Pala had asked for – he had only one water buffalo left to help plough. Satnam watched her fanning her tail now, sitting in what was left of the house's shade.

As a child, Satnam couldn't understand why Bibi had chosen

3

to live here, with the constant smell of drying dung, instead of in their semi-detached in Wolves, with its time-release Glades in every second plug socket. India, as he'd understood it, was a place for leaving. In the years after she returned to Punjab, he had questions for her but didn't know how to ask them. On their clipped video calls, he'd stick to the same few talking points, so that a conversation could be performed, even if little was actually communicated. He knew how to ask about the weather, her plans for dinner and how the buffalos were doing. The only buffalo left now was thin. Her skin hung slack from her ribs. She yawned and looked back at the door as Satnam's parents appeared, followed by the lawyer. He couldn't believe how quickly they were arranging for the land to be sold, just hours after spreading the ashes.

'We've hardly any compassionate leave,' Mum said.

'Not all of us have your free time,' Dad said.

Satnam was still living off severance. He called them over, wondering, as the lawyer's scooter turned down the dirt road, raising dust and fumes, how far down the river Bibi's ash was now, and where it would be by the time they flew back to England. His parents walked through the haze towards him.

'This has to change the asking,' his dad said, looking down into the well.

His mum shook her head. 'My money's on rain.'

Pala arrived that evening to pay his respects. He said the monsoon, like a bad lover, hadn't lasted long. There had been no rain in weeks. The nearby Hawthorn Reservoir was empty and the Hakra co-op had agreed to pool funds to order in paddy water.

'Last day of October and it's the height of summer.'

The men sat down around a dusty bottle of Glenfiddich. Satnam added flat Coke to his glass; his dad and Pala took it neat. When Pala drank, he winced, revealing wrinkles. He was a few years older than Satnam but dressed as a much younger man. How he could wear such tight jeans in this heat, Satnam didn't know. He wondered if Pala still owned the lucky Wolves shirt his mum had forced him to leave behind on their last visit. It seemed like it might still fit him.

'Did you put any of the paddy water in the well?' Satnam's dad asked, in English.

'No.'

'Strange,' his dad said, before switching back to Punjabi. 'So how come you've been away?'

Satnam couldn't follow as the conversation turned, and asked his dad to translate. Pala's nephew was mute. Bibi had given him money to take the boy to a nearby city to see a specialist. His sister and nephew were still awaiting the appointment, but Pala had come home as soon as he heard about Bibi.

Satnam's dad gave up on interpreting and talked to Pala in quick Punjabi for two more glasses. Satnam let it wash over him, the language meaning less and less as it sped past, becoming music. In the last few months, Harp had insisted on giving him Punjabi lessons; she wouldn't date a coconut, and she would certainly never raise one. Satnam had given in when it became clear that Bibi's memory was failing. She might die before he'd ever truly spoken to her, he thought.

'Isn't it weird,' he'd said to Harp during their first lesson, 'that, when describing the language of animals, we say "song": birdsong, whalesong?'

'We're not doing this if you start wandering off.'

The filmi that Bibi listened to felt a more pure form of music because he couldn't understand the lyrics, as did the bhangra Harp liked. At university, Satnam had lived next door to an exchange student who had got him into French rap, and he'd enjoyed not knowing what was being said whenever they hosted pre-drinks, not having to worry if the lyrics were offensive. He thought back to a work trip to Seoul in his Oracle days, stepping into a cinema to kill time before his delayed flight, the film with its incomprehensible dialogue taking on the characteristics of a dream; he thought of how, when the main characters spoke during the sex scenes, whatever they were saying had the potential to be the hottest thing a person could say, which had reminded him, shamefully, of the time when, as a child, his local gurdwara had installed a projector screen at the front of the hall to show translations of the verses that the Granthis were singing. Up until that moment, he'd believed in God because it seemed strange not to – why else would all the adults he knew sit on the floor in silence? He'd assumed whatever was being sung to be transcendent and whatever was written in the holy book he bowed before each Saturday to contain life's cheat codes. But then, reading from the screens, he could understand what was being sung, and he lost his faith. In an instant, he was a different person, and he'd spend trips to the gurdwara evolving his Pokémon and watching the clock. He'd later liken the experience to the time congregations in England first heard a sermon in a language they understood, abstract Latin giving way to lowly English, the high word of God suddenly commonplace, fixed in meaning, mundane. 'Something that could have been anything becoming one thing,' he'd said to Harp. 'There's no way that can't be disappointing.'

Pala and Satnam's dad talked over one another now, getting louder – Punjabi comprehensible to Satnam in slow straight lines, and then indecipherable at the speed a native spoke. Perhaps this was how infants experienced life, all sound song.

'One more?'

'Go on.'

He'd interpreted Bibi more by the tone of her voice than by what she said; he loved her because he couldn't really know her. Occasionally, his parents would ruin his simplified idealisation of her and he'd catch a glimpse of the real person, her questionable views – too many immigrants, too many

6

handouts – or the different ways she liked to push people, especially her children, away.

'You were always your own person,' Satnam's father had said, on the banks of the Sutlej that morning, before he emptied out the urn.

'Good luck,' Satnam said, when the last of the ash was cast out.

'Again?' Pala said now, in English, as Satnam's dad turned in.

'So, he told you about the water?' Satnam said. 'Pani?'

'Sure, bro.' Pala topped up Satnam's whisky with water.

'No, no. *The water.* I'll show you.'

The night sky glinted like new tarmac. Satnam thought back to the first time he'd met Pala and his sister, Reha. After dinner, while the adults talked, they had sneaked out to play, daring each other to take a step into the pitch-black field, to see who made it furthest from the light of the house. They'd lost each other in the dark and Satnam had felt something move against his foot – a snake, a wolf? He wondered if Pala remembered him running across the field, screaming. His lasting memory of that trip was that it had been the first time he'd grasped the concept of time zones, of jet lag. He could vividly recall telling Pala that he existed six hours in the past.

At the well, Satnam lit one of the candles and held it over the opening. The water looked like oil. Pala pulled up the bucket and brought his cupped hands to his mouth as if in prayer. He laughed, drinking another handful and another. He spoke in Punjabi, or maybe Hindi, his speech shifting into the ordered rhythm of hymn, and Satnam noticed a phrase, a word – no, a name – repeated enough that it rose to the surface: 'Saraswati.'

Grinning, Pala switched to English: 'They were right. It's finally happening. It's really happening.'

November

Satnam slept badly; the village's Diwali fireworks continued deep into the night. When he woke, his parents had gone. They'd driven into the city and left him instructions to show around a prospective buyer who was arriving that afternoon. He texted them, asking if they could buy him underwear and a change of clothes. Wrapped in a wet towel, he washed his only outfit – thick sweats that had seemed a good idea for the flight – in well water and hung them to dry in the courtyard. After twenty minutes on hold, he made it through to a real person at the airline who, clearly following a script, told him they were doing everything they could to locate his missing suitcase. Pacing the courtyard, he decided to take off his towel and hang it on the line. There was a simple thrill to being naked outside. He had the house to himself, a good square acre. Even if Pala was in, he wouldn't be able to see anything from the annex. Satnam carried a cot up to the flat roof of the house so that he could sunbathe.

The new height revealed the level landscape, the grids of yellow and gold. Coming here from London felt like a change in aspect ratio, a shift into widescreen. It shouldn't have been this hot so late in the year, but he wasn't complaining. He lay down on the cot and watched the clouds drift above. The still scene was disturbed only by the restless buffalo in the courtyard below, the clucking of Pala's chicken and the odd buzzing of his phone.

Glancing at the screen, he saw a text from Harp.

Just thought I'd check in?

He turned on flight mode and closed his eyes.

She'd always found it somewhat ridiculous that he could fit all his clothes into a single carry-on – 'Minimalism is so 2014' – but, when he'd packed for this trip, moments after the phone call about Bibi, she'd questioned why he was taking so much. 'A raincoat, Satty? Really – when are you back?'

He'd drafted a long message to Harp on the plane but

deleted it before the descent. Unable to sleep, he'd tried to think of Bibi, attempted to grieve, but his mind kept drifting, he kept tuning into the film the man next to him was watching – a heist gone wrong, the hero drawn into violence – kept looking at the woman who was trying to get her baby to sleep as she walked away from him down the aisle, and then averting his gaze when she walked back. 'The fact that children find it easier to sleep in motion,' he remembered telling Harp, on an early date at a gallery, back when they used to do things like go to galleries, 'is proof that humans, for most of our history, have been migratory. Our bodies,' he said, 'are designed for wandering plains. For walking, constant movement.'

'All this because I wanted to get one taxi.' She pretended to take in a nude, stepping back and then leaning in. She'd later say it was best to let him talk himself out when he entered lecture mode.

'Still water isn't safe,' he said, 'it's supposed to flow. We're supposed to move. It's in us like it's in birds, who one day seem to know it's time to get up and leave. All our problems stem from being sedentary. We weren't supposed to settle. You see it in tribes and stuff. Even the word "settle"—'

'I think this is the one. It feels more measured than the others.'

The exhibition's shtick was that one piece in every room was actually a forgery, but was presented as real, so that every painting in the gallery could have been, may as well have been, fake. The lengths they have to go to try to make art fun, Satnam had thought, before carrying on.

'I was reading this thing ...' he said. 'No, it was a podcast, and they think it's because we lack a predator. Like, a predator that evolved with us, to eat us. Or that there was one and we killed it off. And without that threat, we turned inwards. There was no more running. No need to move. We stagnated, built settlements, turned the energy we'd have spent on the beast on ourselves. War and whatever.'

9

Harp moved on to a window, looking at it as if it were also a piece. 'Sounds like you've latched on to a new thing,' she said.

Protestors were passing below, and Satnam and Harp briefly joined the crowd as they left the gallery, moving on to one bar, and then another, in thickening smog. In a mock-speakeasy in Soho, they bumped into Satnam's line manager from Oracle and his much younger girlfriend. All of a sudden, they were on some kind of cursed double date, squeezed into a booth and surrounded by mirrors, his line manager minesweeping an abandoned Beavertown and telling them all about his latest purchase: a freshwater lake in Latvia.

'A lake?'

'People used to buy bunkers. Now, it's freshwater lakes, man. I'll be laughing.'

A month later, after Satnam had completed a trade with a nut conglomerate in the fertile crescent, on the future price of cashews, his line manager called him into a meeting with exciting news from Chicago. 'They're opening futures trading on water,' he said. 'A new frontier. We want you on it, pronto. What's wrong?'

'I don't know.'

'Annual review's in a month, hombre. It'll be reflected. All your good work will be reflected.'

Harp wasn't as excited about his resignation as he thought she'd be. She was already scanning Indeed for him when he got home.

'Let's go travelling,' he said.

'I'm a doctor, Satty.'

'There's Doctors Without Borders—'

She must have mentioned it to Ore, the friend who had introduced them to each other at university, because he messaged Satnam a week later with an interview offer at the start-up he'd just joined, VertiCrop. They were looking for a 'diversity and inclusion champion' for their people team.

'I'd get a referral fee,' Ore said. 'Amazon vouchers.'

Satnam had previously been strong-armed into heading up Oracle's racial equity network during his first appraisal, but this was taking it all too far. He went to the interview to appease Harp, and ended up getting the job.

VertiCrop grew microgreens in controlled UV-lit environments in a warehouse in Tottenham, which they claimed vastly reduced the amount of water and land used, compared to traditional farming, eliminating the need for pesticides and herbicides, cutting the amount of loss and rot in long-haul transport and the carbon footprint of shipping. *Welcome to tomorrow*, the on-boarding literature said. A not insignificant portion of the job was spent deciding on culturally appropriate snacks for heritage days, ordering in the right bunting. Satnam's success was getting religious holidays to be granted as free leave – though, only for HQ employees and not for those on the ground, who happened to disproportionately contribute to the company's diversity statistics. 'Lettuce doesn't stop growing on Eid. Well, no, it would stop growing and that would be the problem.'

It was a few days after Rosh Hashanah and Navaratri that Satnam was let go. His redundancy package included a box of kale and chard, along with a generous severance. He cooked the greens down for dinner and called Harp, who was away on a hen do.

'Wait, give me a sec, I'll find somewhere quiet.'

'I was saying they let me go. They're making cuts. Turns out growing vegetables without sunshine isn't actually that profitable.'

'Maybe it's a blessing. A door opening a window. What did they offer you?'

'I'll be all right for a minute. I think the time will help.'

'What about Oracle? It was a good role—'

'I'm not going back, Harp.'

'Just floating an idea, I'm not saying anything. It's just words. We were thinking about that deposit, is all. Moving in.'

Conversation turned to the housing market, and then the job market, and then the marriage market. She was happy to get a breather from the girls, who, it seemed, had been a bit too liberal with their advice for her. 'Like, hun, you can't "quiet quit" the ICU.'

As she talked about her friends and their jobs – they all seemed to work in marketing, everyone in London seemed to be working in marketing – the fire alarm went off in the kitchen. His pan was smoking, everything charred. Satnam muted himself while he opened the windows, and, hearing Harp go on – she seemed utterly oblivious to the fact that she too had a 'lecture mode' – he started to speak.

'Can you hear me?' he tested.

'At a certain number of shitty boyfriends, it becomes a question of taste rather than fate ...' She clearly couldn't.

'I've been having doubts,' he said, trying it on for size. 'I'm not sure about moving forward. I like where we are, where we've been. But—'

'But, yeah, I'd call it flirting. If it was me. There's girl code, but how far do you go?'

'I feel like you're supposed to know about these things. To be certain. But I'm not.' There was no escaping cliché. If anything, he was thankful for the set phrases. 'It's nothing you've done. It's just this feeling. Or lack of it.'

'I shouldn't say anything though, right? Are you there? Can you hear me?'

He unmuted himself and replied.

After hanging up, he decided to end things the day she got back from the trip. She had such a certain idea of the future, and it scared him that he could just drift into it without ever really knowing what kind of a life it was he wanted himself. The question was at which point in the evening to say anything. At the station, on the bus or on the walk home?

When he did meet her, it was clear the moment wasn't right.

'I wanted to be cute,' she said, as he took her suitcase, 'but

I'm feeling so rough.' The girls had pulled an all-nighter ahead of their 7 a.m. flight. 'I feel like death, destroyer of worlds.'

Satnam went for a walk while she took a nap. He left his phone at home, wanting silence. He was the only dogless person in the park. A bad person, ready to do a bad thing.

With new resolve, he arrived home to find Harp waiting for him in the hallway.

'Your phone was ringing and ringing. So I answered it.'

'What's up?'

'Call your mum, Satty. It's your bibi.'

There was a knock at the gate below and Satnam woke, struggling to adjust to the glare. The knocking continued. He reached for his phone to check the time, but it was dead.

'Hello!' The knocking intensified. 'Oh, hello!'

Was it the buyer? Had he slept for that long?

'For the appointment?' the voice continued.

Satnam looked at himself. He knew he should rush downstairs to put on his clothes and greet the developer, but he didn't move.

He heard the buyer talk on the phone, probably to Satnam's parents, who, no doubt, would soon try to reach him. He figured he could claim that he slept through the appointment. Jet lag. His phone had been dead. It was all essentially true. The man knocked on the gate again, shook the chain. 'We said two o'clock?'

There was a pause. Footsteps. Satnam imagined him giving in, turning back to his car, and let out a long breath. His parents would be pissed, but it was nothing he couldn't weather. The silence lengthened and he relaxed. But then, a minute later, there was the sound of the chain, of a key in the lock, and then a second voice: Pala.

Pala spoke to the man in quick Punjabi, probably explaining that the seller's son must have gone out. They walked across the courtyard, one of them wearing flip-flops. There was the sound of the kitchen door opening and shutting, echoed by the mosquito guard.

Satnam felt profoundly naked.

His pubes sparkled with sweat. His towel and the only clothes he had were hanging on the line in the courtyard. Maybe he could make a dash for his parents' bedroom to get to his dad's suitcase? Or make it to the toilet, which he could lock? But he could hear running water, the shower, which meant they were up there already, right across the hall from the bedrooms. For a moment, he thought they might not come up to the roof, but the generator was up here, as was the water tank, both of which the buyer would likely want to see. Though, maybe not if the man already intended to knock the building down? The two men laughed about something. A window opened, shutters clattered. A few minutes passed before the back door opened. There was the staccato sound of flip-flops on steps, getting louder, closer.

The house was two storeys tall.

Maybe he could stick the landing?

Pala's voice was undeniable: he said something, and something else, and Satnam heard an English word in the midst of it all – 'tank'. He felt himself shrink. He could call out and tell them not to come up, that he wasn't decent, but what if they thought he was some pervert? Coming naked up to the roof – his dead grandmother's roof – to do what exactly? Satnam lay down on the cot, resigned to his fate, and shut his eyes. He left his mouth open a touch, turned a little to hide his penis, but tossed again, debating whether it was more humiliating to show cock or arse.

The footsteps stopped. Satnam tensed. Pala cleared his throat, but Satnam remained motionless. After a pause, the men returned down and, when Satnam finally opened his eyes, a towel was hanging on the handrail in the stairway.

Down in the courtyard, he smiled at Pala and the man.

'There's no sun this time of year, back home,' he said in English. 'I was ... yeah. Hello.'

'Foreign-returned,' Pala said to the buyer, by way of explanation.

'Well, I think I've seen all that I need to,' the man said.

'Not everything,' Pala said. 'You have to see the well.'

When they crossed the field, the man couldn't believe the water had returned.

'Does anyone know?' he said. 'The authorities?'

Due to their limited baggage allowance, almost everything of Bibi's was given away. Locals arrived in their courtyard, quietly picking over her things – the clothes, the pots, the non-perishables. Satnam felt the need to document, to preserve the moment in case it might register emotionally in the future. He could offset his grief. He was conscious that he was yet to cry.

He photographed her things: the TV remote with three numbers worn smooth, her kirpan and kara, the safe under her bed that they were unable to open, stacks of gossip magazines and a stockpile of cigarettes. It all formed some sort of portrait. Maybe, in the end, we were known by our things, like magpies, pharaohs.

'Why on earth do we need a picture of cigarettes?'

'We'll forget.'

'What's worth remembering about her smoking?'

'The fact that she didn't smoke.'

His dad picked up the wooden safe and shook it. Something moved inside. He reached for a screwdriver, trying to loosen the screws on the back. Giving up, he returned a few moments later with a hammer.

Satnam had expected money or jewellery, but nothing inside seemed to warrant being locked away. There were seven large pieces of folded cloth, and in among them a notebook, itself containing a small scrap of red fabric, a bookmark between two pages.

His mum inspected the little red square and put it in the bin pile.

Satnam unfolded one of the large cloths and shook out the splintered wood.

'It's a phulkari dupatta,' his mum said. 'Looks handmade. Rare, these days.'

'Rare?'

'People don't know how to make them anymore. Not like this, anyway – this is impressive. It's forgotten. Old-folk stuff.'

'So, Bibi made these?'

'The only needle she could use was on her record player,' his dad said. 'They were probably passed down or something.'

'So you remember them?'

'Son, I can't even tell you what day of the week it is.'

Satnam took the seven phulkari dupattas out into the court-yard and pegged them to the washing line. They hung still in the dry air as he took photos.

The first was green and yellow, the pattern showing crops, fields. The second was patterned around circular rings rather than a grid, and the third was less detailed: several blue lines weaved together on white cotton, all meeting at one end of the piece, the way the branches of a tree meet its trunk. Satnam's mum unpegged the cloth and turned it upside down, the branches roots: seven rivers coming from one source. The fourth was made up of the colours of fire, while the fifth was completely white. Up close, he could see a white cow stitched at its centre, four white streams of milk coming from her udders. The sixth had an abstract pattern that looked like hair, and the seventh, which seemed unfinished, showed the begin-nings of a spiderweb. In each piece there was a line of gold thread, but other than that one detail, there was such a vari-ance of colour and style that they might have been made by different people.

Satnam tried to capture all seven pieces at once. The breeze returned and they danced like prayer flags. As they moved, Satnam, looking through his viewfinder, saw all the way out of the open gate and across the farm, up to the well, where a blurred crowd of people had gathered and a fight had broken out.

A dozen people were talking, shouting, at once. Pala stepped up on to the lip of the well, and it was unclear if he was trying to calm the people down or rile them up. Satnam assumed that most of the men were farmers: the calloused hands, the dirt under the nails. Several of them were clearly Sikh, wearing turbans and kirpans, and Satnam would have guessed that the others were a mix of Hindus and Muslims. They were filming on their phones, taking pictures of the well. The water level had risen even further. If Pala slipped, he wouldn't have a long way to fall.

Satnam's parents arrived behind him. His father was out of breath, and listened for a few seconds before shouting himself. Whatever it was he was saying had an effect on the crowd. The other men stopped to listen, and then Pala stepped down from the well. Satnam could slowly make out the gist of the dispute, but none of the specifics. There were a few English words that helped: 'groundwater', 'canal', 'government', 'science'. And one familiar sound continued to come up in the argument: 'Saraswati', 'Saraswati'.

Eventually, the people left. One of the women, still holding one of Bibi's old pans, filled it to the brim with well water and walked slowly across the field, careful not to lose a drop.

In the shade, Satnam's dad attempted to explain. Only a few farms in the area had seen anything return to their wells, and many were complaining about the unfair distribution of water. People wanted it shared, for trenches to be dug—

'That's not really it,' his mum said. 'There's all that bakwas about the river.'

'Don't get me started,' his dad said.

'What river?' Satnam said.

'They seem to believe, some of them, that the water is evidence that some river has returned beneath the ground.'

'A holy river. The Saraswati.'

Pocketing a packet of Bibi's cigarettes, Satnam walked out to the well that night to find the lighter stored in the samadhi. He crossed the dark field without his phone torch, and let his eyes adjust. The night, which at first appeared utterly silent, slowly increased in volume to accommodate distant cars, nocturnal birds, insects. Despite the light of the moon, which appeared closer here than it did in London, Satnam failed to see the body by the well.

'Jesus!' he said, almost tripping over it.

It was Pala.

'You're camping out here?' Satnam said.

After the commotion today, Pala explained, sitting up, he wanted to keep watch over the well. Satnam asked what it was that needed protecting, and Pala told him that the water was the body of the goddess – or did he say the mother? – Saraswati.

'A long time ago,' he said, 'here, there was the greatest river ever. The most special river. More so than Ganga. But then Ma Saraswati disappeared underground, vanished. They tried to tell us she was never here, that it was myth. But here she is, returning.'

'Right.'

'I'm not good at putting it in English words, but come tomorrow, you'll see.'

The next day, Pala's sister, Reha, and her son, Emperor, returned from the city. At Pala's instruction, she had cut their visit short, missing an appointment with the language therapist so they could meet the priest. Satnam met them at the well. Reha didn't make eye contact with him and, as Pala hadn't properly introduced them, Satnam didn't strike up a conversation. He tried in vain to play with the child and was glad to be interrupted when Pala's phone rang. Pala seemed to be giving directions; a few minutes later, a Range Rover appeared on the dirt road.

'The Brahmin,' Pala said, for Satnam's sake. He fixed his hair and grinned wildly at his sister, so that she could check if there was anything in his teeth.

It was a large car for such a small man. As his loose-fitting robes whipped around in the breeze, Satnam could make out the contours of his skinny frame. He looked much too young to be any kind of religious authority. Satnam was conservative enough to believe doctors, police officers and priests should be older than those to whom they administered. It felt wrong to take spiritual advice from someone wearing an Apple Watch, to hear of the divine from a man with an uneven skin fade.

Before talking to Satnam or Pala, the Brahmin looked down into the well. He let out a deep breath, almost a sigh, like a builder assessing a job and mentally calculating a quote.

'Yes,' he said, as he drank the water. He then turned to Satnam and shook his hand, without drying it first. 'Kush Bhatt,' he said, introducing himself. He had a deep voice for a man with such a soft handshake. 'It's a pleasure,' he said, in received pronunciation.

Without acknowledging Reha, he turned from Pala to the boy. Satnam was able to translate parts of what was said, piecing together the sense of it, if not the sentences themselves, from the disparate words, like someone making constellations from stars.

The boy doesn't speak.

Kush began a prayer. Pala filled a plastic bottle with well

water. He made the boy drink from it, and when the boy turned away, he held him in place, forcing the water down.

'Speak,' Kush said, after finishing the lengthy prayer. 'Speak!'

The boy, unable to move, cried.

Pala said something, excitedly, which Satnam thought might mean, *It's working!*

'Speak!'

Pala continued to douse him with the water, covering his head. The boy's cry revolved around a repeated sound, which Satnam would have believed meant nothing, were it not for the look of excitement on his parents' faces and Kush's satisfied smile. Maybe it was a word. It might well have been.

That afternoon, Satnam received a call from the airline to tell him his bag had been found and was on its way. The courier arrived the next evening.

It wasn't his. It was the right brand and design, but a darker grey, and the lock was a different make. It was the bag he'd seen disappear and reappear again on the conveyor belt, after everyone from his flight had left, and he hadn't clocked what had happened then, stressed about being late for the ceremony, but now it was clear. Someone had taken his suitcase, thinking it was theirs.

'This isn't mine,' Satnam said to the courier.

'They only pay one way,' the courier said, before driving off.

Inside, Satnam tested his own combination on the lock, pointlessly. He tried to picture the person who'd taken his suitcase, imagining them walking down the airport's empty halls until they reached their connection. They'd be halfway across the world, arriving at home or a hotel by the time the penny dropped. How had they not noticed the colour? They would turn the numbers at random, curious – it wasn't beyond the realm of possibility that they might happen upon the code, 1993, or perhaps they'd reach for a knife. They'd then lay out the contents on their bed, before slowly taking off their own clothes. They'd try on his Calvin's, his Levi's, and maybe they'd fit, as would the pile of identical black T-shirts, his shed skin. He could see them slipping into his life as it had been – as he felt it could be no longer – as easily as he was slipping out of it.

They'd given away Bibi's kitchen knife, so Satnam resorted to using a scythe from the farm shed. He made an incision. He imagined the case filled with cash. Or cleverly disguised drugs. Perhaps he was blundering into some crime story, an ordinary man thrust into the extraordinary. He sighed when he finally got the thing open. He was an ordinary man living an ordinary life. There were piles of clothes – a man's, a woman's – and some kid's toys: a fidget spinner, a picture book about a dog. He laid out the men's clothing. Waterproof-chic. So many pockets and zips. It wouldn't hurt to have some more things to wear. Maybe the new him would be more adventurous, ready for all weather and terrain.

The women's clothes were more fashionable. From the size disparity and the difference in style, it was clear to Satnam that the man was punching. He sprayed the woman's perfume. It was different to the one Harp liked, but smelled the same to him. Deeper into the suitcase he found a set of architecturally intricate lingerie. There were all sorts of straps; it was hard to envision how the thing came together. He wrapped it in a blouse, knowing it would be just his luck for his mum to walk in as he was holding the thing up.

He'd give the women's stuff to Reha. It occurred to him, though, that it might be taken the wrong way if he gave her a suitcase that included someone else's lace panties. But to remove them from the suitcase would surely be worse. Holding on to a stranger's underwear, in his dead grandmother's house? He was losing his mind. On cue, his phone lit up with a message from Harp.

Any news?

He opened the chat. He couldn't do it over text. He wasn't

that man. But to do it face to face? To have to continue the fiction for the rest of the trip?

I miss your voice, she wrote.

He was a terrible person – the worst! To think Bibi hadn't known he had a girlfriend, let alone that he was the kind of person to break up over the phone. She'd known almost nothing of his real life, had never really seen him in his element, only ever accessing a stuttered version of him. He'd known as little of her inner life as she had his. They played their roles. She was the loving grandmother, sneaking him KitKats. He was the good grandson, watering her plants. Perhaps, he thought, as he stared at Harp's messages, the disconnect he felt with his bibi was just a heightened version of his relationship with anyone. How close could you really get with another person? How could you ever really know them? The body was a black box. What was Harp like at work? He couldn't picture her tending to a patient, having a meal with colleagues in the cafeteria. Most times, he was sure he didn't even know himself. He knew he wanted to break up, but he couldn't understand why.

Harp was still online and had no doubt seen that he was, too. At this point, not to act was to act. To leave the panties in the suitcase he gave to Reha was to give Reha the panties. Not to tell Harp it was over was actively to lie. He put the underwear in a drawer, planning to bin them when his parents were next out, and then he began a voice note:

'Hey, I feel terrible to say it like this, I wanted to do it in person, obviously, but then, with the circumstances as they are – I love you so much and I really don't know how to do this, it doesn't come naturally, that's for sure, but maybe, I don't know, a break would be good for me, for us – a pit stop. We're moving in the right direction, it's just, it's fast, right? Everything's moving. Moving so fast. But I know you're in a place.'

When it came down to the finer interactions, language was a blunt tool. The voice note wasn't good enough, but in trying to figure out how to delete it, Satnam sent it, and there it was. Done. Sound waves of his voice saying things that could no longer be unsaid. He threw his phone at the bed and it bounced on to the floor.

'Everything all right in there?' his mum called.

The screen had cracked. A spiderweb. 'All good!'

When Satnam took the suitcase down to the annex the next morning, Pala wasn't in.

'He's at the well,' Reha said, in English.

Satnam made a mess of explaining the situation with the bags, but Reha seemed to understand, thanking him without meeting his gaze. Emperor watched TV, sucking his thumb.

'I'll just leave it here,' Satnam said, conscious of overstaying his welcome.

'I can give you some of Pala's clothes,' she said. 'He told me you don't have anything.' Her English was much better than her brother's.

'Oh,' Satnam said, 'that's OK.'

But she turned into their room anyhow and returned with some kurta pyjamas. 'I don't think he ever wears these.'

As a joke, Satnam walked out to the well in Pala's clothes, to see if he'd notice. He was too busy with a queue of visitors to make the connection.

'Would you help?' he said, handing Satnam an empty bottle.

Satnam filled bottle after bottle with water, which Pala handed out to the visitors. He poured some on the knee joint of an amputee, reciting a prayer. A woman lifted her eye patch and poured water on to the socket. They washed their hands, their faces; they drank.

When the visitors left, Satnam asked Pala about his sister. 'Where's the dad?'

Pala paused. 'He took sulfas.'

'Sorry?'

'Swallowed pesticide.' It wasn't like the old days, he said, when one harvest would lead to another. The crops were designed to be sterile; farmers were forced to buy new seeds each season which wouldn't grow without certain fertilisers and pesticides. Reha's husband had taken out loans to keep up with rising costs and diminishing returns. 'He'd taken it that far, so he could only see putting more into it. And then there was nowhere for him to go.'

They were interrupted by another visitor. Pala muttered a prayer and Satnam lowered the bucket. Another elderly woman approached.

'Where are they coming from?' Satnam asked, when they were alone again.

'Aren't you on SpeakFree?' Pala said. 'I'll forward a link.'

He found his parents packing when he returned to the house.

'Gone native?' his dad joked, pulling at the fabric of Satnam's new clothes.

Pala's message arrived as they sat down for a takeaway dinner.

An auspicious moment for all India! A poor villager's son from UP who passed from IIT with distinctions has created a new app called SpeakFree. Scientists at MIT and Harvard are calling it the best app of the year because it is the first ever app which uses code from Sanskrit. Download now and forward this message to 10 contacts!

The day before their return flight, Satnam and his parents planned to drive to the city to sell the seven phulkari.

'They're probably of cultural significance,' his mum said. 'They'll mean something to someone.'

Satnam hadn't wanted to sell the pieces – the person they meant something to was Bibi. But he didn't have the fight in him. She was his grandmother, sure, but ultimately she was his dad's mum. He had less of a claim on her than his parents did, if he had any claim at all.

'She'd have long forgotten them,' his dad said, ending the conversation. 'She'd lost the key.'

The water buffalo was still sleeping in the courtyard when they left the empty house. They paused at the edge of the plot, watching Pala do his morning stretches by the well.

'The state of it,' Satnam's dad said.

'Someone else's problem soon,' his mum said.

When he got into the car, Satnam was forwarded a message on SpeakFree by Pala: *May the waters, the mothers cleanse us / may they who purify with butter, purify us with butter, / for these goddesses bear away defilement, / I come up out of them pure and cleansed.*

There was a link below the quote – an article about Saraswati, in English.

Our Mother Goddess

We begin with the name. Saraswati comes from 'saras', meaning 'flow' or 'water', and 'wati', meaning 'she who has'. Alternatively, it comes from 'sara', meaning 'essence', and 'swa', meaning 'self'. Saraswati is one who has flow, who knows herself. There are other translations: she who possesses water, she who possesses speech.

Saraswati is best known as part of the Tridevi: Saraswati, goddess of language, knowledge, speech, art, music; Lakshmi, goddess of wealth, fertility, earthly and material fulfilment; Parvati, goddess of power, beauty, love and spiritual fulfilment.

Mind, body, soul.

The origins of Saraswati are the origins of the universe. Upon creating the cosmos, Brahma looked upon his creation and found it lacking. There was nothing but matter. Nothing had shape or purpose. To help give the universe form, he decided to create the embodiment of knowledge itself. From his mouth emerged Saraswati. To call her his muse would sell her short. She less inspired Brahma than told him what to do. She told him how to create order in the world: the sun, the moon and stars. With her teachings, he learnt to hear the melody of the mantras in the cacophony of chaos. He named her Saraswati, goddess of speech and sound.

It wasn't long before Brahma fell in love with Saraswati, his own creation. She avoided his incestual advancements, evaded his looks. Brahma wanted to see her at all times, and each time she escaped his gaze, he sprouted another head from which he could view her. This happened four times, until he could look north, east, south and west all at once. His fifth and final head looked up to the heavens. Saraswati fled to the last place she could be free of his gaze: Earth. She became a river, the greatest of all rivers. But even then, he managed to find her, and so she decided to flow beneath the ground, and disappeared from us all.

Until now.

Satnam's phone buzzed with a call from an unknown number as they approached the auction house. The estate agent.

Even if he didn't have a voice in the matter, it was Satnam's name on the will, his signature they'd need to sell the house, and therefore his number on the paperwork. He passed the phone forward to his parents. As they talked, he pieced together that an offer had been made on the land.

'Just in time!' his mum said. They were flying out the following night. 'You must have made quite the impression on him. It's a decent price. You could finally move into a proper place. It won't be long until you and Harpreet will be needing a second bedroom.'

While his parents argued about where to park, Satnam unfolded one of the phulkari dupattas and flicked through the notebook that had been stored among them. A photo fell out: his bibi and baba, when they were younger. They stood stiffly, in front of the house. Neither of them was smiling. His baba was holding a lit cigarette. Satnam put it back between two pages.

Bibi's handwriting was neat, the lines that her letters hung from so straight that they might have been drawn with a ruler. It didn't have the look of a diary per se, but rather a copy of some other rougher text, presented now without faults. The only thing he could understand from it was the date on the last page. It was from three months ago. Had she lost the key in that short time, or hidden it? He could imagine her tossing it down into the well, trying to keep what they were now selling some kind of secret. He tucked the book under his seat, along with one of the dupattas.

'Were there only six?' his mum asked him, as she unfolded the cloth for a prospective customer.

The following afternoon, he noticed the water buffalo was lying down in the exact same spot. Insects flitted about her mouth and her nostrils. A fly walked across the cool surface of her open eye. He called his parents, who were checking in.

'She was too young,' his father said. 'You'd get nothing for the meat.'

When Pala was called over, he explained that there were no Chamars left in the pindh, and therefore no one to deal with the hide. There was nothing to be done but burn it.

Moving the body was quite the workout. Satnam and Pala dragged it by the legs from the courtyard, not wanting to stink up the house. They left it outside the small hut where Pala kept the buffalo's dung-cakes. He arranged the dried dung-cakes around the body and Satnam used Bibi's lighter to get the rancid fire going.

'I've got to get back,' Pala said. 'Kush needs me. You're OK to handle this?'

The fire skirted tentatively about the body without actually burning it. Satnam doused the fur in cooking oil, but the flames didn't catch. He had an image of sitting contemplatively in front of the pyre, ruminating on the transition of the buffalo from subject to object, from the ground to the air, solid and liquid to gas, but here he was, failing even at this. Denying the animal the dignity she deserved. He broke off some twigs from a nearby tree and prodded the body with the lit tips. No dice. There was too much moisture in the body. It was slowly steaming, rather than burning. He searched in the cupboard under the sink for the whisky, and stuffed a cloth into the bottle. He ignited the cloth and placed the bottle into the buffalo's mouth. He was sweating, out of breath, but finally the body was burning.

He sat before it and tried to meditate. Tried to hold an image of his grandmother in his head, tried to hear her voice. But all he could hear was his own. He could recall photos of her, holding him above a birthday cake, but he couldn't invent an image of her. He lit a cigarette on the pyre and looked the buffalo in the eye.

His parents called him into the house when it was time to sign. The estate agent had put Post-it notes on all the relevant pages.

Satnam picked up the pen and looked down at the dotted line above his printed name: *Satnam Singh Hakra*. He took a breath, and then he set the pen back down.

'Google says traffic,' his mum said. 'We've got to wrap things up.'

'We can't have a repeat of LaGuardia,' his dad said.

'I don't want to sell,' Satnam said, finally.

'Excuse me?' his dad said.

'I'm not sure I want to sell.'

'Satty.'

'I'm not ready to leave.'

'What's got into you?'

'I'd like to stay a bit. Process, I don't know.'

'You've been off all week.'

'Well, my grandmother just died. I'm allowed some rope.'

'She was *my* mum.'

'And?'

'It's not the point. Just sign, so we can get going.'

'I don't want to.'

'What the hell are you going to do here?'

'All I want is a little time.'

'You can't even speak to these people.'

'These people?'

'Bloody hell, your generation.'

'Bally.'

'No, I'm serious. Who does he—?'

Once his parents' car was out of sight, Satnam returned to what was left of the pyre and tossed the paperwork into the embers, his name in the air, smoke. All this was his. He owned the ground he stood upon – the house and the crops, the groundwater. His mum messaged: *Just got off phone with Harpreet. You have a lot to explain. It's hard to recognise you.*

Four and a half hours into his digital detox the next day, he caved and dug his phone back out of the ground. He unsealed the Ziplock bag he'd put it in and found no notifications. Watching YouTube in the courtyard, with the sun and the birds, the clean air, the quiet, he felt happiness glance off him like a breeze. He had happened upon an abundance of time. This was good, he thought. This was where he was meant to be.

Pala woke him before dawn. It was time to harvest.

'Couldn't you use your England money for another buffalo?' Pala said, slashing at the rice crop with a sickle. 'Or, better, a tractor. Green Revolution never reached this farm.'

The moon lit their path through the field, casting a dull sheen on their blunting sickle blades. Satnam ignored the pain in his lower back as he stooped to cut the stems as close to the earth as he could. There was a rhythm to it, like there was a rhythm to everything. Wait long enough and everything repeats. The arc of the universe, he thought, was an orbit. The repetition was coming, even if you wouldn't live long enough to see it. He was on the verge of waxing poetic about doing the work of his forebears on the land of his forebears, but got the sense Pala was on a short fuse. His breathing thinned as he strained with effort. There was smoke in the air already, cutting sharp at the back of his throat. Sweat dripped into his stinging eyes, into his mouth, dampening the cloth he'd tied around his face to filter the harvest air. The sun rose. They reached the well and drank with abandon. You could lean in now and touch the water.

Pala received a call. The conversation quickly became an argument and, as he raised his voice, his speech quickened to a pace that Satnam could no longer attempt to follow. When he hung up, he seemed content.

'What's going on?' Satnam said.

'The scientists are coming.'

They retraced their steps with twine that afternoon, tying the cut crop in bundles to dry in the sun.

'So, they've been this way before, the scientists?' Satnam asked.

'Yes,' Pala said. 'About the palaeochannel.'

The palaeochannel was the underground route of the ancient Saraswati River. Different bodies had been tracing developments along it.

'There was activity in the Shivaliks, movement in Jaisalmer,' Pala explained. He was switching between English and Punjabi, but Satnam could more or less follow.

He looked down into the well as they stopped for another water break. 'But it's not like the water is moving.'

Pala laughed. 'This is why you're not a scientist.'

Within two days, the acre was cleared, leaving nothing but stubble.

'What now?' Satnam said, finally getting to sit down.

'Now? Now, we burn.'

In an effort to reduce water stress, the government tied the sowing of rice paddy to the coming of the first rains. That year, the rains had arrived late. Farmers had stalked the cracked earth, looking up at the simmering sky, awaiting the delayed release. This meant the rice was planted late and harvested late, which meant in turn that there was almost no time at all left to plant the wheat. In normal times, there might have been a fortnight to switch between the crops. But Satnam and Pala found themselves with five days to clear all the stubble from the harvested rice, turn over the acre and plant the wheat. No method of stubble-clearing was as efficient as fire.

Flush out of dung-cakes, they resorted to syphoning fuel from the emergency generator. The fire began to move, turning the stubble black, then white, then black again, grey smoke rising, indecipherable from the grey sky, plots burning for miles, sacrifices to some ancient god. When the work was done, Satnam climbed up to the roof. The horizon, in all directions, was burning. No face covering could keep out the smell and taste of the charred earth come alive in fiery rigor mortis. It was awful, it was beautiful, the land in its death throes, the flowering smoke.

December

The fog lay upon the fields like agricultural fleece. Satnam watched the first of the scientists vanish. It wasn't clear, from talking to them, whether they were geologists, chemists, cartographers. They took a series of measurements, collected samples of soil and water, appearing and disappearing in the fog. Satnam headed out towards them, the hard edges of his body softening and dissolving into white, until he was gone entirely.

The well came into focus. One of the scientists put down their clipboard, and Kush Bhatt dabbed some well water on the scientist's acne, reciting a prayer under his breath. The scientists' speech was dotted with English: 'community engagement', 'town hall', 'funds'. And then, 'Whatever it takes.'

Satnam introduced himself and washed his face. The surface had risen.

'A few more weeks,' one of the scientists said, in English, 'and it will be overspilling.'

'Are you seeing this anywhere else?'

'Between us,' he said, 'yes.'

'What does that mean?'

'There will be more visitors.'

The next arrivals wore uniforms. Their cars were branded with the CRSR logo: Centre for Research into the Saraswati River. Satnam watched the officials take selfies with the well.

'It's a different thing altogether, seeing it in person,' one of them said, wetting his thinning hair and slicking it back with a brush. 'Many months looking at graphs. But this is real life, you know? We're at the heart of it. The eye of the storm!' He took another photo.

'I can take one for you?' Satnam asked.

'No, the angles are better like this, I think.'

They went in for tea – Reha had been cooking all morning. One man had a map of the territory on his tablet. 'So, this here is you, one of the first sightings.' He drew a line, from the mountains in the north-east to the sea in the south-west. 'And this is the ancient route of the Saraswati. From Kailash to Kutch.'

'As you probably know, we're aware of movement in the channels,' another man said.

'Rising water,' said the first.

'And, here, to see it surface – water, where there hasn't been water for years.'

Their smiles were infectious. Maybe it was just the relaxation that came with speaking in English, but Satnam felt at ease.

'I don't need to tell you farmers that water is good news. That fields near rivers prosper. There's no smoke, no mirrors.'

'We've run all sorts of projections – next slide, Ajay, please – and, as you can see, there's only upside for a man like you. To be at the centre of a historic discovery, as well as what might prove to be an era-defining project – a project the likes of which the world has never seen.'

'Project?' Satnam said.

'To bring the river back! To return to the world our great river. It really is a deal that can't be better.'

'And yet—'

'And yet, we at the centre are aware that compensation may smooth the wheels. So, on top of your upside—'

'More upside.'

'You'd be one of the first to sign – that really is a history-book thing. Tell-your-grandchildren stuff.'

They'd superimposed the river on to a map of his land. Ajay's next slide visualised the desert in the south-west turning green. After that were several GIFs of farmers grinning with abundant harvests. The other official wrote down a number on a piece of paper. The money from the deal would far outweigh any income Satnam could envision making from the few square metres he'd lose to the river.

'The last time we visited, a few months ago – was it your grandmother? She was very receptive, too. You come from good stock, I can tell.'

Representatives from CRSR returned a week after Satnam signed, bringing with them politicians and the press.

'Human chain?' Pala called, outside the marquee they had set up by the good road.

Satnam jogged across the field. He dipped empty bottles into the well and passed them along the line of villagers, from right hand to left, all the way down to Pala. From the well, Satnam could hear music, chanting, engines. Kids threw pebbles at the news crew's drone. The marquee rippled with wind.

When they were out of bottles, their makeshift river disbanded, everyone rushing in to find a seat. The tent was so packed, Satnam had to stand. Kush took a while to figure out how to adjust the microphone stand to his height. Once he'd got it down, he was afforded some gravitas by the slight reverb the sound engineer had applied. When he spoke, it seemed as if it were from a great distance, and of things of great importance: the epic past, the uncertain present, the promising future.

A few days after the event, Satnam was able to watch the published footage with the aid of English subtitles, understanding exactly, in retrospect, what he had felt intuitively in the moment.

'Ma Saraswati is central to all our origins,' Kush began. He paused for effect. The camera zoomed in. It looked like he'd had his eyebrows done. 'It was on the banks of the Saraswati River, upon which you now find yourselves, it was on this very land that the rishis first composed the Vedas. This was the very soil that birthed our great nation, our great way of life. Inspired by the mother goddess, the rishis were moved to song, songs that we still sing now, many thousands of years later. And just as their music continues to live, so too shall we soon hear the plentiful waters of Ma Saraswati. Because, friends, our mother goddess has returned to us. It is that simple.

'The reasons for her leaving us, many years ago, are for my esteemed colleagues to say, but the reason for her return is clear. She wants to return our country back to its former greatness, and, in doing so, make this village prosperous. All that we ask of you is that you believe the science and that you help us to gather support and funding to aid the returning of the river!

'The river will irrigate your farms, turn the brown ground green. I don't ask for your faith, for blind belief. I ask that you open your eyes and see the blessings in front of you, on your very doorstep.'

Kush introduced Dr V. M. Singh, a representative of the CRSR, but the video cut to an ad break before the old man walked on stage. Satnam shifted his cot in the courtyard, to reach the moving shade. The glare was still so strong that his reflection was clearer than the video on the screen. The adverts finished, and the applause resumed. Dr V. M. Singh raised the mic.

'I have been an academic in innumerate fields of scientific study, but, if I were to presume to give myself a title, I would say I am a riverologist. I know how rivers work, to put it in plain language. And I have devoted the last few years of study specifically to the Saraswati River, a river that I believe will soon be one of the great wonders of the world, because we as the Indian people will work together to restore it.

'You have all had the blessing to live not just upon the ancestral land of the rishis, of the people of the Saraswati Civilisation, of which my decorated associate General Prakash Ji will be deliberating upon in due course, but, in actual fact, you have the blessing to live above the river itself. To have your farms irrigated by holy water. Yes. As it stands, the Saraswati is running beneath the ground, through palaeochannels that date back millennia! We at the CRSR have known for a long time that the Saraswati never truly disappeared; a better word perhaps is that she went into hiding, a riverine hibernation. For thousands of years, as the greatest of all rivers – much larger than the Indus or the Ganga, even – she ran from the holiest of mountains, Mount Kailash, down through Himachal and past us here, in Punjab, across Haryana and Rajasthan, all the way to Gujarat, where she met the sea in what is now the Great Rann of Kutch. In fact, the Yamuna and the Sutlej were *mere tributaries* of the Saraswati.

'Well then, what happened to our great river? Why did she disappear? Why does a volcano sit dormant? In the scripture it is said that she vanished beneath the ground to evade the looks of Brahma. And, as always, the scientific answer matches that which was written all those years ago. It is proven in the records that an earthquake changed her course, and the river ran dry into the Thar Desert, no longer able to reach the sea. The Yamuna shifted east, meeting the Ganga. The Sutlej shifted west, meeting the Indus. The Saraswati then had to rely upon the rain, and the rains, they were few, and so she charted a course beneath the ground.

'But listen carefully, brothers and sisters. Do you hear that?' The wind shook the tent. 'That is the sound of the river flowing again, the goddess knocking at our door! She is ready to return. I won't bore you too much with the science. The data collected at the International Space Station, the thousands of land surveys, the analysis of glacial movements ... You are honest, hard-working folk. You don't need me, here, to talk about numbers and charts. No, I stand before you as a humble translator, to put the science that I have studied into words that you know. And let me make it clear: this is the scientific discovery of a millennium! If you can help support the campaign for returning our great river goddess, we can chart a path to put India top of the podium! In the spirit of the goddess Saraswati, put reason and logic first. You remember praying to Saraswati when studying at school? Doing a mantra in her name before an exam? Why do we do that? Because she is the voice of reason. Let reason lead your decision, and don't blindly listen to the naysayers and anti-nationalists in the media that may try to lead you astray to further their own perverted causes. Follow *your* cause. The cause beneath your feet.'

General Prakash Ji walked up next, his bejewelled cane more of a prop than a crutch. His suit was tailored in the tradition of nineties NBA players, his moustache styled in the vein of nineteenth-century European explorers. The starched bristles rustled against the microphone as he spoke. Satnam had met him after the event and remembered him smelling like Brylcreem. Unlike the others, he spoke in English.

'We gather here today,' he said, at a volume he might once have used to address his soldiers in battle, 'to *reclaim* our history. A history that has for too long been written by our colonial masters. A history that has been upheld by leftist historians, held beyond our reach. Our history tells us who we are, and yet we subcontract it out of India, to those expert purveyors of poppycock that populate Oxbridge, Harvard, what have you. To this I say, it is our land and it is our story. I want this story told using only Indian facts. Unlike the colonists, unlike the leftists, I have no agenda. I have only archaeological evidence, geographical satellite imagery, carbon dating, genetics mapping, linguistic, anthropological and scriptural evidence – and, above all, a little-used tool when it comes to the study of Indian history: common sense.

'Leftist historians will have it that the great civilisation of our ancient times was the Indus Valley Civilisation. And yet, 80 per cent of the archaeological sites of this civilisation lie not along the banks of the Indus, in Pakistan, but on the banks of the ancient Saraswati – this very land.

'We have long suffered a history of misnaming. The Greeks, led by Alexander the not-so-Great, only made it as far as Punjab and believed the Indus to be the great river of our nation, and they named the land India after the river. But they got the wrong river!

'Next came the Arabs, and they found the Sindhu, our name for the Indus. But they couldn't pronounce the S, so they called us Hindus, our nation Hindustan. Well, they got the river wrong!

'The Indus is a *border* river, a line at our periphery. But the centre of the nation – that, my friends, was the Saraswati. It was the greatest of all rivers, the mother of floods.

'Along this river, Hinduism was born, the Rig Veda, the oldest living, surviving, thriving system of thought and belief on this entire planet! And the Vedic people were direct descendants of the people of the *Saraswati* Civilisation, as it should be called. And we see the early marks of Hinduism in the most ancient of ancient artefacts from Saraswati sites. Whether that's figurines with bindis, doing the namaskar, or worship of a Shiva-like god. We have carbon-dated these great cities to 9,700 years ago. The Chinese, the Egyptians, the Mesopotamians can't hold a candle! And the miracle – let me make it clear – the miracle is *not* the antiquity, but the continuity. The very things we do now were done by our forebears on this very soil, on the banks of the river that has returned to us. With its water will come a renaissance for the modern rishi, development beyond anything you or I can imagine.'

He paused to catch his breath. 'They have dammed our history up. But now we've been presented with an opportunity to break down their walls, to let the river burst through. To let the water flow where it was supposed to. Before they took over, we were the world's greatest economy! And now we have the world's greatest population. And here we have the chance to return our country to its former glory. There are lakhs of acre-feet of sweet water running beneath us. The river will feed your farms, it will green the desert. It's not just the country's history arriving on your doorstep, it's the country's future. All we ask for is your support.'

In the shaded courtyard, Satnam paused and played the video, repeating new phrases.

'Voice of reason, voice of reason.' He felt fraudulent, putting on the accent. But this was who he was, who he was supposed

38

to be, who he would have been were it not for the accidents of history that had led his family to England. 'Thriving system of thought. Thought. Former glory, *former glory*.'

'Are you OK?' It was Pala's sister, Reha. She'd been sweeping round the corner. 'Are you on a call, or … ?' It took a moment to match the voice to her face. He'd rarely seen her without her child, or outside her home.

'I'm trying to learn,' he said. 'I can understand most things, but still find it hard to speak.'

'I trained to be a teacher,' she said. 'If you want help.'

'I didn't realise.'

'I had a whole life,' she said. Satnam offered to pay for lessons, and she laughed, inviting him in for tea. Emperor was drawing on a page of the picture book Satnam had found in the suitcase.

'You teach him English English,' Reha said, 'and I'll teach you Punjabi Punjabi.'

'Deal.'

'I just need to finish lunch,' she said. 'Could you watch him?'

There was an uncanny quality to the child's silence. There was a sense of knowing in his gaze, one you saw in children in horror movies. It felt as if he were conscientiously silent rather than accidentally so, like he had something to hide.

'Hello,' Satnam said, eventually.

Noticing that he was being observed, Emperor discarded the book.

'Can I read?' Satnam said, trying too hard to sound approachable.

In the story, a designer puppy, living in a mansion, dreams of adventure. But every time he's taken outside, he's confined to his rich owner's handbag. Unlike dogs of his ilk, he likes to get dirty, to roll in the mud and jump in puddles. He's bored inside the pristine house, doesn't even like the taste of the fancy food his owner buys him. Watching the outside world through the owner's tinted car windows, he sees packs of stray

39

dogs running free through the streets and wishes he could be among them. So, one day, he escapes. He wanders through the dark, scary streets, until he finally finds the strays. They're suspicious of him, but take him into the fold. They eventually form an unlikely friendship, and the dog starts to get a sense of the hardship the strays face. They often go hungry. Getting dirty is less fun without the chance to then be cleaned. The dog spots his own missing posters around the city, and one afternoon he passes his owner in the street. She's clearly bereft without him. But she doesn't recognise him now that he's transformed into a dirty street dog. He follows her home, and gets into an argument with his pack, who think he is abandoning them to return to his old, spoiled life. Caught between his owner and his friends, he feels totally alone. He calls out into the night, and the owner's ears prick up. She'd recognise that sound anywhere. They reunite. As they return to the house, she puts him on a leash. But he quickly pulls at the lead, and she's dragged out into the street, not wanting to let go. He runs through puddles and on to dirt roads, and she's pulled along – laughing, rather than shouting – stilettos breaking. He runs until he finds his friends. Somehow, the owner realises what he's trying to say. She calls her driver, and they all head back to the fancy house together. The final pages show all the strays enjoying the height of luxury and wreaking havoc in the mansion as the owner laughs along.

It looked more like it was made by a child than for one. Satnam googled the title as Emperor lost interest, but the first page of news articles were about India's stray dog problem. People were arguing that sterilising wasn't enough. There were calls for gunmen. He scrolled, stopping suddenly when he saw a familiar face. It was General Prakash Ji, with his unmistakable facial hair, frozen mid-argument in an Instagram reel. Satnam clicked the link.

'Now, they talk about our strays. Do you know their real name, the dogs – their scientific name? Indian Native Dog.

They are indigenous! You know what they're called by these anti-nationals? Indian Pariah Dog. The *Native* is *Pariah!*'

He went on to the General's profile and flicked through his videos. Emperor sat in his lap, watching with him.

'Everybody knows that India invented zero. But they act like that is the sum total of our worldly contributions.'

Satnam followed a link to the *AlphaAsian* podcast, where the General was frequently interviewed.

'When I hear these anti-nationals speak, it puts me in mind of a dictum from the colonial masters that we seem not yet to have fully shed. "We must do our best to form a class who may be interpreters between us and the millions whom we govern; a class of persons, Indians in blood and colour, but English in taste, in opinion, in morals and in intellect." Cut them out of our government, cut them out of our media, out of every facet of our country. We must Indianise our education system—'

'Ridiculous that tribals can apply for indigeneity, but not a man like me, whose ancestry stretches back to the first Indians, the first men—'

'You can tell that the people of the West, that fallen Rome, are so distanced from the natural world by the space they put between themselves and the fire that drives their lives. It's out of sight, somewhere further up the chain, out of mind. They know their car is faulty when they can actually see the smoke coming out of it! As if, when they can't see it, it isn't there. What they can't handle is that we make the fire, we see the fire, and we are comfortable with the fire—'

Reha came in with the tea, and Satnam picked the book back up. 'See? Dog. Dog. Yes. "The dog is hungry. It's time to feed the dog."'

Reha translated the phrases into Punjabi for Satnam. 'The dog is hungry. It's time to feed the dog.'

'"The dogs had no owners. The dogs were free."'

'The dogs had no owners. The dogs were free. The dogs were hungry.'

41

Satnam searched for the General that night and found lots of videos of him on TV debates. His fiery outbursts had given rise to several memes. Someone had cut together clips so that it looked like he was arguing with himself. Satnam clicked a debate compilation – *Epic Anti-national Takedowns* – and found again the dream of a language that meant nothing, language that was song: a dozen people shouting at one another, over one another, the talking heads increasingly animated, even when muted by the host, who would always come out on top, dismissing factions of his guests, ridiculing them and then getting the last word, shifting into articulate eloquence in an uninterrupted monologue. Tension, release – it was all the same. The people on his screen were shouting about evolution, about Urban Naxals; they were shouting about firmer borders and the dictates of woke, of the brain drain and space exploration; they were arguing about Ayurveda and how the West had lost its soul; they were arguing and agreeing about the significance of the upcoming elections, of the population projections, the dogs roaming the streets turning violent, the violence in the mountains, the violence at the border; but mainly they were saying, 'Let me speak', 'Let me speak', 'Let me finish', 'If I can just finish', 'If you'll just let me finish', 'If I can speak'. Satnam could hear Reha singing on the other side of their shared wall, the baby crying. He played different compilations in separate tabs and turned up the volume until his AirPods were generating pure noise, impenetrable sound. As his mind filled with the words of others, he could finally feel some sort of freedom from his own straying thoughts, all that conflicted doubt.

The man hammered the piledriver into the ground and the white water burst forth. It geysered above head height, covering them all in mist.

'Praise Saraswati!'

'And … cut.'

'I think we've got it.'

It was the third attempt at capturing the footage, and now the director seemed satisfied. Satnam and Pala crowded round the monitor to see it played back. It looked real. You wouldn't have guessed from the footage that they'd had to bury a hose, pump it up to its maximum pressure and perfectly time the releasing of the valve with the falling of the hammer. The final edit would show that the river was swelling, desperate for release. The drama of the video would help capture attention, Satnam agreed. In any case, it wasn't fake, he thought, because the water they were pumping into the hose was all from the real well.

'A stretched truth,' the director said, 'is still the truth. It just reaches further.'

That afternoon, Kush, Pala and Satnam were asked to appear on camera. They shot a Hindi interview with Kush and a Punjabi one with Pala. Satnam watched on, running through his answers to the two simple questions the producer had provided him with, trying not to think about how many viewers the producer had boasted that they could reach.

Satnam stood by the well while the sound man took room tone – the singing birds, the rustling crop. The level of the water was weeks, maybe days, from the lip. *A person chooses their life the way a body of water chooses what it reflects*, Kush had said. *All this has been fated for you.* The last time Satnam had held a microphone was at karaoke with Harp and her friends. Filmi classics, sung by reading phonetics. How distant London felt. If he'd felt a fraud in his previous guise, a trader of futures in the city, what did he feel now? A so-called farmer, caught in the centre of what exactly?

'The clouds are good for the light,' the cameraman said. 'Are you ready?'

'Sure,' Satnam said, clearing his throat.

'We'll remove our voices, sir, so try to include our question in your answer, if you understand? We'll begin … What do you think about the government's plans to bring back the Saraswati River?'

Satnam took a deep breath, wanting to get his answer right, to be clear and concise. But in the moment he took to consider his answer, he became conscious, hyper-aware, of the fact that he wasn't speaking, that now he was failing to speak, and the journalist was looking at him expectantly, and all that Satnam could think about was how he was, all of a sudden, completely failing, utterly blocked, and that, with each instant that he wasn't speaking, it was becoming harder to speak, because he needed to say something of a profundity that would have necessitated such a silence, but he could no longer think of anything to say, and as the silence expanded, a balloon filled with emptiness to the point of exploding, he could no longer remember quite what the question, so simple, had been exactly, and now feared speaking and answering something completely different from what had been asked, feared spouting nonsense, noise, and the journalist glanced at the cameraman and said, 'Sir, it's OK, we're not live. Take a moment, take a water, and we can begin again?'

'There is no surprise it's anti-national presstitutes who naysay and defame. The truth is they still bootlick Britishers, prostrate themselves before the Mussulmans. This is the India they want: anti-progress, anti-growth. But you, the true Indians, have the sense to vote in favour of your country, rather than against it. And, to do so, vote for the return of our mother goddess. Vote in favour of a New Green Revolution, a desert turned green. In favour of wonderful abundance, record new jobs, the world's greatest engineering project. Vote in favour of brand new cities. Indian ingenuity made manifest on the world stage. Return us to our former glory. Vote for Narayan Indra and turn India's most successful chief minister into the prime minister—'

'Can we turn that off? We have a *guest*,' Reha said, making an apologetic face to Satnam as she set the table.

'This is a historic moment right now and you want us to focus on your chicken?' Pala said.

Chicken? Satnam was sure they knew he was vegetarian.

'It's a rerun from hours ago. It's not a historic moment right now. But the food is hot right now.' She came out with three identical bowls. She'd been cooking for hours.

Satnam now noticed, in hindsight, the absence of the clucking sound in the courtyard. If only he could experience an absence as keenly as he could a presence.

'Our mother's recipe,' Reha said, smiling proudly.

Satnam looked down at the bowl. The chicken had been shredded, so the pieces were largely indistinguishable from the gravy. He smiled, and tore off a piece of roti, glistening with ghee, and opened his mouth, reluctantly, eagerly, to eat. He'd broken up with a long-term girlfriend, left his home and his job, left his family, and now he was abandoning his vegetarianism. *Untying a knot is harder than tying one*, Kush had said. Satnam was finding that easy to disprove.

Reha continued to talk as the news looped on mute. 'It's getting dark so early. I don't remember days so short.'

'You say that every year,' Pala said.

'So, what do you think of the student's progress?' Reha asked, nodding at Satnam.

'His Punjabi? He still hardly speaks. You should have seen him the other day, and that was English!'

'I can follow,' Satnam said, laughing. 'I'm getting better at following.'

There were footsteps upstairs. Emperor had woken up.

'I'll handle it,' Pala said.

As he left the room, Reha dropped her voice and switched to English. 'I appreciate you staying close to him. Could you keep an eye?' She paused. 'I overhear things. You could keep him from trouble.'

'I'm not sure I understand,' Satnam said.

'He's easily led. He's a passionate man. But passionate men—'

An alert sounded on both Pala and Satnam's phones at once. It was Kush.

Reha picked up the dishes and left for the kitchen, and Satnam copied and pasted the text into Google Translate.

I need some men. It's time to send a message.

January

On the first Monday of the new year, Satnam and Pala rode towards one of the areas of darkness on the map – a greyed-out plot signifying a landowner resistant to the river works. By the time they were given the instructions from Kush, the owner had already received visits from government officials and CRSR reps, from holy men and friends in the community. But still he refused to understand the environmental and economical benefits the river would bring, let alone the spiritual ones. All reasonable people had consented. It fell to supporters like Pala and Satnam to help the outliers see things a little more clearly.

'You, my friends, are not on the books,' Kush had told them, switching to English for Satnam's sake. His face was filling out a little, Satnam thought. When he sat down, he could tell the priest was developing a bit of a belly. 'You understand? You are not connected to any of this – in any official capacity. You're not part of a body. I'm not telling you to do anything. And no one is telling me to tell you anything. Anything that you choose to do, I'm unaware of. If your interests happen to align with ours, there might be certain protections – is something I'm not saying.'

They accelerated north-east, upriver. Satnam directed Pala. He had a screenshot of the address from their Speak-Free group chat; Kush had a tendency to delete his messages shortly after sending them. Pala had tied Satnam's turban – his disguise – too tight. He could feel the beginnings of a migraine coming on, iridescent floaters wriggling across his vision, microscopic worms on the surface of his retinas. He closed his eyes and the floaters intensified in colour. He'd knotted a hand-kerchief around his face to keep out the fumes but could still smell the sputtering exhaust. The whole motorbike shook. He felt his brain pressing against his skull, his eye sockets. Pala had wedged a phone inside his helmet and, amid the watery sound of rushing traffic, Satnam could make out certain words as he talked to Kush, bobbing buoys, and tried to focus on them, to chart a route between them. Reha's lessons had been working. The way she'd put it, it was less about learning Punjabi than unlearning English. 'More Indians speak English than there are English people. Your old world is small fries.'

They passed billboards for politicians, billboards for news anchors. Signs for immigration lawyers, English tutors. Ads for tractor repairs, face cream, international SIMs, gym member-ships: *New year, new you. Renew now.*

There were two worlds, Satnam thought, as they approached the farm. One where nothing meant anything, and one where everything meant something. He wasn't sure to which he belonged now, but he felt at home, the restless-ness that had defined his aimless twenties replaced by a sense of purpose. Here he was, speeding towards something. He sat bolt upright, the crowbar hidden beneath his shirt an external spine. When they parked up, he kept his face covering on.

Kush clicked the grey land on the digital map and it turned green. 'An extra half-mile – that's a solid start to the week.'

The marquee had become an unofficial office for those invested in helping the river works. There were maps on porta-ble walls, a quote of the day that hadn't been updated in weeks: *While others drift to the sea, strive against the current to the source.*

Officially, Pala and Satnam only came to the office to drop

off kegs of holy water. They rolled them down from the well and picked up the empty containers. It just happened that inside one of the empty containers would be a generous amount of cash, in a waterproof bag. Running a functioning farm was much more costly than Satnam had envisioned. The crop was already suffering after his decision to stop using any chemical pesticides and he was still paying a mortgage on his unoccupied north London flat. Kush was keeping him liquid.

They picked up the empty kegs and were about to leave, when Kush zoomed in on a large expanse of dark grey on the map. 'Our biggest hurdle, as it stands,' he said, 'is here at the New Albion Estate. The Trust is refusing to cooperate.'

'We can pay a visit,' Pala said.

'It'll take much more than a few men. And this, you could say, is an opportunity for a louder message.' He grinned. 'But first, you've got Sen to see to, down the road. Make it a friendly one. He's a good man. Just words.'

Mr Sen wanted to show them the peepal tree. Its loose braid of gnarled trunks turned to roots before they met the ground. It was clearly very old, as wide as four trees put together. Sen's dog lazed in the immense shade, gnawing at a bone.

The intermittent fasting was getting to Satnam. He felt light-headed, tired. But Kush said that was all part of it. You had to start from zero.

'I was sorry to hear about your grandmother,' Sen said to Satnam. 'We knew each other growing up, actually. I'd let her use my bicycle. But then, of course, she left for England. And all those years later she returns! She'd be happy you decided to stay, I'm sure.'

Satnam glanced at Pala. 'Well, there's a lot more happening here than I had going on in London. What with the river and everything.'

Pala straightened up.

'Yes, I know that's why you're here,' Sen said. 'I told the first lot, and the second lot, but I can tell you, too. I won't allow them to cut down the tree. I'd be happy for them to go through the land, if they go around it. The roots go far and need a wide berth. I'm not against the river, if all they say is true. But this tree is older than me, my father, my grandfather, his father. It won't go on my watch.'

'They can't change the course, it's following the palaeochannels,' Satnam said. 'The river is already here.'

'Again, I'd allow it to run through my land, if an assurance was made about the tree.'

'You don't seem to understand,' Pala said.

'I understand perfectly well. I've heard about the Dhaliwals. They said no. Then, all of a sudden, they said yes. And then there's Ahluwalia. He was adamant. But then, go figure, he says he's fallen ill and won't come round, and a week later it's a yes. But my position is simple. I'd happily give you my thumb print, if you redraw the course.'

Satnam ran his palm along the coarse surface of the bark.

'If the people come back,' Satnam said, 'sign the papers. It'll make everything easy and smooth. We wouldn't want things to get complicated.'

Pala grinned and shook the man's hand, firmly. 'Your dog looks in need of a good meal, uncle.'

Satnam and Pala visited New Albion with Kush, to scout out the property. Satnam remembered visiting the gardens both times he'd come to Punjab growing up. A half-hour drive from Hakra, it was the thing to do.

On his first visit, the avenue of giant, grafted oaks that led to the entrance felt miles long. He had jumped in the central fountain to cool off after playing stuck-in-the-mud on the flawless lawn. Everything in that memory was in bloom, and he was running. His one clear recollection was that the old stone statues of naked men that lined the avenue had been wrapped with cloth around their waists to protect their modesty. He remembered his parents laughing.

The second time he came to New Albion, he'd brought his DS. The grass was yellow; the fountains had to be switched off. In the wonky shade of the once-square hedges, he'd played *Mario Kart* until the battery died. With nothing to do, he walked up to a sign and read the visitor information. The gardens had belonged to Sir Bernard Hawthorn, an English diplomat. There were photos of what the land had looked like before he purchased it. Two small hills acted as natural bunds at a bend in a stream. Covered in deciduous trees, it was a rare patch of land not yet farmed: 'virginal', in Hawthorn's words. He had bought it sight unseen, wanting a retreat from the city, and expected it to be flat, like much of Punjab. 'I had in mind a land like my father's, out in Suffolk,' Hawthorn wrote. 'Somewhere with a long, level horizon, upon which the mind can rest. What I found instead was a godawful wilderness.'

The maps Hawthorn had consulted hadn't included contour lines. Rather than settle, he paid a landscaper to see what could be achieved. Locals were hired to dig at the hills, flattening the small valley. The stream was dammed. English evergreens and oaks were dug up near Lowestoft, shipped to Karachi and brought up along the Indus and the Sutlej to Hawthorn's land, which he named New Albion, after the story of Albina. 'This queer land is beginning to look like my dear old England,' he wrote.

When Hawthorn's son inherited the land, he had more baroque visions. He'd never been to Suffolk; his only trip to Europe had been to Paris, and it was the gardens of Versailles he hoped to replicate on the land. He turned the flat land into a carefully patterned garden and commissioned a series of nude male statues, after the Greeks in the stories his father loved, to line the promenade that would lead to his standout feature, a fountain. There was no water available on the land, so he had a pipe made that ran from the Hawthorn Reservoir to the New Albion Estate. It was a marvel to the many business associates he hosted.

When the country gained independence, Hawthorn left for London, a place he knew nothing of, and the gardens were left untended. A historian in Delhi petitioned the new local government to preserve the gardens as a feat of human engineering, and Hawthorn's servants, who'd been squatting in the house since his sudden departure, were evicted, along with those displaced by the new border who'd taken refuge in the many rooms of the main house. The historian set up a trust and turned the gardens into a tourist attraction.

The promenade wasn't as long as Satnam remembered. The sun-bleached sashes had been removed from the statues, and so, too, on closer inspection, had the statues' penises. Each cock had been crudely chipped away and sanded down, leaving an area of blankness in place of the manhood of Zeus, Apollo, Poseidon.

'It would have more impact if we did it before Vasant Panchami,' Kush said, glancing up at a security camera.

'Won't people be busy with the harvest?' Pala said.

'True. A few weeks earlier?'

'Does that give us enough time to plan?'

'The beauty of something like this,' Kush said, lowering his voice as they passed a dozing guard, 'is that you don't need a plan. All I need you to do is to start to put the word out.'

Pala spat into the empty fountain.

'I hope I don't have to doubt you two,' Kush said. 'I don't want to have to keep defending your abilities, if I'm asked.'

'What do you mean?'

'That Sen, who you visited. He's still refusing to sign.'

They took a detour on the drive back to buy dog treats and a cage.

*

The sight of the pressure cooker on the hob in Reha's kitchen had Satnam salivating. He could feel his stomach tighten like a muscle.

'How long will it be?' he said.

'Any minute now.'

He stood in the kitchen's doorway and ran through the Punjabi phrasing in his head before speaking. 'What was she like here, my bibi? To you, what was she like?'

Reha paused, increasing the heat on the pressure cooker. 'She was very nice.'

'No, really,' Satnam said. 'Honestly.'

Reha met his gaze. 'She was a very serious woman, I suppose. Exacting. She was always going on about how much better it was back in England. No one could quite understand why she was here.'

Sen's dog barked in Satnam's courtyard, straining against its chain.

'Neither could we,' Satnam said.

'But you're here. Why are you here?'

'Did she care about the house? The farm?'

'I wouldn't say so. But she cared, I suppose, about how it had been kept in the family so long. She was proud of the phulkari. They had been passed from mother to daughter, over and over. For someone so serious, she could be surprisingly sentimental. I think that's why the memory loss got to her so much – she wasn't sure what it was she was forgetting.'

Before he could respond, he heard Pala shouting outside. 'Come! Come! Quick!'

'You see! Do you see?' Pala cackled.

The water was running over the edge of the well, dripping – flowing, even – down its sides and running in right-angled rivulets along the grouting of the brickwork, before turning out into the mud.

Satnam lit one of Bibi's candles. 'I can't believe it.'

Reha filmed the sight and put the video on SpeakFree. Within minutes, Kush had forwarded it back to Satnam and Pala. Prayer-hands emoji. *On my way!*

'Do we collect it?' Satnam said, when Kush arrived. 'So it doesn't go to waste?'

'No, no. Now, we let her flow.'

They sat beside the well, and Kush led an impromptu puja.

The water steadily edged downhill, away from the farm.

The river was real. It wanted out.

Satnam chanted along with the rest of them, more humming than singing, so as not to get the words wrong. The water slowly softened the ground. They drew words with twigs in the mud, Satnam practising Punjabi letters, while Kush sang of the first creation.

Then, Reha screamed.

'God! The cooker. The pressure cooker!'

She'd left it on and forgotten all about it. Heating up this long, the thing was surely minutes, seconds, from becoming a bomb. Emperor was asleep in the bedroom above the kitchen. They ran towards the house, fearing the worst. While Satnam might have hoped he was the kind of man to storm into the kitchen and kill the hob, the thought of arriving at the moment the pressure cooker finally blew, exploding dal and metal shrapnel, made him slow down as he approached the house, letting Reha and Pala go in first.

Reha came out, crying with relief.

'The power cut! There was a power cut,' she said, incredulously.

The boy was fine, the house was fine. The electricity had gone, cutting off the hob. They sat down in the dark, training their phone torches on the ceiling – the emergency generator had no fuel inside it.

'She was looking out for us,' Pala said. 'She's watching over us.'

53

February

Due to the numbers, real fires were discouraged. The women carried plastic candles above their heads, flashing in different primary colours, as they progressed through the dirt. It had been Kush's idea to have the parade walk through the excavated bed of the future ancient river. The men held up floats, idols of Saraswati covered in garlands and tinsel, tin foil shining red, yellow and blue, as the drummers, who'd been adamant that they didn't need to rehearse, verged on free jazz. Behind the politicians were the schoolkids, waving flags, fighting over kazoos. Satnam stepped out of the procession, climbing what would one day be the river's bank to take photos. Everyone was wearing yellow. It was Vasant Panchami, the fifth day of spring, the day of the Saraswati Puja. Already, in the distance, yellow kites were flying.

Satnam FaceTimed his mum.

'I just wanted to show you,' he said. 'It's quite the party.'

The screen froze as she spoke.

'What?'

'I said I'm glad—' The buffering continued.

He maintained his smile, in case she could still see him. 'Hello?'

'—wondering when?'

'Sorry?'

He called time and hung up, checking his SpeakFree notifications. As the celebration had fallen on a Friday, clashes were anticipated at Bhoj Shala. The ancient site to the south, which housed a temple for Saraswati as well as the graves of several Sufi saints, was open to Hindus on Tuesdays and Muslims on Fridays, with the exception of Vasant Panchami. Military police were in place, but at dawn the crowds were already overwhelming them, the site experiencing more than double its usual capacity.

There would be no such scenes along the river, Kush had insisted. Everything would be calm and pious. It was less a scene of piety, though, than a raucous party as the early after-noon procession continued on past Satnam. At the back of the parade, the farmers shifted into a bhangra rhythm, dancing and passing around bottles of river water that contained – Satnam realised when he was given a sip – straight vodka. A season of work in the fields was done, and the harvest was here. No god or second coming would disturb the jolly. Satnam took another swig and walked on with them, though his harvest wasn't yet ready. He'd stuck to his guns, selling off all the farm's stores of fertilisers, herbicides and pesticides. When he'd gone to a seed store to find native crop to plant for the next season, Pala had rolled his eyes. A Singh put his arm around Satnam now and forced him to dance as they fell further behind the procession.

'Drink, drink,' he said, and Satnam happily obliged. It would only help him carry out the plan, he figured.

'You're late,' Pala said as they met outside the marquee. 'There's two seats for us at the back. Once the cameras pan to us and pan back, that's the signal. Then, we go.'

Where the whole village had filled one marquee previously, three tents had to be joined together to accommodate the number of visitors now. It was clear that many had arrived from outside the state, some taking train journeys that had lasted multiple days. There were news crews from interna-tional channels, someone from the BBC, *The New York Times*.

Satnam took his aisle seat in the back row. The speeches began, and Satnam, much closer to fluency but a little desen-sitised to all the hyperbole, tuned out much of what was said. He'd kept hold of one of the holy vodka bottles and continued to work through it. The people on stage talked of the upcoming elections, in which a young chief minister, Narayan Indra, was running for the first time. He was tough on crime, on drugs, and would be strong on the border. He was going to flush out the terrorists and the anti-nationals. And, once the external threats were neutralised, he would solve any issues around food and water scarcity and unemployment by doing something truly era-defining: bringing the Saraswati River back to life.

As the event wore on, it became difficult to distinguish the holy men from the politicians, the scientists from the historians. The Puja was about worshipping your ancestors, it was repeated, paying dues. Satnam thought briefly of Bibi; he knew nothing of her parents, their parents. Pala elbowed him as the cameraman approached, and Satnam focused on the speaker.

'Praise Saraswati, goddess of speech! Oh, praise Saraswati, goddess of thought! Goddess of science. Goddess of music. Goddess of time. Oh, Vagdevi, goddess of all that flows, we feel you flowing here beneath us. The earth is not so solid as it looks; we feel you rushing, we feel you with each unstable step. Come before us, great mother, mother of all rivers, and let us flow with thee. Praise Bharati! Praise Mahavidya! Praise Mahavani! Arya, Brahmi. Praise Bijagharba, Veenapani! Oh, Sarada, Vageshwari. Sing for Gayatri, for Satarupa, she who has seven forms—'

Satnam registered his and Pala's faces as they appeared on the big screen, and smiled. Then the feed cut back to the speaker, a child from a local school, who'd prayed to the goddess and achieved perfect results in her latest exams. That was their cue.

Satnam wanted to stay where he was, to abandon the plan. But this was no place for an argument.

They slipped out the back of the marquee and headed for the truck. Checking that they weren't being followed, they drove towards Sen's farm.

'There's clouds, man,' Satnam noticed. 'Dark clouds. I say we cancel.'

'Cancel?'

'There's got to be another way.'

'"You have to be the change you want in the world",' Pala said. 'Jay-Z.'

Pala parked up and took the kerosene from the back. Satnam watched through the windscreen as he walked up to Sen's peepal tree. He didn't like it. But what were his options? He could either watch Pala do what he was going to do, and be complicit in not stopping him, or he could help and the thing would be done more quickly, and they could get away faster. He'd already come this far. Whatever he did, he was involved. Implicated.

'Fuck,' he said, before opening the truck door.

He set fire to a twig and held it up to the low branches. Once the fire had assumed some life of its own, the two men rushed back to the truck and sped down the dirt road, back towards the celebrations. The clouds made it hard to see any smoke in the rear-view.

They took their seats in the marquee a few minutes before the event finished, clapping along with everyone else, just in time for the camera to pan once again back to them. They cheered. Their faces were on the footage twice. That was undeniable. They had been here.

While Pala and Reha sat Emperor down in the annex to try to teach him to write his first word, a custom on Vasant Panchami, Satnam went up to the roof with one of the free yellow kites the organisers had handed out. A short prayer was printed on one side, and on the other an advert: *With generous support from the Laal Guru Foundation.*

On the roof, he could see hundreds of kites fluttering in the tumultuous air. He unwrapped his yellow pagh and scratched his itching scalp, and put Bibi's phulkari around his shoulders as the temperature dropped. The wind formed music on the surface of the kite as he let it loose. It hung in the air a beat before soaring up. He took a photo to send to his parents. He hadn't replied to their last few messages on the group chat.

His mother had sent a link to an article about the Saraswati. *It sounds like it's getting out of hand,* she said. *Everything's OK out there?*

His father had messaged underneath: *You agreed with your mother to call once a week.*

Satnam hearted the link and replied with his photo, *Sorry we cut out – all good here! Not much to report.*

March

It didn't matter how much milk and honey was mixed in, the urine left an aftertaste. Satnam chased the shot with a scotch and then Listerine, wincing, waiting for his vision to change, for a shift in perspective. They were sitting in a circle, seven of them in total, waiting for the all-clear. Other than Pala, Satnam knew no one.

'Is it happening?'

'I don't feel anything.'

'All I feel is that I just drank Kush's piss.'

'Maybe the dose wasn't high enough.'

'I'm not drinking any more, I can tell you.'

'Wait. I feel something. Buzzing.'

'That's the call, you idiot. Pick up the phone. Let's go.'

They filled the cars and drove towards New Albion. The lights were growing, and the people shrinking. The dog was barking.

Kush had discovered the mushrooms growing in a cow pat in the dug-up riverbed. Crouching next to the shit, he recognised them as fly agarics, as signs, and sent a photo to his teacher, Laal Guru (known online as the YouTube Yogi), who gave him detailed instructions. Both Kush and Laal

Guru subscribed to the theory that the fly-agaric mushroom, which grew along the Saraswati River, was the soma of the Rig Veda, the soma that the rishis, the seers, would grind into a juice and consume. One shaman, the scholars contested, would take the drink raw, and his followers would drink his urine – the shaman's body having detoxified the drug in digestion – allowing them to access the godly plane, to have visions of the world beyond, moving them to sing by the holy river, capturing what they saw and heard of the divine in metered words. The same practices, Satnam had read, having researched ahead of the ceremony, were seen among the Sami of the far north. They'd filter the mushroom juice through a reindeer, and kneel to eat the yellow snow. The reindeers would dance, fly, pull sleighs through the air. The fly agaric could be traced to the Nords, too, the berserkers. Men wearing bearskins or wolf hides would consume the juice in preparation for battle, turn into werewolves. Satnam watched the YouTube debates. Many believed soma was a plant, a creeper, but there was archaeological evidence that supported the fungal theory: at several Indus Valley Civilisation dig sites, figurines had been found with fly-agaric mushrooms growing out of their heads, in their hair; there were traces of spores in burial grounds.

'It's about connecting with roots,' Kush had said, carefully decanting the drink into shot glasses. 'Living the lives of our forefathers. Seeing, too, the visions of the rishis. Let this light a fire in you for tonight. So you can do whatever you do.'

Satnam read the scripture on his phone, but the words kept moving as they turned on to the dirt road. *We have drunk soma and become immortal; we have attained the light.* It was hot and his shirt was darkening with sweat. *Thou, Soma, art preeminent for wisdom; along the straightest path thou art our leader. With all thy glories on the earth, in heaven, on mountains, in the plants, and in the*

waters, with all of these, well-pleased and not in anger, accept, O royal
Soma, our oblations.

'Can you feel my heartbeat?' the teenager, Vijay, said to
Satnam.

Satnam touched his neck, slapped his face. He was just a
kid. 'You're good, bro.'

The men in front were arguing over the radio station. The
windows were down, dark farms blurring.

And Soma, let it be thy wish that we may live and may not die.
Guard us, King Soma, on all sides from him who threatens us.

When the music came on, it was accompanied by the growling in the boot: Sen's dog. Pala was telling everyone his new
favourite story. After the power cut, he and his family had
moved into the main house with Satnam. And, in the guest
room, in one of the drawers, he'd found a lingerie set. 'Now,
either it belongs to our very own Satnam Singh Hakra,' he
said, 'or it was his grandmother's!'

Accepting this our sacrifice and this our praise, O Soma, come, and
be thou nigh to prosper us. Well-skilled in speech we magnify thee,
Soma, with our sacred songs: Come thou to us, most gracious One.
Soma, be happy in our heart, as the cow in the grassy meads, as a young
man in his own house. Save us from slanderous reproach, keep us, O
Soma, from distress: be unto us a gracious Friend. Soma, wax great.
From every side may vigorous powers unite in thee: be in the gather-
ing-place of strength.

Everyone was laughing and Satnam was feeling good, really
good. He punched the headrest in front, banged on the door-
frame in time with the pulsing EDM.

Wax, O most gladdening Soma, great through all thy rays of light,
and be a Friend of most illustrious fame to prosper us. Wealth-giver,
furtherer with troops of heroes, sparing the brave, come, Soma, to our
houses. To him who worships, Soma gives the cow, a fleet steed and a
man of active knowledge, skilled in home duties. These herbs, these
cows, and these running waters, all these, O Soma, thou hast gen-
erated. The spacious firmament has thou expanded, and with the

light thou hast dispelled the darkness. Do thou, God Soma, with thy godlike spirit, victorious, win for us a share of riches. Let none prevent thee: thou art Lord of valour. Provide for both sides in the fray for booty.

Satnam repeated the last line out loud, laughing as the music gave out to the news.

A crowd had gathered at New Albion. The demonstration, the newsreader said, was about removing the shackles of empire; it was about confronting the past. 'We're here at the scene, as peaceful protesters gather to call for the shutting of New Albion Gardens.' They cut between different interviews, and Satnam put his face against the window, but there was no glass, and he felt the wind in his hair and it felt good.

'Think of Europe, now, where there are no cultural moorings of civilisational identity, there is only secularism. They've killed their own identity and, where there is no identity in the consciousness, something else will fill the gap, because a vacuum cannot exist.

'We came into this land from nowhere, children of the soil always. We are the indigenous. If anything, we win the war of woke: brown, indigenous people whose way of life is under threat. We gained independence several decades ago, and yet we are not truly free until places like New Albion Gardens are gone. Until all the English gardens are gone. All the Mughal gardens. When they came here, they knocked down our temples to build mosques and churches, and yet, now they're gone, we not only let their structures stand but protect them! That protection ends today.'

The wind wasn't wind but still air they were passing at speed. There was no mention of the river or the Trust's refusal to sign, which had been their assurance when inviting the journalists. Help had come from above.

Parked cars blocked the road ahead. Pala and the driver were discussing a man who was going viral on SpeakFree for spreading conspiracy theories about the river.

'He only lives a few miles away.'

'Just forward it to Kush – he'll know what to do.'

The driver pressed down on the horn.

'We won't make it in time.'

Eventually, they turned off the road into a field, and Vijay was still speaking: 'It's getting louder, it's getting louder!'

The cage shook in the back, the dog growling as the car jolted over the ploughed land. They turned the car around as they parked at the edge of the treeline, for a quick exit.

The boot lifted up and the growling intensified. The dog was all teeth. Nobody wanted to be the one to open the cage.

'Sorry it came to this, my guy,' Satnam said, looking the dog in the eye and lifting the cage out of the car. They'd planned to return the thing to Sen, but then Sen had vanished. No one knew where he had gone. Now, it meant they had some added protection. Satnam stood behind the cage. He'd open it and it was up to the others to grab the metal lead.

Satnam spat on the ground, his mouth producing too much saliva. The trees were expanding in all directions. There was infinite grass, when you thought about it. Infinite grass! He lifted the metal grate and the dog bolted out. It was too quick for the men, running across the dark field and down the road, and they were looking around, dumbfounded, and everything was moving. There was the sound of its metal chain clanging on the tarmac, and then there was nothing.

'Man.'

They paused, as the field stopped spinning.

'Let's just continue on,' Pala said, picking up the giant watermelon.

They entered the woods and came upon the fence bordering the back of the estate. They could hear the chants coming from the crowd outside the front gates, multiplying. Satnam pulled up his face covering, his breath hot and wet. Pala climbed partway up the fence to impale the watermelon on one of the barbed spikes. It held. Then they vaulted Vijay up. Gripping the watermelon, he jumped over the fence. The security booth was empty, all available staff manning the front gates. Vijay pressed a button in the booth and the back gate opened.

Inside, it was clear the stately home was caught between conflicting aesthetic ideals. There were animal heads on the walls, shrines on the mahogany furniture. The others checked upstairs. It was Satnam's job to go down into the basement security office. Thankfully, it was empty. Footage of the protestors played on the CCTV screens. They were holding up placards, shouting into megaphones. The men were pressed up to the fences, punching the air. Satnam turned off the cameras – he'd watched a tutorial on YouTube in preparation – and looked for the control panel for the front gates. He called Pala.

'Ready?'

'I'm really starting to feel it, bro. I feel fucking *invincible*.'

'Ready?'

Satnam unlocked the front gates.

He paused, looking at the black computer screen. He couldn't hear anything from above. He was about to leave when he remembered the footage. He couldn't figure out how to erase it – his head was pulsing, his hair itching under the turban – so he just unplugged the laptop and carried it up with him.

'Time to go,' he told Pala on the phone, the stairs changing size as he stepped on them. He was stretching over great distances, climbing out of the basement.

'Come up, come up,' Pala was saying. 'We're all upstairs.'

Satnam came out in the main hall and could hear them laughing.

'We should go,' he called.

'We're up here!'

They were howling. Hitting their chests. Through the windows, Satnam saw the crowds.

'You've got to see what we found,' Pala said.

'The stairs are weird, man,' Satnam said.

'What?'

'The stairs!'

'Hell, yeah!'

He got on all fours and found it easier. The carpet was so soft. He stopped to inspect a painting of the English countryside. In the foreground, a peasant was bent over next to a stream. In the background, a landlord posed for a portrait, facing away, with nothing visible of the painter behind the easel but their legs. Satnam felt he was experiencing the stairway beyond language, his thoughts were just vibes, and the vibes, they were good. He stroked the wooden bannisters. What artistry! How much work it must have taken to craft each one, the wood spinning in the lathe, ribbons peeling away. He had come such a long way, he thought, looking down the stairs. The carpet smelled like old jumpers. Hugs.

'Bro?'

Pala helped him up to the library. The books were changing sizes. He opened one by Helena Blavatsky, which was fun to say, but the words were just shapes, insect ink.

'Blavatsky. Blavatsky.'

He moved the book closer to his face and Pala called to him. The rest of the men were gathered around a box, laughing.

'You have *got* to see this.'

Satnam looked inside, at a loss for words.

The box was filled with stone penises. The men emptied them out on to the antique coffee table. They were skilfully made, flaccid.

'From the statues,' Satnam said, eventually. The Trust must have kept them when they were removed from public view.

A firework went off outside, drawing them all to the window. The crowd had overcome the promenade. Suddenly, the window smashed, multiplying, and Vijay laughed. He'd thrown one of the rock cocks at the glass. The sound of chanting entered the room, along with the wind. They were shouting about traitors, about Urban Naxals; they were shouting about termites.

'Maybe we should go,' Satnam said, feeling nauseous. 'The plan—'

One of the other boys had grabbed a penis and threw it at the next window. Another, at the mirror. Then they were running around the house, smashing glass.

'We need to go.'

'If you want to go, go,' Pala said. 'I'll take the computer.'

'Don't leave without a souvenir,' Vijay said, handing him one of the faux-Grecian penises. Satnam put it in his pocket.

New Albion was only a few miles from the pindh. Satnam was trying to keep things the size they were meant to be. His shoes, the road, the trees. He could hear the fireworks behind him, champagne bottles popping. He thought back to yesterday morning, his unexpected visitor: the buyer had returned with an improved offer. Satnam had let him speak through the fence, not responding. 'I know you're there; I can see your silhouette. Just hear me out, at least. I drove all this way.' The man eventually gave up, sliding a business card under the gate. He was probably going door to door along the river route, Satnam thought, imagining his farm surrounded by apartment complexes, high-rises.

The walk was doing him good; his mind was clearing. He must have been sobering up. His phone buzzed and he assumed it was Pala. But it was Ore, back in London. A person from a past life.

Hey man, been a minute! Pints soon?

He held the phone closer to his face, to check the message was real, but then, in the dark, he heard the clink of metal on the road, a breath. He stopped, turned. He heard the breathing, louder now, and then the metal. Little padded feet – the dog. He was tripping, he told himself. This wasn't real. A growl, the sound of metal, like dropped coins. He turned and saw the dog's eyes in the dark, its teeth. He ran.

He wasn't sure whether to stay on the road or head off into the fields. The chance of a car coming and scaring the animal kept him on course. There was nothing but flat land on either side of the road, and no notable landmarks to speak of, bar the streetlight he was now approaching. The dog was gaining on him fast. He couldn't outrun him. He wouldn't give in. He pulled the penis out of his pocket as he ran; it would do more damage than his fist. As he reached the streetlight, the dog pounced on his leg, biting his thigh. He fell forward and rolled as he landed – the pain was real – and then he lashed out at the dog with the rock, hitting its hide again and again. In the stark fluorescent light, its teeth were yellow, almost green as it snarled. Satnam grabbed the chain and wrapped it around the pole of the streetlight, trying to improvise a knot while the dog was momentarily stunned. It ran towards him and he dived into the field, landing awkwardly. It was at his feet and he scrambled in the dirt, managing to get beyond the radius of the chain and the circle of light. The knot held as the dog strained at the leash, barking. Satnam tried to run, but had to limp. He was alive. This was real. He spat out mud.

Fifteen minutes later, he accepted a ride from a stranger. He asked if the man had seen a dog up the road, but the man didn't know what he was talking about. He looked around and got in, covering the wound in his thigh. The dark concealed the blood.

'Seen what's going down, up the road?' the farmer said. 'Madness.'

'Yeah,' Satnam said, eying the rear-view.

'Were you—?'

'No.'

'So, which way is home?' the man said, shifting in his seat. 'I'll take you as far as I can.'

April

The flights were grounded on account of the smog. The south-easterly winds had funnelled the smoke from Punjab, where some farmers were still burning their fields, through Haryana, where miles of land for the Saraswati had now been secured, down to Delhi, where Satnam awaited take-off. From the window seat, he could barely see the next plane over. He checked his SpeakFree feed. Exit polls were already predicting a landslide for Narayan Indra. The New Albion Trust had dissolved, donating their land to the local government to form a public park. Pala had messaged him a photo of their tar-black field, and Satnam reacted with a thumbs-up. Kush's daily quote read: *Greatness is always an alloy of good and bad.*

After take-off, Satnam asked the air hostess not to wake him for food when she passed in the aisle. He searched his bag for the painkillers for his leg. It felt like the fasting was working. He was a vessel. An empty vessel. A hollow mould into which a person could occasionally be poured. He took the pills, wrapped the phulkari around himself and was out until the descent.

He'd lost almost two days. All travel is time travel, he thought, limping up to another queue. In the slow-moving line, he switched to his UK SIM. The passport machine wouldn't recognise his face scan, so he was moved to another line.

'I'm here to sell my flat,' he told border control, after being questioned.

'The beard suits you,' the agent said, scratching his chin. 'It's taken me months just to get to this.'

It was late, and the Tube towards central heaved with drunkards. Satnam ran through a mantra in his head, trying to stay inconspicuous as the football fans began to sing and the beggar shook her paper cup. The air was hot and thick, as if they were passing through some vast exhaust pipe. The carriage rattled, the screech of the wheels drowning out the away fans, and then came to an abrupt stop in the darkness between stations. There was a long pause before the driver gave an update, but the intercom was obscured by white noise, the driver's monotonous drawl indecipherable.

With no signal, Satnam pretended to sleep. He counted repetitions of the mantra in his head, but failed to meditate, tuning into conversations around him.

'A tenner someone's offed themselves.'

'They always say signal failure, whatever it is.'

The driver piped up again, but nobody could understand him.

Satnam pretended to wake up from his fake sleep, yawning. Looking for anything to fill his mind, he reached into his rucksack for Bibi's blue notebook. He'd printed the Punjabi alphabet on the back page, and, flicking back and forth from the first page to the last, he attempted to begin a transliteration. He managed the first two words – a title? – *Heer Ranjha*, and typed them out in his Notes app. He didn't recognise either word, sounding them out in his head. He tried and failed to recall the exact sound of Bibi's voice. *Heer Ranjha*, he repeated in his head, with no idea. He checked his transliteration, certain it was correct, and moved on to the first line. A few words in, he became too tired to think. He put the book away. The driver spoke nothing again; from the intonations, it seemed that, whatever had happened, nothing had changed. The man across from him, a slick City worker, the sort who could have worked at Oracle, dramatically finished his paper.

'Swap?' he said, gesturing at the free paper next to Satnam with his neatly folded paid-for one.

Satnam dutifully read the man's paper. It was the same old circus. He skipped ahead to the world news.

India's River Idi-Odyssey.

He skim-read the piece, remembering why he didn't normally read the news. The article claimed the return of the water along the Saraswati route was simply due to the increasing speed at which the Himalayan glaciers were melting. The journalist went on to suggest that the river project was somehow an act of war: by diverting water from the Punjabi rivers that fed the Indus across the border, the Saraswati might cause a future drought in Pakistan. You couldn't really write a story like this, Satnam thought, from outside of it. Unless the reporter was on the ground, up close, he didn't really need to hear what they had to say. Especially when they wrote with such open disdain – at one point, they claimed the chief minister had actually changed his surname to Indra to help with his PR. Satnam turned the page, and, seeing a short article next to the longer opinion piece, he snapped the paper shut.

A man's tongue had been cut out by thugs in Punjab.

Six men had been arrested.

The Tube driver spoke again and finally there was movement.

Six months of mail had piled up behind the door to his flat. Satnam released the trapped air and used a campaign flyer from an election he'd missed to scoop up the dead insects on the windowsills and take them to the bin. He almost gagged, opening the bin – maggots, grey furry mould. He limped over to the kitchen window for fresh air. A fox walked down the empty road. He could see the TV in the flat opposite. He shut the curtains. The plugged sink in the bathroom was full of water, almost green in the light of the naked bulb. Short strands of hair floated on the surface – he'd shaved in a rush the morning he'd left for the airport. He pressed the plug and opened the box of contact lenses by the sink. He'd grown so used to his reduced sight that wearing them now hurt. He blinked at his reflection, straining. The place would need a deep clean before he called any estate agents. He checked the bedroom. Harp had made the bed before she left. Dust covered the bedside table like frost. He was about to enter the basement when his phone vibrated.

Kush Bhatt has left the conversation.

Satnam looked at the group chat's members. Only he and Pala remained.

He stepped down into the basement and his ear popped. It smelled of damp. There were watermarks on the walls. His phone vibrated, and vibrated again, messages coming in. Then he saw the mould. It had gathered in a patch on one wall, like some dark portal.

Finally, he opened SpeakFree. Several people had forwarded him the same article: *Six men linked with tongue attack released on bail.* He expanded the image: the men were wearing saffron-coloured garlands. Second from the left was Pala. The furthest to the right was Vijay.

He didn't know what to do. He had all this confused energy but no outlet. He opened his contacts and scrolled up and down. He hovered over Harp's name and called her. It rang – she hadn't blocked him – but she didn't answer.

When he heard the tone for voicemail, he opened his mouth, paused.

He imagined her listening to the message and hearing nothing but him breathing, like some creep. He had to say something. But what?

'Hey, I'm calling because I'm back in London and thought, you know, I hope you're well. Things have got confused I think, out of scale, and I'm not sure … but if you do hear this, don't feel in any way like you need to respond. You don't owe me anything, I know that. I did a bad thing. With us, I mean. And I can't undo it. But if you wanted to speak, I don't know.'

He hung up and sat down on the basement steps, looking at the circle of mould. He could hear Pala's voice. He could see it all so clearly, the scene unfolding the evening he'd left the farm for Amritsar, for his connecting flight to Delhi. He could imagine Pala heading out as Reha did Emperor's night-time routine. The wind in his hair as he rode to the others, who would have gathered at the edge of the contested land. The increased dose of soma. The chanting. The Glenfiddich. Slapping each other, getting psyched, before heading up the path. Forcing the door and entering the small room, not quite square. The man cowering in the corner, eyes wide, calling the police. Not only had he refused to sign the river rights on his land, but he had taken to social media to talk about the Saraswati, to air his conspiracy theories.

'Why ring them? We are the police,' Pala might have said, before scanning the room, water dripping from the drying dishes, a pile of tattered school textbooks propping up a TV antenna, the spinning fan above a blade short.

And they probably grabbed the man and pinned him down to the cot. The wood creaking under their weight, Pala grinning as he took out the scissors.

'You regret what you said?'

'I'm sorry,' the man might have said. 'I'm sorry, I'm so sorry. I take it back. I take it all back. I was wrong. I was so wrong. I didn't see. But now I do. I'm so sorry. I swear—'

He was punched on his right temple, according to the reports. One man likely grabbed his bottom jaw, holding his mouth open. Another knelt on his forehead, causing bruising. Their victim would have kicked and struggled, no doubt, to bite, but the men had no injuries. Perhaps there was a gag. Or they rendered him unconscious before Pala attempted his first incision.

Satnam could imagine his neighbour looking down into the dark well of the man's throat, spitting. The barber's scissors gleaming cold against the hot, wriggling tongue – a purple deep-sea creature – cleaving the thing from its root. Likely, the man would have almost choked on it, but his attackers pushed him on to his side – that was how he was found, face down in the red sheets – before running out into the dark, leaving the tongue writhing on the floor, moving as if it were still in the man's mouth, still a part of the sound he made, that animal sound, that song.

HEER RANJHA
1878

It was the same old stories they wanted, over and over.

The family had gathered in the courtyard. You could cook a roti on the sunlit tiles, which they might have done if they had any flour. Sejal sat between her mother and sister, and carried on with her needlework. Her little cousins continued to debate about which story they wanted her aunt to tell.

To Sejal, a story was like an ear of corn: once you'd consumed it, all that was left was husk. But people these days were indeed chewing on old husks. It gave the semblance of eating, even if there was nothing to swallow. The kids would leave the cleaned-out cobs in the sun, until they were dry as bone, and then they used them as toy daggers. If you got hit by one with enough force, it left marks like teeth.

Sejal understood the desire for familiarity and routine for the very young and the very old, but, now she was sixteen, she couldn't relate to it. Once you knew where a story was going, what was the point of continuing? It had been two summers since the story-wallah had come through the village with fresh material, and in his absence they were stuck with the same few qisse that her aunt could remember. Inside, they were all the same, the way one carcass was identical to another: *two people connect across a divide, and the divide swallows them up.*

In the qisse, something happened each day; people's lives changed. But all of Sejal's days were more or less the same: she and her family performing their parts on the farm like dancers doing giddha, a pattern to it all, as if written in cloth. Of the acres of land they farmed, of all those open fields, they only ever walked down the same few paths, which deepened and widened like riverbeds.

Sejal was destined to live the life of her mother, who had lived the life of her mother. As soon as her sister's wedding was completed this week, attention would turn to her – such was the need now for money, such was the need for food.

Her little cousins finally voted for the story they wanted their aunt to tell: 'Heer Ranjha!'

How they were so energetic, Sejal didn't know – they'd had nothing but watered-down buffalo milk and a single cob between them since yesterday. If the rains didn't come soon, the family would have to eat seeds, next year's yield.

'There isn't enough thread,' Sejal whispered to her mother, as the children formed a circle in front of her aunt.

'You'll be fine,' her mother said, without looking.

Sejal was working on the last dupatta of her sister's wedding set: a sataranga. She was on the seventh colour of the phulkari now – gold. She watched a spider crawl across the fabric, passing from flower to flower, waiting for the inevitable shriek when her sister spotted it. How many nights had she heard her sister's call for help, found her marooned on a stool, held captive by the smallest of spiders? Sejal the saviour trapping it in a cup and releasing the thing outside.

'You killed it?' her sister would ask.

'Of course,' Sejal would lie.

Her sister's husband would have to deal with the spiders and lizards come Sunday. Not that Sejal imagined many cobwebs in his house with the painted walls.

The world is a web and Waheguru is the thread, she remembered her mother saying, when she first taught her to sew. *One side of the cloth is day, and the other is night, and the needle is you.* She was connected to the spider on the fabric and the silk stitching, to the silkworms who made them and the mulberry leaves which they had eaten, taken from a tree a bird might call home for a night, before flying up into clouds that would soon be rain. How to show all that on a phulkari? All her sister wanted was flowers.

Even though Sejal knew this pattern inside out – it was one of the first her mother had taught her – she worked slowly. She liked to imagine the wedding being delayed if she didn't finish the phulkari on time, her sister kept home for as long as she continued to weave, the pattern on the khaddar increasingly intricate until it was as detailed and messy as life, could show all the women here in the courtyard, her aunt telling 'Heer Ranjha' yet again, her sister listening to it for what might be the final time.

'A long time ago, not far from here, lived a village chief. He had eight sons and two daughters, and Ranjha, his youngest, was his favourite. While everyone else worked on the land, the chief let Ranjha loaf and play music.'

Her aunt was a faithful storyteller; her wording and intonation never changed. She told stories the way Sejal's mother wanted her to sew – each phulkari a perfect replica. *Why the same pattern again?* Sejal would argue. *Wasn't that the point of the Angrezi machines?* Whenever Sejal strayed from the path of the set pattern, her mother would have her undo the work and begin again. But Sejal believed a pattern could incorporate any mistake: if she messed up the fiftieth stitch, she could go on to mess up the hundredth. Perhaps her mother thought that in teaching her to follow a pattern, she might grow to follow her routine, to repeat each day as dutifully as her own mother had: wake, wash, feed and milk the water buffalo, sweep the courtyard, start the fire, the tea, the breakfast … Maybe Sejal's dream of breaking away from that – to work for the seamstress across the river, to venture beyond the pindh – was just part of the greater plan: the pattern could incorporate the mistakes. Hadn't her sister sworn she would only ever marry if it was to someone beautiful? Now, she was marrying an old man for the sake of a buffalo and two chickens. That was the cost of her life.

'When the chief died, his land was split among his children. Because his siblings had worked hard, and Ranjha had done almost nothing, he was given a barren plot where little could grow. And because he had been so spoiled, he didn't know how to farm. He went from being rich to becoming destitute. He abandoned his land and ventured off to play music. He had no idea where to go, but when he heard word of a great beauty in the land of the Sials, he decided to find her.

'At the Chenab, he realised he had no money to pay the ferryman. He took out his trusty flute and began to play. The song was so beautiful that crowds gathered and the people paid for his crossing.'

Sejal's sister rested her head on Sejal's shoulder.

'On the other side of the river, lazy as he was, Ranjha found a resting bed and went to sleep. Little did he know, the bed belonged to Heer, the beautiful woman he had heard rumours about! She regularly came to the river with her friends. When they all arrived that day and saw Ranjha in Heer's bed, they shouted at him to wake up. He and Heer locked eyes … They were instantly in love.'

Sejal's sister looked up at her and they grinned. Sejal covered the spider with her hand, but it crawled up into her palm. She wondered what it would taste like, if it could push away her hunger, even briefly. Did the famine affect spiders, too? Was the thing on her hand as hungry as she was? She thought of the birds who usually ate their leftover roti – what were they eating now? The mornings were quieter. Normally, flies would flit about the faces of their two water buffalo, but where were they now? Before her sister could look down and see, Sejal squeezed her hand shut. She brought the spider up to her mouth and ate it. It was like swallowing a hair.

'Heer and Ranjha made a plan to see each other again. Heer persuaded her father to hire Ranjha on their farm. And, like that, the son of the village chief became a cowherd, taking water buffalo from Heer's house to the forest on the banks of the Chenab.

'On his walks, Ranjha played the flute, enchanting the buffalo to follow him without ever wandering off. And, deep in the heart of the forest, the buffalo and other animals would dance to his music! Such was his gift of song. Seeing this wondrous sight for herself, Heer fell even deeper in love. They got married in secret in the forest, and every day Heer brought Ranjha lunch and they ate together among the trees and the animals, husband and wife, and they were happy.'

Normally, her aunt would then go into a long description of all the wondrous food the couple ate, detailing the brilliance of Heer's cooking. But today, for the first time, she skipped on.

'One day, after spending the afternoon in the forest together, Heer went down to the river to get some water. While she was gone, her uncle approached Ranjha. He suspected Ranjha, a lowly cowherd, of having an affair with his high-born niece. The uncle disguised himself as a faqir and asked Ranjha for some food. Ranjha shared some of his lunch with the old man. The uncle recognised the taste immediately – only his niece could cook like this!'

Sejal licked the golden thread and put it back through the needle it had fallen free of. Her aunt raised her voice as she described how Heer's uncle told her mother about the affair: 'The family name was in ruins! The only option was to marry Heer off, far away. She was matched with one of the Kheras on the other side of the river.

'Heer, of course, refused. She and Ranjha were married in the eyes of God! Ranjha was actually the son of a village chief; he wasn't really a cowherd ...'

Sejal's aunt paused, knowing she'd arrived at the kids' favourite part.

'Her mother cut her off,' she said. '"If I'd known you'd grow up to be such a whore, I'd have put you in a box as a baby and tossed you in the river. If I'd known how you'd ruin our name, I'd have pushed you down into the well." After the fight, Heer was married off to a son of the Kheras. Even at the wedding, she resisted, debating with the qazi that it was against Islamic law for her to be married against her will. To which the qazi told her it was against the law too to resist the will of her parents. She was married.'

Sejal's sister picked at her cuticles and ate the dead skin. It was a trick they'd learnt the last time the harvest failed.

Their aunt was in full flow now, their very own Waris Shah: 'The issue of love is that its current is too strong to be confined within social order. It flows wherever it flows.'

Sejal's mother ran her fingers across the phulkari. Her left hand, permanently clenched into a loose fist, lay on her lap. The story behind her injured hand had changed throughout Sejal's childhood, depending on what it was her mother was chastising her about. It was injured because she was playing with the water buffalo when she shouldn't have been, or because she got too close to the fire when cooking, or because she was climbing a tree even when she had been told not to.

'You'll need to get more thread,' her mother said now.

However the injury had actually happened, Sejal's mother had never been able to sew. Nevertheless, she'd learnt the technique and the patterns from Sejal's grandmother. 'If I didn't learn,' she'd told Sejal, 'who would have taught you? And then what would my granddaughters know? And their daughters?'

This particular pattern was Sejal's great-grandmother's. Flowers with interlacing stems, locked together by their thorns. 'However far the women of this family go,' her mother had said, 'wherever it is they end up, whichever families they're married into, they'll know our phulkari, our own patterns that you can't buy in any market, that no one else can replicate. Pass every stitch down.'

'Yes … it flows where it flows,' her aunt repeated now, after a rehearsed pause. 'Heer was unhappily married, and each night, in bed, she longed for her beloved, her Ranjha. She prayed to be with him, and he prayed to be with her. He heard rumours of where she had been taken and took on the guise of a chaste yogi to be able to travel towards her.'

'What's "chaste"?' one of Sejal's cousins asked.

'When Ranjha arrived in Heer's new village, he sat by the common well and stayed there, day and night, waiting to see her. Local women spread word about his good looks. When Heer's sister-in-law described him, Heer knew instantly who it was. She confided in her – and told her how she had been married against her will.

'Her sister-in-law was shocked and she agreed to help reunite Heer and Ranjha.'

Sejal had always thought that the story should have ended with Heer and Ranjha reunited in the woods, running away together. But her aunt went on: 'When the lovers escaped, they were chased by the Kheras and captured. It was decided that Heer would be returned to her husband, and Ranjha banished. Hearing the verdict, Ranjha fell to his knees and struck the earth. He called upon God to punish the Kheras and the villagers, and all who stood in the path of his and Heer's love. And as he raised his arms to the heavens, a fire burst out in the village! People ran out to the river to try to extinguish the blaze. All agreed that the flames were a sign from above: Heer and Ranjha were supposed to be together.'

Sejal finally reached the end of the thread. Her mother fetched a small pot of yoghurt that she could trade for more silk at the general store.

'It doesn't matter,' Sejal's sister said. 'I think it looks nice as it is.'

'Don't be ridiculous,' their mother said. 'It's not finished. You two go on together.'

In one way, Sejal was glad to leave before her aunt finished the story. She hated the ending of Heer Ranjha: the couple finally happy, celebrating their wedding day, only to be given a box of poisoned laddu by Heer's disgraced parents. Heer takes a bite of the sweet and dies in Ranjha's arms. Unable to bear life without her, Ranjha finishes the laddu and dies, too. Some stories went on too long, Sejal thought. If it didn't end in the woods, it should have ended at the altar.

They walked downhill towards the river. The store was on the other side of the Beas.

'Maybe you'll be able to come and visit,' her sister said, biting her nails. 'You could come and stay.'

'Yeah,' Sejal said. Her sister's new home would be several days away. 'That would be nice.'

'How much is there?' her sister asked.

Sejal opened the pot. The watered-down yoghurt smelled deliciously sour.

'I suppose we only really need a little bit of thread,' Sejal said.

'They won't know how much was in there to begin with …'

'… And business must be slow; they'd take what they can get.'

'So …'

Sejal shut the lid. 'No. No. Mum would kill us.'

'And I thought *I* was the boring one.'

They walked on. Sejal had all sorts of questions but didn't know how to ask them. Growing up, she'd assumed she would have her sister by her side for life. But to marry so far away! She could probably now count the number of times they would see each other again on her knuckles. There was so much to talk about, so little time. 'So, you're happy with all of this?' she asked. 'It feels right?'

'It doesn't look like River Baba is here,' her sister said, looking at the crossing point. 'How long's it been since we crossed?'

'A month, at least.'

'You don't think he's—'

'He was *old*, old.'

River Baba was a friend of their grandfather's, and always let them cross for free.

His replacement, a tall young man, about Sejal's age, wore fine clothes. When he smiled at Sejal, she looked down. He introduced himself as Jugaad, in a deep voice.

Sejal's sister explained that they usually crossed for free and didn't have any coins.

'Well, what's that you have there?' he asked.

Sejal opened the pot and gave him a spoonful.

He held her hand to help her on to the boat. Facing them as he rowed, he was careful not to look at Sejal. While he looked back to see the opposite bank, she allowed herself to regard him.

Her sister leant on her shoulder again. 'Finish the story,' she said, 'one last time.'

'The wedding was great fun and Heer and Ranjha were happy, so happy. They bought fertile land along the Chenab, and Ranjha worked hard every day, singing the plants from the soil, herding his animals with his flute. Heer raised many gorgeous children, and met her younger sister often, and the two of them would have lots of fun, and the kids would play in the green fields. Heer and Ranjha happily grew old and fat—'

'Fat?'

Sejal caught Jugaad's eye as he smiled, and then the world dimmed. They all looked up. A cloud! A dark cloud.

A speck of rain on her arm. And another. Rings blossomed on the surface of the river. Jugaad put down the oars and reached his hands out. Raindrops ran down his brows, his sharp cheekbones, his jawline. Droplets clung to the thin hairs on his arms like dew on grass.

The three of them laughed. They drifted with the current, bobbing up and down. Sejal opened the pot and they each took handfuls of the thinning yoghurt, eating with abandon. They licked their fingers clean and turned their heads up to the sky, their mouths open in silent howls, tasting water, after all this time, fresh water.

If she hadn't run out of thread, if her sister wasn't getting married, if River Baba hadn't died, Sejal might not have met Jugaad. And if the clouds hadn't arrived, and the rain hadn't fallen, if the fate of the village hadn't changed, maybe nothing would have passed between them. All the generations after them, all those branches, it was all down to two people meeting, beginning to talk. It was the same old story for everyone, a dream of a story that doesn't end, that always changes, a pattern large enough to hold everything within it.

BEAS

As the crickets' soft autumn hum is to us
So are we to the trees
As are they
To the rocks and the hills

'Front Lines', Gary Snyder

1. Camp Justice, Diego Garcia

Katrina had long insisted, with diminishing conviction, that she would meet her person in the *real world* and not on the apps, and so was at times more willing than her friends to entertain the attention of strangers – especially if the man in question looked anything like Jay. He put down his newspaper and looked across her at the view through the plane window, the islands they were still circling. 'Vantage of the vulture,' he said, in a voice that reverberated.

Any attraction Katrina might have felt over the duration of the flight was now tempered by the fact that he was American. She smiled, and he took her silence to mean she hadn't heard him.

'I said vantage of—'

'I wonder why we haven't landed,' she said, glancing down at *The Times*. A group of garlanded Indian men were grinning: *The Saraswati Six Cleared Amid River Turmoil.*

When she looked up, he was looking at her. His eyes flitted

83

back to the window. Like her, he seemed to be in his early thirties. He wore no uniform, but something about his posture and build said military. Then again, this was supposed to be a civilian flight, the first non-military service to the Chagos Archipelago in several months. He had claimed their shared armrest, his elbow crossing the border between their seats. The face of his watch was turned to the inside of his wrist, not out, and had already been set to the local time below. The second hand glided smoothly without stopping.

They didn't know then that the reason the plane was unable to land was that a family of feral donkeys had dozed off on the runway on Diego Garcia. In a few months' time, the donkeys would become a central part of their shared lore, major players in the origin story they would occasionally bring out at dinner parties. 'See, if the wild donkeys hadn't been placed under protection by a new British environmental act, the soldiers would have shot at them as they used to and the plane would have landed on time, and Kat and I probably never would have spoken.'

Katrina would then take the thought experiment a step further. The two of them would never have talked if the donkeys hadn't lived on the island in the first place, and the donkeys wouldn't have arrived on the island if the Chagossians – who had been enslaved by the French and made to work on coconut plantations – hadn't been freed. Once they were working for themselves, on their own land, they turned to animal labour, donkeys. But the Chagossians wouldn't have been freed were it not for France losing the Napoleonic Wars on the other side of the world, which wouldn't have happened unless ... and so on, etc.

Here, Jay would take the baton back and say that the Chagossians wouldn't necessarily have been on the island were it not for the French taking them from the east coast of Africa to grow coconuts, to harvest oil, to light lamps in the west. But, then again, the French wouldn't have known about the islands were it not for the logs of a Portuguese captain, Diego Garcia, whose ship had been waylaid by a storm in the Indian Ocean hundreds of years earlier and happened upon the archipelago, his crew likely the first mammals to leave marks in the sand.

Their dinner-party routine sometimes ended at Diego claiming the land as his own and promptly abandoning it, never to return, but normally the couple would go on to reveal the other chapter of history that led to the redundant donkeys turning wild and camping out on the runway, delaying the landing long enough that Jay plucked up the courage to start a conversation. The fact that all the native Chagossians were brutally rounded up by the British in 1976 and forced into an illegal exile that was yet to end. Several generations were squeezed into cramped hulls, along with the animals that the British didn't gas, bound for the Seychelles, Mauritius and the UK, never to live on their own land again. Diego Garcia, the largest island of the British Empire's newest colony, was then rented to the US military for the establishment of a strategically located base, named Camp Justice, from which the Americans could bomb much of the eastern world. If the Chagossians still lived on their land, still farmed, if their children still climbed trees and invented games, if they could still fish their waters and feed scraps to their pets that could still run along their beaches, if they could tell stories and laugh and sing around fires, in front of TV sets, in bed, could still drink on porches and smoke and fuck and fall in love and raise children on the land of their grandparents and their grandparents and their grandparents, then there would have been no Camp Justice and there would have been no Jay and Katrina.

'So, what are you in for?' Jay said, once they'd introduced themselves. 'Inciting jihad?'

The person across the aisle, one of the Filipino contractors that filled the rest of the plane, gave him a look.

'Pest control,' Katrina said. 'Yellow crazy ants.'

'Yellow crazy ants,' Jay said.

'Yellow crazy ants,' she said. 'The true arseholes of nature. I've studied them long enough to feel good about being called an exterminator.'

'What makes them crazy?'

'You really want to know?'

'Captive audience.'

'They're what's known as generalist invaders. When they arrive in a new ecosystem, they decimate it. There's been a sighting here in Chagos.' She briefly met his gaze. 'Which is bad news. Essentially, their queens go off in search of new terrain and find new resources around which they build new colonies. But unlike other species, they join up their colonies in these crazy-ant empires – supercolonies, with multiple queens. They eat everything, spitting out this acid. Worms, spiders, frogs. Nesting birds, lizards. They'll wipe out one species, and then the whole chain collapses. Which, on an island like this … It's growth without end.'

'Until you come in.'

'Exactly.'

While they spoke, Katrina attempted to guess Jay's ethnicity. His name could have belonged to any continent. His skin tone didn't give any exact answers, nor did his hair. She couldn't determine race from his accent, his brown eyes. She didn't know if everyone played her little game of origination when they met new people, but were too polite to acknowledge it, or if it really was just her and the boomers. She figured the question of where a person was from was as important a means of understanding someone as anything. But convention held that you had to ask what someone *did*, rather than who they were or where they were from – you had to stick with verbs, not nouns, all of us active agents determining our own futures, not passive accidents of history, mediated by the world into which we were thrust.

What Jay *did* was work as a trail designer for the US military – she'd got something right. The officials at Camp Justice

86

wanted a series of trails built on Diego Garcia and the smaller islands surrounding it, which could be used in training exercises. 'It's nice not to have a desk,' he said.

She was trying to figure out a follow-up question when he asked: 'Where are you from? If you don't mind—'

'Port Louis,' she said. He nodded, but it was clear he didn't know where that was. 'In Mauritius. And you?'

'Orange, New Jersey,' he said. 'And, before that, Trinidad. Well, not me – my mum.'

Just like that, she had an opening into the conversation. And the light was just so that the small coincidence chimed like fate. She told him her family legend, that her ancestors had left India to go to work in Trinidad, but never made it past the boat's first stop in Mauritius.

The stewardesses came out with complimentary drinks to apologise for the unexplained delay. Which was the moment, they would later say, that they knew.

'Eyes,' Jay said, as they touched their plastic glasses together, grinning. 'Eyes.'

'I thought I'd save you,' Jay said, offering her a drink out on the deck of the Island Room. Katrina's BritRep sponsor had abandoned her with a group of marines at the welcome mixer, and she'd been roped into rounds. Everything was spinning nicely. The world was a dark place with unfathomable depths, but how good it was to float a while on the surface of things, to be happily drunk in good company. She knew she was sitting on stolen land, but it was also true that she was smiling, flirting, that some of the hairs on her right arm were raising as Jay brushed his fingertip across the scar on her elbow.

'I got caught in the lines, sailing.'

The bell rang for last orders and they walked down to the beach, passing the *No glass bottled drinks* sign with a bottle of white.

'I can't believe you've never been for a night swim,' Jay said, taking off his shirt.

'Yeah, no thank you,' she said, watching him strip. 'I'm not a risk person.'

He turned and ran into the dark sea. She took a swig, trying not to think about his body.

A few sips later, she began to worry. She couldn't see him. The waves were loud; she wouldn't hear him if he called out to her. She walked towards the water, running through even-tualities: calling the soldiers; forming a search party, torches illuminating the white veins of foaming waves; the bloated body washing ashore weeks later ...

But then Jay appeared, completely naked, hands cupped to cover his modesty. 'I lost my damn briefs! Can you?'

She threw him his jeans. His lips were still wet when they kissed, tasted of salt. If he had pushed to come back to hers or for her to go to his, she would have agreed. But he only asked once. 'I have to sleep,' she said. 'The eradication programme starts tomorrow.'

While Jay hiked around Diego Garcia recording potential routes, Katrina studied the maps of colonies that the BritRep heading up the invasive-species committee had put together. The worst outbreak was on the Salomon atoll, north of Diego and east of Peros Banhos. Perhaps the ants had reached the area via a civilian yacht which had illegally moored off the coast of Ile Anglaise, an island rarely visited by BIOT officials. From there, they could have travelled on flotsam south to Ile Boddam, and later boarded a US vessel down to the Great Chagos Bank. She was flown to and from the islands by hel-icopter, but didn't have clearance to take any photographs, so described the landscapes to Jay when they met for dinner each night, the only civilians in the mess.

She was grateful to have taxing work to fill the days she

would otherwise have spent overthinking their situation. They were two adults having casual fun, and that could be that. They had no past, and knew from the start that, after their three months in Chagos and their return to their separate countries, they would have no future; all they had was the present, and she was OK with that, really – fun was fine.

After taking wind readings, she went up in one of the Seabees' choppers and used the university's dispersal machine to spray the tropical forest below with AntOff. As it fell, she imagined what it would look like from below, volcanic ash. The acid-spewing colony, attracted to the granulated fishmeal in the ant bait, would consume fipronil, an insecticide which caused a hyperexcitation in their nerves and muscles.

'What a way to go,' Jay said, when she showed him a video. 'Pure rapture.'

Looking out at Salomon, Katrina thought of Jay's auntie spasming in church, in the story he'd told her, claiming to be possessed, to be taken by the spirit, and, as Katrina pressed release, she imagined the souls of the ants rising from their glitching bodies – no, they definitely sank.

'If there is a hell,' she said to him in bed, 'it's crawling with yellow crazy ants. And the god that designed them.'

'To hunt,' Jay said, 'the predator has to think like its prey. Empathy has its roots in killing.'

'You're saying I think like an ant?'

'A crazy ant.'

On her third visit to Salomon, circling Boddam, she looked away from her monitor and spotted a small speedboat bound for Peros Banhos.

It didn't look military.

There was a flag flapping in the wind aboard it, but she couldn't make out the colours from where she was.

'What's that?' she asked.

When the helicopter pilots didn't reply, she realised they had cut the radio. They were discussing something without her hearing, and then they carved a new course, swerving suddenly back towards Camp Justice.

Katrina craned her neck to look back at the boat. From this height, the drama of the ocean and its giant waves were flattened; the boat looked insignificant. It was a wonder that so small thing a could have caused such a stir; when she arrived back on Diego, it was clear that something was very wrong.

The next day, her BritRep sponsor met her for breakfast.

'You've been making great progress. Well done for finishing work on the northern islands. My colleagues tell me it's a done deal.'

'Excuse me?'

'The northern islands are good. We'll have someone come round with your flight details.'

'But Peros Banhos, you said there were sightings on Peros Banhos. I haven't even been down on the ground.'

'Katrina, we've been very happy with your work. You'll have the full honorarium.'

'If they take Peros Banhos, who's to say they don't make it to Diego? We agreed on months. This is bigger than politics. This is—'

A flight was called in for the next evening. The pilots and crew arrived in the morning with hours to kill, and turned heads on the beach. Katrina and Jay watched them swim. She could tell Jay was making a concerted effort not to look at the stewardesses. Shifting a touch in the sand, Katrina couldn't see a single building or sign, couldn't see any uniforms or evidence of the military base, and if she had taken a photo, she thought, and found it again decades later, she might have remembered the idyllic scene as belonging to some perfect holiday. But, somewhere nearby, the queens were moving, their colonies crawling over carcasses. She'd only been here for two weeks. She should have had at least three months on the island with Jay. But now they had only a couple of hours.

'I think we should go somewhere we can talk,' Jay said. 'I can tell my sponsor I forgot some equipment on one of the routes.'

He managed to get the car keys, and they drove around the atoll, past the Ground-Based Electro-Optical Deep Space Surveillance Centre, on the road towards Sunset Point. He parked up on a soft verge and they headed into the jungle, following the trees Jay had marked with red spray paint. The silence between them bloated with possible meanings. Finally, far enough from the road, he began to speak.

'Have you tried reading any news?' he said.

'Not with any success.'

'My internet's out, too. Anything could be happening out there.'

She'd hoped he'd brought her on the walk to talk about the two of them, but now she realised he wanted to get out of 'downtown' before talking about the island. It was shameful, selfish, to equate her small life with whatever was happening out there, but she couldn't control what her body felt.

'I mean, there's no torture laws here, right,' he said. 'Maybe that's the boat you saw. It could be anyone. They could be doing ... anything.'

She didn't know what to say.

They lost and gained height along the path, crossing a small stream and then winding up an increasingly rocky incline. Soon, they were above some of the younger trees, could see the wildlife in the higher branches.

'My last trail,' Jay said, 'I was working with this guy who claims his great-whatever was a Texas Ranger, a frontier guy. This was the 1870s, he said, and barbed wire had just been invented? Up to then, the rich people in the east, they'd hire cowboys to safeguard their livestock. But then, barbed wire is so cheap, they're suddenly redundant. It was his job

91

to protect the fences; the cowboys were going around with wire-cutters.'

Katrina refused Jay's hand when he offered to help her over a boulder. She wouldn't bring it up, she decided. It wouldn't be on her to raise anything.

Jay continued, walking ahead. 'Now, unlike buffalo, the cows needed to travel south in the winters, trampling grazing grounds. No one owned that land and they could move freely. But then the fences. Apparently, in one year a single factory produced enough barbed wire to circle the world ten times. Don't quote me on that.' He turned to her. 'Are you OK?'

She nodded.

'Well, anyway,' he said, quieter now. 'There was this awful winter. Hundreds of thousands of cows running south in a blizzard. The fastest of them hit the fences first, bled to death. The ones behind them, with nowhere to go, were forced into the bodies of the dead. Those in the middle suffocated, those in the back froze.'

He held up a branch so that she could pass under it.

'I don't know, it just feels like more and more things make me think of those cows.' He looked as if he might say something else, but stopped himself.

Slowly, the breeze returned, carrying the calls of birds, and they emerged into a clearing, with a vista of the glittering British Indian Ocean Territory waters framed by the dense foliage. Facing this way, there was nothing but greenery and sea, a view that could have belonged to any age. Jay leant in for a hug.

'Don't touch my back,' Katrina said. 'Your trail's made me sweat.'

He paused, looked her in the eye. 'What are we?' he said. 'Where do we go from here?'

They connected to the Wi-Fi at Changi Airport, after transferring from Paya Lebar Royal Singapore Air Force Base. It was an hour until Jay's flight to New York, six hours until hers to Port Louis.

They scanned the news, expecting some declaration of war that would have justified their expulsion from Camp Justice. But there was little of note in the headlines. Another American school shooting. A boat landing in Italy, completely empty. A forest fire the size of Wales in Australia. Melted permafrost had revealed the world's most intact mammoth skeleton. India's new prime minister, Narayan Indra, had been sworn in, drinking water from the newly surfaced Saraswati River during his inaugural speech. She could only find news of Chagos by specifically searching for it.

'I don't even have your number,' she said to Jay. 'I'll forward you this article.'

A group of tourists had recognised an Indian actor, Amit Das, waiting for his flight. They asked for autographs, and soon a small queue formed in front of Katrina and Jay's seats while they scrolled.

They'd been wrong about the prisoners. Wrong about a war. The reason they had been sent home early from Diego Garcia was because a small delegation of native Chagossians had chartered a boat to Peros Banhos. Citing the UN ruling that Chagos be returned to the exiled Chagossians and that the UK had no sovereign claim to the archipelago, this was the first time they had visited their homeland without a British escort. On board were seven Chagossians, an English journalist and cameraman, and two Mauritian politicians. The US and UK forces were powerless to react with cameras rolling. The islanders were filmed dropping to their knees on the beach, kissing the sand and then entering the dense bush.

Deserted since the seventies, trees and plants had grown through the buildings' windowless openings, their empty doorways. The islanders cleared debris and droppings from the roofless church, taking photos, singing. The politicians were filmed planting a flagpole, raising the Mauritian flag.

Once the right photos had been taken, it was clear that it was time to leave. Six of the seven headed towards the boat. But one woman, Marianne, refused to leave. International law said this was her land. She had the UN and the ICJ on her side. She was going to sleep on the island, her island.

The group attempted to reason with her – there was no running water, no safe shelter, no means by which to communicate with the outside world. When it was clear they wouldn't succeed in getting through to her, they decided to return in a few days and collect her. There was one clip of Marianne being interviewed by the journalist. Katrina gave one of her AirPods to Jay and they watched it on her phone.

'How will I live on Peros Banhos, you say? It is inside my body. My mother knew this land. My children will know this land. They will grow old on Peros Banhos, on Diego. They will die, as I will, as my mother couldn't, in Chagos.

'I have been in courtrooms, I have been in protests. I have camped outside the Houses of Parliament and the International Court of Justice. I have held up signs, I have been in newspapers. But it has achieved nothing. The only place to protest is here. On the land. With this air in my lungs, with coconut flesh in my gut.'

Jay's flight was called on the tannoy. Katrina watched him slowly remove the AirPod. She and Jay would have had two and a half more months of dinners and afternoon hikes, if Marianne hadn't laid claim to her native land; so much more sex, so many late-night conversations, kisses with morning breath, breakfasts at the mess.

'Well,' he said.

'OK,' she said.

He looked up at the board, paused. His knee was shaking.

'If you could go anywhere on that list,' he said, 'where would you choose?'

New York, Bangkok, Tokyo, Wellington, Karachi, Dubai, Cairo, Paris.

When she answered, he looked up flights.
And she googled accommodation.

2. Longyearbyen, Spitsbergen

Jay's – and, in turn, Katrina's – obsession with Mount Kailash, the sacred source of the Saraswati River, began after landing in Longyearbyen, the world's northernmost settlement, during the season of the midnight sun, for their honeymoon.

They planned to stay in the old coal-mining town for a few nights before heading out on a hike, starting at the Svalbard Global Seed Bank, the Doomsday Vault, where a million seeds were stored underground, then making their way into the interior to get a sight of the receding glaciers, and round to the abandoned 'city' of Advent. Jay had done the route when he was in his twenties, and thought he could lead the hike himself, just the two of them.

'I'll just need to rent a gun,' he said. 'Everyone I knew here had one, for the polar bears. They're all gone now.'

'The bears?'

'My friends. People come for a few seasons, then go.'

She agreed to the holiday, so long as they went with an official guide.

'You're questioning my masculinity, here.'

'Cute.'

It wasn't exactly the kind of hotel room Katrina had imagined having for her honeymoon. But Jay wasn't the kind of man she had imagined marrying. They had sex, showered, had sex. They woke from a nap and it was still light, and amid the cool sheets there was an overwhelming sense of bliss.

'I have, like, zero idea what time it is.'

They laboured over the mechanics of the coffee machine.

'I think the water goes in here – no, here.'

'Maybe you twist it? Are you sure it's on?'

They drew the curtains and whichever switch they tried, it

turned the wrong light off or on; there was no conceivable logic to the wiring. Everything had been building to this moment, she thought, as Jay went about the room wearing nothing but complimentary slippers, trying different switches; her whole life, the lives of their parents and theirs, and so on, to the Big Bang and whatever came before that, had all been building to this flickering moment, and this, and this! The play of light through the net curtains, the pile of pillows. The smell of sweat and the hot pressure of the shower, a single travel-sized bottle of conditioner containing enough far-off ingredients to have made a medieval man rich. Every moment gave on to another and another, like those atoms splitting and multiplying in petri dishes, and love had lowered her threshold of wonder to such a degree that there was beauty in their blurred form in the mirror, the snatches of fresh, cold air through the spinning extractor fan, beauty in the texture of a towel, the wild pattern of moulted hair on the glass partition, a footprint appearing and then disappearing on under-heated tiles.

Jay laced Katrina's hiking boots, and she looked down at the swirl of hair, or lack thereof, from which the rest of his hair seemed to originate. It looked like a hurricane as seen from space, an approaching front. All his other hairs subtly pointed away from it, like grass bending in wind. His body was end-lessly fascinating to her, and she couldn't envisage a world in which she tired of it. He kissed her stomach as he finished the left shoe, and she thought of all the millions of microorganisms that lived within him. There would likely have been hundreds or thousands of generations inside his body, vast family trees, empires and civilisations of minute beings, which, in making out and fucking, would have also crossed over into her body in a kind of mutual colonisation. Their skin, when touching, less a border than a permeable membrane, a site of crossing.

Snow from their boots turned to water under their table at breakfast. They ate well and stepped back into the cold, walking south to the crossroads. The few cars on the main road stopped as a reindeer approached, faces pressed to windows to see the great beast bow its head, sniff the grey slush and pause in thought. Finally, it continued on, and the engines started up again.

Katrina and Jay arrived at the crossroads early, debating the interior life of reindeer. They built a small snowman, kicked its head in. They had expected a group of hikers on the tour, so, when Edward arrived in the cab, they were surprised to find it empty save for the driver. Spending their honeymoon hiking as part of a group was one thing, but hiking with just a third wheel? Jay gave his *I was right* look as they got in.

'Enjoy the last of the heating,' Edward said, from the front. He passed back a map and ran over their route.

If anything, Katrina thought, it would be a story. Life, as she saw it, was about accumulating anecdotes, trading them at house parties and double dates. The value increased as the distance between teller and tale decreased, so that to tell a very interesting story you read in the news was worth less than the somewhat interesting story of a friend of a friend, which in turn was worth less than something that actually happened to you. Already, the present moment in which they were driving away from town was overlaid by a possible future in which Katrina was describing it, and so she became especially attuned to telling details that could serve to give her account a sense of authenticity. How, for example, would she render their guide, Edward? For starters, she hadn't expected him to be East Asian. Chinese? He was middle-aged, but in good shape – good-looking, she might add, to get a fake rise out of Jay at their future drinks. She wouldn't need to bother to describe the landscape – they'd have photos, evidence. Nor would she really need to discuss the route. What an anecdote required was some sort of drama, and she was imagining a sighting of a polar bear, hearing the gunshot ring out and seeing the spray of red blood on white snow as the warning shot accidentally made contact.

She wiped the fogged-up window as the car stopped. The

Svalbard Seed Bank was built underground, and all you could see from the road was its entrance jutting out like the opening of a futuristic mineshaft.

'Beneath our feet,' Edward said, while doing a gear check, 'is the result of 13,000 years of agriculture. Pretty much all the food in the world.'

It didn't take long for the small entrance to disappear from view. Soon, they settled into a relaxed pace, marching through the snow, dragging their gear behind them on sleds attached to their waistbands, as if they were huskies. And, as the view opened out before them, with a revelatory power that didn't dilute, so too did the conversation.

Edward had been in Svalbard for a year, leaving China and his job after he'd secured a lucrative contract with the government. 'The joke is,' he said, 'I started out building bridges, but made my fortune in fences.'

The company he worked at specialised in fences that could withstand extreme weather and high altitudes. Normally they worked in other countries, but since Narayan Indra had been elected in India, Edward continued, and had promised to build a new river, the Saraswati, which would divert water away from Pakistan, there had been a renewed focus on the highest water tower in the world, the Himalayas. As India's northern border melted into China's southern border, and more usable land was revealed, Indian troops had been encroaching on Tibet. China had sent more soldiers to the hills, and so India had further increased its presence. There had been several brawls, soldiers, not cleared to shoot, fighting with sticks studded with nails and baseball bats wrapped in barbed wire, with rocks and bricks. And so it was decided that a physical border would be built where the natural one had sufficed for thousands of years. Edward had overseen the bid and, he said, earned himself a break.

'But why Svalbard?' Katrina asked, as they came upon a crest of snow and a new view of the valley.

'Have you ever heard of Zomia?' Edward said.

Jay did the nod he did whenever he clearly didn't know something.

Zomia, Edward explained, was the world's largest non-state region. 'Though, I suppose it's an academic construct rather than a tangible reality.' Edward had learnt about the place in a report he'd been given in the midst of the bid. 'It stretches from the Hindu Kush through the Himalayas – as far west as Afghanistan, as far east as Vietnam. I think, on average, as a region, it's three, four thousand metres above the sea. That high, almost everyone is nomadic, living beyond the reach of government.'

An estimated 450,000 people lived in Zomia, and while they technically belonged to countries like India, Nepal and China, they received little or no governmental support or intervention in the form of healthcare, infrastructure, schooling or law enforcement; they didn't vote, didn't pay taxes. 'For hundreds of years,' Edward continued, 'the mountains were a refuge for people fleeing oppression. The Bon, for example – they ran from the Buddhists in Tibet a thousand years ago, and live in the highlands to this day. They roam freely, following the seasons, their yak. And then, boom! A fence. The yak are penned in, the pastures halved. Families and communities separated. And, with the man-made border, Zomia becomes a thing of the past.'

'If it wasn't your company, though, surely it would have just been someone else,' Katrina said.

'It's true,' he said, 'but, on reflection, I thought it would be nice to find a place in the world where these lines mean less. And that was Svalbard. No visa.' He coughed. 'Low tax.'

The conversation turned, and Katrina and Jay did their bit about how they met. She told Edward about Marianne, their short time on Chagos.

'What happened to the ants?' he asked.

'No doubt continuing to spread. No one responded to my emails.'

'And the woman?'

'According to the news, she returned to England, to Crawley, for health reasons.'

'Ah. Of course.'

Edward pointed to an indistinguishable spot on the white plains, where they would bivouac. Dinner meant adding melted snow to dehydrated beef stew. The sun dropped towards the horizon, but didn't touch it, as if magnetically repulsed. Travel, Katrina believed, allowed you to experience the world in a purer present than that which you could access in your everyday life. Her commute to the lab would be overlaid with all the hundreds of times she'd completed that journey before, so that the pattern on the bus seats, or the faces of her co-workers, would, in a sense, be invisible to her. Perhaps she could experience something purely only once, and then each repetition was more of an attrition, a kind of erosion. Though, perhaps in the case of Jay, repetition became addition.

As they walked on, she wondered if someone born here would call this flat expanse beautiful. Growing up, the paradise of Mauritius was commonplace to her. It was only on weekends, when she'd accompany her mother to the resort after church, following her from room to room as she cleaned, that Katrina could understand people going there for its beauty. The water in the pools was so perfectly blue. She'd inspect the mess the people left, the clothes, the towels, the tissues. She had a distinct memory of picking up what she thought had been a plastic tube containing glue, before her mother squealed. Whether the condom story was real or not it was hard to say, but she'd repeated it often enough to friends that any fiction had subsumed reality. She could remember holding it up to her eye, the thing dangling around as if alive.

The sea always seemed more beautiful from the balconies of those hotel rooms, through the eyes of the resort's visitors, than it did from her home, in a small town further up the coast.

There were no deckchairs or parasols on their stretch of beach. Once, she'd seen some Europeans in their town and couldn't fathom why they'd driven up so far from the resorts. She'd asked her mother, who'd explained that sometimes the tourists didn't want to be tourists. They wanted to feel like locals.

'Like us?' Katrina had said. 'We should swap. They can have my room and I'll have their suite.'

'Either way, it's me having to clean your room. Will you *please* put those clothes away?'

Katrina was thinking along these lines, or feeling these thoughts on a level just below articulation, as they built their tent. Almost anything she could see right now, she had not seen before. Surely there was something universal, she thought, in the pleasure of untouched snow, of diving into an undisturbed pool, writing on a brand-new blackboard.

She and Jay struggled into their respective sleeping bags. The tiredness she had felt in her feet and legs as they walked now pooled out across her whole body as she lay horizontally. Jay shifted towards her, a merman on land. Their synthetic clothing brushed against their synthetic sleeping bags, which brushed against their roll mats and, in turn, the tent. He pulled up her hat and kissed her.

'I love you.'

'I love you.'

'I'm hard.'

'That's a shame.'

'What if I was, let's say, to de-cocoon?'

'I would say it's freezing.'

He unzipped his sleeping bag and rubbed his hands together, breathing on them to heat them up. His long johns were skintight.

'Edward is right there,' she whispered.

'He'll be fast asleep.'

'I'll need to thaw first.'

'We'll huddle.'

He unzipped her sleeping bag. They made out. She pulled down her trousers only as much as necessary.

'Just don't touch me,' she said. 'Your hands are freezing.'

'I could put on gloves.'

'How hot.'

The logistics were less than ideal, but they managed to make some inroads.

'I love you.'

'I love you.'

Their thermal clothing rubbed together, creating static and white noise. Jay moved glacially, aware of Edward's proximity. Their lightweight tents were within a metre of each other. Something about safety, polar bears. Edward should have been asleep, but there was no way to be sure. Jay adjusted, and found a more forgiving angle. Katrina felt the snow compact beneath her roll mat. She grabbed his hair, breathed in his ear. The wind picked up. It was still so bright, and Katrina wondered if they would form some kind of silhouette on the outside of the tent. They kissed and the coldness of his nose against her cheek made his tongue seem even warmer. Her mind was wondering as she looked up at the blue tarp – did people of the far north have a similar amount of sex as people in the Amazon? The same amount of children, on average? What did temperature do to libido? Terrain? She thought of Jay during their time on Diego Garcia, the ceiling fan she'd look up at while he went down on her, the pearls of sweat on his head. She thought of him that first night on the beach.

'Are you close?' she said. 'I'm getting close.'

He smiled, quickened. The fabric was making more noise now, but that could have been anything, someone tossing in their sleep, fluctuations in wind. There was a brief moment when she didn't care if Edward could hear, and then she was imagining him listening in, touching himself in his sleeping bag. Jay was kissing the top of her head, and all she could see was his chest, his fleece rubbing against her cheek, her nose.

She was as far north as she'd ever been, would ever be, with a man she loved more than anyone she ever had, ever would, and it was hard to take the burning, melting world seriously; it was nothing to her – she was happy, brilliantly, selfishly happy, and in this world within the world that they had now built for themselves, all was good and green.

'I'm there. I'm there.'

They made good progress the next day, beginning to bend back west. The addition of their new audience member turned any conversation Katrina and Jay had between themselves into a kind of performance. Katrina ran faster in busy parks than she did in empty ones. She had better posture when someone sat next to her at the lab. They walked on, their sleds wiping their tracks clean, and she imagined the scene as viewed from above, from a drone, the two of them led across the tundra by their guide. At what point, she thought, did a person first imagine themselves from a bird's-eye view? She began to lag behind the men and was glad when Edward suggested they camp. She dehydrated the lentils, and Jay offered Edward his metal flask.

'A bevvy while we bivvy?'

Katrina turned in early, going through the day's pictures inside the tent. There was no wind that evening, and she could hear Jay and Edward talk as if she were still out with them. Their conversation turned from Zomia to the Saraswati River, and from the Saraswati to its source, Mount Kailash. Then Edward said something that made her open her voice-memo app and press record.

'He only told me this when he knew he was dying, as if that offered some amnesty for the secrets he'd long held. And he made me promise that I would tell no one the story until I too thought my time here was up. He was strange like that. And, well, I didn't say this yesterday, but the main reason I came to

Svalbard, the reality is – I have a few years at most, perhaps months. And you seem as good a man as any to pass this story on to. All your talk of the Saraswati must be some kind of a sign ...'

In the early 2000s, in the midst of the mobile-phone boom, Edward had met a man on a visit to a tungsten mine. He was new at the company, having just finished his studies abroad, and working on a bridge that would link the new mine to a new road, along which the metal could be transported to the relevant factories. 'And as a man is wont to do when travelling for business, I frequented a local bar.

'On my last visit to the bar, I got talking with a lonely regular, bought him a drink. I was leaving that backwater the next morning and feeling merry. He was a retiree, and in such bad shape that at first I doubted the validity of his story, which he told me only after several stiff drinks. When the bar closed, I offered to walk him home. He was an interesting man, and frail, and we were heading up the mountain roads in the dark when he began to speak. He told me, and these were his words, "My friend, I am living the life of a ghost."'

The man – Edward used no name – had once been a celebrated mountaineer. By his thirties, he'd climbed any peak worth its salt in the Chinese heartland, and most noteworthy mountains in the Himalayas. But he had his one white whale. His ultimate goal.

Kailash.

It was the mountain that would make him famous. In all recorded history, it had never been climbed.

The virginal peak, many believed, was the centre of the world and all life on it. Our axis mundi. Anyone who had trekked up to Lake Mansarovar, which was the ancient source of the Saraswati River and one of the highest lakes in the world, would look upon the face of Kailash and see it as the archetype upon which all peaks were based. It was smaller than Everest, but harder to climb. Each face of the mountain was ever-changing, the ice always shifting, so even if a route up Kailash had ever been established, it would have long disappeared. It was one reason among many that nobody had ever reached the peak and returned alive.

'To the Hindus,' Edward said to Jay, 'Kailash is the abode of Shiva. The god continues to live, physically, some believe, in or on the mountain, in pious solitude. And from his frozen hair, from the mountain, stem the rivers – Ganga, Brahmaputra, Indus, Yellow, Mekong, I could go on. The waters over a billion people rely upon. The convergence of the mountain's four faces – supposedly made of crystal, ruby, gold and lapis lazuli – helped to form the centre of the world, and the mountain is located at the heart of six ranges, which fan out from it in the shape of a lotus. It is, some think, a gateway to heaven, but to climb the mountain would be to disturb the destroyer's peace, to trespass upon the sacred.'

The man told Edward that it was also a major site of pilgrimage for the Buddhists, the centre of supreme bliss. To Jains, it was the mountain on which Rishabhanatha, the first Jain tirthankara, attained nirvana. To the Bon it was the nine-storey Swastika Mountain, the centre of the universe and the Tagzig Olmo Lung Ring. As the physical heart of several of the world's largest and oldest religions, the Chinese government, after assuming occupation of Tibet, had decided to prohibit anyone from climbing the mountain.

The man Edward met, and a group of his climbing friends, paid enough of the right people to look the other way and made it up to Mansarovar without a hitch. They had planned an alpine-style ascent along the mountain's south-eastern ridge. They followed a stream north from the lake and established a base camp in a shielded valley. They had timed the climb with both the weather and the coming pilgrimage season in mind. Several times a year, the area would be busy with Hindu, Buddhist and Jain pilgrims circumambulating the mountain clockwise, and Bonpos doing so anticlockwise.

They made their ascent at night, when the ice was less volatile, leaving their cook at base camp with a radio for reporting approaching weather systems and instructions not to call for any help, and to assume them dead and leave if they didn't return within five days.

'The problem was,' Edward said, 'they dropped the corresponding radio that first night. So they couldn't communicate with the cook, and had no way of knowing about the shifting weather fronts.' They took a chance on it and forged on, quickly reaching the ice wall. The mood was good among the three climbers. No one alive, or dead, had ever seen what they were seeing now.

'I don't remember all the details,' Edward said. 'But, when they were halfway up the ice wall, the storm hit.' It was impossible to climb up or down to safety, so they knocked screws into the ice and tied themselves in place. When the weather cleared, it became apparent that the man lowest down on the wall was dead, his body hanging from his screw. The other two continued up. They couldn't let him die for nothing.

A fog fell upon the mountain, and in the low visibility they clipped two ends of rope to each other, taking turns in the lead. The air thinned, and the headaches and visions worsened. But they reached the peak. 'It was too overcast to see anything. So they lost some height, waited a few hours and returned. And, that second time, it was a success – they could see for miles. The centre of the world!'

Coming down from the peak once more, they felt a little surer of their route and picked up their speed. But something had changed as the man's friend led. The visibility worsened again. And then the slack rope between them became suddenly taut. The man fell on to his back, dragged at incredible speed down the slope. He hit a rock hard and was flipped on to his front, allowing him to reach to his back and pull out his pickaxe, which he swung out into the ice. There was a jolt as the rope became taut again. He tightened his grip on the rubber handle, tried to steady his breath. He called out to his friend but could only hear the wind. The axe creaked in the ice, straining with the weight of the two men. He called out again. Had the slope been shallower, he might have been able to take the weight on one arm and attempt to pull his friend up.

He couldn't condemn him. Nor could he agree to die along with him. The two things were true at once, pressing at each other. But, along the fault lines of life and death, there could only be one truth: preservation.

He swore. He waited. He called out. His friend was either already dead or bound to die, and he was bound to him, and would go with him. He removed one foot from the ice and attempted to loop it under the rope, to see if he could move it at all. He couldn't.

To live, he would have to kill.

He kicked his crampons into the ice again, and gradually reduced his left hand's grip on the axe, taking all the weight on his right. Then he quickly reached for his penknife, almost losing his grip in the process. He grabbed back on to the axe handle, knife in hand, and picked out the blade with his mouth. His breath was fast, and he salivated on the knife's plastic grip. If he wasn't quick, it would freeze to his lips. His arms were searing with pain. The option was one death or two, that's what he reminded himself. One death or two. Gathering his strength, he let go of the axe with his left hand once more, but when he finally managed to put the blade to the rope, all the weight pulling down on him suddenly vanished.

His friend had cut the rope himself.

In an instant, his fate had changed from becoming a murderer to becoming a survivor. He managed to reach back now for his other axe, and climbed up the slope to a small ridge where he could rest. He descended the rest of the way the next day, sure the mountain would kill him. But he made it to base camp. He passed out in the tent and woke with his hands cuffed to a hospital bed.

The cook had caved and called for help, worried about the others. 'The authorities gave him two options,' Edward said. 'Either he went to jail to set an example not to climb the mountain. Or he would be given a new home, far from anyone he knew, where he could live freely under a new identity, but on the condition that he was officially pronounced dead in his own province. The group's fatal failure would then become the example. What would his mother prefer – a son who died heroically, doing what he loved, or a son who rotted in prison, a disgrace to the family name?

'The decision was easy for him. But he didn't want to live and to die with no one ever knowing the truth. And the truth was, he claimed, after his friend had cut the rope and he'd climbed back to safety, he'd seen someone else on the mountain. A tall, dark figure. He was facing away from him. The wind blew, and then he vanished.'

Katrina pretended to be asleep when Jay eventually entered their tent. She didn't get a chance to discuss the story with him until they arrived at Advent and Edward went down to the water to call in their ferry. Jay and Katrina walked around the razed mining town, nothing remaining of a human world but traces of wood, almost a century old. Looking across the Adventfjorden to Longyearbyen, finally out of earshot, she asked Jay how it went last night after she went to bed.

'Oh,' he said, 'nothing much to report. Just general chat, but I was wiped. He's a talker.'

She didn't understand why he wouldn't offer up the story Edward had told him. Was it that it had left such a small impression on him that he didn't think it worth telling? Or was he really going to stand by Edward's request for him to keep the story to himself? She thought they kept no secrets at all between them. When she'd been called for jury service, she'd told him every detail about the case. If he could keep Edward's story to himself, what else was he able to hide? It was small, she knew that, and she would be overreacting, she believed, to call him up on it. But it was efficiently irritating, like a little stone in her shoe, or a paper cut on her knuckle. Then again, if he could be accused of keeping the story to himself, as per Edward's wish, then she could be accused of withholding the fact that she had been eavesdropping. Was she now thinking like a married person? The kinds of couples she and Jay had long mocked? She would let it go.

'You OK?' he said, as they watched the small ferry arrive.

'Yeah.'

'You sure?'

'Yes.'

'I love you.'

'I love you.'

He helped her aboard, and, facing backwards, she watched the effect of the boat on the still water, the ripples going on and on, fading but never truly disappearing.

3. Jambhoji Sacred Grove, Haryana

When Jay eventually told her the Kailash story a few years later, over the phone, Katrina had almost forgotten about it. She was watching children race paper boats in a puddle in the dug-up trench of the future Saraswati River. She had flown to India to investigate a yellow crazy ant sighting at Jambhoji Sacred Grove, on the Haryana side of the Rajasthani border. From the edge of the grove, she could see the Saraswati River site, the fencing bent and opened up by schoolchildren. If she ducked under the fence and turned right, along the trench, she would in theory eventually reach the Shivalik Hills and then the Himalayas, and in turn Lake Mansarovar and Kailash, the mountain Jay was now discussing from back home in Brooklyn. She had barely slept, waiting for news about his appointment.

As was their routine when she was called away for work,

they had cleared a weekend to spend time together at home before she left. Jay no longer travelled. He worked a desk job in Parks and Recreation. When they knew that they wouldn't be able to have each other with their usual regularity, they would revert to younger versions of themselves, full of energy and desire. Katrina joked that those weekends felt like the two of them were partaking in an illicit affair, the empty days structured around sex and takeout food, one person packing a suitcase and leaving when Monday came. Lying next to him, she realised the whites of his eyes looked yellow. Was it the light? She wouldn't have thought that noteworthy if, after sex, she hadn't seen his urine before she sat down to pee. It was dark. She'd booked a doctor's appointment for him – he'd never have gone of his own accord.

'Remember that man Edward, from our honeymoon?' Jay said now, on the phone. She could hear wind coming through on his end, birds. Maybe he was going for one of his morning walks in Prospect Park, which made her even more sure it might be bad news.

'Yes,' she said, trying to keep her voice even and calm.

'He made me make this promise. He had this story to tell me, but I had to swear I wouldn't tell anyone until – well, it's strange, he said he was only telling me because he knew his time was up. And the person who had told it to him only did so when he was dying. I don't know why I didn't just tell you; it's just a small thing. But it felt wrong to break the promise to a dying man, even if we'd just met.'

'What are you talking about?' she said. She wanted him to tell her the news straight. There was no time for stories. Was it jaundice? What had the doctor said?

'He had this story about Kailash. The mountain. And I'm thinking – now, I don't have the time—'

'No.'

'It would be a place I'd want to go, if I could pick one more place.'

'Jay?'

'Yeah.'

'What is it?'

'Pancreatic.'

She immediately started googling, putting him on speakerphone.

'How long?' she asked.

'It's unclear.'

'There must be—'

'It's too far down the line.'

'Jay.'

'I know.'

'I'm getting the next flight home.'

'No. No,' he said. 'No. I want to come to you.'

'What?'

'India. Nepal, whatever. *Mount Kailash*. That's where I want to go. One more adventure.'

He proceeded to tell her Edward's secret story, and the details came back to her. She acted like it was all new. It was only after he'd finished that she managed to get out of him some of what the doctor had said about his pancreas.

He went up to New Jersey for a week to see his mother. At least Katrina had the ants to keep her busy. Jarnail, the grove's elderly caretaker, would check in on her each afternoon with fresh tea.

Jambhoji Sacred Grove was named after Guru Jambeshwar, the founder of the Bishnoi religion. He was an animist, believing in the pervasiveness of God in all things, in a world in which the human and the non-human could prosper together. There were several protected forests in his name, but the grove in southern Haryana was particularly significant, not just to the small population of Bishnoi in the area, but to all farmers with land near it. The preserved trees regenerated the dying aquifer below, which fed their wells – though the water was now officially attributed to the Saraswati.

The forest, Jarnail had told her, was important to Sikhs as well as the Bishnoi. It was believed that the grove contained a tree that Guru Nanak Dev Ji, the first Sikh guru, had meditated underneath. It was unclear which tree within the forest it was, so all Sikh visitors treated each tree as if it were the specifically holy one.

It was a delicate ecosystem, and Jarnail did everything he could to keep outside species out. When he discovered that the new ants he'd spotted were invasive, he lost it. 'I know exactly how they arrived,' he'd told her on her first day. 'Indian Indiana Jones.'

Ancient ruins had been found on the grounds of the protected grove, dating back to the Saraswati Civilisation, as it was now being called. Researchers at a local university, led by Dr Radha Johns, had received government backing to forgo the protections around the grove and excavate a clearing. 'It can't be a coincidence that the crazy archaeologists arrive, and then the crazy ants appear.'

Katrina showed Jay the ancient dig site when he arrived. They looked down into the empty hole in the earth, a few metres of substrate separating their world from that of the ancients.

'I think I'd want cremation,' he said. 'Or that thing where they turn you into a tree.'

'Stop.'

'I'd want to be evergreen. None of that deciduous bullshit. I'm talking Jay Smithson Sacred Grove.'

They ducked out of view of the river workers and made out against a potentially holy tree.

While she sprayed down the colonies with AntOff, Jay researched ways to get up to Kailash. You had to be part of an organised tour. 'The best option,' he said, 'that leaves soonest, is to join the Laal Guru Foundation.' The religious organisation arranged trips up to Kailash, which their leader,

Laal Guru, the YouTube Yogi, called the holiest place on earth.

The yogi's face, strangely familiar, appeared on the website's background. He wore a loose white turban that matched his sparse beard. He could have made as much money off his skincare routine, Katrina thought, as he did off his meditation courses – he had a warm smile, perfect teeth. They watched some videos in which he hiked to Kailash, and scanned his website. He'd worked in Hollywood and Silicon Valley, briefly, as a corporate spiritual adviser, before returning to India. He was profiled in the *New Yorker* and photographed for *Vogue*: 'The Aesthetic Ascetic'. Suddenly, she remembered where she recognised him: he often appeared on her Instagram's *Explore* page.

They subscribed to his programme and bought tickets for a Kailash tour, receiving push alerts of the guru's daily wisdom and targeted Ayurvedic ads. The tour wasn't cheap, especially with Jay's medical fees taken into account. When she realised all the colonies had been decimated, they still had a few months until the hike.

'My contract will be up,' she told Jay, at the edge of the grove. 'So, we should probably think about going home.' They watched an old man prostrate himself near the river's construction site, crawling forward, inch by inch.

'But they pay a day rate, right?' Jay said.

She arranged to meet Jarnail for lunch the next day to discuss the invasion. As she waited for him to arrive, the dhaba quickly filled with students taking a break from one of the protests. They rested their placards on the wall outside, next to Katrina's table.

Say NO to Water War!

Climate Justice Now!

Dying glaciers = 'reincarnated' river

All the men looked at her. Their gazes were hard, unwavering. When one man finished his food and left, he continued to look across at her, even as he drove his motorbike away. She checked her phone again; Jarnail was late.

When he arrived, he read the placards. 'Even the eco-warriors know this is the best spot for chole bhature,' he said.

Now that he was sitting next to her, she felt the eyes on her turn to other things.

'I would have thought you were an eco-warrior, too,' she said.

'I'm not a hippie. I like the trees because they are sacred, not just because they are green.'

She told him that the colonies had spread further than she had first imagined, that she'd need more time.

'The bastards,' Jarnail said, glancing at the students as they laughed. He licked his fingers and sighed. 'However long you need.'

She spent the following mornings wandering through the grove, chasing the ghost infestation, pouring pesticide down the toilet, in case Jarnail checked. She'd meet Jay after his yoga in the park, also run by the Laal Guru Foundation.

'Doing OK?'

'I'm all limbered up,' he said. 'Do you want to go back to the Airbnb?'

They spent the afternoon in bed and planned a weekend trip over a decadent dinner. The next morning, she went out to buy breakfast and returned to find him dead on the rug. A follow-along meditation video was still playing on his laptop.

'Your centre,' the instructor said, over the drone of a veena, 'is not necessarily corporate. It could be your solar plexus, yes, or your head, the space between your eyes, your heart, but it could also be your home, your mother, your husband; it could be your place of origin, even a place within time. Focus on your centre, whatever that means to you, and—'

4. Lake Mansarovar, Ngari Prefecture

The other pilgrims and I were already weathering our bowls of gruel, awaiting Laal Guru's daily sermon on Zoom, when Katrina walked in. I shuffled aside on the floor so that she could sit next to me and the other women. She picked the sleep from her eyes and made a start on her porridge.

'Coffee?' I asked.

'Please,' she said.

Katrina and I had become quick friends in Haryana, which had seemed an unlikely outcome to me, given the way in which we met. I'd sought her out as an interview subject for a long read I was working on about Sejal and Jugaad, two characters from the classic Punjabi qissa. I had recently discovered that they were not only real people who had actually existed, but they were people to whom I was related. They were my ancestors and, I believed, Katrina's.

When we initially spoke online, I gave Katrina the same spiel I'd given to my editor.

'Several months ago,' I said, 'I received a call telling me that my father was dead. I was surprised to find we still lived in the same state, given how many years it had been. I was invited by his executor to meet my father's other daughter, a half-sister I'd never known about.'

I suppose the shock my half-sister felt on hearing about my existence was even more than what I experienced when finding out about her, for she had been raised by our father, had known him her whole life, while I had met him once, the day after my twelfth birthday. When he first told her about my existence, she thought he was losing his mind as he neared the end, and blamed the medicine he was on. But a few weeks later, she was confronted with the inclusion of my name on her father's will.

My mother had been a teenager when she had a brief affair with my late father, who was in his forties. When she became pregnant with me, she was cast out of her family as a fallen woman, and he returned to his family without anyone ever knowing.

'What was he like?' I asked my half-sister, who appeared more like an aunt to me, being fifteen years my senior.

'He worked dutifully at the tax office,' she said, 'and, on weekends, he did his history. He was an amateur historian. Like you, he wrote.'

It was family history that interested him most, she said. He had created an intricate family tree, which she showed to me on her laptop. I read the bottom row of the diagram first, and did not find my name. I scrolled up. The top row said, *Sejal and Jugaad of Hakra*. Beneath them were several children, named after rivers, and it was from the last of them that there was a continuous line down to my father and, therefore, me.

It was a lot to take in; I remembered the story of 'Sejal Jugaad' from elementary. I often went to a friend's house after school, a girl who'd moved to Dharamshala from Punjab, and it was her mother who'd play us television versions of old qisse. Several of the real details my father had discerned matched those in the television series: I could almost see Sejal and Jugaad dancing through the cornfields.

My half-sister also showed me a large box containing several printed copies of the qissa 'Sejal Jugaad'. Some dated as far back as 1903, and were collected, according to the inscriptions, by a woman called Saraswati Sanghera.

I called a friend of mine, who worked as a photo researcher for a rival paper, and she gave me suggestions of which archives to visit if I wanted to do more digging. I'd recently been moved from current affairs to the travel vertical. My political reporting had brought a lot of site traffic, with most of its engagement in the form of hateful comments. I'd recently caused a bit of an online stir after reporting on one of Indra's favoured ministers. On his campaign trail, he had claimed that he'd cleaned up all the rivers in his district. To prove his point, he drank a glass of water directly from one of the streams and was hospitalised within two hours. Apparently, my article about the incident was callous; I was politicising an old man's health, had no regard for human decency and so on.

The new management wanted to take a less combative stance with political reporting. In my younger days, I would have seen this as some great injustice, would have said something about the fourth power crumbling, but the truth was I was tired. Tired of the late nights in the empty office, all the waiting around courtrooms, all that darkness. I'd almost come around to the idea of redundancy when I was offered the travel role. There was funding from the tourism board to promote activity along the planned route of the Saraswati River. I figured the new management didn't want to fire me because I'd been one of the students the old and much-loved editor-in-chief had sponsored to study journalism at university. 'It's a lot of time on the road,' my new manager said, 'and so many of our writers are tied down. But you ... you know.'

'Sure.'

'Can you drive? They can offer a car.'

'Yes,' I lied.

I'd just finished my intensive driving course when I found out about my father. I didn't call my mother, and, after that initial decision, continued to keep up the lie, not telling her that I was using my new free time to drive to the archives and continue my estranged father's research. She lived up in the hills now, dressing like a tribal woman and offering herself as a guide to tourists on hiking trails, selling them souvenirs when they reached their destinations. She'd gone all in on this new lifestyle, and seemed to enjoy the quiet, that horrid rickety shack. When I did occasionally go out to visit her, it was as if she were starting to believe she was actually from one of the hill tribes, that this was the real her, and all the preceding years in Dharamshala had been some kind of dream. To call her and tell her about the man who had so violently upended her life, to yank her out of her fantasy into the reality she'd escaped felt needlessly cruel. Just as I was raised not knowing about my father's life, she would live on knowing nothing of his death.

I could churn out the travel articles over breakfast, often inventing details about certain festivals, villages or hiking trails when I couldn't be bothered to drive out and see them. So much was on Google Maps, my subeditors never really noticed the difference. Or, if they did, they knew it was all equally inauthentic. I still left the house each day for one of McLeod Ganj's hippie cafes; none of my housemates would have known I was putting aside my real work for my own new project. At first, they thought that moving on from the long hours of political journalism might revive my dormant dating life. My ex had ended things because I was constantly having to check my phone for updates, and would often have to call off one of our dates, mid-meal, mid-hike, to rush back and deliver a piece. But all my free time now went on to this new project.

If anything, when I started searching for the real historic Sejal and Jugaad and my connection to them, I was looking to disprove my father's research, to undo his work, render it redundant. But most of the evidence he'd collated was legitimate; he must have been working on this for years. Once I understood that he was right, I wanted to see if I could fill in the rest of the tree, see if I could find any descendants of those other branches, from the other six siblings, chart some kind of family. I signed up to Helix, a genetic mapping service, and sent a strand of my hair off to be processed.

The first step in my research was to find the farm in Hakra. I was surprised by how much there was online about the village: apparently it was one of the places where the waters of the Saraswati had originally resurfaced. Amid the articles was a profile of a farmer called Satnam Singh Hakra, who owned the farm that first saw the water's return. He was pictured drinking at an old well. 'We like to see history as a story of linear progress,' he said, 'but I don't think it's so simple. Where we learn something, we forget something. What we gain in technological advancement, we lose in traditional knowledge. So this water, at a time like this, I don't know – everything doesn't have to be forward.' It was his aim, he said, to return to old ways of farming, to grow only native crops and do away with fertilisers and pesticides.

When I searched his name, there was a report about an appearance he'd made in a Punjabi court as part of the trial of the Saraswati Six. He had been asked to give a character statement about one of the thugs, named Pala Chauhan. He claimed that Chauhan was a religious man, a family man, a good friend. 'I can't believe that he could be capable of what he's being accused of,' Satnam said. 'I can't see it at all.'

Satnam's land matched several descriptions of the farm in the qissa: an almost square plot, with a well in one corner. Energised, I set off on the long drive the next day.

The road into Hakra was backed up with trucks carrying building materials. At the edge of the village, an old man pointed me in the direction of what he called 'the Angrezi farm'.

There was no answer at the gate. It took me a few minutes to come to terms with the fact that I'd driven all this way for nothing.

I figured I might still be able to see some of the farm from the outside and walked around the construction site on the neighbouring plot, where large foundations were being dug, to look in at what might have been the field owned by Sejal and Jugaad. It was overgrown and unruly, with little in the way of deliberate cultivation save for a row of young peepal trees at the edge that demarcated the farm from the newly dug trench of the Saraswati River. The trees looked as if they'd just been planted, the soil around their roots darker than the rest of the field. There was just enough water in the riverbed for it to be muddy, and amid the muck I spotted shards of smashed glass, blue plastic bags. I turned along the bank, with the farm on my right, until I came across the well at the corner of the plot. A small path wove through the grass towards it, and, figuring there was no harm with no one at home, I walked along it.

I drank through cupped hands and paused, waiting for some kind of revelation, some feeling of connection. But this was land like all other land. Even if I did have a legitimate family tie to it, did that really differentiate it from its neighbouring plots? This was just water in my hand. It was just grass.

I was starting my car up when I got the Helix notification about Katrina. She appeared as a match, sharing some portion of genetic code with my half-sister and me – enough for us to be considered distant relatives. I sat in the driver's seat a while, before turning off the engine and writing a note for Satnam. I posted it through his letterbox, and then reached out to Katrina on the app. She had replied by the time I arrived back in Himachal Pradesh, saying that she'd signed up to the genetic mapping project for quick money at university, and hadn't thought anything would ever come of it. I carefully worded a reply, explaining the premise of my project, hoping that we might be able to speak on a call.

I'll actually be in India in a few months, she'd messaged, mentioning that she would be coming to Haryana for work. We scheduled a lunch but then she didn't respond to any of my messages in the days before we were due to meet.

Then she called me, hyperventilating. 'I don't know what to do,' she said. 'I don't know anyone here.'

When Jay's mother flew out, I drove the two of them to the crematorium. It was my first time driving with other people in my car and I was nervous. At one junction, I stalled badly and, as the surrounding cars sounded their horns, it took everything I had not to cry. I managed to get them there on time, and sat in my car as Jay was turned to ash.

Would I have helped Katrina to the extent I had, I thought,

making arrangements with the undertaker, translating for her, if I had no link at all to her? If she had come up to me in the street? While I was certain I had done a good, charitable thing, I felt conflicted about the fact that, as I was experiencing the drama of Jay's death, I was also thinking about how it might fit into the project I was working on. The reality in front of me – Katrina's mother-in-law breaking down in the parking lot, being comforted by Jarnail, an old man Katrina had been working with – offered itself as material I might one day tweak. I expected not to hear from her after she returned to America, but a month later, she called me again.

'I'm caught in two minds,' she said, after catching me up. 'On the one hand, to do it without him, to go to Kailash, that would feel wrong. But then again, it's what he would have wanted, I know that. And I could take him there,' she said, referring, I supposed, to his ashes.

'It might bring closure,' I said. 'A closing of that circle. I don't know.'

She paused. 'This is going to sound crazy,' she said then, 'but why don't you come with me? Take Jay's ticket and come with me.'

'Mountains are living beings, no?' Laal Guru said, in the video they played for us during breakfast. 'They grow and shrink as we do. You've heard the maxim, you cannot step in the same river twice? Well, and I'm sure your brave Sherpas will agree, you cannot step upon the same mountain twice. In all the blessed times I have visited Kailash, both I and the mountain itself have been different beings. And so, each time, I had to empty myself of all ego.'

I offered the rest of my porridge to Katrina. She finished her bowl, and then took mine. I typed a few notes on my phone. The travel editor had covered my costs and wanted a kind of diary of the trip to the source.

'You must allow the journey to wear you down to nothing. You are nothing in the face of the mountain. To receive Kailash, to receive Saraswati, you must be empty – a vessel. You are a speck of dust in the face of such might. Not even a blip in the timeline of this great being.'

Katrina and I had already agreed not to make eye contact during the woo-woo parts of the tour, so as not to break our cover as proper pilgrims. I had already learnt that her poker face was as bad as mine, that we had a similar sense of humour.

The trip involved crossing into China through Nepal. The plane that took us out of Nepalgunj was three seats wide. It landed on the Simikot airstrip, which was flanked by sheer drops. People cheered on landing, it was that kind of crowd. We set off early the next day, walking as far as the Karnali Valley. Katrina said she recognised the village we walked through from one of Laal Guru's videos. In it, he stopped to photograph the different locals he passed. A police officer, a fan of the podcast, recognised him and asked for a selfie. The officer left and reappeared later on in the video with his baby daughter, so that the guru might bless her. I couldn't quite fathom how a seventy-five-year-old man could walk the route we were on. Perhaps there was some truth to the long-term benefits of daily vinyasa, some credibility to his holiness, or to the story that he had communed with an alien race of giants, as he often claimed. I was grateful to see the cars waiting for us at Karnali, which would ferry us up the two-kilometre pass to the Hepka Valley.

The air thinned up towards Tsong Tsa, visibility becoming so poor that our group leader, Jeremy, decided to cut the day short. The campsite, further north in the Limi Valley, had to be disassembled by the Sherpas and brought down to us. Katrina gazed off at the path disappearing into the fog and I imagined her thinking about Jay, of the paths he'd left around the world, all those soldiers marching, of the unfinished work she'd told me about in Chagos, paint cracking on tree bark. She was still so young in grief.

Eventually, she joined us in our chanting, as we waited for the adverts to play out on Laal Guru's podcast – 'for those suffering from feelings of hopelessness, inability to focus, indigestion ...' – continuing to repeat the day's mantra, which would purify both our ancestors and our descendants: 'Om Namo Narayanya.' The repetition of the sounds created a groove in the mind, which deepened.

Finally, Laal Guru's voice came through on a recording from a few weeks ago, projected into the future: 'Take, for example, this river forever in the headlines. People are saying India is "creating" a river. But how can this be accurate? The Saraswati in its previous form was not destroyed, it did not vanish from the earth, because nothing can. The water that flowed down her channels then has been flowing all the same, all around us. It still enters the sea, the air, it's in our rain. The droplets on the window, who's to say they were not once part of the Saraswati, the Rhine, the Tiber? The government may be reshaping a vessel for it, but the river is the river. It never went away. Everyone is searching for a creation story, but there is no such thing. There are only *conversion* stories, stories of change.'

We made our first sighting of Kailash's south face from Lapche and set up camp – or, rather, the Sherpas did. We watched the light fade, the white triangle of the holy peak becoming visible only by its negative space, a wedge of dark emptiness amid the manifest stars. It was hard not to be affected by the starlight, but to talk about the stars, to describe them, was as useless as attempting to photograph them. So many of the lights were exploding, dying, I thought, as I leant back and looked up, this might be the last night that they'd ever give off any light – or, rather, the last time they would be visible here, having disappeared months or maybe years in the past. The sky seemed to expand the more I stared, the dark giving on to more dark, and lying on my back beside the remains of the fire and the dying chatter, looking up at this visible past, I was reminded of a visit to a planetarium as a child, sunk in a beanbag, watching the steady spectral zoom towards our blue orb at its beginning, and I remembered watching Pangaea come apart, India drifting from Africa towards Asia, the two plates thrust-faulting, creating the mountains around me, which were still growing, blocking out starlight, and the valley I was lying in, sinking into, rock that was once underwater, home to bottom-dwellers looking up to the heavens as dead fish descended, offerings from the sea-gods, picked clean, their eyes separating dark from dark, never to see stars, mountains, people, stuck like I – we – would always be in their own limited Umwelt, unable truly to imagine a world different from their own, beyond the portion of the sea floor they saw as home, dying, millennia ago, knowing nothing of air and the birds that drifted in its invisible currents, nothing of the land, just like I would die knowing nothing of the world as it appeared to the mantis shrimp, or as it smelled to the Labrador, dashing through a park off its lead, able to sniff a history of long-gone scents, or as it was heard by the vampire bat, whose ability to hear was only trumped by its prey, the greater wax moth, whose sense for vibration might allow it to feel even the faintest reverberation of a distant call in its wings, a call from the past, as each present sound ripples on into a future, and perhaps somewhere beyond all this lay a creature who could sense all these echoes, the sound of my waterproof as I shifted and the fire's breath, the wash of the distant stream eroding rock and the slow creaking of the hills, who might interpret the sound of pickaxes deep within rare-metal mines, interpret the music of calls on hold and the steady thrum of cruise-ship engines, as well as the buzzing moon-like glow of their cabin lights luring migratory birds from their routes home, and the beat of insect wings as they veered towards the headlights of cars, the veined shadows their spread-eagled bodies cast across the rain-slick road still humming with the aftershock of seismic charges from gas prospectors using sound to see like the bats, who'd fled their roosts to escape the noise of LEDs, leaving the insects and frogs that they would have hunted to grow more confident in their mating calls and, no longer haunted, to sing not just for continuance but for the sake of the song, for the feeling of shaped air leaving the throat, and somewhere still, to those who believed, were the distant reverberations of the first song of Saraswati, singing the cosmos from the void, singing shape and meaning from matter, the sounds then echoing now, everything that vibrates continuing to vibrate or turn into heat, the past around us still in the warming air, the words of the dead slipping between our bodies like ultra-black fish in the deep, disappearing from the dark into the dark, leaving a supple wake.

'Pee partner?' Katrina said, yawning.

I realised we were the only two pilgrims still out by the fire. 'Honoured,' I said.

We'd been told only to venture from camp in pairs. I fetched my Shewee from the tent and we walked off, wearing head torches. She squatted and I pointed my artificial penis out into the dark. When we were done, I bent down to tie my shoelaces and noticed we had the exact same make of hiking boots.

'Are you a five, too?' I asked.

She nodded. 'Same shoes, same size. Maybe that's more evidence for your project.'

We were surprised to see a light on in our group leader's tent when we returned – a blue lantern, illuminating the surrounding snow. As we neared it, we could hear the muffled tones of a voice on the satellite phone, a clear sense of panic. Then, Jeremy's voice, stressed: 'But what do we do? What do you say we do?'

More crackle from the phone.

Jeremy emerged and walked briskly to the large tent the Sherpas shared. He woke the Sherpas and talked in a language Katrina and I didn't know. There was no way I could sleep now. We sat by the fire and were silent.

When Jeremy eventually came back out, we asked him if there was any news.

'You should be sleeping. Sleep. Tomorrow, things will clear.'

In the morning, I struggled to wake in time for breakfast. Jeremy finally gathered everyone for a meeting.

'There seems to have been a confrontation at the border,' he said. 'They told me on the radio there's a lot of tension. The Chinese. The Indians. It's to do with some water treaty, the river, I don't know. It doesn't matter. We've been encouraged to cut our trip short and turn back.'

There was a pause. A nervous laugh.

'No,' one pilgrim said.

'You said it's only one more day away,' said another. 'We'll get to Mansarovar and then turn.'

'I'm hearing things are serious,' Jeremy said. 'This shouldn't be taken lightly. Our pilgrim visas might not carry the weight they usually do.'

'A vote?'

'We can't split the group. My first duty to you is safety,' Jeremy said.

'Hands raised to continue on.'

Almost everyone raised their hand. Even Katrina. I didn't move.

Jeremy sighed. 'I think we should act on the advice. We don't know what's happening out there. It's an active situation. Moving parts. I'm hearing talk of gunfire.'

'I can't speak for others. But I have been saving years to come here. I've been training months. I know for sure this is my one chance. I'll be going on to the lake, even if I go alone.'

There were a few nods among the pilgrims. A consensus formed: they would speed on to the lake, and, instead of staying three nights there as planned, they would turn back after one.

The Sherpas grew frustrated. They took Jeremy aside. One of the pilgrims, the Brit, joined the argument.

'I'll personally pay you extra. Cash, as soon as we're back in Nepal. Can you translate that for them? *Cash*.'

'He's saying about his family.'

'What's the number? Let me know the number and I'll—'

Two of the Sherpas abandoned the group, taking with them an elderly woman whose energy had already been flagging before the news. The other three agreed to continue with the group for an extra fee. Despite not raising my hand in the vote, I decided to go on, too. We had come all this way. I didn't have any signal to check in with my editor.

We made fast progress that afternoon. It was unclear whether the stream we were following was flowing to or from the lake. When we finally reached Mansarovar, my first thought was about my feet. I was done in by blisters. My next thought was second-hand embarrassment about the pilgrims, the way they dropped to their knees, how they sang. That my first reaction to the splendour was irony irked me. It truly was a spectacular view. I wished that I could have been like them, could have experienced beauty in its pure state, in the present. To react to it with my body, rather than filtered through so many layers of thought! I looked again at the view and it was beautiful. I stared until the clichés rang true.

Katrina and I helped the three Sherpas set up camp, allowing the true pilgrims their moment. The lake was larger than I had imagined, and Kailash's peak looked almost diminutive across it. The guides made tea and it was good to drink, to eat and talk, at the highest point of our trek. The hardest work was done. Katrina looked out at the peak, perhaps thinking of Jay, or of the situation at the border.

During the evening prayers, the satellite phone continued to sound with warnings. 'We've alerted them to your presence, so they know not to—'

As the night began in earnest, we saw lights in the distance. Jeremy scrambled around in his tent for the paperwork. Everyone else prayed. I felt a deep and undeniable dread in the pit of my stomach, rising within me as the cars approached, and catching like acid reflux. I could taste it in the back of my throat. The Chinese soldiers left the headlights on, and in their glow read through the forms Jeremy presented. Our fate was to be decided by teenagers! In the car, they radioed their superiors. During the long wait for a verdict, panic spread among the pilgrims. Katrina, though, was noticeably calm. Eventually, it was decided that the soldiers would escort us to the Indian border in the morning.

'The Indian border?' I asked, as the soldiers set up their own camp next to ours. 'But we came through Nepal.'

'That's what's been decided,' Jeremy said. 'And seeing as I bloody well just do what other people say—'

'And what do we do when we get there?'

'I knew we should have turned back,' someone else cut in.

'It's ridiculous,' the Brit said. 'Utterly ridiculous.'

It was decided that the group would listen to a Laal Guru sermon and then go to bed. Katrina wandered off, and I followed her, several metres behind, fed up with wisdom. She was holding a freezer bag. At the edge of the black lake, she crouched down and emptied it out into the water. She filled the plastic bag with water and turned that out too, to ensure that every last bit of ash was gone. The sight of her silhouette against the lake, that tangible absence on the reflective surface, continued to play on my mind the next morning, as we were driven off-road to the S207, which we followed until its end in Burang County. We made camp further south, in Murong, and then trekked the next day to Dingsong via Duolong. The path frayed at Donggu Yingqu and one step, among the thousands of steps I was taking each day, took me from China into India.

A few hours later, Katrina pointed into the distance, at what I could only describe as a white tower. It was as tall as the Qutb Minar and made entirely of ice.

'An ice stupa,' Jeremy explained. In the winter months, when snow was frequent and water was readily available, villagers would pipe water down from the nearest peak and send it up through a vertical pipe. At the top of the pipe, several metres in the air, the water was shot out through a sprinkler at night. The diffuse liquid would freeze as it fell, and stick to the pipe. With time, ice grew on ice, until a densely packed stupa formed. Because of its shape, it would melt very slowly when the summer came, creating a steady and reliable flow of meltwater for the locals. It projected resources into the uncertain future, levelling the divide between winter and summer. We walked up to it, as if encountering a relic of an alien race. Katrina joined me as I lay down next to it; looking up, I felt a sense of vertigo. It was like a well that rose above the ground rather than being dug into it. And this inversion lent it an unearthly air, as if we had not crossed the border from one country to another, but from one world into the next.

5. Mool Sarovara, Nanda Devi National Park

We rose quickly, almost vertically, the passing peaks abstracted on the reflective surfaces of our foil heat blankets. The chopper would take us to Munsiyari, where a coach would drive us on to the new town of Mool Sarovara.

In our extended absence, a narrative had formed: *Hindu pilgrims detained on holy route by Chinese forces as border battle intensifies.* I just wanted to get home, but it became clear that we didn't have much of a choice about going to Mool Sarovara. I could escape political reporting, but I couldn't escape politics. The small town, still essentially a construction site, was deeper into the mountains, and further from our route back to our normal lives, but the government wanted to capitalise on the press. As pilgrims, we would now pray at the new lake, the 'new source' of the Saraswati River, on the Indian side of the border. I managed to get through to my editor, who was keen for me to go along with it all and send back some words each night.

The sun set behind the peaks as we flew, the sky an intense and varied blue through the glare-resistant tint. We landed on a school playground in Munsiyari. A representative from the Centre for Research into the Saraswati River met us on the makeshift helipad and led us to our coach. Because of the border, she explained, Mansarovar and Kailash, the spiritual sources of the ancient Saraswati, couldn't be reached by the river works. But, in any case, she continued, as we walked to a bend in the road, the science was clear that the source had shifted across the border and could now be found in a recently formed lake in the Nanda Devi National Park. 'The Saraswati starts in Uttarakhand, heading north to Himachal, then out through Punjab, Haryana and then Rajasthan and Gujarat.'

The camera crews were waiting for us. I pulled my scarf up like Katrina had, covering my face. We rushed out of the coach and entered the largest of Mool Sarovara's new hotels. The CRSR had left their leaflets in each of the rooms. The town had been built with funds allocated to the river works, as part of the regeneration of the entire Saraswati route. It would become a tourist destination once the river began to flow, as pilgrims flocked to the new springs. The source, the literature claimed, had sprouted around the same time as the water had been detected along the river's ancient palaeochannels. A glacial lake had formed in Nanda Devi, almost ten times the size of nearby Roop Kund.

Several cities would be built along the Saraswati River's route, the largest of which would be New Lothal, at the river's mouth. Some governmental functions would move to the coastal city, the leaflet said, which was inspired by Lothal, the location of the world's first port, built in the time of the Saraswati Civilisation.

I met Katrina in the hotel bar, after she'd been for a night swim in the basement pool. There wasn't yet any beer on tap, so we went for wine. The bartender had moved recently to the town, abandoning the flock of sheep his father had expected him to tend to after his death.

'There are herds this high?' I asked.

'Sure. Sheep, cows. They come up for the summer when the grasses appear. And there are more grasslands now there is less snow.'

When we ordered a second bottle, Katrina asked me again to share what I'd discovered about her family in my research. 'Tell me where I come from,' she joked.

'Sejal and Jugaad,' I said, again, 'had seven children, all named after the rivers of Punjab. Their eldest daughter, their second child, was called Beas, and she was your – let me get this right – great-*great*-grandmother?' According to the records, soon after her marriage to a man from a neighbouring village, Beas and her husband moved down to the coast, where the two of them were spirited away by the British. In a ship log I'd seen in an online archive, Beas and her husband were bound for Trinidad. They were recorded leaving Karachi and arriving at Aapravasi Ghat in Port Louis, Mauritius, where they were to transfer to a larger ship, better suited to the longer and more arduous stretch of the voyage past the Cape and on to Port of Spain. But they disappeared from the records on that second ship, not recorded as boarding in Mauritius or deboarding in Trinidad.

They might have found work during their short dock, or perhaps one of them had fallen ill over the course of the journey and couldn't go on. Maybe, strolling through Port Louis, they lost track of time and missed their connection. Or they fell out with a friend on board and vowed not to return. Perhaps they were kicked off the ship, had committed a crime. Or maybe they changed their minds about going to the other side of the world, wanting to stay at a distance from which they might feasibly return home – not that they ever would. There were endless possibilities that didn't appear in the records, but what was certain was that they took on a lodging in Port Louis and ended up having three children, two of whom survived.

The next day, certain I had enough for the piece, I made

arrangements to get to Gairsain, Uttarakhand's summer capital, but Katrina wouldn't return my texts. I found her in the hotel bar. She was talking to the bartender about a local farmer who had gone missing with his herd.

'In all likeliness,' the bartender said, 'something has happened.'

'You think he's dead?'

'He was an old man. It's not impossible. If he has kicked the bucket, they'll probably send a search party out for the cows. A helicopter.'

As the bartender made my cocktail, I asked Katrina about which bus she'd like to get the next day.

'I'm not sure I'm ready to leave,' she said.

'Oh.'

'It's nice here, don't you think? I think it's a good place to clear my head.'

I would pick apart the nuances of the tone in which she delivered that line a day later, after she'd WhatsApped me the audio recording she'd made of Edward and Jay that night in Svalbard.

Passing this on, she said.

I listened to the recording in the bath. It was strangely intimate, Katrina's husband's voice in the room. He spoke more than I expected, Jay, often interrupting the flow of Edward's meandering story. As he laughed, I remembered that Edward had only told Jay the story about Kailash when he knew he was about to die. And Jay had only ever revealed it to Katrina when he knew the same. Why had she sent it to me now? I got dressed without being properly dry and went down the hall to knock on her door. There was no answer. I checked the lobby, the pool and the bar.

'She said something about a walk,' the bartender said.

I figured she might have gone up to the lake, the new source, and I put on my hiking boots. The way was easy along the newly paved path. My blisters had become callouses, and the adrenaline lent me much-needed energy. The lake still looked like a building site, diggers frozen around its perimeter. It began to snow, and snow heavily, and not finding any sign of her, I turned back towards the hotel.

There was talk of movement in the hills on the lobby TV. Apparently a landslide further north had revealed a pit of bones, frozen for so long that scraps of perfectly preserved flesh remained. Even hair. Jeremy and I formed a search party and we set off in different directions.

I walked clockwise around the source, staying in touch with the others via radio. I veered away from the lake and turned north. My breath thinned as I headed uphill, towards the glaciers. I should have waited for backup, for a local who knew the terrain, but Katrina had been missing far too long to delay any further. I hugged the side of the hill, coming out in a new valley. The lake disappeared from view and I began to walk down, snow cascading with each step. The mountains, pockmarked with dark cryoconite holes, cast crisp shadows. I spotted a patch of darker snow ahead and sped towards it. When I reached where I thought it had been, there was nothing of note, and I thought the valley was playing tricks on me, the light. The dread within me had morphed into desperation. I had to find her. Everything ached. I was getting increasingly light-headed and beginning to consider turning back.

But then I came across a footprint.

I dropped to my knees. I yelled out and my voice echoed on the surface of the hills.

With renewed determination, I followed this trail for several minutes, until I looked back and realised that I was leaving identical prints. Katrina and I had the same shoes. The same shoe size. Was I following her, or following myself? I looked around, utterly disorientated. The mountains seemed to move, to dissolve and reappear in different configurations. I sat down, dizzy, and looked up, stunned, to see a cow, a white cow, drifting through the air. It was suspended by a harness and a long cord from the chopper above, floating serenely over the white valley.

Katrina looked up and saw it too, from where she'd fallen into the hidden crevasse, that deep well, the white cow drifting up above, held for a moment in the narrow view she had of the blue sky, before vanishing beyond the ice.

SASSI PUNNU
1879

It was only after Jugaad met Sejal that he was able to see his future as something to run towards, rather than a refuge from the past that he had been running from.

They met twice a day as he ferried her across the river, to and from her work at the house of the seamstress. But the length of the boat ride was never enough. There was always more to discuss. If only the river were wider.

'I'm no storyteller like you,' Jugaad said, when Sejal asked him to tell her about his childhood. 'I don't even know any stories.'

'You're telling me you don't know *any* stories,' she said. 'Everyone knows *some* stories.'

'My parents never told me any growing up. They were quiet people. I didn't go to a school.'

'No stories at all?'

'Why don't you tell me one, then? It's nice listening to your voice. Tell me one.'

He tied the boat to the post as they arrived. Rather than get up to leave, she stayed in her seat, facing him, and began to speak.

Long ago, in a great land, the queen gave birth to a girl so beautiful she was named after the sun: Sassi. The king called upon an astrologer to predict her destiny. The astrologer fell silent before hesitantly reading out his prophecy: Sassi would lead a life of anguish, deception and desperation, and would die helpless and destitute out on the dunes, determined to follow love to a disastrous end. The parents were horrified; this was no life fit for a royal. That night, they placed their baby in a small boat filled with gold and silver coins imprinted with the royal seal, and sent her off alone to float downstream.

A poor fisherman found the baby and the boat. He and his wife had been trying and failing to have a child for years. Now, here was a gift from the gods! They adopted her and used the gold and silver to build a house and give Sassi a happy childhood, with servants and tutors. Intelligent, beautiful, she was the envy of all high society when she came of age, visiting theatres and exhibitions. At one gallery, she was transfixed by a painting of a handsome prince, Punnu, from a foreign land in the west. She'd never thought she was one to care about men, but she couldn't stop thinking about him, and returned to see his picture day after day.

The artist who'd painted Punnu noticed Sassi admiring the portrait, and asked if he could paint her, too. What resulted was another masterpiece. Hearing praise about the work, the king bought the painting without having seen it. When he did look upon Sassi's beauty, he ordered the artist to bring her to him. He wanted her as a second wife.

Sassi and her father visited the king, and when they met, the king noticed that her father had a gold coin imprinted with his own personal seal. There was only one way he could have come across such a coin ... The king was standing in front of his long-lost daughter! He asked that Sassi be returned to him and his wife immediately. They had mourned the loss of their daughter for years.

It was all a shock to Sassi. If she really had been abandoned, then how dare they ask for her back? She loved her adopted parents and would never leave them. Not even for the king and queen.

The king was disgraced, and he ordered the artist to take the painting of Sassi away. Returning to his studio, the artist placed the portrait next to that of Punnu. The two of them together were a sight to behold. That night, he rode off through the desert, heading towards Punnu's kingdom in the west to show him Sassi.

Punnu fell for Sassi's portrait, just as she had fallen for his. He set off at once for Sassi's city, accompanied by a caravan of hundreds of men and camels. When the caravan arrived at the edge of Sassi's city, a festival began to mark their marriage.

Punnu's father, the king in the west, heard about his son's marriage and was furious. No son of his would squander the family fortune for the sake of a lowly fisherman's daughter! Especially one from a foreign land of old enemies. A prince should only marry into royalty. He sent a group of henchmen across the desert to find Punnu and bring him home.

Sassi and Punnu luxuriated in one another's company. They spent days and nights in their tent in the middle of a vast camp. Punnu adorned his wife in the finest silks, diamonds, pearls ... With her intelligence and her royal blood, he knew she would make the perfect queen. Punnu had heard all sorts of tales of love in his time, and had written them off as exaggerations. But, feeling the way he did now, it seemed the stories weren't extreme enough. He and Sassi drank their evening tea after a decadent feast, not knowing that the tea had been laced with a powder that would send them both into a deep sleep.

Sassi woke in an empty bed. She stepped out of the grand tent, which had been in the centre of the camp, to find herself surrounded by nothing but desert. Where had everyone gone? Had it all been an elaborate dream? She didn't know what to do or where to go. Where was Punnu?

Unsure, she walked back home across the hot sands. Her parents attempted to console her, letting her know that

Punnu had decided to return to his kingdom in the west. Sassi couldn't understand it. Someone had to be lying to her. She ran away from home, ran out on to the dunes. She walked for miles and miles towards the land of the setting sun. The immense heat made the necklaces and bangles burn on her skin and she ripped off her pearls and her diamonds, her gold and silver; she tore away her silk clothes and walked naked on the sand. The winds carried her last cries across the desert plains: 'Punnu, Punnu, Punnu.'

When Punnu finally woke up, his hands were tied. A camel was pulling him in a sheltered cart. The whole caravan was travelling across the desert. He couldn't see Sassi, he couldn't remember deciding to leave.

'Sassi!' he called out, and it was a servant who explained how his father had ordered that he be brought back alone. He begged his servant to free him, and he escaped that night, running east across the dunes towards the rising sun. He walked for days and nights, his resolve holding strong against the mirages and the hallucinations, until he spotted something glinting in the sand. A silver necklace. He walked on and found his wife's pearls, her gold bangles. How he cried! He tried to dig up the sand, looking for her. He was all out of water and had no food. He continued to dig and finally he found her body. He lay down next to her, exhausted, and let the wind cast the sand back down upon them as he embraced his wife. No one was witness to his final words: 'Sassi, Sassi, Sassi.'

Jugaad looked Sejal in the eye. 'I wish it had ended with them at the wedding.'

'Me too!'

'You have a nice voice,' he said. She didn't reply. 'For telling stories.'

'Now it's your turn.'

'Won't your parents be expecting you home?'

It was getting dark.

'Tomorrow?'

'Tomorrow.'

Jugaad wondered whether to make something up about his past so that Sejal might be more impressed by him. But when he sat in front of her on the boat, he found it impossible to lie. 'I was born a landless Chamar, near a hill station to the east.'

When the rains were good and crops flourished, his family suffered. And when the land turned dry and the livestock died, they celebrated. Whenever a cow or buffalo dropped dead, he and his father would be called for. They'd skin it, deal with the corpse and the meat, tan the hide, work the leather, making belts, shoes, saddles. Jugaad did most of the work; his father was normally recovering from the previous night's drinking. His mother had to think of new places to hide the money when it came in. When times were especially hard, their emergency fund would become visible at the bottom of their sack of rice.

He hadn't properly thought of running away until he wandered into a forest one day, at fifteen, and saw a dead body: an unclaimed buffalo corpse. He waited a few minutes, trying to check if anyone was around. Then he got to work quickly. He made a series of careful slits with his knife, and removed the skin from the carcass. The meat was rotten, worthless. He dragged the hide deeper into the forest and dug a hole to bury it. If anyone found out that he'd claimed goods from somebody else's property, his family's debt would worsen. If there had ever been the hope that they might work themselves out of their current predicament, his being called a thief would put an end to it.

After days of thinking, he returned to the forest to dig the hide back up. The smell was deeply unpleasant. He beat what was left of the hair off it. When it was smooth as skin, he took it down to the river to clean. Then he sewed up the cuts and slits, the eye sockets, nostrils, mouth, udders, vulva, anus. The only opening he left was in one of the rear legs, where the hoof had been, which was where the body would be inflated. It took so long to fill the hide with air, he almost fainted. But eventually he'd inflated it enough that it was buoyant – a beri. He held up the buffalo-balloon, his pass to a better life. With it, he could traverse any body of water. He tested it on the river and, sure enough, it acted as the perfect float. With his beri tied to his back, like an enormous rucksack, he walked on to the cross-roads and then to the train tracks. He walked until he came to the hill station. It was as hot as he'd ever remembered, and he figured the Angrezis would all be retreating to the hills and would be willing to call upon the services of a hunting guide.

The white men were intent on killing as much as they could. At the very least, they had to kill twenty-one beasts; that was the tally a rival group of friends had reached. Jugaad carried their things and helped them navigate the foothills, which would have been difficult without his beri. Each gunshot sent birds into the air. They only stopped to inspect the body if the animal was rare, otherwise they just walked on, leaving behind a trail of rot. The rivers here were hard to ford, so at each crossing he'd untie his prized beri. First, he'd place their things on the buffalo hide and swim across the river. Then, he'd return for the men. One by one, the whites would climb upon his back and he'd swim them across, using the beri to stay afloat.

At first Jugaad assumed that they were high-born, educated men. But one of them, who'd been in India long enough to learn some Hindi, explained that, in England, they were probably as low as he was! They had worked on trains, shovelling coal in engine rooms for hours a day. And then they were recruited here as specialists. Now, they were rich enough to afford servants like Jugaad.

Sometimes Jugaad would be asked to cut the horns from the bodies, sometimes their genitalia. Once, he was told to scoop out the eyeballs, which were used in batting practice. As the men approached their target number, they grew increasingly cruel. One deer died standing up, held in place by a thick bush. One of the men took his musket and pushed it into the deer's anus. They laughed as he pushed it further and further still. That night, he gave Jugaad the gun to clean. The men drank heavily and fell asleep. Jugaad searched through their things, taking three bags of money and all their maps and compasses. He pushed the bags of money into the blow-hole of his beri, before inflating it up and sealing the opening. He tossed the maps and compasses into the river, and then jumped in himself. Holding on to the beri, he let the river's flow take him.

As time wore on, he lost feeling in his feet and legs. But no matter how cold and numb he became, he did not let go of the beri. He didn't steer off on to a bank to rest or warm up, he did not allow himself to stop, because he knew that, as soon as the hunting party woke and realised what had happened, they would come looking. And he did not have a strong enough imagination to foresee what it was they might do to him if they made it back alive and found him.

He held on, simply held on, fighting sleep, dodging rocks in the rapids. Sometimes he'd be close to drifting off, but would jolt back awake when a change in the current made the money in the hollow belly of the beri jingle.

It was only when the sun rose that he pulled into the river-bank. He didn't want to be spotted by any fishermen, and had come upon a town. He stripped naked in the sun, trying to get some feeling back in his limbs. He moved about, getting his blood to flow again, and when his clothes had dried he put them back on. He unsealed the beri and took out the money. He put pebbles into the opening, making the thing heavy enough that it would sink, and threw it into the river. He kept enough money for new clothes and hid the rest inside his turban. From the river, he could see the distant dome of a gurdwara. After eating his fill of langar, he set off in search of a tailor, and came out looking, and feeling, like a new man.

But no distance would be great enough for him to feel safe from the white men. So he bought a boat off an old fisherman and continued on downstream. His dream was simple enough. He wanted some land of his own. He rowed from village to village in search of work, entering the flatlands of Punjab. Eventually, he heard about a job: an elderly ferryman had passed away. He laughed. It was his destiny to live a life of crossing. He headed on down the river, drawn by the current towards Sejal.

'And that's how the story ends, the two heroes sitting in a boat as night comes on.'

'That's how it ends?'

'Well—'

'That's no place to end.'

RAVI

It's always a new river,
Always the same old train again
'The Waters of Caney', Jody Stecher

The Shining of Karakum

Heading from Mombasa towards the interior on the brand-new lunatic line, approaching the severed heart of the Great Rift and leaning against the train window, Nathu experienced the same reversal of perspective that had once captured him as a child: rather than feeling like he was moving through the world, it was the world that was moving past him. All within the carriage was still and new; it was the landscape beyond that was animate, the plains. He could see the dusty pane as if it were a slit in a spinning zoetrope, the light strobing between the uniform trees, planted as part of the Belt and Road development. This was Nathu's first venture beyond his neighbourhood in almost a year and so far nothing had gone wrong. Despite that, he still felt like he was speeding towards a mistake, or rather that trouble was rushing towards him.

Trouble in the form of Radha Johns.

She'd messaged that she was through security at Jomo Kenyatta, and then she sent him a YouTube link with a caption: *Not far from this*. In the video, a medium claimed to have divined the meaning of the ancient Saraswatian script simply by looking at it. She'd locked herself in a windowless room for days to meditate upon the runes and had come to a revelation in a fugue-like state.

'The symbols began to move and resolve themselves into meanings—'

The video buffered as the train entered one of the new tunnels built by the Chinese. It was frozen on an image of a small seal found at Mohenjo-Daro, the largest site of the Saraswati Civilisation. Nathu recognised it, though in his time it had been known as the Indus Valley Civilisation or the Harappan Civilisation. The seal depicted a man with the horns of a bull, sitting in lotus position. He had three faces, an erect phallus, and was surrounded by beasts who bowed towards him, as if bending to his will.

When Nathu had studied the Harappans forty-five years ago during his undergraduate degree, the Indus script – now the Saraswatian script – had been the only ancient language yet to be decoded. Ancient history had changed in myriad ways since then, but that one fact remained. Until the script of the Saraswatians was deciphered, little could be known about them for certain. If his memory served him right, they were thought to be a peaceful people because of the absence of bones bearing marks of trauma. They had mastered the manipulation of water, that much he knew: irrigation, reservoirs, sewers. He had written a small piece of coursework about the possibility of an animist belief system, such was the pervasiveness of animal/human imagery in Indus finds, the man with the horns of a bull.

His reflection vanished as the train re-emerged in the light. The medium continued with her nonsense and Nathu wrote back to Radha: *That one video has probably two hundred times more viewers than the entire readership of my life's work put together. Perhaps it's her you should be hiring, not me.*

When he'd first received an email notification from his long-dormant LinkedIn account to tell him that Radha Johns had viewed his profile, he was surprised not only how much he remembered of her, but also how little he'd thought of her over the years. For two summers, she had been central to his married life with Akeyo, but then one day she was gone.

Radha had entered their lives as a worker on one of Nathu's projects near Lake Turkana. She was ten years younger than him and Akeyo, with the short slim build his wife normally went for. When Radha came to a gathering after a particularly gruelling week on site, Akeyo pulled Nathu aside. 'I like the one with the bob,' she said, grinning. 'The Indian.'

'You seem to have a type,' he joked. 'She's a visiting PhD. Not anyone I'm advising.'

Like Nathu, Radha was an early riser, and the morning after her first night with Akeyo, back in Nairobi, he found her at the kitchen table. He'd thought he was the only person awake, and was embarrassed to be seen in his boxers.

'I hope you don't mind, I helped myself,' Radha said, picking up her coffee mug. He nodded and she continued, 'Could you please explain your situation? I really don't want to be getting into anything unwelcome. I was very drunk last night.'

He sat down. He would see her soon at the faculty, and would see her every day when they left again in a few weeks for the dig site. 'The situation,' he said, 'is that Akeyo is a lesbian and I am uninterested in having sexual relationships. Something with my chemistry. I don't feel things for women – or anyone, for that matter. Well, I feel – just not, you know. Akeyo and I had been good friends for a long while, and both her parents and mine were pressuring us into marriages. Getting married to each other solved a lot of problems.' He paused. 'Well, solved problems for her. My parents severed ties. Not wanting me to be out of caste.'

'So, you've never—'

'We live very happily together.'

The secret that Radha and Nathu held from the rest of the team allowed for some intimacy between them during the dig at Turkana. They became friends, and when Akeyo came up for long weekends, they were happy, the three of them, in their unorthodox house built upon what had been the cradle-site of the human species. He hadn't seen Akeyo fall for any other woman so hard. When they would go on their long drives together, the house would be eerily silent without them.

Early one morning, over a year into the relationship, Nathu saw Radha distraught in the kitchen.

'Can we go for a walk?' she asked.

They crossed the Kipande Road and entered John Michuki Memorial Park, heading downhill towards the Nairobi River. Following the path towards the National Museum, Radha finally got to her point. She'd received a job offer to work for a company that mediated between engineering firms and museums when it came to archaeological finds on commercial dig sites. The money was impossible to ignore. But the offices were in Rome and Istanbul. 'I shouldn't do it, should I?'

'I'm the wrong person to ask.'

'What would you do?'

'I can only speak for my career, but a role like this doesn't come up often. And you're the one who applied for it. You knew it would involve a move. Perhaps your answer already lies in the fact that you sent off the application?'

He had underestimated Akeyo's reaction to the news. If anything, she was normally too clear-headed about the ends of her affairs. But, usually, she was the one ending them. The campus was quiet over summer break, and work wasn't keeping her as busy as it did the rest of the year.

'Did she tell you about it, the job? Did you know?' she asked.

Hugging his wife, his closest friend, Nathu lied. 'She told me the morning she told you. She was so sad, too. And I told her not to do it because what you had was special. And she was so unsure, I thought she wouldn't go through with it.'

146

A few months later, when Akeyo was finally herself again, enjoying life after their move to Mombasa, he found a letter with a return address in Rome, forwarded on from their old house in Nairobi. It was addressed to Akeyo, but, arriving home before she did, Nathu carefully opened it. He scanned it quickly, scared Akeyo would return from work. Radha wrote that her feelings for Akeyo hadn't subsided. Rome seemed more accepting than Nairobi or Delhi. She'd seen women walk down the streets arm in arm, had spotted two men kissing. She wrote that she wanted to see Akeyo, to show her what she was working on now – a Roman bathhouse uncovered in the foundations of a budget German supermarket. Nathu didn't remember much of the letter now, save for one phrase which had stuck with him: *My love for you is like the shining of Karakum*. He put the letter in his jacket pocket and sat at the kitchen table, waiting for his wife. Would he tell her? He had to tell her. But what if she left him? Moved to Italy? Who would he be without Akeyo? It wasn't until three in the morning that she burst through the front door, giggling, followed by a woman he didn't know.

'Oh, you're up! This is Grace.'

He kept the letter in his bedroom. And it stayed there for two days, until Grace finally left. At which point, Akeyo told him she'd found the one.

'She must be about twenty,' Nathu said. 'She looks like an undergraduate!'

'I wouldn't expect you to understand.'

'But, seriously ...'

'Just be happy, I'm happy. I'm moving forward and I'm grateful.'

He assumed he'd give her the letter once Grace inevitably left the picture. But, even though she wasn't really up to Akeyo's standard – he couldn't quite figure out what her job was, if indeed she had one – Grace stuck around. Nathu and Grace eventually became friendly, if not friends exactly, and he presided over their secret marriage in the living room. Their friends sat on the floor to watch the couple share their vows. After the ceremony, Nathu remembered Radha's letter, and added it to the bin bag he filled up after the party.

While Akeyo's marriage to Grace was filled with drama, her marriage to Nathu was steady, straightforward. He couldn't imagine his life without her company, their dinners, their walks, couldn't imagine the weeks spent on dig sites without their phone calls in the evenings. How could he face faculty dinner parties or evenings out with friends without her presence? How could he finish his papers without her second opinion, her rigorous edits? Akeyo worked in the university's administrative office, and while they often left for work at different times, depending on his lecture schedule, he always tried to meet her for lunch. They'd eat, do a lap of the green, and then return to their separate offices. And then, last spring, he waited on their bench and she did not arrive. He finished his sandwich and walked around to her building. The receptionist said she hadn't seen her, and upstairs they had assumed she was ill. He was anxious throughout the length of his office hour – in which no students turned up – and he left early to see if she was at home.

Akeyo's body was still in her bed. He thought back to the morning, the closed door he'd ignored, thinking she deserved a lie-in. The coffee he'd left in the jug for her was still there when he arrived home. Why, of all mornings, was that the one he didn't say goodbye?

Several days later, when he got through to Grace, who had been away visiting family, she'd already taken everything out of the account she and Akeyo shared. She told him to let her know the plans for the funeral, but, when the day came, she avoided him and left the church early without going on to the community centre. When Nathu arrived home, drunk, in a taxi, he saw that his and Akeyo's car was gone. The TV had disappeared, as had the laptop. There was no cash left in the coffee can. The shampoos and conditioners had been taken, the bottle of champagne Akeyo had been given by work. Her clothes were gone. The magnets that Akeyo had collected had been taken off the fridge, apart from one, a novelty magnet in the shape of a flamingo from Lake Nakuru, under which a note had been placed: *I have only taken what is rightfully mine as her real spouse.* G.

When one of his university colleagues came round to pay him a visit, a few weeks later, he was shocked to find Nathu's house so empty.

The truth just wasn't a feasible option.

'It was saddening me,' Nathu said, 'seeing all her things. I think she would have wanted me to give them away.'

'Time is the best doctor,' his colleague said. 'It's not right to do this now, I know, but I thought you were owed a heads up, seeing as you haven't been in to hear anything. I've been trying to call you.'

Nathu had always paid the mortgage and Akeyo took care of the bills. But now that Grace had control of her accounts, the landline hadn't rung since the funeral.

'They're talking about cuts,' his colleague continued. 'Big changes.'

Nathu was given the opportunity to re-interview for his job, to fight his case, but when the day came, he stared at his suit hanging in the cupboard and decided to stay home. He didn't feel able to reaffirm who he was, what he had to offer. To argue why what he had been doing for decades had any importance. He ordered a new television and had spent much of this last year in front of it.

But then the notification from Radha, and later a message: she had a layover in Nairobi and wanted to meet to discuss a job opportunity. He scrolled through her LinkedIn page. She was heading up the newly created Saraswati Centre at the Archaeological Survey of India and had become somewhat famous for positing the existence of a Rosetta Stone for the Saraswati Civilisation, which she called the 'East/West stone'. In several articles, she explained that objects inscribed with the Saraswati script had been found in Mesopotamia – the land between two rivers – and that Mesopotamian finds had surfaced along the ancient route of the Saraswati. Perhaps the most telling piece of evidence for Radha was what was known as the Gilgamesh seal, a Saraswatian carving showing one man fighting off two lions – a scene straight from the Akkadian epic. It was clear that both civilisations were seafaring, and clear too that the lapis lazuli that was found all over the tombs of the Mesopotamians' other trading partners, the Egyptians, was mined in only one place at the time: modern-day Afghanistan. The blue stone must have been traded down through the land of the Saraswati and up through Mesopotamia before reaching the Nile. These were extensive two-way trade routes, Radha contended, routes where goods, money and culture were all exchanged. And so, along these channels, Radha maintained in her articles, one would likely find an object containing both Saraswatian and Mesopotamian scripts. If such an object were found, then the whole puzzle of the Indus/Saraswati language would finally be solved. They needed as little as one sentence to be translated for the rest of the script to be decoded by AI. The systems, she claimed, in a profile titled 'Indian Johns: The Legend of the Saraswati Stone', had been trained on the formation of all other ancient languages, and had been fed with every Saraswatian symbol – all that was missing was a single line to be cross-referenced. At which point, the civilisation, which for so many thousands of years had remained silent, would begin to speak again.

As the conductor passed down the carriage, Nathu's phone buzzed with another reply from Radha, still talking about the medium who was going viral on social media. *She's been reposted by an official at the Department of Science and Technology*, she said. He reopened the video and watched it in full.

The medium was 'reading' an inscription found at Dholavira. 'Here they talk about a "Shava", a great god. Shava – Shiva. It's all connected. Reading this language is more proof, if we needed it, that our current ways go back several thousand years further than thought. It makes it definitive that we are not only the people of this land, but the people of all lands, that from our culture sprouted the cultures of the rest of the world ...'

The train slowed as it approached Konza. The station had been renovated along with the new line, but no futuristic architecture could keep out the dust. The last time Nathu had been here, the last time he had left Mombasa, he'd stepped off the train to get food for Akeyo. It had been the final ever running of the old Uganda railway, the line that his great-great-grandfather, Ravi 'John Henry' Hakra, had helped to build.

He and Akeyo had travelled to Nairobi on the Friday, and stayed in their old neighbourhood in Ngara, before returning to Mombasa on the Monday. As the old train had rattled along its metre-gauge tracks, Akeyo had asked him again to repeat the story of Ravi, a story as worn-through in their marriage as the cracked leather seats upon which they were sitting. He had been happy to tell it again, happy to spend time with her alone, the whole carriage theirs, the whole of the plains.

They had looked out at the same view he was seeing now, but one thing was different about it today. Nathu could see the old narrower tracks, stretched out on the plains like a great fallen ladder. In some sections, people had hacked them apart to sell on the metal. But floating above those rusted bones was the memory of Akeyo, alive, drifting through the air, how she looked out the window while she spoke, picking the stuffing from her seat with her short nails.

'Say it like it's your first time telling me,' she had said. 'Like we just met on the train.'

*

151

Ravi of Hakra was named, like all his siblings, after a Punjabi river. His eldest brother had been named after the Sutlej, near where they lived, and, once his parents had named their first daughter Beas after another river, they continued in the same vein. Ravi was raised to have an equal share of the square farm as all his siblings, but he forwent the inheritance to pursue his dreams of seeing the world. Stopping at a crowded bar in town after a busy market day, he sat next to a drunk British sailor who seemed eager to talk about his travels. Ravi asked what the world was like beyond India. 'Africa is to the Hindoo what America has been to the European,' the man said. He wrote down a name and an address in Karachi, in exchange for another Patiala peg. Within a few weeks, Ravi was heading down to the coast.

His timing couldn't have been worse. Karachi was in the throes of a great plague, and Ravi was forced to quarantine along with thousands of other workers in Budapore. The scale of death at Budapore was such that he was tempted to turn back, but he had signed himself away, and, in any case, didn't want to be the one to bring the invisible killer to Hakra. He coughed and coughed, covering his mouth with the red cloth his mother had given him, cut from a large piece she had split evenly among his siblings. He survived, and then endured the long, cramped voyage to Mombasa, where he was designated to become a pile-driver on the Kenya–Uganda railway. It was a costly line, linking Mombasa and Lake Victoria, and some in British Parliament had already nicknamed it 'the lunatic express'.

As was the case for many colonial infrastructure projects, the line had been designed to make the extraction of resources from the interior more efficient and cost-effective. It wasn't about joining up communities but about creating a direct channel for goods to flow down to the coast, where they would travel on to the Western world.

'All was well and good on the line,' Nathu continued, sounding like his grandfather, 'until the workers came upon the Tsavo River. Which is where they encountered the lions.'

Here, the thread of the story frayed. This would have been 1898, with the rail works stopping for a bridge to be built, thousands of Indian workers forming a camp eight miles wide at the point the river bled out into swamp. But, to Nathu, the timelines didn't quite work. There was a thin chance that Ravi had made it all the way up to Tsavo in time for the end of the lion drama, but the likelihood of him being involved in the episode to the extent that his grandfather claimed was low. Too low for a man in his line of work to allow for. Akeyo thought differently: a story with lions was more memorable than one without them.

'There are different theories about the lions' unnatural taste for human flesh,' Nathu went on. 'It was either caused by the rinderpest outbreak that had decimated the plains and removed the lions' normal food sources, meaning they were so hungry they'd eat anything, or the lions of the Tsavo had become accustomed to scavenging on the dead bodies of slaves tossed into the river and swamp by the caravans heading to the coast.

'See, the very reason the railway was being built was to reduce the cost of the long journey through the interior, to reduce the loss of property. The bodies the lions were eating were the reason the men were in Tsavo trying to build a bridge. The railway would put an end to the perilous crossing, the caravan raids. Well. Whatever it was, thousands of tired men had just camped upon the scavenging grounds of two very hungry man-eating lions.'

The men fought over who could sleep at the centre of the camp. Ravi, who had established himself as one of the hardest workers on the line, wielding a hammer in both hands, slept near the heart of the camp, while many of his peers were less fortunate, pitching tents near the fiery border of the swamp, keeping watch. One by one, they were picked off, dragged screaming into the shadows.

'The lions were shot, and Ravi survived. When he reached

Lake Victoria, the inland sea, he was supposed to ride one of the first full-length trains to Mombasa, and then travel on to India, but he stopped off at the brand-new town of Nairobi and never got back on the train.'

'I prefer the version where he fights the lions himself,' Akeyo said. 'The version you said your dad would always tell.'

Nathu laughed. It was, perhaps, one of the few positive memories he had of his father, the way he'd embellish their family origin story. According to his father, Ravi had taken a hammer in one hand and a knife in the other and had run at the lions while his superiors shot their rifles. This version was the one that had stuck with Nathu's younger nephews and nieces, and perhaps they still believed it now, wherever they were. It had been an early education, Nathu thought, in the fact that all history was historical fiction. A story had a longer life than a fact.

If Nathu had ever become a father, perhaps he would have intensified the story of Ravi 'John Henry' Hakra as his own father had. The story would morph into a more durable shape: Ravi the lion-killer outliving Ravi the piledriver. Whatever had or hadn't happened in Ravi's life, it was undeniable that he had helped in some way to form the tracks Nathu and Akeyo had been moving along then – the very tracks that he could see now in the parallel distance.

The new train finally came to a stop in Nairobi. It was so much faster than the old one that Nathu didn't fully trust he had arrived.

Nairobi itself was part of Nathu's family's twisted lore. It had sprouted from the swampland a few years before Ravi arrived. Nathu's mother always liked to note that, in its early years, it had been almost entirely populated by Indians and a few whites, a fact she seemed to be proud of. *Now, the city is gone*, she used to say.

In the years since Nathu had last returned to the city, it appeared to have changed, but only in cosmetic ways. Flux was a defining characteristic of any city, provided it wasn't embalmed by UNESCO – shopfronts were supposed to change, neighbourhoods to evolve, the population to move and morph. A city's character was rarely impacted by what happened on the surface. Often, he would hear friends bemoan the death of a loved neighbourhood, the end of a certain era, such and such bar or restaurant closing to become a betting shop, a nail parlour, the same way every generation would announce the death of 'real' music, which was always the music of their youth, or the end of 'proper' manners, the manners by which they were raised. To Nathu, a city changed the way a body did: every part of it was always dying and being replaced, but the essence of the self remained. Within a decade or so, every cell within him was reborn. In nine years, if he made it that far, he wouldn't physically be the same man Akeyo had hugged, but he would still remember the feeling of her body against his, the smell of her hair.

Akeyo would often counter him on this reasoning. What he said was true to an extent, but at some point all the dwellings he'd spent decades studying as an archaeologist had been completely abandoned, had they not? The heat of the water in the pot rose until the frog boiled.

It was impossible not to walk through Nairobi now without thinking of her. He was utterly disorientated in Ngara, on a street where he and Akeyo used to go for meals out. There was a hole now where their favourite restaurant had stood, foundations being laid for something new. He'd learnt nothing about death from her passing, nothing at all. He looked down into the pit and then answered his ringing phone.

Radha was waiting for him at a rooftop bar. She'd already ordered for the two of them.

155

He was surprised to see that she'd taken to dying her hair, having never seemed concerned about her appearance. Admittedly, all his preconceptions of her were several years out of date. Like most archaeologists, she'd subscribed to the unofficial uniform – khakis, light jacket, a thin scarf. But she wore subtle signs of her improved lot: gold jewellery, the ripe cheeks and wrinkled neck that Akeyo had taught him indicated Botox. He wondered if his wife would still have been attracted to her now.

'I was so sorry to hear about Akeyo,' Radha said, quickly, as if to get it out of the way. He'd told her about the death when she'd first messaged. 'It's been quite something to get my head around. I can't imagine, for you.'

'Speed was a blessing.'

'Of course.'

'I think it's better not to know if it's coming, maybe.'

Radha nodded, and, not knowing what to add, changed the subject. 'I read everything you published,' she said. 'Reading your stuff really did make me want to return to Turkana.'

'You remember the house where we all stayed, near the lake?' he said.

'Of course.'

'When Akeyo and I went back, a couple of years ago, it was completely submerged. The whole building, roof and all. The lake's been growing so fast, people are being forced to move. The question is not whether to go, but how far to move, and how to possibly afford it. Even the shrines they had, you know, where they'd pray for rain, even they were underwater. We took a boat out on to the lake and our guide asks, "How long have you been married?" And Akeyo says, "Thirty-five years," and he says, "I'll take you thirty-five years out into the water." He took us so close to the church spire that you could reach out from the boat and touch the cross – wait, I have a photo somewhere.'

He handed her his phone.

'Surely it'll shrink back down eventually?'

'Ordinarily, yes. It grows and shrinks; there's a satellite-photo montage showing how it's changed over the years, and the lake moves like a mouth talking. But these last years have been different. It just grows and grows. I'm … I'm waffling on. How have things been with you? I know nothing.'

She had very quickly moved from Rome back to India, where she married a man and had a child. Now, she said, they were essentially separated, she and the father, who ran a successful construction firm, but not in any official ways. 'He had his women before me, and continued on. I had mine. I was there to provide a little family prestige. A good name. It suits us both, to be honest.' Their son, Nish, was working in construction too, though his father had ensured that he started at the bottom of the ladder, so that he too could be a 'self-made man'.

'Nish is working on a stretch of the Saraswati River, up in the foothills,' she said. 'He's helping to dig up the riverbed. Both our lives are defined by moving dirt.'

She went on to explain how busy her work had been, with dozens of new ancient finds being discovered by the river workers. 'We're in a constant war. According to law, as soon as a find is spotted, we take control of the site. They're in such a rush, and we're so scared of rushing. It's just like it was in Rome.'

'You're butting heads often, then?'

'Often enough that they're trying to change the law. At first, the prime minister celebrated all the progress we were making with the finds. But, with what it's doing to the river work's schedule, the delays, there's been this change of heart. Indra was in the news himself asking why we had to stop to protect every little scrap of pottery, each spoon. "What is the significance of yet another pot, yet another water pitcher, when we have found so many already?" and so on.'

'I suppose rushing is something you are going to have to do.'

'Exactly. For now, the funding is good. Very good.' She paused. 'Are you still working?'

'No.'

'But you'd be interested in coming out of retirement?'

He thought of all the money Grace had taken, the steps he'd made this year to live within smaller means. How long had it been since he had tasted wine like this? He took a long sip.

'You were such a great mentor to me,' she continued. 'And we need all the help we can get in the search for the stone. At the moment, money is no object. It's a bottomless pit.'

He nodded.

'Just think about it,' she said, swilling the last of her wine around in her glass before finishing it. She checked the time on her phone. 'I'm afraid I haven't got long until my connection. I'll email?' she said.

'You should know,' Nathu said, 'Akeyo never received that letter you sent. I'm sorry, I am. But she was with someone and I thought she was happy, and I thought it would derail her. If I could do things again, I might do them differently. It's not that she didn't want to reply, it's that she never knew there was anything to reply to.'

It took a moment for Radha to understand.

'I did wonder,' she said. 'It was unlike her to be silent!' She smiled. 'I think that letter was the only time where she didn't get the last word. In any case, I'm glad she found her person in the end. It all feels like a different world. I can't even remember what I might have said.'

He contemplated telling her about what Grace had done after Akeyo's death. But it was nicer for Radha to think that there had been a happy ending, for that to exist as a reality in the world.

Radha left, and Nathu ordered another glass of wine. The prospect of one last project did excite him. An opportunity to be part of something concrete, something that could impact the field. His lasting contributions to the academic world would otherwise be his final few papers at the university, which might as well have been written on water.

The next day he continued west on the line to Equator, the place where Akeyo was born, and the place where she had wanted to be buried. As per her requests, there was no marking on the grave, so it was impossible to know exactly where she was. She might have been directly beneath him now, or a hundred yards away. And so the plains as far as he could see were imbued with a kind of significance. Any step he took led him closer to her, further from her.

'I'm going to India,' he said out loud, sitting down. 'I'm not so sure when I'll be back.'

A light wind lifted the top layer of dirt off the ground.

'I think about you every day,' he said to the brittle weeds, the ants. 'It's not sadness, I'd say. It hurts, but it feels good to hold you in my mind. Sometimes, when I'm sitting in the armchair, there are noises from the neighbours, and it feels like you're in the kitchen. And I can kid myself that you might just walk through the door.

'I've tried cooking your best meals. You'd probably laugh, watching me. I read and reread the instructions on the recipe, and by the time I look up from the screen, something's burning.'

The shadow of a bird progressed across his field of view.

'You know, I was reading up about these deep-sea archaeologists, specialising in shipwrecks and so on. And they were explaining how the gaps in the wood of a sunken ship fill with water, and if the wooden parts are removed from the sea too quickly, the whole structure disintegrates as it dries, literally breaks to pieces. So, they have to fill up the gaps in the wood while they're under the surface, with some kind of epoxy, some resin. And I was sitting there, thinking I could hear you, and it occurred to me this whole grief thing works a little like that. I'm a wreck of what I once was. Without you, there are all these gaps in me, Akeyo. Gaps in my day. In my head. And I've been scared that surfacing from this grief too quickly would break me, so I've just been staying down in it. You'd be embarrassed by me. And I think it's time to fill in those spaces with something else, is what I'm trying to say. Some work might do that. It'll be strange; I know we both always wanted to go to India and never did. And I'm sorry you can't come with me.'

He leant back on to the ground and covered his eyes with his left arm. The whole of the world was beneath him. He spoke about Radha, his new employer. 'She seems to have lived a good life. Very high up in the field, and she has an adult son now, believe it or not. He's working on what they've called the Goddess Valley Dam. A huge thing, to feed that river you first told me about. Radha showed me a photo, and on the surface of the dam they've carved a relief of this Saraswatian seal, a man with the horns of a bull. Must be metres and metres high. And I was reading about it, after Radha left. There was a construction worker, and for whatever reason – they don't seem to believe it was an accident, or a fall – he decided to jump into the dam, as it was being built. He climbed up a crane and jumped down into the wet concrete below. The witnesses said he looked like an Olympic diver, fingers steepled above his head. It said in the article that the concrete at the heart of the dam never truly dries, and that his body, suspended in it, might continue to move, millimetre by millimetre, at something like the rate that tectonic plates move, down, deeper still—'

There was a vibration in the ground, a rumbling. He sat up and opened his eyes. Adjusting to the glare, he made out the distant form of a train, the new lunatic express, a blur on the horizon. The ground hummed as it approached, and he stood and waved, imagining how he would appear to someone inside looking out, suddenly vanishing. As quickly as the train arrived on the flat plain, it was gone, dust rising in its wake.

The *Continuance*

Entering the convergence zone of the Indian Ocean gyre, streaming Ethiopian tezeta on his phone while sonar pulsed down into the depths below, Nathu looked out of his porthole at the thin film of particulate garbage, the miles of polythene shine. This was his third day in isolation, quarantined in his cabin with a virus that had yet to manifest any symptoms.

The team were scanning the midnight zone for signs of the wreck – the wreck of the *Continuance*, which they believed might house the long-sought East/West stone. Looking out at the glittering surface, he imagined the ship falling through the water column 150 years ago, seen by a thousand eyes as it sank, a sign from a foreign heaven. His attention turned from negative to positive buoyancy as the research ship entered the Indian Ocean garbage patch proper and actual objects came into view, greyed by extended exposure to the elements. Caught adrift in the churn of the South Equatorial Current, the plastic objects – crisp wrappers, fishing nets, energy-drink bottles – were undergoing a slow metamorphosis, less an aquatic afterlife, having served their brief purpose, than a floating purgatory. Abstracted from their original work, they existed and didn't exist, slowly breaking down within the shimmering epipelagic zone, until one day they would coat the stomachs of fish eaten by fish eaten by fish. The boat cut a course across the floating ruins like an Arctic ship through melting floe. Nathu longed to be free of his confinement, of this low-ceilinged cabin, but every test he did came out positive. If what he had spread through the ship, the whole expedition would require rescheduling. And there was much more than just money riding on them finding what they were looking for.

Their mission was to send an unmanned submersible down to the seamount upon which the wreck of the *Continuance* had been detected. The submersible had been retired after being used by scientists in the Clarion-Clipperton Zone, so they had got it at a good price – according to the team, tens of thousands of dollars was cheap. Its last mission had been to collect as much data as possible about the thousands of unknown species on the seabed before the mining nations began their dredging for polymetallic nodules. Whether it was the Clarion rift or Katanga, Turkana or the new Saraswati Valley, man's legacy upon the earth would be to overturn it, to seek out what pressure had produced in its depths. And the story of the East/West stone, as it was already being told, before it had even been found, was sedimentary, one layer of history pressing down upon another to produce something new.

There was a knock at the door.

It was too early for dinner.

'Yes?'

Takehiro, the ship's navigator, had just tested positive, too, and would have to isolate with Nathu. He pulled down his face mask, revealing an apologetic smile. Nathu paused the music.

'No symptoms,' Takehiro said, answering Nathu's first question.

'Me neither. You can have the top bunk.'

Takehiro stooped in the cabin, one of those tall, thin men, ill at ease with their size.

'Sit, sit,' Nathu said. 'Do you play cards? I'm desperately bored.' He dealt out two hands. 'So, what's the news out there in the free world?'

'They claim they've found it on the sonar. A few minutes from stopping now, probably.' As he said that, the boat did indeed stop. Plastic crap sloshed up against the window and there was the guttural groan of the anchor being deployed.

When their dinner arrived, Takehiro produced a bottle of sake.

'Emergency supply,' he said.

Nathu's day was turning around.

They drank and Takehiro told him about his last few months

aboard the ship, 'speaking to whales'. Swedish scientists had used AI to form phrases of whale song, and he was part of a team tasked with locating pods to which the ship would then communicate. There was a speaker on the hull sending out different calls, and a receiver recording any responses. Those responses would be fed back into the data set until a more complex understanding of the communication could be formed by the model.

'So, they were talking back?'

'As far as I could understand, the whales were talking to the machine. And the machine was talking to the whales. But the people couldn't understand the whales and couldn't understand the machine. I'm not sure.' He laughed. 'I just navigate. Like this trip, I don't understand really what it is about.' He asked Nathu to explain, and, with little else to do while they waited for news, the older man obliged.

Unlike many of their colleagues, the team's search for the East/West stone hadn't taken place in the field or in museum collections, but in the library. They found a description of a stone slab inscribed with two languages, one above the other, in the eighteenth-century diaries of Major General Sir Alexander Cunningham, who had discovered the stone retracing the steps of Jean-Baptiste Ventura, a Bonapartist who had become Governor of Lahore. Ventura had been inspired to search stupas for loot by the travelogues of Abu Rayhan Muhammad ibn Ahmad al-Biruni, the world's first anthropologist and the inventor of time as we know it, and of Xuanzang, later known as Tripitaka, who, like Faxian, had been searching for Buddhist scriptures he could bring back to China. Cunningham had received funding to establish the Archaeological Survey of India on the basis that he could prove that the religions of the Orient were all considerably younger than Christianity. But when he found the stone, he recognised one of the two scripts as Sumerian, which meant it was of high antiquity. If the other crude language were local, and pertained to Brahmanism, it would challenge his thesis. He arranged for the stone to be sent to London where it might be studied by Indologists. It was loaded on to his ship, the *Continuance*, along with a holdful of treasures bound for Bloomsbury. When the ship set sail, Cunningham stayed behind in India to oversee a dig at Taxila, a ruin that had been a thriving city in the time of Faxian. It turned out he'd owe his life to his busy schedule. Drawn into the gyre as it sailed south through the Indian Ocean, the *Continuance* was set upon by pirates who had been tipped off about its loot. They took the silver and gold, the ivory work and the jade, as well as the guns, ale and biscuits. But who, in the midst of a battle, would steal a heavy stone tablet with no known value?

The pillaged ship sank and remained undisturbed for 150 years, until an unmanned autonomous vessel, tasked with mapping the sea floor, passed by. There were fifteen such machines systematically exploring the midnight zone, drifting about of their own accord like marine Roombas, sucking up raw data that was fed into a deep learning model, which could then alert a central organisation to sites of possible significance.

'As you probably know, coordinates of shipwrecks can't exactly just be made public,' Nathu told Takehiro. 'There's 60 billion dollars' worth of precious metals in wrecks. So research units have to provide their motives and apply to find out if a specific ship they're interested in has been located on the confidential map. There are all sorts of fees and, if there's a match, they can pay for the exact coordinates.'

'So, all this, on a ... ?' Takehiro couldn't think of the right English word.

'Hunch? Yes. It's a kind of space race. Just with one side competing against itself.'

Already the misinformation about the Saraswati language was rife, with different papers being published every few weeks to generate press attention, which could be counted upon whether or not the work was peer-reviewed. Radha had been clear on her parameters: there was no watertight truth until there was a Rosetta Stone.

'My fear is that, even if we do make a genuine discovery, we might not be believed.'

Takehiro took one last swig and set the bottle down on the floor. 'But you believe in the work being done here? It's not strange, maybe, that the only two people quarantined, they're the only two people not from India?'

'I think we've both had too much to drink.'

They moved to their bunks, and Nathu looked up at the abstract shapes of light on the cabin's ceiling, cast up off the moonlit plastic outside the porthole. The sake bottle, which had fallen over, rolled from one end of the cabin to the other with the waves, and Nathu, unable to sleep, thought back to his last week on land, at a fundraising event that Radha had hosted under the guise of her son's twenty-first birthday party.

Radha's son, Nish, had come down for the event from the Shivalik Hills, where he was working on the Goddess Valley Dam. But, after the cake-cutting, the young man disappeared from the party. Nathu had found himself stuck in a circle of colleagues which had formed around the newest head of the Archaeological Survey of India, General Prakash Ji. He was Radha's new boss, stationed strategically close to both the hors d'oeuvres and the cocktails. The General's first dictate had claimed that he wanted to run the survey like the military, protecting 'the borders of our past'.

Radha had sent Nathu some of the General's books, flimsy and inflammatory polemics in which he claimed all language, and therefore culture, originated in India, that India hadn't been invaded by Aryans but that the Aryans were Indian. In his latest book, he claimed that the Saraswati 'Empire' was the world's first 'pristine state', meaning it hadn't grown out of something before it, but had formed from nothing.

His moustache gives Cunningham's a run for its money, Radha had texted, when they first heard about the appointment.

But, at the party, she was buttering the General up: 'A *Pristine State* was certainly ... thought-provoking. Are you writing anything new?'

The General handed her his empty plate before replying. Nathu counted the medals on the General's suit and zoned out. He looked around the party; the ratio, he believed, between the amount of schmooze and the amount of booze was irreparably skewed. And this was him several Scotches in. He decided to play the age card and make for an early exit.

But he had got lost in the labyrinthine layout of Radha's husband's house, its rooms within rooms, rooms which seemed to serve no purpose, rooms with sofas that seemed never to have been sat upon, adjoining bathrooms that might never have been used. What would a future archaeologist make of this? He stopped to admire the ivory tusk of a woolly mammoth, mounted in the library. The framed certificate beneath it claimed it was almost fully intact, and had been retrieved from the melting permafrost of Russia's far north, where mammoths had lived contemporaneously with the Mesopotamians.

'It's not actually that valuable,' a man said, shocking Nathu. It turned out that there had been someone sitting on the sofa in the gloom, after all. He turned and recognised Radha's boy, Nish. 'The ivory from Russia is much cheaper than it is from the poachers. Mammoth is worth less than elephant.'

Nathu nodded. Nish asked how Nathu knew his parents, and upon hearing that he was part of the search for the East/West stone, provided his opinion on the matter unbidden.

'It's less about being 100 per cent right,' he said, 'than it is about being first. The stuff Mum says, nobody believes on the ground. I work with real people, but everyone she knows –'

166

he gestured towards the party – 'they don't know the real country.'

It was hard for Nathu to take the young man seriously. They were sitting in the mansion he'd grown up in and he was talking about the proletariat.

'We believe what we already believe, and then just seek out the facts that confirm that belief. And there are enough facts in the world to back up any argument.'

'That's quite a pessimistic world view,' Nathu offered.

'Like, what does it matter if a pot was made 2,000 years ago or 4,000 years ago? Does that really change anything?'

'Sure. It matters to me.' As he had many times before, Nathu felt vindicated that his life was better for its lack of children. To raise an idiot, an idiot you would have to put up with for the rest of your life – in snatches, he could understand how his father resorted to violence. He, of course, had thought his own father to be an uneducated fool. Perhaps this was just the way of the world, the young always insulting the beliefs of the old.

'Mum can do all her work in offices, but I'm on the ground, right, and we see what actually happens. Half of the finds, it's protesters against the river – Muslims, mainly, and Punjabis – they're planting fake archaeological finds along the river's route. They take stuff from their backwater museums and bury it, and, when we get to that stretch and dig it up, we have to stop, weeks, months, and the longer the delays, the stronger their cause gets, right – they'll march and ask why all these crores were spent on the delayed river project when they could be going to whatever it is they want.'

'So, either you think we're clueless, or that we're in on some conspiracy?'

'It's not that.'

'If you believe that the river is returning along its ancient route, then wouldn't you believe the ancient sites to be real?'

'You're not really listening to me.'

Nathu felt a little sorry for the kid. Two parents at the top of their fields, perhaps too busy to have raised their only child closely. A pendulum swung from generation to generation, and whichever extreme might be seen in the parent was inverted in the child to an equivalent degree, so that perhaps the grandparent and grandchild resembled each other more closely than the parent and child. Nathu would have much rather been raised by his grandfather than his father. He had often wondered how different his life would have been if he'd married Akeyo when his grandparents were still alive, if their opinion might have changed that of his parents, who had presented an ultimatum after they met her: either he could marry the Black woman and start his own family without them, or he could continue in their line and marry someone of whom they approved. He had wrongly assumed that any marriage would please them, but it was a twisted point of pride to them that, for all the generations the family had lived in Kenya, they had never married outside of the community – their blood was Indian all the way through.

Nish had been talking, talking about the river works, about Prime Minister Indra and how the country could only be led by an alpha, someone to take the bull by the horns, that the state had languished too long in the hands of betas, who would never allow it to reach its full potential. 'It's ridiculous, now, that you are branded as some kind of weirdo online if you're proud of where you're from. God forbid you like the place you live!'

If not enjoyable, the interaction was proving to be somewhat interesting. Learning about Radha's son offered some kind of portrait of her in relief, and so he entertained Nish and spoke on, talking about the difference in national pride between the immigrant and the native, which led him to the story of Ravi 'John Henry' Hakra.

'... and the captain said to John Henry to pick up his hammer. The riflemen scared the lions out of their hiding spots, and when one of the lions came at him, he thrust a knife up into its throat, and came down on its skull with the hammer.'

'Lions aren't actually that hard to fight,' Nish said. 'In terms of, if push came to shove and you had to choose between the big cats. You could do worse.' Perhaps sensing he was being needlessly difficult, Nish started again. 'It's impressive you can trace your family back so far, though. I don't know anything about my grandparents' parents.'

'My theory,' Nathu said, 'is that an immigrant has a ready-made creation story. An origin story. I was there, then I came here, and now you are here. There's a clear point at which the story can begin. There's a need, too, you could suppose, to lay a stake in the ground. My parents cling to where they're from, even though it's been so many generations that no one in their right mind would call us immigrants. But your parents – well, it's more diffuse.'

Nish showed him an app on his phone called Helix. 'Mum bought this for my birthday. Apparently, before, they could trace a family back maybe four generations at a push, with spit or hair or whatever it is. But this one claims to be able to reach seven generations with its genome mapping. They can track cousins of cousins, huge genetic webs.'

Nathu looked at Nish's results. There was a map of the world showing where his genetic code originated. And a list of users, just anonymous numbers, with whom he shared enough code to technically qualify as related. 'If you pay for premium,' Nish said, 'you can reach out to them.'

'Would you download it on my phone for me?' Nathu asked.

It was only now, unable to sleep as he floated above the *Continuance*, listening to the percussion of Takehiro's bottle moving across the floor and the steady rhythm of his breathing in the bunk above, that Nathu's results came through.

The first thing he noticed was that his genetic map didn't just show South Asia – there was also a prominent strain of East African code in him. If only the technology had existed before his father's death! There were specks of Afghanistan, Mongolia. The world had globalised several times over.

The second thing that caught his attention was a message about a match with another Helix premium account. He accepted the terms and opened the correspondence.

It was night in McLeod Ganj when I received an alert, but I'd been awake, wrapped in several layers on my balcony, watching drunk backpackers, who had been unable to leave the state since the lockdown, find their way back to their homestays. A chorus of riled-up dogs sounded their chains. The yellow light of the pizza shops and bars, open despite the restrictions, rose above the hills like a haze. I recognised the sound of the notification from when I had found Katrina, and my heart rate quickened.

I could see that Nathu had filled in what he knew of his family tree, and when I saw the name he'd included five generations back, I texted Katrina: *A match! Ravi(!)*

I would FaceTime her the next morning, during the hospital's digital visiting hours, but I had to share the news with someone.

She replied within a minute: *!!!*

She was recovering quickly, already ahead of her physio schedule. While at first I thought she had left for that solo hike with some kind of dark premeditation, she told me that what had drawn her out of the hotel, off the path, was the idea that she might take more risks and allow a little recklessness into her life, that she might be more like Jay. But when the ground gave way beneath her and she fell into the narrow crevasse, she realised that she couldn't become him, and that, to keep his memory alive, she needed to continue to be the woman he had loved. Caught in the tight embrace of the ice, she understood that Jay could be left in the mountains, as close to heaven as one could get on earth, and that, when she made it back down to sea level, he could continue on up here, a figure in a blizzard. She unclasped the small pendant she was wearing, a capsule in which she had kept a pinch of Jay's ashes. She slipped it inside her glove, so that she could feel it on her palm, and she said goodbye. It was when she dropped it down into the icy depths that she began to call out.

She should have been sleeping now, but I sent her screenshots from the app. The estimation that Nathu had put against Ravi's birth and death lined up with my rough timeline. It was certainly possible, then – probable, even – that this person was also a direct descendant of Sejal and Jugaad. He, Katrina and I all shared a specific splice of genetic code, connecting us across continents.

When I found out about his voyage to the *Continuance*, I imagined Nathu stepping into the submersible himself, or at least issuing commands from the quarterdeck. But Nathu only heard the mission had been a success when breakfast came the next morning. He watched the actual footage of the mission along with the rest of us, when it was published upon the ship's return to land.

The film began with the submersible being lowered into the water. In a small screen in the top-right corner, we could watch the raw data, showing stats on depth and pressure. The colour slowly drained from the submersible's visual feed, the camera showing nothing but black at the depth at which an eyeball would burst.

While I skipped ahead and changed to double speed, Nathu watched in real time, mentally calculating the dollars disappearing with each second. He tracked the moving dot of the submersible as it approached the fixed X of the *Continuance*. He hadn't realised its lights were on, because there was nothing for the light to bounce off. Until—

'Oh my.'

Jutting out of the mid-Indian ridge, in the heart of the midnight zone, was the epic Victorian wreck. There was an unreal quality to the light, the wood returning green and grey. The image was impressively detailed. It seemed the back end of the ship must have been heavier as it fell, as the bow protruded almost vertically, so that the angelic figurehead, remarkably preserved, had the appearance of attempting to fly back to the surface.

The submersible rotated around the ship from a distance and, after a full revolution, it approached. Up close to the bow, with the intensity of the light increasing, you could almost make out some letters carved into the wood: *Cont.*

I had imagined a pile of scrap wood. Nothing resembling an actual ship. Nathu, who had been privy to more research and the initial scan the deep-sea mapper had provided, was nevertheless still shocked at the ship's condition. The theory, as described on the film's voice-over, was that the sails of the *Continuance* had stayed intact during its descent, parachuting its fall. This slow fall, coupled with the fact that it had only encountered a relatively small amount of damage from the pirates, who perhaps had initially hoped to take not just what the ship contained but the ship itself, meant the wreck had fallen on to the seamount without breaking apart.

Nathu had paused and replayed the video as the submersible encircled the ship a second time, up close. Large anemones drifted about the broken deck, floating over a group of sea squirts, small bubbles of processed liquid, from which, the narrator claimed, we were all in fact descended – the sea squirt being mankind's oldest ancestor with a spinal cord. Parts of the wood were patterned with bristle stars and in places he spotted sea lilies, moving as if in a light breeze. Somehow, down here, they could piece together a livelihood, extracting nutrients from what looked to Nathu to be nothing but utter desolation. If, up on the surface, we were wiped out, all this down here would survive.

At this point, an ROV was deployed from the larger submersible. It was a brand-new model, the size of a football, that the team hoped would be able to navigate what was left of the ship's interior. The controller of the ROV was renowned in the world of eSports and had been practising for this moment for weeks (it was hoped the added publicity that came with his involvement would help with funding). He piloted the mini drone through an opening towards the back end of the ship. The footage had the quality of a dream, the ROV gliding through strange non-spaces that would have once been cramped rooms filled with sailors excited to be homeward bound. I skipped through what was several hours of footage, but Nathu watched it all, ignoring his back pain. Then, the moment arrived on both of our screens: the ROV's cold blue light touching the slab of stone, filling the carvings with shadow. I saw an inscription in the shape of a fish, one the shape of a snake. Nathu recognised the symbols at once, and beneath this Saraswatian language he saw the unmistakable cuneiform of the Mesopotamians.

It wasn't a long sentence, but it was enough.

The image was instantly scanned and fed to the model. Experts on Akkadian knew the line's meaning already, which was confirmed via the AI, and once the letters were isolated and mapped, the dominoes began to fall and all of the thousands of Saraswatian finds that had yet to be understood started to move. Meaning spread through the archives with the speed of a virus. The sentence was all over the news by the time Nathu's ship returned to land, docking in front of a cheering crowd; it was already being written on school blackboards, quoted by government officials, typed into museum catalogues:

A cow is worth seven chickens; a pot is worth ten beads.

A Pristine State

'Today, we change the weight of the earth. When *Varuna II* takes off in under an hour, our planet will become 400 tons lighter, and our future unspeakably richer.'

I was stuck in traffic in the back of a rickshaw, listening to the radios echoing from across the jam, all tuned to the same station covering the launch. People were crowding around shopfronts to see the rocket on television screens; some workplaces had opted to allow early lunch breaks for employees to catch the coverage. The whole country was looking up, as if towards an incoming asteroid, a call from the heavens. And, like the voice of a god, Indra's speech reverberated up and down the road, his inflated sense of gravitas punctured only by the horns of impatient drivers, edging forward by the inch.

When I finally made it to the terminal, the coverage was playing on all the airport screens, too, sounding from the phones of security guards, baristas and those of us queuing at the gates. While we waited for take-off on the plane, I watched the news on the tablet of the man in front of me, who was playing it without wearing earphones.

'This day you will describe to your grandchildren,' the news anchor said. 'As the rocket penetrates the atmosphere, just know *that* is the moment our New India comes of age—'

An air hostess asked him to turn off the tablet.

I looked out as we rose – from a certain vantage point, all landscapes look like plains. Nothing could be gained from surfaces. I had little to do other than read the scholarly work that Nathu had forwarded me, but I didn't make it past a single abstract. At a certain point, all language is plains. Instead, I read what had loaded of my social-media feed before I turned on flight mode, stopping at a tweet that read: *These are the Golden Aleph records, developed in association with space agencies worldwide, containing a sound clip of every known language on earth, which is approximately seven thousand. The lightweight records contain a spoken sentence in each of the languages, and will be sent into space via the* Varuna II *explorer.*

I'd heard about the Golden Aleph on TV. In one segment, a reporter had breathed through a 3D-printed reconstruction of an ancient Saraswatian larynx; certain models could approximate the sound of Saraswatian speech, and it wasn't as if anyone was around to prove how accurate it was. Now that an audible version of the language and its alphabet had been created, it was being uploaded to translation apps and students in the country were able to learn Saraswatian alongside Sanskrit. The first recording was used for the Golden Aleph project, the new old language sent to the outer reaches of the solar system. It was supposed to call back to the *Voyager* records sent out in the seventies, I guessed. It marked the start of a new age. A shifting axis.

We were somewhere over the Thar Desert, not far from beginning our descent, when the pilot spoke on the intercom.

'We understand that the countdown for the launch of the *Varuna II* has begun. If you look out of the left-hand windows, you might be able to glimpse a sight of it, any moment now.'

There was a clacking of seat-belt buckles and all of us on the right-hand side of the plane stood up. The row across from me was empty and I managed to take the window seat. A layer of clouds stretched out below, flat as the sea. And then the distant rocket burst through it, too quick to see, followed by an immense movement of smoke and air, which sent ripples across the cumulus. We all cheered. In the moment, I had no articulate thoughts, no opinions, just a brief and sudden sense of awe, a human reaction to the natural order of things being overturned. For once, I didn't want to think first, I didn't want to politicise it – all it was to me was beautiful, the children jumping in their seats, the sound of prayers.

When we landed at Jaisalmer, I watched the rocket clip replay on my phone, waiting for my luggage to be brought from the plane. It seemed like the small airport catered to a single arrival and departure each day. By the time I'd got my bag and found Nathu's address in my emails, I was one of the last people in the building. Then, I felt an unfortunate turn in my stomach and sought out the restroom. A significant amount of time passed before I re-emerged. I followed the sign for the taxi rank. But all the cars were gone. There was nobody outside the terminal.

There were no rickshaws. No motorbikes. The few cars in the car park must have belonged to airport staff, or people who had parked up before departing. When I reconnected to the airport Wi-Fi, I found out that there was no Uber or Ola. I was googling local taxi companies when my phone died. Was this some kind of elaborate prank? I looked around and saw nobody at all.

I was – and I had no better word for it – fucked.

But then I heard a noise, some footsteps. I found a cleaner just as she came out of the ladies' toilet. As the last person in there, I felt an instant pang of shame. I explained my situation, hoping she might have a phone charger, but her phone was a different brand to mine.

'Do you have someone to call?' she asked.

I didn't know Nathu's number. 'Just a taxi?' I said.

She called her brother, who called a friend who owned a three-wheeler. Then she told me to walk on to the crossroads and wait. Something about her tone of voice encouraged me to trust her. If this was how I was kidnapped, I told myself, I had only myself to blame – myself and Delhi street food.

The cleaner was kind enough to give me a bottle of water. 'It's not far,' she said. 'Otherwise, he has to pay entrance.'

I headed out into the flat heat. Not even the wiry scrubs, which somehow clung to the unforgiving earth, gave any shade. I took off my backpack and dragged it along behind me. This was a different planet to the hills where I lived. It was madness to think that Himachal Pradesh and Rajasthan belonged to the same country. I stopped at the crossroads and took dramatically small sips of the water, scared of running out. I'd had barely a tenth of the bottle when the three-wheeler arrived, blaring filmi music – Arushi. You could hardly go a day without hearing Arushi. I didn't follow music, but she was impossible to ignore. If it wasn't her songs, it was the adverts;

if it wasn't the adverts, it was the news. Our entertainment reporter joked that she was essentially an Arushi correspondent. 'I'm busier than whoever reports on Indra!'

The driver barely said a word, as if this situation happened all the time, and maybe it did. We sped along the road. The songs, the breeze – bliss!

The road was too narrow for two vehicles to pass comfortably and, whenever we came upon oncoming traffic, we swerved off on to the bumpy verge, the rocks and the dirt beneath the tyres sounding like loose screws. Eventually we joined a wider road and a wider one yet again, and then at last there were buildings, almost windowless, and in front of some of the buildings temporary housing, blue tarp drawn across wooden poles, and then there were schoolchildren, there were trees, driveways, bicycles, and we were turning into Jaisalmer, where the streets narrowed again, sandstone buildings blocking the view of the fort, which appeared in brief snatches down the passing alleyways in which cows dozed and children played. We parked at the entrance to the fort and, after I paid the cleaner's brother's friend, I was met with the calls of vendors, women selling tat and men offering tours of the fort, which I entered on foot. My shoes slid on the incline, and at the top of the hill I was serenaded by the clanging of hammers on stone, men knocking fresh cobbles into the ground worn smooth by the persistent passing of tourists and motorbikes, one of which rattled as it pulled along a trailer of emptied oil drums. I followed a pariah dog down one of the narrow alleys and asked a vendor where I might find the Hundred Year Haveli. I peered through open doors as I walked, generations sitting on cots in darkened rooms. Brightly coloured tobacco pouches hung around shop entrances like garlands. Second-hand books left by backpackers on a communal shelf – Lonely Planet guides, Kipling, Shantaram – had fallen victim to the pigeons in the rafters. In every tourist shop I saw the face of Bob Marley, and rates for camel tours. At last, I came upon Nathu's haveli. After showering, I met Nathu on the roof, where my hair quickly dried.

'Do I call you cousin?' he said, extending his hand. 'Looking at you, I feel I should be saying niece.'

'I think cousin is right, actually. We're the same number of generations away.'

Perhaps I was searching for a likeness where there was none, but we had similar noses. He spoke with the received pronunciation of a child of Empire, and kept his sunglasses facing backward from his ears, as if he were looking in two directions at once.

'I suppose that would mean your folk took their time,' Nathu said. 'My parents had me very young.'

'My father was very old, my mother very young,' I said.

'What are they like, then, this aunt and uncle of mine?'

I told him how I was raised solely by my mother. For getting pregnant before she married, she was abandoned by her family, barely eighteen. My father, I said, I'd only met once. I showed him the family tree my father had started, and some photos from his files.

'He was actually an impressive historian,' I said.

'And you're continuing his work?'

'It's become a bit of an obsession.'

'I knew quite a lot about my family,' Nathu said, 'even if we don't talk. But my wife, whose people had been in Kenya so long, she knew almost nothing about hers. It's a question of parameters, maybe. Back far enough, we're all brothers and sisters and so forth.'

'All children of Genghis Khan.'

'Exactly. We're all from Turkana.' He moved his chair into the shade. 'So, you've met others?'

'One,' I said, telling him about Katrina. 'And there's another I know of. But he hasn't replied to any of my messages. He's in Punjab, a farmer.' I showed Nathu the website Satnam had recently launched. The Hakra farm was now acting as a seed bank for crops native to Punjab. Any farmer could arrange to pick up seeds for free, as long as they then shared a portion of their next harvest's seeds with others.

'It's beautiful,' Nathu said, scrolling through pictures of the farm on the gallery page. 'Ooh, bitter gourd,' he said, zooming in. 'Akeyo loved that.'

He told me about her, trusting me enough to elaborate on the particulars of their marriage. Had we been inclined to share our inner lives because of our genetic proximity, or because, by contrast, our lives were so distant? From here, we could part and never again impact one another. There was freedom in that. When our giant thalis arrived – cooked by the porter in the tiny rooftop kitchen – we both ate with our left hands.

'I'll take you to the collection,' he said, after his last bite, 'and then the pit. And then the dig site.'

The collection was a warehouse, at the line where the city limits met the plains. Inside, there were hundreds of crates. A few of them were red, the majority were blue. Next to the crates was an even larger collection of heavy-duty jute sacks.

'Red is museum quality. Blue is worthy of study. And the bags are about to be buried.'

'Buried?'

'We can't collect everything. Keeping everything is keeping nothing.'

He wanted to show me one of the red boxes, but I was drawn to the sacks. Several men were loading them on to a truck.

Nathu saw me looking and took me over to one that was yet to be tied up.

'Here, take whatever you want. A piece of history.'

I picked out a shard of clay the size of a jigsaw piece and put it in my pocket.

'Do you have a coin?' he asked.

I was a little confused, but handed him one.

'It's so that, if a future me digs it up and thinks they've come

179

across an epic discovery, they'll know that all this was found and reburied this year.' He paused to inspect the coin. 'Or, according to this, three years ago. OK, make a wish.' He dropped it into the bag and tied it up.

I helped him carry the bag out to the truck. He was strong and agile for his age, his back hunched, I supposed, from a long career of looking down at the ground. While he talked with the workers, I inspected some of the blue and red crates. I had a hard time distinguishing the characteristics that decided which piece would end up in which box.

We eventually followed the truck out into the desert, until we reached a large hole in the ground. There was little sense of ceremony to what Nathu called 'the funeral'. The bags were dumped into the pit and covered with dirt.

We watched for a few minutes before getting back in the car. Nathu opened up a newspaper as we were driven on.

'This is saying the Colorado is almost dry. Half the world has too much, the other not enough.'

The Jeep turned on to a dirt road, stopping a few minutes into the sand. We would have to walk the last part of the route. As we climbed a large sand dune, I got my first look at the maze-like dig site.

'A metre is about a thousand years,' Nathu said. 'Before the river ran dry, all this would have been green. They would have had too much water to use, and this here, we think might have been a place to store it, from one winter to the next summer.' He pointed to the larger hole in the ground, where several workers were on their knees. 'Who knows? Maybe it will turn that way again. Like my grandfather used to say, "Everywhere that water goes, it's already been."'

Hearing Nathu say that line, I grabbed his forearm and hugged him. He was understandably confused. But I explained the connection, that it was a line in the qissa of 'Sejal Jugaad' – more evidence that we were in fact connected.

'Sister!' he said.

'Brother!' I turned back towards the site, grinning. 'So this was a water tank? And what else?'

'I feel I can talk to you openly,' he said. 'I haven't told anyone this and it goes nowhere.' He lowered his voice. 'We've been encouraged from above to label this a shrine. A site of religious importance.'

'But is it?'

'It's hard to say what it is. It might be. The survey seems to think that the only way to protect a dig site if it lies along the construction route is to claim that it is a site of religious significance.'

'And you're comfortable lying?'

'I'm not *comfortable*.'

'But you're going to do it.'

'If it means stopping a find being bulldozed. I mean, this is four thousand years old!'

'But wouldn't people need evidence?'

'You can make all sorts of sentences from the same collection of words. The language is modular – at least, we think it is. It can be cut in more than one way. Most of the writing we find is about tax. No one wants to read about tax rates. The East/West stone was about fixing the price at a market.'

Hearing his ambivalence, I thought about the conspiracy videos that had surfaced about the Saraswatian language. One had gone viral a few weeks ago, claiming that the East/West-stone footage had been deepfaked. Part of the conspiracy's evidence was that Nathu and Takehiro, the only non-Indians on the ship, had both been quarantined with the virus at the time of the submersible's deployment. The evidence was nowhere near concrete, and the backlash to the claims was overwhelming. It was racist, it was discriminatory, people just couldn't accept that a non-Western country could have made such a discovery, and so on. *Look at the shadows!* the comments said. *They don't move with the light. And the objects don't properly sink. It's basic physics.*

'It's nonsense,' Nathu said, when I mentioned it. 'I was there. Crazy people.'

He paused as if to say something else, but thought better of it. I let the silence grow and eventually he spoke.

'Part of the reason I've stayed on, you know, after the success of the stone – beyond the money, which is obviously helpful and somewhat needed – is because Radha, who hired me, wanted me to stay. If I'd left right after the discovery and in the midst of the conspiracies, it might have added to the narrative. You know what, let's get in the shade.'

We walked down the dune towards the marquee, following our elongated shadows, and he explained that many of the workers were volunteers.

'They come here because they want to. It's better they're part of an organised dig than going off on their own. It's like the whole country is looking for something it's lost.'

Inside the gazebo, Nathu talked to the site operator, who then went outside to call the workers in for a break. I watched the news play out on the operator's laptop, muted footage of the *Varuna II*'s launch on loop. We joined the queue for tea, and I looked at the finds that had been laid out on one of the plastic tables. Among the mess of shards were four perfectly square cubes, made of smooth stone.

'Weights for market. You would have paid by weight and they'd put the stones on the scales.'

For the first time, the site appeared to me to have been a real place, once busy with real people. You could see not only the workers fashioning the weights from rock, but the merchant placing them on the scales, doing mental maths; you could see the merchant's child stacking them up on a quiet day, making a tower and knocking it down.

There was a sudden commotion.

One of the workers spilled their tea, while pointing at the laptop. 'Volume! Quick.'

We all turned to the screen and saw a blurry clip of a concrete

182

dam exploding. White water burst out of its centre. The footage shook as the person filming it ran away. The sound came on.

'—just in from Kurukshetra, the Goddess Valley Dam has burst. The scale of the damage is not yet known, but we will keep you informed as information comes in. To confirm, the dam in the Goddess Valley has burst. There is widespread flooding in the locality. Emergency forces, including the army, are being deployed—'

A second clip showed the explosion from a different angle. Another showed the violent water surging downhill.

'We will bring you updates as and when they come in. The scale of the damage is not yet known—'

The news channel abruptly cut back to its coverage of the rocket launch, cutting off the anchor mid-sentence. We all waited, confused, worried, for the segment about the dam to return, but after the repeated clips of the launch came the ads. One of the workers switched to another news channel, which was also showing the *Varuna II* launch and nothing about the dam. The next channel was the same.

Nathu's breath had quickened. His eyes were wide. I sat him down and attempted to calm him. He was trying to open his phone, but kept getting the passcode wrong.

'VPN?' he said, urgently. 'Do you have a VPN?'

I changed my phone's location to Sydney and tried to load the news, but there was no stable connection.

'It's better up the dune. At the top.'

I had someone watch him – he needed to steady his breathing – and I ran up the hot sand with some of the others. We raised our phones to the sky, the black screens shining. Then the alerts came through. In the Australian news I saw images of the dam. Estimations of the death toll were already arriving, rising. In a higher-quality video I could see the image of the man with horns, the ancient Saraswatian god, sitting in lotus position, at the heart of the dam – I could see the carving exploding into chunks of concrete. There were maps of how far the water might surge along the Saraswati route, which towns and cities were in danger, which villages were already gone. The workers next to me, who didn't have a VPN, could only see footage of people clapping at the launch control room, crowds cheering for the *Varuna II*, and the weather.

I ran down to Nathu, who was watching the rocket launch and launch again. He was attempting to get through to Radha, he told me, through uneven breath. 'Her boy,' he said, as the people cheered. The phone rang, but there was no answer. In the end, there was nothing but the tone.

MIRZA SAHIBAN
1879

They packed light, their only luxuries Sejal's sewing kit and a pot of seeds she'd stolen from the farm. Jugaad helped Sejal off the jetty and she took one last look around at the only world she'd ever known, blue in the moonlight, before sitting. They pushed off downstream.

If it wasn't for her aunt's stories, Sejal might never have known that eloping was an option. Might never have known that there were options. And it was her aunt's voice she could hear in her head now: *Those who turn from their parents are cursed to see their own children turn from them.*

But what of the parents who turned from their children? Her mother had refused Jugaad, saying no daughter of hers would marry a Chamar. They came from an endless line of Jats, and she wouldn't allow that chain to be broken in her lifetime.

Sejal hadn't slept properly since she'd realised an entire moon cycle had passed without any blood. She had waited for the bleeding to come, but another month had gone, and suddenly it was harvest time already.

Resting in Jugaad's lap as he rowed with the steady current, she finally drifted off, more certain, now they were doing it, that this was the right thing to do.

When she woke, it was light and Jugaad was rowing slowly.

'I can take over,' she said.

He protested a little, before allowing her the oars. He lay as she had, his head on her left leg. Once she'd found a rhythm, she looked down. How handsome he was!

Farmland gave on to farmland, the clear river reflecting the first stirrings of the day. She would never have thought that running away could be so calm, so quiet. That it could be so easy to stray off the set path of her life and find herself in this other, freer world.

She ran her hand over the top of Jugaad's pagh, feeling the money pouch that he'd tied to his patka. When he woke, he smiled. They couldn't see any people, any houses. Jugaad stood up, his full height surprising to her even now, and he howled as loud as he could. Sejal laughed and joined him. Together, they screamed.

After a few days, they stopped by a cornfield. The corn was taller than Jugaad and they ran through the dense crop, giggling. They stopped to kiss, and Jugaad ran his hands over her body. This was freedom, she thought, as he unwrapped her. He placed his clothes on the ground for her to lie on. Sweat dripped off his face and on to hers. It tasted of salt.

Afterwards, they gathered as much corn as they could carry and ran back to the boat.

They passed people fishing, filling pots and washing clothes, children diving and swimming. All of them were strangers and would have assumed that Sejal and Jugaad were a married couple. These people couldn't have known their families, their trades, their castes. The two of them were simply passing through.

The river widened as it met the Ravi. The current strengthened, and as the late afternoon light started to fade, they decided to find somewhere to rest. They set the boat on its side to make some shelter from the night wind and started a small fire.

'Let's have a story, then,' Jugaad said, turning the corn on the fire. The purple and red kernels absorbed the firelight like jewels.

'Not if you fall asleep again. I'm so awake.'

'I won't. You have my full attention.'

'Long ago, in these parts, lived Sahiban, the most beautiful woman of the Khiwas—'

'Are all the stories about the most beautiful and the most handsome?'

'You want to hear about ordinary people?'

'I suppose not.'

'Sahiban, the most beautiful woman of the Khiwas, had an intellect that astonished all who met her. None more so than Mirza, her handsome classmate. The two quickly fell in love, but when Sahiban returned home after her schooling, she was engaged to marry someone else.'

'Of course.'

'When Mirza heard about the wedding, he chased after her on his legendary stallion, the fastest horse there ever was in the land of the seven rivers. He caught up with the wedding party on the eve of the marriage and got word to Sahiban. Hearing that he'd travelled all this way to find her, Sahiban sneaked away in the middle of the night to meet him. You're burning the corn, you're burning the—

'The couple rode away on Mirza's horse. They only stopped once, in a place not unlike this, to consummate their secret marriage. Once they were finished, Sahiban was eager to get back on the road. She knew her brothers would come looking for them, and she feared what they might do, with the family's pride at stake. But Mirza ignored his new wife. He wanted to sleep. He was stronger than her brothers and was not afraid. No one was more deadly than he was with a bow and arrow.

'Sahiban couldn't sleep. She was strung between two posts:

romantic love and passion for Mirza on one side, and filial love and tradition on the other. She wished she could be loyal to both.

'They had sex again in the morning, and on the forest floor Sahiban could swear she heard sounds in the woods. Her brothers! She pushed Mirza off her. They needed to run. But Mirza said he would not run his whole life. He would stay and fight. He told her to fetch his arrows. Acting on pure instinct when she found his quiver, Sahiban broke all of the arrows. She couldn't just let her husband kill her brothers.

'The brothers surrounded the couple, and she tried to reason with them. But they would not hear her. Her eldest brother shot Mirza, and Mirza, recognising Sahiban's betrayal, pulled out one of his broken arrows and ran at the brother, killing him. The two fell to the ground in a deadly embrace. And Sahiban didn't know what to do; she couldn't move at all.'

Sure enough, Jugaad had fallen asleep. Sejal looked up at the stars, listening to the dying fire. In her aunt's telling, Sahiban ended up taking one of Mirza's broken arrows and stabbing herself. But that didn't make sense to Sejal. She preferred to think of the heroine continuing to run. Running from her brothers, who wanted to drag her home. She could imagine her taking Mirza's stallion and galloping towards a distant land. A place where she had no past, a place where she might begin again.

In the morning, they rowed further downstream and came to a small village called Hakra. They asked around about land, and followed one villager's directions over the hill, finding a farm which was almost perfectly square, planted with bright yellow mustard, ripe for harvest. It was much smaller than Sejal's family farm, but there was a lot of water in the well.

It didn't take much to convince the old farmer to sell. His son had moved to Rawalpindi 'to work for the government,' he bragged. '*Interpreter.*'

They camped near the river as the farmer finished his harvest, and watched the village busy itself for Vasant Panchami. They introduced themselves as a Jat couple from far away who had sold off their infertile land in the hope of beginning again.

Within a few weeks, the land was theirs. How happy they were! On their first day, they walked up to the well at the corner of the square plot and drank. They washed their faces, splashed each other, still laughing, short of breath. They stripped off to wash themselves. Looking down, her stomach was already showing signs of growing. Jugaad grinned and produced what he called a wedding gift. It was a bar of scented soap wrapped in wax paper. They ran the soap over one another and took turns tipping bucket after bucket above their heads, laughing from the cold.

CHENAB

In every deliberation, we must consider the impact on the seventh generation ... even if it requires having skin as thick as the bark of a pine.

Saying based on Law 28 of the Constitution of the Iroquois Nation

Raag Deepak

It was one thing to advocate for direct action, and another entirely to act directly. While Gyan had supported the movement since Lake Mead, she had never imagined herself on the front lines. But here she was, parking her car on the side of the dirt road and hiking through the old growth towards the residency, guitar in hand. As she unlocked the safe box to get the keys, she knew she had crossed a threshold: she was now aiding and abetting the resistance. But that couldn't be worse than what she'd been doing the rest of her life: aiding and abetting our oblivion.

The residency was housed in a decommissioned fire-lookout tower, in the BC boreal forest south of Jasper and east of Banff. She left her guitar at the bottom of the fifteen-foot ladder and climbed up above the canopy. She caught her breath on the deck, taking in the view of the valley, the old growth bald in patches since the arrival of Jenkins Timber. Her only job had been to book the property and keep up appearances: unlike the others, she had no priors.

The property was owned by an endowment to the arts, and was available for creators to rent to help develop their practice. Gyan hadn't written a song since she'd left the band, but was still scoring films. In her application, she'd detailed her current project, a new soundtrack to H. P. Carver's *The Silent Enemy*, which was being reissued a hundred years after its release. She'd said she was in desperate need of inspiration and hoped the landscape might help, which wasn't untrue.

She checked the cupboards, the drawers. The lookout was small and square, with panoramic windows and a balcony that wrapped all the way round. There were no cameras. The original logs of the fire-watchers were still clipped up next to the thermometer. It was almost thirty degrees. She inspected a map of the territory, tracing the shape of the Elk River north. There was a larger map of Canada on the opposite wall, the forest stretching on as far as Newfoundland in the east and the Yukon to the west. Even with the windows closed, she could hear the birds.

In the morning, there was a call from below.

'Goldilocks, let down that hair!' said a man's voice. She peered down and he gave the hand signal. He looked like a college student. She hoped they weren't all going to be younger than her. 'This your guitar?' he asked.

'Yes,' she shouted down. 'I didn't know how to get it up. Coffee?'

'Tea.' He climbed up.

'So, what do I call you?' she asked.

'I got "Peyto". You?'

'"Huron",' Gyan said.

'Gotta be the nicest hideout I ever saw.'

She poured his tea, and he brought out a full bag of sugar from his pack.

The guidelines said not to question a fellow volunteer about their past, or to ask anything that would result in identification. But they weren't robots.

When Peyto had joined the movement as a teenager, he'd already dabbled in ecotage. 'Me and a friend would break into golf courses at night. Pour concrete into the holes. Didn't last long: they started paying for twenty-four-hour security.'

'So, you hit their profit line.'

'Created jobs, I suppose.'

Gyan cooked tadhka beans on the camping stove, the smell of onions filling up the small room.

'Man, I love Indian food,' Peyto said, as he emptied the fifteen-inch nails from his bag. 'Last few times I did one of these, we ate like shit. Chickpeas from the can.'

'This is my first time.'

'Once you see how easy it is, you'll be, like, why isn't everyone doing this?' He picked up one of the nails. 'See, this is for one cedar, and each cedar is what, like, fifteen grand?' He began to count out the long nails, putting them in three even piles. '… Seventy-five, ninety, one hundred and five, one hundred and twenty …'

After lunch, the other two volunteers arrived together. The older man was to be called Erie, and the younger woman, who looked to Gyan to be around thirty, would be called Nipigon.

'There's a guitar, here,' Erie called up. He sounded Quebecois.

'I didn't know how to bring it up,' Gyan said, embarrassed. 'It's mine.'

Erie sent Nipigon up with some rope. She knelt beside Gyan to tie one end to the ledge and tossed the rest down. Her thin legs were covered in blond hair. Gyan had had her legs lasered when that was the done thing; she'd visited her aunt in Surrey after her eighteenth and it had been their secret. Now, she imagined people like Nipigon judging her for shaving. She liked to think that, had she been a teenager in this new world, without the glossy mags, she might have embraced her natural hairiness, but that was easy to do in theory.

Erie looped the other end of the rope through the guitar case so they could hoist it up. They repeated the process with Erie's duffel bag.

'Jesus, what's in this thing?' Peyto said.

He unzipped the bag to reveal the flare guns and hammers.

'Everything from that ridge to that stream,' Erie said, looking through his binoculars. 'That's the Jenkins claim.'

'Half a day's hike, would you say?'

'It'll have to be less.'

Monday was Victoria Day. The team at Jenkins Timber would be off for two days in a row, having the Sunday as usual and then attending Pete Jenkins' annual cook-out on Monday afternoon. It was a family tradition, and even if his mill could now process 350,000 board feet of lumber a month, he wanted to retain that family feel.

'We'll leave at dawn and be back in the afternoon. In Alberta by the time they get out of bed.'

Erie gave the binoculars to Gyan.

'You radio if you see anything, anything at all.'

There was little distinguishing the claim from the rest of the forest. Erie had split it into three sections on his map, so that he, Nipigon and Peyto could cover as much ground as possible.

'Ninety nails, three hammers, ammonia, sugar ... spray?' Peyto said. 'Who's got the spray?'

Nipigon unpacked the spray cans. Once they'd spiked each tree with a fifteen-inch nail, they would tag it with an S, so the timber workers would know not to cut it down. A nail in a spiked tree could break a chainsaw or explode a wood-chipper; the shrapnel could injure or kill. Their mission was property destruction – a vigilante carbon tax on extractive businesses – not violence.

Nipigon was more strict about following the rules on talk, and revealed little about her life. She clearly wasn't here to make friends. The group listened to the radio while Gyan cooked. The death count from the Indian dam was still rising. The newscaster explained that Prime Minister Indra had blamed the incident on ecoterrorists. There was a sound clip of him speaking in Hindi, dubbed with an English translation: 'We will find the culprits and will punish them to our highest level. There is no room for those who counter our advancement. We will put an end to this green jihad.'

'I'd be impressed if it were true,' Erie said. 'But all evidence points to problems with the construction.'

Indra continued, 'But still, let us not lose track. This is a sign. A clear sign our mother goddess is desperate to return, to flow again.'

'Well, cheers,' Nipigon said, lifting her wine glass and breaking her silence. 'The only good dam is a broken dam.'

'And a beaver dam,' Peyto said.

'And a beaver dam.'

'So, you'll play us a song?' Peyto said.

Gyan did the usual dance before opening the case, tuning up. 'Don't worry, I won't sing.' While they talked, going over the plan once again, she messed around on the fretboard, straying into her version of 'The Two Sisters', then 'Willy O'Winsbury' and 'The Golden Vanity' – music that had been around for hundreds of years, background noise in the room.

'We leave nothing at the site,' Erie said. 'Sundown, we get to my truck, I drop you off at your cars, we're all on our separate ways and none of this ever happened. We destroy the burner phones and never resume contact.'

'Copy,' Nipigon said. 'I'm going to bed.'

The other three went out on to the deck to finish the wine.

It shouldn't have been as temperate as it was outside. The night sky looked right out of the residency's brochure.

Now that he'd gone through the plan several times, Erie seemed to relax a little. Without them really asking, he told them that he'd been there when the movement lost steam in the nineties. After all the arson, the public had turned on the cause. They were deemed the most dangerous terrorist threat in North America. 'I started to see us acting out as part of the machinery, you know. A by-product of the system, rather than the thing that would dismantle it.'

He had joined the movement, he said, after meeting someone in the crowd of one of his drag shows. In the early nineties, he'd performed as part of a vaudeville act in Montreal. 'Madame Demoiselles, that was my stage name. We took over this old antique shop on Atateken, in the Village. The owner hadn't found a buyer yet, so all his old Chinese finds would be pushed up to the front of the shop, pretty much blacking out the windows. The show moved on when he sold, and I stopped performing. I walked past it not so long ago. It's a fucking axe-throwing bar now.'

Erie's act had been inspired by the War of the Maidens in nineteenth-century France. 'All these farmers, they had always known the forest as a commons. It belonged to everyone; they could all take their animals into it to graze, and so on. Then, a new act was passed in favour of big paper and big charcoal, meaning they could now stop people using the woods, as the trees were more profitable if they were farmed.

'Now, the people weren't having it. They continued to use the woods, but were repeatedly forced back. So, they started to resist, and turned to violence. As the whole area got more hostile, the men started to dress as women – corsets, wigs, make-up – so that they might sneak across enemy lines and lure them into some false security. These charcoal workers were lonely men. They'd seduce them, and then ... Bam!'

'This is real?'

'History! I painted some toy guns black. Stuffed my corset. I'd do a little striptease in character and then start shooting. Ecotage avec décolletage. You might not believe it, looking at me now.'

'Oh, I can believe it,' Peyto said.

'And, at the bar, after one of the shows, I got recruited.'

Peyto told Erie how he'd got involved. His original crew were spread across the state, now. 'One of my friends is going up Banff way, and another's doing a job in Prince George. It might be the busiest week I remember. It's finally starting to speed up.'

The mention of Prince George caught Gyan's attention. That was her home town, where her parents still lived and where her mum worked at a pulp mill. She tried not to give anything away. 'Oh, yeah?' she said. 'What kind of stuff they planning?'

'More intense than what we're up to, sounds like. They're going to try to shut this one operation down.'

'Intense?'

'Yeah, I mean, they're pouring all their shit into the rivers, the pulp mills. It's gonna be great. And, because we're all, like, hitting in the same week, it's going to flood the news.'

There were lots of pulp mills near Prince George, Gyan thought. The likelihood of her mum being affected—

'So, I told you my origin story, and Erie told us his,' Peyto said. 'What's yours?'

What had happened to Gyan at Lake Mead might, in centuries past, have been considered a kind of religious awakening. She had quite literally seen a sign, and almost instantly decided to change her life.

She'd been down in Nevada to see Tansen, her old band, headline a benefit by the lake. Mead, which had once been America's largest reservoir, was now empty. It was still famous as a tourist attraction because of its 'bathtub ring', a white mineral layer left behind by the water that had disappeared. It showed a kind of ghost lake, a trace of what had been. And, across the arid lake bed, the skeletal remains of sunken ships stuck out at dramatic angles, seeming to burst forth from the ground like the first bones of the rising dead. Backstage, before Tansen's set, she saw someone spray-painting words on to the bathtub ring: *Wenn du mich siehst, dann weine.*

The phrase, she later learnt, was taken from a German hunger-stone, hidden in the Elbe River. If the water level dropped and the stone became visible, the townspeople would know famine was imminent. There was a fuss in the news about the graffiti, the defacement of a national treasure. The consensus was that a destructive act like that didn't help anything, and that it only hindered a cause the general public were already in favour of. The paint was meticulously scrubbed from Lake Mead, but a trace of the letters could still be seen: *If you see me, weep.*

The aim of the benefit was to raise money for the legal fees of Native American tribes taking the seven states of the Colorado River Basin to court. After another year of meagre rainfall in the ongoing megadrought, a line had been crossed: the long-depleted Colorado River would barely reach Mexico, let alone the sea. The river's fresh water was divided in a series of compacts, the acre-feet of flow shared between key stakeholders: seven US states, and countless cities, farming companies, tribes. The Imperial Valley, fed by the All-American Canal, had senior rights in the lower basin, meaning it could withdraw its water first, before the desert cities, which had sprung up where no water had reached before, and doubled and tripled in population. In a good year, everyone got their share. But these were bad years. The river's water had been over-allocated.

Just as a person whose life savings are stored in a bank about to collapse will rush to withdraw all their savings at once, causing the bank to fail further, so the Colorado stakeholders all attempted to withdraw their full share of the water before the water was completely gone. They caused a run on the river. And, like a run on a bank, it was disastrous. Clem, Tansen's lead singer and Gyan's oldest friend, had described it to Gyan as a kind of fucked-up game of musical chairs. 'There's more people than there are seats. And when the song finishes, someone will find themselves without anywhere to sit.'

Peyto searched for Tansen on Spotify, and put on their most popular track. Clem's voice played out from his phone: 'Can you feel it coming? I can see it coming. Look at the horizon! I can feel it coming!'

While the music played, Gyan told the two of them the story behind the band's name. It was her idea to form the band; she'd had the name in mind before she even floated the idea of music to Clem.

Tansen, a sixteenth-century Indian musician, was renowned for his voice, which was so powerful he could enchant elephants, move birds. He was appointed Emperor Akbar's court musician, and on a whim the emperor asked him to perform the Raag Deepak, the song of fire. If performed correctly, his stomach would boil and flames would emerge from his mouth and nostrils, his body eventually turning to ash. He had no choice in the matter: the emperor's word was final.

In preparation for the performance, he taught his daughter, Saraswati, the Raag Megh Malhar, the song of the clouds. If she performed her raag while he burned in the palace courtyard, the rains would save him. But, at the last minute, the emperor's men decided to host the performance miles down the river, for fear of the fire damaging the palace. Tansen had no opportunity to tell Saraswati. The emperor and his court sailed down the river, leaving Tansen on one bank, while they sat at a safe distance on the opposite side. Tansen opened his mouth, breath becoming song. Hot tears streamed from his eyes, hissing as they hit the ground. He sang forth the smoke, sang the flames, and the emperor sat rapt as Tansen began to ignite. At any point, they thought he would stop, but Tansen would not finish singing until he came to the end of the song. The river between them began to boil.

Saraswati arrived at the palace, running through its vast halls and courtyards, looking for her father. She thought she must be too late, or that her father had been marched away and executed for refusing to obey the emperor's command. She dropped to her knees and sang her raag, mourning her father. The sky darkened. Rain attacked the palace, flooded its halls, and she sang with such passion that the clouds spread across great swathes of sky and the storm raged across all the lands, reaching Tansen. The emperor could barely see the singer for all the steam rising and the rain falling, but he could hear the raag's last verse. The river had all but disappeared between them. Tansen walked across its bed towards the cheering crowd, and the whole town feasted on boiled fish that night. By the time Saraswati had finished her song and been reunited with her father, the rivers were filled again with rain.

'So, it was your band?' Erie asked. 'But then you quit it?'

Gyan woke after the others had left. It was hard to fathom that an act of terrorism was taking place in the forest. She sipped her tea on the deck and looked out, listening to the birds singing. She thought of her mother and made a call on her personal phone.

'What's happened?' her mum said.

'Just checking in,' she said. 'You're OK?'

'Oh, you know – same old.'

'Work's OK?'

'Sandra's retiring, so at least one of my prayers has been answered.'

'Maybe you should take some time off this week. Extend the holiday.'

'Funny.'

'It'd be good for you and Dad. Call in sick, play truant!'

'You're being strange, Gyan.'

'What time do you normally finish?'

'Tomorrow? I'll be home for six.'

'Call me on your drive back?'

'OK, honey.'

They said their goodbyes and Gyan scrolled through her phone. The death toll in the Goddess Valley continued to rise. Numbers were losing their meaning. There weren't enough roots to hold the soil together. Some enquiries pointed towards an issue with the concrete. But the government spokespeople continued the calls for terrorists' heads on sticks. She should have been firmer with her mother. Maybe she should have told her the truth.

Gyan scanned the claim for any signs of the others, seeing nothing but trees. She'd have happily spent the day sitting out there, but eventually she resigned herself to the fact that she should indeed be using the free time to work.

She pulled up *The Silent Enemy* on her laptop. By the time the silent film was released in 1930, the sound era had begun. A spoken introduction was filmed in New York and placed before the opening credits: the viewer passing from a modern medium to one that was already redundant. Gyan played the speech, by Chauncey Yellow Robe, as she tuned her guitar:

'This picture is the story of my people. I speak for them because I know your language. In the beginning, the Great Spirit gave us this land. The wild game was ours to hunt. We were happy when game was plenty. In the years of famine, we suffered. Soon, we will be gone. Your civilisation will destroy us. But with your magic, we will live forever. We thank the white men who helped us to make this picture. They came to our forest, they shared our hardships, they listened to our old men around the campfire. We told them the stories our grandfathers taught us. That is why this picture is real. Look not upon us as actors. We are living our life today as we lived it yesterday. Everything you see is as it always has been.'

She skipped through the visuals to reach her problem scene. The Ojibwe tribe, in Canada's frozen north, are starving for lack of game. After six years of abundance, their seventh is one of hardship. The chief sends his best hunter, Baluk, off in search of food.

Baluk is one of two suitors for Neewa, the chief's daughter. The other is Dagwan, the medicine man, who uses Baluk's absence as a chance to bad-mouth him. When Baluk returns empty-handed, Dagwan has reason to celebrate. But Baluk maintains the chief's favour, and the chief agrees to Baluk's plan to march north in search of game.

The way is hard and people die from cold, from exhaustion, starvation. Approaching death, the chief meditates alone, high on a mountain, and there he has a vision of the future, of cattle. When he returns, he appoints Baluk as the new chief, and then he dies. Dagwan is angered and starts to manipulate the tribespeople with the aid of magic, launching a propaganda campaign that scapegoats Baluk as the reason for all their trouble. Wasn't it the march north that was killing them? Wasn't it his leadership that had brought about their demise?

Baluk sends his closest allies away to broaden the search for food, telling them to send smoke signals if they spot anything. While they are gone, the rest of the tribe, stirred up by Dagwan, turn on Baluk, ignoring the old chief's prophecy. Dagwan calls for him to be banished for his crimes, but Baluk opts for an honourable death instead: death by fire.

It was here that Gyan was stuck. In the film's pivotal scene, Baluk sits atop his pyre and bangs a drum. While he keeps time, he sings, the flames licking up at the edges of the screen.

The tribe looks on in horror as he drums, and the original score plays up the drama, all crashing symbols and screeching violins. If she could have it her way, the scene would be completely silent. Maybe the whole film should be; she was starting to see her music as some kind of manipulation, telling the viewer how to feel. She skipped on and watched the end of the film.

As Baluk begins to burn, another fire appears on screen – a smoke signal from the other hunters. They've found the game. Baluk is rushed off the pyre, just about alive, and leads the tribe towards the smoke, towards the crossing of the caribou. The game is plenty, and they feast, eating in a new settlement made out of caribou skins. Dagwan is banished, forced to endure the coward's death, to walk on, unarmed and without food or tools, into the wilderness, alone. In the last frame of the edited reissue, all is white save for his black silhouette, as he ventures on into the nothingness.

Gyan could see no movement on the claim. There was only her and the birds, her fingers wandering around on the fretboard. She used to get so frustrated with Clem always offering his feedback while she wrote, but now she missed his second opinion. She returned to the scene on the pyre, playing out different themes as the images looped. Baluk, played by the tall and muscular Buffalo Child Long Lance, continued to sing. There were hours until the volunteers were due back, hours to get the last few movements right. But she set aside her guitar and took out her phone. She was old enough to consider surfing the web an activity in and of itself, and liked to spend time searching things, clicking through hyperlinks, not that anything really 'clicked' anymore. *The Silent Enemy* led her to Yellow Robe, who led her to Long Lance.

Buffalo Child Long Lance was born the year Sitting Bull died and Jim Crow began. His parents – Croatan, Cherokee,

Lumbee, White, Black – had been born into slavery, and Long Lance ran away from home as a teen to join a Wild West show. He learnt Cherokee words from the *Buffalo Bill* performers and took on a new name. He moved to Canada after the war and, working as a journalist, earned the trust of Mountain Horse, the Blackfoot chief, who named him Buffalo Child and adopted him into the Blackfoot Confederacy. Famous for writing about Indian society, he returned to America a celebrity, 'one of the few real 100 per cent Americans', with 'New York in his pocket'. He was a hit with women, who liked the sight of him in his tuxedo as much as they did the postcards of him in shops, which showed him in a contradictory mix of Crow and Blackfoot clothing. The staged photos drew suspicion from Native Americans.

'Soon I might stop writing about Indians,' Long Lance wrote. 'It is the most thankless job I've ever tackled.'

But he kept writing, inventing origin stories. He was working on his autobiography when he travelled to Banff for an affair with a white woman. When her husband's Black butler walked in on them together, Long Lance struck him repeatedly with a hot iron poker. He ran back to the east coast, this time claiming that he had in fact been the *chief* of the Blackfoot, and that he himself had fought in the Battle of Little Bighorn. His autobiography became an instant bestseller. What readers didn't know was that he had taken the foundational stories that Mountain Horse had told him and retold them in the first person, making himself the hero. Feeling his grip on his identity slipping further still, he ventured to Hollywood and was given the lead in *The Silent Enemy*, in which he played a chief cast out as an outsider. The problem was that his co-star Chauncey Yellow Robe doubted his Native authenticity. Yellow Robe hired a private investigator, Ilya Tolstoy (grandson of the novelist), to discover Long Lance's true race. It was determined he was Black. Long Lance was cast out of both his Native and white circles. He was later found dead from a gunshot wound.

Gyan clicked through to a page about Buffalo Bill, about the silent era, about the first film score, about D. W. Griffith, Lillian Gish. She refreshed her social-media feeds. There were fires in New South Wales. Fires near Half Dome, fires in Newfoundland. An embassy set alight. Yachts were exploding off the coast of Monaco, off the coast of Maine. An Olympic swimming pool had been filled with red dye. A congresswoman was sprayed with Easy Cheese, parliament doused in manure. Bricks were going through windows. Birds were falling out of the trees. Dog paws were burning on pavements. The wheels of tar-sand workers' cars were being stabbed; they were having to commandeer school buses. The National Guard had been posted to the mines. Spitting had become a serious offence. People holding hands and singing were hit with water cannons. Gas drones were attacked by kites.

Some of the first silent films were shot in Thomas Edison's Black Maria studio, acts from *Buffalo Bill's Wild West* show rotating on a circular stage in the darkness. In one, a group of Sioux men, young and old, apparently performed the Ghost Dance, a couple of years after the massacre at Standing Rock. Either Edison had stolen what had been a secret ritual, or they were doing a different dance and Edison had misnamed it for better marketing. Gyan watched the dance on a separate tab and played her music over it. It was twenty-five years before this silent film and just after the typhoid epidemic of 1867 that Hawthorne Wodziwob, a Paiute elder, had a vision of a new earth and was given the idea for the dance.

The prophecy spread, morphed. To the Lakota, it was about renewal, a Spirit Dance, mistranslated. John Fire Lame Deer later said that it was about dancing a new world into being: 'There would be landslides, earthquakes and big winds. Hills would pile up on each other. The earth would roll up like a carpet with all the white man's ugly things – the stinking new animals, sheep and pigs, the fences, the telegraph poles, the mines and the factories. Underneath would be the wonderful old new world as it had been before the white fat-takers came ... The white men will be rolled up, disappear, go back to their own continent.'

During the solar eclipse of 1889, Gyan read, trying to stay awake, Wovoka – aka Jack Wilson – had a similar vision, a vision of the Lord, and, in the light, he saw his ancestors and was given the Ghost Dance and told to take it to his people. He gathered disparate tribes and the dance spread across the plains. The dance bringing the tribes together was enough to put it on the radar of the US government, who believed its performance to be an act of terrorism. The papers spread panic, and both coasts feared the dance as a threat to the country. As the pace quickened, some dancers would enter a trance-like state and experience visions as they sang, 'I see my father / I see my mother / I see my brother / I see my sister.'

Gyan scrolled on. Pictures of the remains of bodies had gone viral after a peat bog had been excavated. The couple were impeccably preserved, and had died, it seemed, in an embrace – an embrace that had lasted four hundred years. There were fears of ancient virus strains resurfacing in the churned-up bogs. There were things lurking in the permafrost, in the ocean bed. A Black Maria was slang for a police car.

It was getting dark and there was no sign yet of the others. Gyan checked her watch. They were supposed to have arrived an hour ago. Every time she thought she had an idea, some motif, it would elude her as soon as she picked up the guitar. The perfect phrase was always just around the corner. Perhaps the others weren't going to come back; maybe they'd been forced to run. She would never make contact with them again, left in the watchtower until the residency ended in a fortnight. Or maybe something had gone wrong and they were stuck on the claim and needed her help. She tried to radio – there was nothing but static. She replayed Baluk's scene and picked at the muted E string, sounding ghost notes in time with his drumming.

The moon was out of focus, blurred by clouds. Gyan tried to discern any human sounds among the dark noises. She cooked the crew's dinner, heating her hands over the hob. She couldn't get through to them on the radio. She was tempted to try to leave them a message on her burner phone, and was beginning to regret her involvement in all this – what if something had gone wrong and she was now culpable in it? – when at last she spotted light in the woods. She took out the binoculars and saw three head torches. She rushed down the ladder and out towards them. It was almost one in the morning.

Peyto had twisted his ankle. Erie and Nipigon were helping to hold him up.

'We're going to have to be quick,' Erie said. 'Don't worry, he's fine. Will be fine.'

They laid him down in the dirt and Gyan brought out water, food and the ammonia. They ate while she cleaned the hammers. Everything they'd brought with them would be dumped, but they had to be careful not to leave any trace.

'Better a twisted ankle than a bad cut – you'd have left all your DNA.'

'There's no way they would trace our DNA,' Nipigon said.

'When it's hundreds of thousands of dollars, they might,' Erie said, grinning.

'Well, it's Peyto being too careful that has turned the plan upside down,' Nipigon said.

He'd been wearing boots two sizes too big for him as an extra precaution. One of his friends had previously got caught out by his shoe size and tread. 'I said I'm sorry,' Peyto said, 'I don't know what else to say. I'm sorry. I'm sorry—'

'But you all got the job done?' Gyan tried to lighten the mood.

'Oh, sure. Ticked off the territory. This one only had five nails left when he fell, and we did those, too.'

'You must be spent.'

'Epsom salts tonight. Well, tomorrow. Whatever.'

'A cold beer.'

Gyan wiped down the spray cans. Strange, two of them were almost empty and the other felt full. She paused. 'I think maybe one of you didn't use as much paint.'

They were confused.

'Two of these are really light. But one isn't,' she continued.

Erie looked at Peyto, who looked at Nipigon.

'Please tell me you were both leaving the tags,' Erie said, exhausted.

'Well, you saw mine,' Peyto said. 'I wouldn't not tag them.'

'I must have just been doing smaller S's,' Nipigon said. 'Using less paint.'

'But you were marking each spiked tree?' Erie said.

'Because if you weren't—' Peyto said.

'If you're lying—'

'Oh, for— What's the point of spiking the trees if the spikes don't actually *spike*?' Nipigon said. 'The point is to *hurt* their infrastructure. Break their saws, break their chippers. Cause damage. We have to hurt them for any kind of message to be heard.'

Erie was furious. 'The point is to save the fucking trees! We saved the fucking trees. *You*— I mean, one saw hits one of your hidden spikes, the blade will fly off. That could be a death, you hear? You kill a person. The *movement* kills a person. *We* kill a person. That's in the news, national, international. Now, anything anyone else does, any progress, that's set back, I don't know, fifty fucking years, do you understand?'

'It's not going to kill anyone.'

'You're an idiot.'

'This isn't their only claim. We can't spike every single tree, but if we actually hit the machines, we triple the effect. So what if one of the men gets injured? If they know the job comes with serious danger, they'll stop signing up to help the fucking devil. If the companies can't get people to work for them—'

'Please, stop talking,' Peyto said.

'You're going to march back with me, and you're going to tag every tree you hit, you understand?' Erie said.

'Absolutely not,' Nipigon said.

'I'm not asking.'

'By the time we get there, it's dawn, and they'll be coming back,' she said.

'Then pack your stuff and fuck off right now. I want you gone. Now.'

'How will you get Peyto back to the truck?'

'Go.'

Gyan was about to intervene. Nipigon's car was parked the furthest away. She'd needed a lift from Erie on the way in. How would she get there in the dark? But, seeing Erie this angry, Gyan didn't want to disagree. Peyto looked down at his ankle and stayed silent.

Nipigon went up to the fire tower to get her pack.

Erie swore again. 'It was all so easy. This was supposed to be a walk in the park.'

Nipigon descended within a minute and Gyan and the others watched as she walked away, alone, into the woods. For a few moments, her lone head torch could be seen bouncing off different trunks, but then it was gone and all was dark.

Erie checked the time.

'You really believe that about the spikes?' Gyan said.

'This movement doesn't work if there's a single death. It's that fragile.'

'Can we leave them an anonymous message? Call it in or something?'

'Not now, and not here. It's all traceable.'

Peyto sighed. 'What you'd have to do is get back and change the sign we left up.'

'I could go,' Gyan said. 'You must be so tired, Erie.'

'No, no.'

'And you need to get him to an ER.'

'You don't know the way.'

They decided Gyan and Erie would leave Peyto at the foot of the tower and rush back to the claim. Gyan brought down some blankets for Peyto and took the unused spray can with her. She tied carrier bags around her shoes to alter her prints and borrowed Peyto's head torch.

Erie took the flare gun out of Peyto's bag and handed it to him. 'Now that we know the radios don't reach,' he said. 'If something desperate happens, shoot.'

It should have been cold, but Gyan and Erie were sweating. Their breath was short as they forded streams and climbed small crests, and for long stretches at a time they did not speak.

Finally, Erie stopped and checked his map. 'OK. Everything to the right, now, should be hers.'

Sure enough, none of the trees were marked with paint. They scanned the trunks with their torches.

'I can't believe we didn't notice,' Erie said. He ran his hand up and down a tree trunk and stopped when he found the head of the nail. There was no way they could find them all in time. 'She must have put them in at the height she thought they would chop. She actually wanted to hurt someone.'

Gyan spray-painted an S on to the tree.

'The only saving grace,' Erie said, 'is, if we can spot them, so can they.'

Gyan sprayed another tree. They reached the clearing where the bright yellow machinery was stored, approaching the edge of the claim and the large poster that Peyto had stuck to the entrance of the site. The sun was beginning to rise, touching the tops of the JCBs.

'What's the big one do?'

'The yarder? Once the trees are cut into logs and the logs are choked by that chain, it's the yarder that pulls them up here.'

They worked their way round the clearing to the site entrance.

Jenkins Timber! Several trees on this claim have been SPIKED with ceramic, non-ferrous and / or brass spikes to save them from felling. A white 'S' marks each spiked tree. These spikes do not harm the tree. DO NOT use a chainsaw on these trees or you risk breaking your machinery and causing injuries.

They decided on a message to add underneath: *At least thirty trees on your claim have been spiked without being marked. So DO NOT attempt to cut down ANY trees on this claim.*

'Perfect,' Erie said. 'Can you pass the pen?'

Gyan checked her pockets. 'Wait, I thought you had the pen? I don't have one.'

'Merde!' Erie went through his pack. 'It rains, it pours.'

'Do you have a pencil?'

'This is it for me, the last rodeo.'

'Wait, the site office – that might have one? Surely, they'd have a pen.'

The sky was lightening.

'OK, you stay here.'

Erie adjusted his face mask and ran up to the office, a shipping container with a door and a small window. The door had a combination lock, so he picked up a rock and smashed the window.

Gyan eyed the dirt road, nervous. The birds were singing. She could hear Erie knocking things over in the office. Finally, he climbed back out of the window, triumphant.

'It's fancy,' he said.

She took the fountain pen off him and started to write.

The pen was dry.

'It's not working.'

'Shake it.'

'I'm shaking it! It's not working.'

'Shake it harder.'

'I could try and scratch it into the paper.'

There was a rumbling sound in the distance. An engine? The wind?

Gyan unscrewed the pen to take out the ink cartridge. She opened it up, her hands shaking, and then spat into it. She shook it around and spat again.

'Quick,' Erie was saying. 'Hurry.'

No, it was an engine. Something was coming up the dirt road.

Gyan shook the pen. Some ink flowed up to the nib. She hurriedly scribbled the message in as few words as possible. It was definitely a car.

Some spiked trees not marked sorry don't cut DON'T CUT!

She dropped the pen and ran.

'Fingerprints!' Erie said. He ran back for the pen and then sprinted back to her, and they dipped into the tree line just before the car sped up to the site entrance.

As they crept back into the darkness of the woods, Gyan glanced back and saw the glowing tip of a cigarette and the silhouette of one of the workers, standing at the gate.

Once they were safely out of earshot, they ran. As they crossed one of the small streams, she saw a bright red flash in the distance. A flare.

'Was that?'

'Peyto.'

They ran towards the fire tower, the flare fading, lost in the dense forest.

When they finally reached the tower, Peyto was lying down with his eyes shut.

Gyan's head was pounding; she ran to him and put her fingers to his neck to check his pulse.

'The fuck?' he said, waking up.

'Oh, sorry.'

'You're OK?' Erie said.

'Yeah, man. You sort the message?'

'We saw your flare. What happened?'

'What? I didn't send any flare.' He opened up the gun. The charge was still inside it.

'Then who?'

'We need to get out of here,' Erie said. 'It's going to take us a while, with your foot. Someone's already at the claim, the rest won't be far away – after that, the police. Gyan, quick, your clothes.'

She climbed up to the lookout and got changed, stuffing everything she'd been wearing, anything that might have been seen on the CCTV, into the plastic bags that had been covering her shoes. She threw on a dress and dropped the bags down.

'So long, sister!' Erie said, helping Peyto up.

The central part of Gyan's instructions was to stay in the lookout tower for the duration of the residency so as not to arouse suspicion. She woke after a short sleep, thinking of her mum. If Peyto's friends did indeed hit the pulp mill where her mum worked, how could Gyan live with herself, having known of the danger but failing to warn her, whiling away the time in a forest retreat, writing music? She looked out at the dark Jenkins claim and called the residency manager, telling her there had been a family emergency and that she was sorry to have to leave so soon. She hiked back to her car and found its familiarity oddly reassuring. The smell of the seats, the click of her key in the ignition. She joined the main road and slowed when she reached the T-junction. Turning left would take her home to Vancouver, and right would lead her to Prince George, the place she was from.

Gyan rarely visited her parents. They came down to Vancouver and Surrey every summer, which suited her. Prince George itself depressed her, a grid of flat buildings on the wrong end of the Fraser. It would be a long drive, but time alone was what she wanted, the anonymity of the highway. She put her Spotify on and sang along to whatever it threw up – 'Courting is a Pleasure', 'Annachie Gordon', 'Adieu False Heart'. And then the AI DJ put on one of her old Tansen songs, 'Om Hum'. She stopped singing. If she began to reminisce about the days of the band, then she would start to regret leaving it.

When she'd left, Tansen were known as a one-hit wonder; there would often be an exodus at their concerts after they performed 'River at My Door'. Gyan felt as if they had evolved into their own middle-aged tribute act and nothing had driven that home more than her drunkenly getting with a twenty-something fan. He'd ended up in the same bar as the band after a show in Seattle, and had told her how much he admired her songwriting, how the new album was his favourite yet, and how he wrote himself and was hoping to record his first EP ...

It was only when the tour was over that she realised she was pregnant. She rarely envisioned a life in which she had children, and had never considered the prospect of raising a child alone – a child who would never know their father. On the day of her scheduled abortion, she went down in her building's elevator only to come straight back up. The doors opened, closed, and opened again.

She'd taken it as a sign: quit the band, have a child, enter into a second adulthood. Perhaps she'd move back to Prince George to be close to her parents, her son having a childhood not unlike her own. She would work on solo material, pare everything back. Go for walks with friends from prenatal, arrange playdates, breakfasts at IHOP. She could imagine the boy's first pair of ice skates, teaching him the ukulele.

She carried him to full term, and he lived for a minute and a half.

The doctor encouraged her to name him, to help with closure.

Her parents went to the gurdwara for the naming ceremony on her behalf. They jotted down a list of fifteen options after the Guru Granth Sahib Ji was opened at random: the first letter of the first word on the left-hand page would be the first letter of the boy's name.

H.

She pulled into a gas station and put on Tansen's latest album. It was three years old now and had been released two years after her stillbirth. Clem had urged her to rejoin the group, he missed her, but she'd refused, watching from the sidelines as their album, *Raag Deepak*, actually charted. For the first time in their careers, the guys were both critically and commercially successful. It was a new sound, more intense and direct, and it was undoubtedly their best work yet. Where Gyan's tendency when writing was always to complexify, to add in extra movements, little diversions, the songs were stronger for being more straightforward. Perhaps Gyan would have been less jealous if they'd replaced her with a man, but to pick a woman ten years younger than her? One who looked like that? The worst part was that, when they'd met at the Lake Mead benefit, she'd been perfectly lovely. It was she who had introduced Gyan to the graffiti artist, who had ultimately sent her down this new course.

The last time Gyan had been in Prince George, she'd performed at the Rivers Day Festival in Lheidli T'enneh Memorial Park. The park lay where the Lheidli T'enneh had lived, until their houses were burned down by settlers, who had come north as part of the fur boom, and then the gold rush, and stayed on for the timber and oil. Lheidli T'enneh, Gyan remembered from school, meant 'at the confluence of the two rivers', the Fraser and the Nechako. The concert had been Gyan's first attempt

214

at performing after her split from Tansen, and she'd seen it as a kind of homecoming. Her parents met her backstage after her set of folk standards. 'It's a lot more quiet, just you,' her mum said. 'I was looking forward to a boogie!'

She passed the town sign now, which dated back to the first trappers, and the town's mascot, Mr PG, a giant smiling man who looked like he was made out of timber. His body was actually made from painted sheet metal and his round head from an old septic tank. She took the 97 as far as the Spruceland Mall, where she turned towards her parents' bungalow in Heritage.

The sprinklers on the front lawn were mid-cycle, the spray darkening the stones on the small path that went from one end of the grass to the other, with no conceivable purpose. Gyan had called it the path to nowhere as a teenager, and that had been the title of one of her first attempts at a song. No one answered the door. She walked round to the back of the house, to see if anyone was in the kitchen, but all the lights were off. The swing that her dad had hung from the oak tree was still there. Her dad had repainted the seat back when she'd told him she was pregnant. Her mum had found her old cot in the attic, her first pair of mittens. She sat on the swing for a few minutes while she tried to call her dad, and then realised where he was likely to be in the early evening on a Tuesday: the gurdwara, opposite the mall.

She'd rarely seen the car park so full. She didn't have a chunni with her, so used her hood to cover her head as she entered. The main hall was packed; she sat at the back. Men were giving impassioned speeches. She didn't have to look for her dad, who stood behind the Guru Granth Sahib Ji doing the chaur sahib seva, rhythmically waving a whisk tail made of yak hair over the holy book. He'd been doing the task since she was a child, and she remembered being confused at first that he could do it even though his beard wasn't white. Her mum had explained the role of the chaur sahib: in the old days, men of significance would be fanned with the yak-tail whisk to keep them cool on hot days and to keep insects away. When the Sikh gurus rose to prominence, their followers would fan them while they gave their sermons. And when the book of their teachings was instilled as the final, eternal guru, devotees continued to wave the whisk tail. But it had always struck her as strange, watching her father fan the book in the depths of Canadian winter. There were no flies here, and if a book could get hot, it certainly wasn't overheating in Prince George.

The first time he took on the responsibility, the family had braved the freezing weather to take refuge in the gurdwara. They'd moved as many of their belongings as possible up into the bungalow's attic: the Nechako had frozen solid, and the ice had formed a dam over the Fraser. The cold water, with nowhere to go, flowed on to the town's streets.

They slept in the gurdwara for two weeks as the floodwater damaged their bungalow, and while she and her mum huddled in a sleeping bag most evenings, her dad continued with his fly-whisk. From the upstairs hall, she could see the white river and the murky roads, could see kids paddling canoes down past the mall, someone casting a fishing line out from their apartment window. She wanted to be outside, but her parents wouldn't let her leave the temple. Then, her father was called by the mill to go back to work. A plan had been agreed for the mill to pump out its hot waste water directly into the river, with the hope that it would help melt the ice. In the end, it was a mixture of the hot pulp run-off and the unauthorised civilian ice blasts – sticks of dynamite chucked from the banks – that broke the ice dam, and soon the water that had covered the city grid was flowing as it should down the Fraser. Her parents took her to visit cousins in Surrey while the insurance was sorted and the bungalow began to slowly dry out. And, when she returned, her parents would still go to the gurdwara most evenings, part of a new routine. As a young child she was made to go with them, opting at least to go to the kirtan music lessons, where she could mess around on the harmonium or on the tabla. Then, as a teenager, she'd get to have the house to herself when they left, and she'd have boys over or spend the evenings writing her garage rock – 'Path to Nowhere', 'Ice Blast', 'Dehumidifier'.

He looked fully at peace now, her father, eyes closed as he listened to the speech, fanning the whisk tail with metronomic accuracy. He was the one who taught her to keep time.

It took a few moments for Gyan to understand that the event was a fundraiser for those affected by the bursting of the Goddess Valley Dam. And while people were donating on the contactless reader in front of the holy book, the speakers weren't really talking about the victims, nor were they focusing on the perpetrators. The speeches focused on what they deemed the root cause of the disaster, the Saraswati River.

'A river is a natural thing, no? So this is no river. It is a glorified canal, no different from the types they built in the eighties and nineties, and the purpose now is the same as the purpose then: take sweet water out of Punjab. Seeing the Sikhs prosper, seeing the Muslims on the other side of the border prosper, it cannot work for this government. So they will divert our water, make us beholden to other states to pay a premium, just to be able to farm the food that we then have to sell at government price back out of state. Everyone is focusing on the lives taken today, but I am trying to warn you about the lives lost tomorrow. Our brothers and sisters back home will suffer. We must do what we can to apply pressure.'

There was the sound of general agreement. What pressure could be applied from overseas, Gyan wasn't sure. Most of the people in the hall had probably only visited India once or twice. She herself had never been. A man who looked half her age took the mic. He spoke in English.

'This river is the latest aggression in a long-standing war on our land, on our people. They treat us like we are not a part of India, and then, when we demand independence, the right to govern ourselves in our own country, they call us terrorists. It doesn't satisfy them that the majority of voters are Hindu, that the majority of the culture is Hindu, that the history taught in schools is Hindu; they want the very soil itself to be claimed, the geology. A river holds no religion. It is only water.'

Gyan couldn't take the boy seriously. He was a teenager from Prince George calling for independence from a country on the other side of the world. One thing shared between the oppressor and the oppressed is absolutist language. Throughout all the speeches, her father showed no emotion; he waved the whisk tail, paused, waved it again. Discussing Indian politics in British Columbia, Gyan felt, was as absurd as batting non-existent flies away from a book. Why did they care so much more about what was happening there, than what was on their doorstep? How many generations did a community have to be in a place for them to no longer feel like visitors, bound one day to return?

At last, the speakers stopped and the music began. Whoever had set up the mics had got the levels all wrong, and what came out as the septuagenarians sang was an almost punk level of distortion, not far off the crap Gyan had made as a teenager. Her father gave up his shift, carefully leaving the hall along his remembered route, and she followed.

He was shocked to hear her voice.

'Gyan? Are you OK? What's happened, hey?'

She held his hand, so that he could confirm it was her before him. 'I just thought I'd drop by,' she said, regretting it. No one dropped by after a ten-hour drive. 'I was missing you guys.'

'But you're OK?'

'I'm OK.'

'You went to the house?'

'Yeah.'

'Your mum will be done with work soon. Can you call her so that she knows not to have to pick me up?'

When her dad had stopped working at the pulp mill after his eyesight began to fail – he'd inherited choroideremia – her mum had started working in the front office. The reversal seemed to have served them both well, Gyan thought: a man who had worked so long getting his rest; a woman who had been confined so thoroughly allowed a life beyond the house.

He took her arm, and she led him out to the car and called her mum.

'You're home?' her mum said. 'What's wrong? What's happened?'

Gyan paused. 'How's work?'

'Fine, fine.'

'You're finished?'

'No, I have to cover for Sandra. Another hour or there-abouts. You *are* OK?'

'Yeah.'

'OK – oh, phone's low, I'll see you soon.'

On the way home, Gyan's dad told her about the marches. A group of farmers in Punjab had broken into the dug-up route of the Saraswati. They were marching 'upstream', trying to disrupt the river works.

'Police are firing at them with water cannons. One way to fill the river. *Everywhere that—*'

'*—water goes.*'

'Exactly.'

Gyan pulled into their drive. 'I'll come around,' she said, getting out to open his door.

Inside, she made tea.

'Hey, Alexa,' her dad said. 'Play "River at My Door".'

The Alexa replied: 'Playing "River at My Door", by Tansen.'

'Neat, huh?' her dad said. 'Bobby set it up for me.'

The tea on the hob darkened and bubbled. Gyan searched the local news and found no mentions of any violence, any activism. She refined her searches and found that, half a year ago, someone had tried and failed to set Mr PG on fire. She wanted to call her mum again and tell her to come home as soon as possible. But to do so would involve revealing the fact that she had taken part in the same kind of action she was trying to protect her mum from. And, of all the people on the planet that she'd want to tell the truth to, her mum was bottom of the list, along with Pete Jenkins and the police. Perhaps she could invent some other emergency, a decoy – she could cut her thumb trying to slice the ginger. She was overreacting, she knew that – knew that, even if her mum's pulp mill was targeted, it was likely to be a non-violent action, harmless.

Her dad sang along to the song, drumming on the table. 'I'm on the oat milk now, Gyan; your mum's got me on the *oat* milk.'

She refreshed the news. The tea came to the boil and the song changed. She gave her dad his cup.

'She's hidden the biscuits somewhere. Would you find them for me?'

Gyan went through the different cupboards, and found the biscuits along with the cleaning equipment. 'Cleaning drawer,' she told her father. 'For next time.'

He tapped the button clock on the table, which announced: 'The time is six twenty-four.'

Gyan's dad took a nap after they finished the takeout. She still had no word from her mum. She called and called again, but went straight to voicemail. There was no news about Prince George. She resorted to calling the pulp mill's reception desk, but no one answered. She paced the room.

'What's eating you?' her dad said, from his armchair.

She hadn't realised he was awake. 'Oh,' she said.

'You can tell me.'

After making him promise he wouldn't tell her mum, she told him about the Jenkins action and about what Peyto had said about Prince George. 'What do I do? Call it in? I can't find anything that says something has happened. But it might be about to happen. She's not answering her phone.'

Her dad stood up and slowly walked towards the table. He tapped the clock: 'The time is eight fourteen.'

He took a seat and sighed. 'Should we drive over to the mill?'

Even if nothing bad was happening, or if something bad was happening and there was nothing they could now do about it, it was soothing to be at the wheel, to be moving rather than waiting. They crossed the Nechako and drove north.

'You know,' her dad said, as she pulled off the 97, 'you're not the first radical in the family.'

'I'm not a radical, Dad.'

'Well, you know what I mean.'

'I know about your chacha's side. The communists, right?'

'Before that, even,' her dad said. 'My grandfather – your great-grandfather – he was a Ghadarite.'

'A Ghadarite?'

'When the first person in our family came over here,' her dad said, 'it wasn't just for making a buck. The story my uncle told was that it was about lying low. Going undercover.'

It was a story I would later confirm with Gyan, showing her the archival evidence I'd found. Sejal and Jugaad's second daughter, Chenab Kaur Hakra, Gyan's direct ancestor, had ended up in Canada, but had originally planned to live in America with a husband she'd never met. The man she married was called Garbaksh Singh, but was briefly known as Great Teacher.

When Garbaksh was a child in Lahore in the late 1800s, the British clairvoyant, Alfred Critchley, a close friend of

221

Sir Bernard Hawthorn, noticed him in the street and determined that his aura was utterly untainted. He took the child to the Lemurian Society of Lahore, a social club for Darwinians who believed in the existence of Lemuria, a continent that bridged the gap between Madagascar and India, from which all the people of the earth had originated. The first people of Lemuria had travelled north to India and west to Africa, before the Ice Age ended and a great flood made the continent disappear. It was agreed at the society that Garbaksh had a Lemurian aura – meaning he came from an unspoiled line of Lemurians – and that he would grow up to be their spiritual teacher. There was no mention in any records about his parents, or about how exactly he was adopted into the society. A year later, Garbaksh was taken to California to meet the society's founders, who, borrowing Helena Blavatsky's lexicon, would confirm him as part of the Great White Brotherhood, a Great Teacher on a par with Siddhartha Gautama and Jesus Christ.

But there was a problem. The voyage was delayed due to unfavourable weather conditions and, by the time Garbaksh arrived in California, a different child, from Mexico, had ascended. The society's founders weren't quite sure what to do with their almost-guru, but Critchley was adamant that he stay. Surely their new Great Teacher needed a friend his age with a similarly untainted aura.

The problem for the Lemurian disciples was that, the more Garbaksh was educated, the more he acted out. He encouraged the Great Teacher to mock them, giving fake visions of the future – 'I see a great fire, a fire spreading around the world and turning all to smoke and ash! Nothing will escape the coming heat!' The two boys started to barricade the doors of their lodgings at night to stop anyone from entering. If someone managed to get in, they would scream, 'Devil! Devil!'

An auxiliary aura test was carried out on Garbaksh and impurities were indeed discovered. His ability to channel the original Lemurians had been hampered. He was cast out of the society as a teenager.

The one benefit Garbaksh had gained from the society was the ability to speak English, which turned out to be crucial to his survival. After a few nights sleeping in a San Francisco park, he noticed a group of Indian men passing through. Remembering his Punjabi, he called out to them. When they realised he could speak fluent English, they saw an opportunity and took him in.

The men, a mixture of Sikhs, Hindus and Muslims, worked at *The Ghadar*, a secret revolutionary newspaper with the slogan 'Angrezi Raj Ka Dushman', *Enemies of British Rule*. As Garbaksh's English was better than theirs, they got him working with local suppliers for paper and ink. It didn't take him long to get swept up with their vision of a new India, an India without the white men and all the ugly things they had brought with them, an India the way it used to be, the way it would be again. But words could only take them so far.

As they began to form a plot, there was only one thing on Garbaksh's mind. He wouldn't die without having been with a woman. He had one of the Ghadarite elders write home to his old village, Hakra, and a girl was sent for.

When Chenab heard the news, she was desperate to leave, like her siblings. Her parents tried to stop her; they'd already lost one daughter overseas. But Chenab had been raised to have a strong will. She boarded a steamer to San Francisco, with a few possessions wrapped in one of the intricate phulkari dupattas her mother had made her. Inside the bundle, her money was tied up in a section of red cloth that her mother had split evenly between her children. When Chenab had children, she was told she would have to split that red cloth again among them, and they would do so for their children, and so on.

There were several Indian men waiting on the dock, all wearing suits, but only one holding a sign. It must have had her name written on it, for she recognised Garbaksh from his photo, the hair slicked back with oil. He grinned and stepped towards her. How glad she was to see his teeth! She'd been having nightmares of a man with a crooked smile. He was a little dark, but, then again, wasn't she? She didn't want to be darker than her husband, because then what would he think of her? She wore her mother's phulkari to their small wedding ceremony, conducted by one of Garbaksh's co-workers in the large room that housed the printing presses. Garbaksh printed off a single special edition of the newspaper, with the headline: Happy Couple Married. The front page showed his photo next to the one of her that had been sent to him. She didn't understand how it had moved from the photo-wallah's back room on to this paper on the other side of the world.

She loved to watch him at the printing press, his nimbleness with all the different letters. It reminded her of seeing her mother at the loom, a person who could perceive a pattern where you saw nothing. His good looks helped to make up for his general destitution. They slept in a small room adjoining the press, and oftentimes, when they consummated their new marriage, the ink on his hands would leave prints on her skin that she wouldn't notice until the light of morning. She could talk to him the way she used to talk to her sister Beas, the two of them whispering in the dark. She told him about her life back home and, one morning, lying on her chest, he told her the plan for the guns.

German spies had sent a shipment of guns to New York, and Irish mobsters had forwarded it south to Galveston. It had travelled west by rail, and was due to arrive in San Diego in a fortnight. The Ghadarites planned to take the guns to northeast India, where the revolt against the British would begin.

'All their attention is on Europe. They're so stretched. This is our chance.'

'I'm much too young to become a widow. I don't like it.'

'We're just delivering the shipment. We won't see any battle. Think of me like a postman.'

They drove down to San Diego to see the ship and, confronted with the sight of the dilapidated *Annie Larsen*, Chenab begged Garbaksh not to go through with the mission.

'That boat won't launch a revolution,' she said. 'I'd probably see you sink from here.'

'They're going to get a bigger ship up the coast; we'll sail from here and meet that ship out in the ocean, move the supplies over. It's all thought through.'

The idea of losing her new husband in such a foolish way, and being marooned in an alien country with no money or work, pushed Chenab to do something she didn't think herself capable of. When Garbaksh was busy with the others, making arrangements in San Pedro about the larger ship, the SS *Maverick*, Chenab walked into a police station with several copies of *The Ghadar* and a pile of letters from Garbaksh's correspondence with the German spies. She had painstakingly translated a sentence, using her English–Punjabi dictionary, that read: *I will tell you the names if you promise our safety.*

She pointed to *The Ghadar* and then to the sentence, keeping the correspondence in her purse.

'Jackson, got another crazy. This one's yours.'

'Say, I took the last one!'

Eventually, they called a superior, who had already heard rumours about a shipment of guns. He handed the affair over to the CIA, who sent a representative to meet Chenab the next day.

There was a white man and an Indian man, and the Indian spoke for the American.

'You can tell us anything and, whatever you share, it'll never come back to you. We can keep you safe. We already know some of the insides of the case.'

'Me *and* my husband.'

The Indian spoke to the American. The American slowly nodded.

'And your husband,' the Indian confirmed. 'But only if you give us the story.'

Chenab and Garbaksh were picked up far from the print house and driven north, through Oregon and Washington to the Canadian border, while the other Ghadarites, evading the police by a matter of minutes, managed to set sail.

The *Annie Larsen* missed its rendezvous with the *Maverick* three times, and the shipment of guns was eventually seized by British forces. As part of the diplomatic scratching of backs between the Brits and the Americans, Chenab and Garbaksh were given Canadian passports and allowed to cross the border past Seattle, into a kind of witness protection.

Garbaksh had been silent for much of the drive, no doubt conflicted about what Chenab had done. The way she had explained it, the police already knew about the plan and were placed to intercept the *Annie Larsen*. If she hadn't cooperated, or if they had told the others about the sting, then the two of them would have ended up in jail as well. She had chosen the lesser evil, and now, arriving in the deep green forests of British Columbia, they were free. She unfolded her red cloth, and counted out their money.

A small section of that red cloth was framed above Gyan's parents' mantlepiece. It was about the size of a postcard. Had Gyan had any siblings, it would have been cut into two credit-card-sized rectangles. And if she had given birth to two children, they might have inherited a section of the red cloth not much larger than a postage stamp. And what would have happened after them?

Her dad was still speaking when Gyan's phone rang. She pulled up at the side of the road to answer.

'Mum?'

'Hey, where are you guys?'

'Where are you?'

'At home. I've been here waiting for my phone to charge.

Thing lasts about five minutes and needs a half hour to turn on.'

'Oh, thank God.'

'What was that?'

'Nothing.'

'Where are you?'

Her dad cut in: 'We just went for a drive. I wanted dessert.'

'Dessert? Gyan, his blood pressure.'

'We can pick something up for you.'

'I was late because I was picking stuff up for *you*.'

When they got home, they saw she had indeed bought all sorts of food for Gyan and her dad. 'If you'd given me notice, I would have had this ready for you,' she said. 'And you wouldn't be eating that takeout crap.' Her mum looked at her. 'Was it another break-up? You didn't even tell us there was anyone.'

'I'm just here to see you guys.'

They sliced a cake, and her mum asked her dad about the programme at the gurdwara. While they discussed the latest on the Saraswati scandal, Gyan walked up to the fake fire-place. She wasn't sure why she was tearing up, but didn't want her parents to see. She pretended to examine the framed red cloth, and then began to look closer at the faint abstract pattern of red on red. The more you looked, the more you saw. She felt a sense of vertigo: to think this rectangle of material had touched so many hands, all in a direct lineage. To think it might all end with her. What had it survived? She could see it on the boat from India to America, could see it in the Canadian woods. One of her ancestors coming home after a shift at the charcoal kiln, hands blackened by work, washing up, wiping their face with it. Could see it folded into wallets, packed into cardboard boxes, moving from house to house. Could see Chenab stuck in a wooden hut as an oil fire raged on the hob, reaching the walls, the ceiling. Garbaksh rushing home through the woods, abandoning his axe as he saw the smoke. Arriving as glass showered down, the woman he loved in the bedroom window, covering her mouth. How she'd rifled through the cupboards to find the cloth that held their money; how she'd had to abandon everything else they'd accumulated, the furniture, the clothes, the gramophone and the records beginning to melt, song turned to meaningless sound, and the phulkari that her mother had laboured over with such love, gone, as she looked down at her husband, who yelled, 'Jump!' Gyan could see it all, could see the cloth unfurling in the air, hot dollar bills dancing like the first leaves of fall.

Raag Megh Malhar

Briefly, the room lightened as Dagwan walked away, alone, into the snow, and all Gyan had to pull off now was the final movement, a return to earlier themes. Not repetition, *accumulation*, she could hear her old music teacher say as the credits began. For the first time in a long while, she was playing without thinking, not creating but releasing.

The audience clapped, and the house lights came up. They'd initially sold out, but the theatre was half empty. The forecast had kept people at home, or convinced them to leave the province.

Gyan gave a short bow, and a chair was brought out for the audience Q & A with Ed, who'd steered *The Silent Enemy*'s nitrate restoration and rerelease. She was expected to stay on stage in case anyone had questions for her. She put down her guitar, feeling exposed without it.

'I don't know if this is a question exactly,' someone said, taking the roving mic, 'but, you know with restoration there's this ability to release a film into a context that the artists couldn't have imagined, right? Latent themes in the original maybe come out more prominently, and I suppose what I'm asking is, did you find something in the film speaking louder now than it did when it came out?'

'Thank you, thank you,' Ed said. 'Though, I should say I can't speak to what it was like when it came out – I'm not quite that old.' Polite laughter. 'The thing that sticks with me, seeing this material that was filmed over a hundred years ago, loosely based on Jesuit writings hundreds of years before that, is this sense of prophecy.'

Gyan scanned the crowd for recognisable faces as he contin-ued to speak. None of her friends had turned up. Her pulse was still quick from the performance, and she took several deep breaths to try to focus. Ed was going off on a lengthy tangent.

'... Tiresias lived for seven generations, and lived first as a man, and then for seven years as a woman, before becoming a man again. And, long story, he went blind, and Zeus gifted him a different kind of sight: prophesy.'

There was a reason everyone called him TED-Talk Ed.

'Now, Tiresias is probably the first known augur, someone who could divine the future from the language of birds. He could hear omens and premonitions in their calls. The problem was that he was cursed so that nobody who heard his warn-ings ever took them seriously. He strayed between binaries, man and woman, alive and dead, seeing and not seeing, could see the world of the gods and the world of men, and still was ignored ...'

It was only when Gyan was scanning the back row that she saw someone she recognised. From this distance, she couldn't be entirely sure it was him. But then he made eye contact and grinned.

It was Peyto.

The guidelines had been clear: never resume contact in the real world. But there was no way his being here in Vancouver was a coincidence.

'And, of course, one of the early warnings we received but ignored was H. P. Carver's *The Silent Enemy*. A hundred years ago, it never really got its dues, arriving just after talkies. But it feels as fresh now as it did then, in no part because of the fact that the prophecies in the film, which were ignored in 1930, are still being ignored now.'

Ed fielded a few more questions, first about how the film handles the theme of fake news, and then about the process of working with the nitrate stock, which was notoriously flammable, and then about his other projects. When someone finally asked Gyan a question, it was about Tansen. 'Do you think you'll ever rejoin the band?'

'Oh,' she said. 'Thanks. I don't think so.' She realised she was supposed to expand on the answer, and felt the weight of the room's silence as she paused. 'I'm finding this kind of work very rewarding.'

The assistant walked up the aisle to hand the mic to the next person.

'Um, I guess I should say this now, as I've just checked my phone, but the news is saying the storm is coming earlier than expected – it's the wind or whatever. Just in case people wanted—'

There was the noise of others opening their bags, checking their phones, and then, one by one, people started to file out of the cinema. As more people got up from their seats, the manager came out on stage and told Ed and Gyan that they too had better get going; the situation had changed quickly while they were all in the dark.

A category-five atmospheric river, almost 2,000 km long and about 700 km wide, which had been snaking its way through the air, from Hawaii towards the west coast of Canada, had gathered a tailwind and would hit Vancouver several hours earlier than had been expected. The airborne river was carrying twenty-five times more water than the Mississippi and would let it all loose when it hit the mountainous coast. Vancouver was perfectly placed for flooding. The subway had been shut, so floodwater wouldn't enter the metro system, and people all over the city were moving valuables up to higher surfaces or packing them into cars that they could drive east.

Unlike her parents, Gyan lived well above ground level; Tansen royalties (or, rather, royalties from their one hit song) had paid for a small one-bed in a False Creek high-rise. Her plan had been to go for drinks after the performance – unlike many of her friends, she'd had no intention of leaving Vancouver. This wasn't her first 'once-in-a-lifetime' storm; her apartment was stocked with enough to wait out any flooding. But there were two things she noticed when she emerged from the dark screening room and into the bright foyer: the drains were already overflowing outside and Peyto was waiting for her by the door, eating popcorn.

'Sorry, I didn't know it was the kind of movie you're not supposed to eat in. I got legit hushed.'

'Oh, Ed, this is an old friend,' Gyan said. How to introduce him?

'Earl,' he said, offering a salty hand to Ed.

'I'll leave you to it?' Ed asked. 'I was supposed to go to Costco this morning, and didn't, and now the doomers will probably have wiped the place clean. Pray for me.' He left, vanishing behind the fogged-up window.

'*Earl?*'

'Yeah?'

'That's a terrible code name.'

'It's my actual name.'

'Funny.'

'No, really.'

He tipped the box of popcorn into his mouth to finish it off.

'What are you doing here?'

'I would say we need to talk privately.'

The bar next door wouldn't let them in. Instantly soaked, they ran to an overpass for shelter. They were enclosed underneath it by two walls of rain. All the shops and restaurants were shutting down or were already closed, and the traffic around them had slowed to a standstill, windscreen wipers moving on fast forward. The air was warm; if they weren't already drenched, they might have been sweating.

Gyan only lived a few blocks away, but she couldn't just invite Earl back to hers. He was still, in effect, a stranger. Once the sidewalk was empty, he finally told her why he'd sought her out. 'You remember Nipigon, right, from the woods? Well, I was doing something out in Alberta, up towards Fort McMurray, and I'm just scouting out the police station, getting my bearings, and who do I see on the notice board outside? It's her face on a missing poster. Claire Boucher was her real name.'

Gyan paused before she spoke. 'How long has she been missing?'

'Since we ... you know.' He sighed.

Gyan slowly nodded.

'Do you remember the flare?' Earl said. 'You said you saw one, but it wasn't me.'

He hadn't been able to track down Erie, but Gyan had made the mistake of discussing her music, which had made her easy to trace. When he returned from Alberta, he found out that she would be doing the film concert.

'It's been eating me up, man. It's been months and they haven't found her. They don't even know where to look. They've been doing search parties in Alberta.'

'And then the fires.'

'Exactly.'

They'd spiked Jenkins Timber towards the end of May, on Victoria Day, and the fires had arrived shortly after, in the peak of summer. If Nipigon, or rather Claire, had indeed injured herself in the dark wilderness and somehow died out there, then her body was likely ash. The one upside, the news reports had been continually saying, was that the autumn's atmospheric river would cut out the summer's forest fires. The thought of her family searching for her in the wrong province – Gyan started to shake.

They had all ignored the lone flare. But at least Earl and Erie had been forced to leave quickly. Gyan could have gone looking for her that night, or the following morning, instead of leaving for Prince George. But the truth was, she hadn't even thought about the flare, with everything that was happening. She'd forgotten about it entirely. Claire wouldn't have been alone in the woods if she hadn't been cast out by Erie, who had only the welfare of the timber workers and the movement's public image in mind. In saving the people they opposed, they'd condemned one of their own.

'Apparently, it's seven years of no news for someone missing to be called dead.'

'She might have gone off-grid,' Gyan said. 'I don't know, moved to a commune. She's probably going around the country in a camper van. She seemed like that type. I just don't know what you want me to do with this.'

'I'm, like, shouldn't we tell somebody? Anonymously?'

'Can we really be anonymous?'

'I don't know.'

'Either way, the result is the same. Whether her body is found or not, it's still a body.'

'You're the one who just said she might still be out there.'

She stopped herself from raising her voice. Stopped herself from saying anything at all. She got a phone call from her mum. She let it go to voicemail and then got one from her dad.

'I thought you would want to know,' Earl said. 'I thought you might be able to help.'

She didn't know what to say.

'I thought you might *want* to help,' he said.

She nodded, and then, without saying a word, and without looking back, walked off into the rain, and then ran.

*

233

She burst through her building's spinning doors. Water dripped off her clothes and off her guitar case as she walked unsteadily to the elevator.

Her apartment was on the twenty-first floor and had a balcony, though not one with a view of the water. She showered, dried, and called her parents, from whom she'd had several more missed calls.

'I'm OK ... No, really, there was just all this traffic after the gig, but I'm fine, the apartment's fine, it's all going to be OK. Has it reached you? ... Will it? ... No, I mean, it's certainly something – it's really going for it! I've not seen the city like this before.'

There was commotion at the gurdwara, her mother said, because some of the younger men had travelled to India to join the protests, and one of them had been arrested, and the community had heard almost nothing about his situation, where he was being held or on what grounds. 'There's people who are stupid by accident, and then there are those that are stupid on purpose. They're just lost, these kids, and these idiots are leading them astray.'

While her parents continued to talk, she googled Claire Boucher. She looked different in the pictures, less serious, but there was no doubt it was her. She was younger than Gyan had thought. Apparently, she fostered dogs, had an identical twin. Her social-media accounts were still live, and, while her mum told her about the worsening situation along the Saraswati, about some other terrible thing Indra had done, or planned to do, Gyan scrolled through Claire's dormant Twitter account. Most of her tweets were about ice hockey. Ice hockey or music: Coldplay, Taylor Swift. She'd seen Beyoncé twice. The closest thing to a clue that she was in any way involved in the movement was the fact that she followed Greta Thunberg. Gyan had only known her for a matter of hours, and only through a fake name, and yet it seemed she knew a side of her that her grief-stricken family didn't. She expanded a photo the family had posted: her two parents and her twin sister, and her dogs, standing in front of a picture of Claire. The twin had shaved off her hair to stop volunteers mistaking her for her sister.

'... In any case, it doesn't look like a sale would even be possible,' her mum said. 'The estate agents have to tell them about the flood risk, which makes them think about the insurance. We'll be stuck here forever.'

'But it's our home,' Gyan said, tuning back in.

'It's too big for us without you here.'

'And it's good for Dad; he'd have to relearn everything. It's a blessing there's no stairs.'

Her dad took the phone from her mum. 'I'm on your side,' he said. 'It's just the money. I always said I could do that job with my eyes closed. Maybe I can go back.'

'I can help you guys out, you never asked,' Gyan said.

'I remember when we first saw this place,' her dad said. 'Now, that was a great day. Finally, the two of us moving out of my parents' house.'

'Best day of my life,' her mum said.

'All this space, and you know what it came down to? What got us over the line?'

Gyan pretended not to know the answer. She liked hearing their voices and wanted them to keep talking as she looked out at the city transitioning to night. Orange rain emanated from street lamps. 'No, Dad. What was it?'

'Of all things, dear, it was the humble spruce beetle.'

She smiled.

'You see, times were hard at the pulp mill, people buying in paper from elsewhere, undercutting us. And I could barely pick up a shift some weeks. And then, out of nowhere, a gift from the gods. The spruce beetle, needling its way into trees all over the territory. They spread fast. And all these premium-grade logs were suddenly worthless. Couldn't make any kind of quality board after the beetle had touched it. And what happens to worthless timber?'

'It gets pulped.'

'I was working double shifts! I basically lived at the mill.'

'Which left me alone with your mother,' her mum said. 'At first, I cursed those beetles.'

'And with that windfall came the house, and with the house came you, and so on. You'd have had a different life, I'd say, if it weren't for the spruce beetle.'

Gyan slept on the sofa that night, as the storm wore on. The wind made all kinds of music on the glass, whistling up and down the pipes. She thought it would be over by the morning, but when she woke, the rain was even stronger. She sat up and heard bird-song. It wasn't a sound she associated with the apartment, and it made her think of her childhood, of Prince George. She looked out on to the balcony and saw four small birds, cowering from the storm. She knew nothing about birds and downloaded an app that would identify them. Apparently, they were house sparrows. She googled what you should feed them.

She could hear the wind in the plughole of the sink. The skyscrapers seemed to sway. The water on the streets was brown and moved with a strong current. She cut an apple, a banana, and took the plate out to the balcony. The wind sent a chill through her body and slammed the door behind her. She was instantly wet. Her presence sent the birds into a panic. Seeing her, they fluttered around, and then, seemingly all at once, made the decision to flee, deeming the storm less of a threat than she was. They were whipped away by the current. She stepped to the edge of the balcony to try to see them, and was utterly drenched. She opened her mouth and tasted the water as it fell on the apartment blocks and the office towers, fell on the roads and on the train lines, filling gutters and blocked-off chimneys. It defined the surfaces of all solid things in the Fraser Valley, and redefined some too, causing mudslides as it ran off the burnt soil, bursting the banks of the rivers and their tributaries; it doused the fires to the east, steam rising with the smoke; it fell on the mountains and gathered momentum on smooth rock, seeping into underground lakes, hidden aquifers; it fell on the tired wings of birds, on the hard shells of insects; it filled ashtrays left out on windowsills, filled the troughs of farm animals, flooded crawl spaces and the burrows of field rabbits, pooling in potholes, spewing out of the concrete mouths of imitation gargoyles; it disturbed the algal blooms in the crater lakes of old volcanoes, fell into the cooling towers of nuclear reactors, into the open mouths of mines; it crossed the coastal mountains, crossed the Rockies, fell in BC, fell in Alberta, drifted north along the Athabasca River towards the polar air, from Edmonton up to the vast tar sands, where it fell on the miles of hot bitumen, filled the enormous dumps of heavy-haul mega-trucks, hit the tailings ponds that threatened to overspill, rippling at regular intervals as the bird blasters sounded to stop migratory ducks touching the toxic surface; and somewhere, not much further east, at some invisible border, the rain stopped and there was land it did not reach, burning trees that it could not touch. Fires in Saskatchewan, in Manitoba, in Australia, in the Amazon; fires in Europe, in the Middle East; there were fires all across Asia, smoke signals that couldn't be deciphered; polling stations were burning, supermarkets, there were yachts on fire, fires spreading through cruise ships, devouring apartment blocks, city parks, flaming torches held up by protesters, protestors dancing in front of the White House, calling a new world into being, the old world, and there were people gluing themselves to the gates of Parliament, across the Abbey Road zebra crossing; people were playing dead in Brussels, forming human chains in Hong Kong; they were throwing pigs' blood at the UN headquarters, throwing tomato soup at the works of old masters; people were starving and people were going on hunger strikes, workers' strikes, general strikes, they were out in the streets, and people couldn't get to work, couldn't get to hospital; people were dying on the streets, dying in their unheated homes, dying of thirst; the children were forgoing school, painting signs, banners, they were singing, they were chanting, and the farmers had downed their tools, driving to the capital in tractors playing music and they were dancing and taking wire-cutters to construction fencing, they were pouring down into the dug-up riverbed, as dry as stone, and walking upstream, into the water cannons, into the clouds of gas, and on, and on the steps of the Red Fort a woman sat down, her sari dripping with oil, her hands shaking as she struck a match and went up in flames, sitting still at first, in a poise of calm defiance, horrified onlookers gathering, taking out their phones, only to film the woman stand up and run, screaming, towards the panicked traffic, the words trapped in her throat as she tried and failed to call for help, to call for someone, a name, for a new beginning, a chance to start again, for the world as it had been, and would be again, calling for a father, for a mother, calling for a brother, a sister, a son: *Hansraj, Harbans, Harbhajan, Hardas, Hardeep, Hardharam, Hardit, Harkiran, Hari, Haraman, Harnam, Harsajaan, Harshbhir, Harveer, Hukam.*

SOHNI MAHIWAL
1886

Stories helped distract them from hunger. Almost seven, Sutlej was old enough to tell qisse to his younger siblings, Beas and Ravi, allowing Sejal to sleep and Jugaad to drink. Her stomach had never grown this large the other times – Jugaad feared twins. As an only child, he'd always wanted a large family, but another two to feed for what was likely another dry season, another spoiled harvest?

'Long, long ago, before you or I were alive,' Sutlej said to his siblings, 'there lived the most beautiful woman – Sohni. She was the daughter of Tulla, a master potter, and lived on the banks of the Chenab, not far from here.'

Jugaad took another swig. He supposed Sejal would want to continue with their family tradition, naming their children after rivers. That would mean the newborn would be called Chenab. And, if there was indeed a twin, a Jhelum. He'd heard that that river was running so low that boats were grounded at some bends.

'Working in her father's shop, Sohni would paint and decorate the pots. She was very skilled and their business thrived – at that time, the river was a big trade route, and people knew to stop at Tulla's for the most brilliant pottery. One of these tradesmen was Izzat Baig, a very rich, very hand-some nobleman from the north.'

Jugaad just needed a few more pegs of whisky before he could do what he had to do. The conditions wouldn't get this perfect again. Sejal was asleep, the kids would go down in a few minutes. The full moon was out and, most importantly, Imtiaz, the owner of the neighbouring farm, was away for what might be days. What Jugaad hoped would be weeks.

'Izzat Baig stopped at Tulla's shop on his travels and saw Sohni working in the back. He fell in love, just like that – that's how beautiful she was. He liked looking at her so much that, every day he was in the village, he returned to buy another pot. Surely, at some point, people asked: "Why does one man need so many pots?" But he did all this just to get a glimpse of the beautiful Sohni.'

'Mum tells it better.'

'Shut up, Beas.'

'Maybe we can wake her up.'

'Don't you dare,' Jugaad said, taking another drink. 'Quiet. Listen to your brother.'

'Seeing the handsome Izzat Baig every day, Sohni fell for him, too. They were soon in love. Izzat Baig was supposed to return north with his caravan, but he told them to go on without him. He wanted to stay with Sohni. To do this, the noble Izzat Baig offered to become a servant for her father.'

'Stupid.'

'He took on the job of buffalo herder and adopted a new name: Mahiwal. He spent his days caring for her father's water buffalo, just so he could spend time with Sohni. The two fell even more deeply in love, and wanted to get married.

'The noble Mahiwal, now a servant, asked Sohni's father for his blessing. He wanted more than anything to marry Sohni.'

Jugaad could see that Ravi was starting to drift off. He just needed the others to do the same and then he could head out.

'Sohni's dad was outraged. There was no way a daughter of his would marry anyone who wasn't from their caste. Who would inherit his business? He immediately arranged for

Sohni to be married to a potter. The marriage party arrived and poor Sohni was taken away from Mahiwal, and they were both very sad.

'Mahiwal, giving up on society, became a faqir. He took on the life of a pauper, aimlessly wandering around, until he saw someone drinking from a pot that had the most beautiful design on it. It was the kind of artistry that he knew only Sohni was capable of. It bore one of her distinct signatures.

'And so, years later, the lovers were reunited. Mahiwal set up camp on the opposite bank of the Chenab, so that he wouldn't be found by Sohni's husband. At night, when her in-laws were asleep, Sohni would sneak out and go down to the river. She would take one of her pots and, using it as a float, she would swim across the wide river and meet Mahiwal.

'They met every night, Sohni sneaking across with her special pot and Mahiwal catching fish and cooking them for her. He was so eager to please her that, one night, when he couldn't manage to catch any fish, he decided instead to cut off a piece of his own thigh and cook that for her. It was only later that night that she saw he was bleeding and realised what he'd done. She only fell more in love with him.'

'Disgusting—'

'While Sohni's husband was away, someone saw the couple gathered by the fire one night, and rumours started to spread in the village. The story reached Sohni's sister-in-law and she decided to follow Sohni and see for herself. Sure enough, she saw her brother's wife use one of her pots to cross the river at night.

'Should she wait for her brother to return home? Or should she take matters into her own hands? She decided on the second option and, the next day, while Sohni was busy working, her sister-in-law swapped Sohni's special hard-baked pot with an unbaked one. The designs were exactly the same and, at night, Sohni wouldn't notice the difference. She took the unbaked pot down to the river. The current was strong, but she didn't mind – it was easy to cross with her float. She stepped into the river as usual, but, as she started to swim, the unbaked pot began to dissolve in the water. She panicked, thrashing around in the river. Mahiwal, seeing his love in danger, dived in.

'But Mahiwal's leg was still badly injured, and he couldn't swim as well as usual. He couldn't reach Sohni. She struggled in the water, flailing. She sank beneath the surface, and, unable to use his leg, Mahiwal lost control, too. They both drowned in the river, and their bodies were discovered miles down-stream – reunited in death.'

Beas had fallen asleep, too. Sutlej had finished the story talking to himself. Jugaad got up and tucked the boy in, using the blanket that Imtiaz had given them the previous winter. Their neighbour was a good man. Jugaad looked upon his sleeping family and blew out the lights. Picking up his spade and his bottle, he walked out.

He arrived at the edge of their plot, the border between his land and Imtiaz's. Both farms were having bad years. There wasn't enough water to go around. And Imtiaz would be away for a while; his son, in Lahore, was seriously ill. If the letters were right, the son would soon be dead. But he had a good job as a clerk, earned well. Enough to support his wife and children – and, Jugaad figured, his father. Imtiaz would survive. But if Jugaad's crop failed again, what would become of Sejal, of Sutlej, Beas and Ravi? What would happen to the unborn children? He had to do what he had to do.

On Imtiaz's side of the border ran a small canal, distributing his share of the water. Jugaad used the spade to knock mud into the canal, blocking its flow and diverting the water into the channel on Jugaad's land.

The makeshift dam held. His neighbour's water joined his own. A month of double flow might just salvage things. He'd break the dam before Imtiaz returned and no one would ever have to know.

JHELUM

Crescat e fluviis
Strength from the rivers

Motto of British Punjab

Harsimran's suit was delivered to his holding cell dripping wet. It had been dipped into the floodwater outside by the courier. The hangers had been removed by guards, and Harsimran, in what little time he had left, attempted to wring the dirty water from the fabric. The leather shoes would be a bad look, but what choice did he have? He'd lost mass during the long wait for the trial – the Indian courts were overrun with cases – and the suit hung loose on his shoulders, despite the damp. The handcuffs didn't pinch like they had when he'd first been brought in.

This was the first day of proceedings about the incident at Saraswati Land and the public seating was full. Harsimran failed to spot his wife, Jasleen, as he was led to his seat. He turned around to try to find her, and the people looked back at him with disgust. When the door opened, their expressions changed and a hush fell over the room: Amit Das had walked in. It was clear just looking at him that he'd paid bail. He was wearing traditional saffron robes, and his skin was glowing. Was that make-up? Harsimran tried not to show any emotion at all as Amit sat on his side of the room. They were both listed together as defendants, even if it felt now that Amit was his true opposition. As they waited for the judge to appear, Harsimran took stock of his predicament, and thought back to the origins of it all, back in Singapore, when he first met Amit.

They were the same height, barely five foot seven, had the same shade of skin, the same deep-set eyes and thick unruly brows, but at that time you wouldn't have said the two men looked alike. If Harsimran sparred in the middleweight category on Mondays, Amit would box featherweight. Harsimran's lats were so large that Jasleen couldn't wrap her arms all the way around him, though she got close when he returned that night and told her the news about Amit.

'Is he the same in real life?'

'He's got good hair,' Harsimran said.

'Of course that's what you'd notice,' she said, running her fingers across his bald head.

He explained the process to his wife, the casting director telling them to assume different poses while she took photos, the flash briefly obscuring the Singapore skyline spread out in front of them. They reached up, bent over, sat down. The producers on Zoom from Mumbai nodded in Harsimran's direction and spoke to the casting director: 'What does this one do?'

'He's an actor, too.'

'An actor,' Amit said to Harsimran, a few minutes after the verdict, as they entered the private gym's changing room. 'Anything I might know?'

Harsimran played 'the Brute' in an acrobatic superhero watershow at a children's theme park called Wild Wild Wet. 'I don't think so. Just bit parts.'

He'd been in the troupe so long, he was certain his agent had forgotten about him. But then the call came. She'd been asked about stunt doubles for a five-foot-seven South Asian man, and she had Harsimran on the books. When he'd found out who this mysterious studio had wanted him to double for, he'd googled Amit with Jasleen.

According to the internet, Amit Das had studied at RADA in London, after completing an undergraduate degree in Cambridge, and went on to perform in a string of off-West End plays. He struggled to secure many TV gigs in the UK, apart from the odd appearance in a soap, and moved back to India for better opportunities. He found success in comedy. He was a chef saving a failing restaurant from closure, a college student who'd invented a bad-mouthed robot, and the monkey in an animated film Harsimran's niece had rewatched several times. They streamed his most recent film, where he played a teacher-turned-stand-up-comedian.

'He's gorgeous,' Jasleen had said. 'You should be flattered.'

Harsimran couldn't understand it. When the casting director had got them to run on treadmills, Amit was out of breath in a minute. The two of them sat on exercise balls afterwards, waiting while the producers talked. Amit appeared content not to engage, but Harsimran tried to start a conversation.

'My wife's a big fan.'

'Do you reckon she'll like *Punisher*?' Amit said, and laughed.

'It does seem like a departure for you.'

'There's better money in action,' Amit said. 'And she likes to cast against the grain.' He nodded to the door. 'Creates a PR story. Skinny comedy actor gets superhero-ripped.'

The studio flew in Surge Gainsburg (better known by his handle, @AlphaSculptor) from LA, who was famous, Jasleen told him, for his work with Marvel. Each morning at five and each evening at eight, they met at the gym in Amit's apartment building. Harsimran had to sign an NDA – the studio wanted to keep Amit's transformation under wraps, to maximise the effect of the reveal.

'Har-sim-ran is the benchmark, you understand,' the Alpha

Sculptor said. 'This is the body of a hero. Wait, is Punisher a villain? Anyway, Har-sim-ran will be *maintaining*. I want him no bigger, no smaller. But Amit, the plan for you, my friend, I got one word for it: *gains*, baby. Gainesville, Massachusetts.'

The split was push, pull, legs. The Sculptor was a kind of mad professor – he attached electrodes to Amit's pecs which sent vibrating pulses into the muscle fibres, forcing them to expand and contract at impossible speeds. Even Harsimran hadn't trained at such intensity – the Sculptor managed to get him doing Bulgarian split squats, which he hated, forced him on to an attack bike. His solo mobility training came as a sweet reprieve.

'You spend more time with Amit than you do with me,' Jasleen said, as he came home from the gym and collapsed.

When the Sculptor returned to LA, it was down to Harsimran to supervise Amit's training. The Sculptor texted them their workout and diet plans.

Before their first session alone, Amit had a strange request. 'I feel like I need to go new recruit, you know what I mean? Get into character. I've got clippers at mine?'

'You want me to shave your hair?'

'Yeah, a new start.'

Harsimran's entire apartment could have fitted within Amit's master bathroom. Looking out at the cityscape through the toilet's panoramic window, he could probably see the Arab quarter, find his building.

He placed a towel around Amit's shoulders and got to work.

'You know, when I got called up for national service,' Harsimran said, 'I was precious about my hair and didn't want to cut it. So, I pretended to be a devout Sikh – turban, everything.'

Amit laughed. 'I suppose you knew you had to enjoy it while it lasted.'

'Exactly. All the men in my family are bald, and I had this thick, luscious hair. But, anyway, I turn up and, day one, they put you with your team, right, and who's there? A friend I had back in the cadet corps – we grew up together! He's like, "Damn, bro, you found God all of a sudden?"'

'Did you enjoy serving? What was it like?'

'Let's just say, I went in with my life all planned out. I was going to join the police force, like my father, his father, etc. Then I came out and attempted to become an actor.'

'Well, you're an actor now!'

'I fall from great heights.'

'And you're very convincing at it.'

He finished up, and they went upstairs to train core. Lying down on a yoga mat, Harsimran looked up at the ceiling mirror. It was already becoming a little harder to tell the two of them apart.

The second time Harsimran visited Amit's apartment, they'd been rowing for miles. Three quarters of the way through the distance the Sculptor had set, Amit gave up.

'Can we get a drink?' he said. 'You can come to mine.'

They steadily worked their way through an eight-pack of low-cal ProBru, attempting to throw each empty can from the designer sofa to the kitchen bin.

'You know, I had to have this professionally cleaned,' Amit said. 'The sofa.'

'If the packaging is right, we've each drunk the protein equivalent of six eggs.'

'You know me, I'm flying back and forth for shooting. I'm barely here, normally.'

'I feel disgusting.'

'But, with a place like this, it has to be maintained. Schedules change; if I come back at random, I want it to be clean.' Amit took off his socks and picked the bits of fluff from between his toes. 'So, my cleaner comes here every fortnight when I'm gone, to keep things in order. And I was off on a shoot and had planned to stay on in India with a girlfriend, but that all fell through, so I cut my trip short. I come back and what do I find? My cleaner and her husband, asleep, naked in my bed!'

'No.'

'I didn't know what to do. She's crying, and she's insisting on cleaning everything. I don't know why I felt so bad! She crosses the border each time she comes here, crosses back to Malaysia each evening—'

'Well, not every evening.'

'Once, she came in with her hair basically like mine is now. She'd sold it all off to some wig maker.'

'We should have done that for you, the other week – made an extra buck,' Harsimran said, crumpling his can and throwing it into the sink. 'How do you know it didn't happen more than once?'

'It did! I finally checked the CCTV.'

Harsimran looked around for a camera. 'Pervert.'

'There was one time when her husband put on one of my suits. Can you believe? That was from Savile Row! And they used the tie—'

'What did you do with the footage?'

'But, yes, the moral of the story, my dear friend,' Amit said, turning serious. 'What I've been trying to tell you … is that I wouldn't sit on that part of the sofa, if I were you.'

The pizza arrived – 'Fuck cauliflower crust!' – and Harsimran began to think of the long route home. His signature payment was yet to come through, so a taxi was out of the question. He didn't have the energy to walk. He zoned back into Amit's endless chatter.

'So, I was watching this doc, right? And it was about why us Indians are naturally high in fat and carry low amounts of muscle mass, why we're so susceptible to diabetes. It's the British. Our very bodies carry the story of their plunder. You know, they manufactured all those famines across India – 1877, 1878, whatever – and, because of that, over so many generations, Indian bodies started to store more fat for rainy days, or the opposite of rainy days, I suppose, and they developed less muscle, as muscle requires so many more calories to maintain, but before the British—'

'You're blaming your slow gains on colonialism?'

'That's exactly what I'm doing. Your body is a blip, when you think about it.'

'It's in the family, they say,' Harsimran said, yawning.

'How come?'

Harsimran shut his eyes and listened to the cracking sound of Amit's can missing the bin.

'How come?'

Harsimran didn't want to walk home. He kept his eyes shut and relaxed his body, slowing his breathing. After a few more moments, he tensed as Amit shifted position and touched his ankles. Harsimran kept his eyes shut as Amit moved his legs up on to the sofa. He felt the weight of a blanket being laid on him.

When it was time to leave Singapore, Harsimran imagined border control joking about his and Amit's likeness, but they went through different queues, and sat in different classes, and made their own way from their separate hotels to the first day of filming. There was chaos on the lot when Harsimran arrived. The production using the studio before them, in an early-morning slot, had been held up by cow vigilante activists. They'd been shooting the death scene of a farmer in *Bund*, a historical drama set during famine time, and the director was adamant they use a real cow.

The activists insisted they were peaceful observers, simply watching to ensure the safe treatment of the cow. The director wouldn't begin until they left. But security didn't have the authority to remove the observers, and the police, when they did arrive, didn't see any issues.

No one had thought to tell Harsimran and the other stunt doubles that the filming had been rescheduled by two hours. They sat together in the sun, listening to the commotion inside. The director could be heard shouting, 'But you wouldn't be here if my surname wasn't Khan! That's a fact—'

'So, you're Punisher?' the one woman in the group said to Harsimran. 'I'm the love interest.'

'I didn't think that character had many stunts.'

'Well, I have to fall from the skyscraper, remember?'

'Of course.'

'What's he like, Amit Das?'

'He's chill. We're bros.'

Much of the first half of the film required both Harsimran and Amit on set. In the less intense action scenes, a Texas switch was all the director needed. This involved Amit hiding out of frame while Harsimran roughed up some thugs or fell down the stairs, and then appearing in shot when the action was done and it was time to *act*. But, as the plot progressed and the action intensified, they seemed to cross over less and less. Instead of doing a Texas switch, the director opted for more camera lock-offs for the real action sections, where they'd shoot their parts of the same scene separately, the different footage brought together by the editor.

In Harsimran's killer scene, the Punisher drives a motorbike up a ramp and, suspended in mid-air, grapple-hooks on to a ledge of a ten-storey apartment block on fire. He crashes through the window of his love interest's bedroom and, grabbing her, runs through the opposite window. He takes the impact of the fall, protecting her, and she panics, thinking he's dead. She gives him the kiss of life – their first kiss – and he lives.

Harsimran was swapped out for Amit for the kiss. He took some lion's mane in the stunt trailer for the soreness. The detonators had failed to go off inside the exploding glass the first time he'd hit the tempered pane, and his head had bounced right off.

He wiped away the make-up that they'd used to cover the bruise and checked the script. One more scene.

In Harsimran's final appearance for *Punisher* – a post-credit scene that sets up a sequel – the character floats six feet up in the air, in lotus position, on fire. The rigging was simple enough, and when he'd first read the script he'd assumed the flames would be CGI. But the thing with fire, he was told, was that it was impossible to accurately replicate with CGI – 'It's the final frontier.' The point being, Harsimran found out, it was much more cost-effective to use real flames.

He put on three layers of fireproof underwear that an assistant soaked in flame-retardant Zel Jel. The assistant then helped him put on a rain suit and, on top of that, a fire suit, and finally a suit of thin cotton. He could hardly move. They applied another round of Zel Jel and then he had to get into the Punisher's costume, a kind of exoskeleton that was already heavy enough. He practised his breathing – he'd need to hold his breath for the duration of the burning, so as not to inhale any smoke – and got rigged up. As he was lifted up, he thought of that Indian woman in the news, who'd self-immolated when her husband, a farmer, had been killed in the Saraswati protests. She'd changed her mind as the flames raged, wanting out, but still died – still, somehow, inspiring a string of copycat suicides, people setting themselves alight across the country. One of them, Jasleen had told him, was a student who'd got some of the highest grades in his state, but he hadn't been able to get any work because an administrative error at his university meant he hadn't technically graduated. After the stunt, Harsimran gained a new appreciation for the depths of their despair.

When he burst into flames, everyone on set shouted a countdown for fifteen seconds – the longest amount of time that a human could be safely on fire (anything longer than that and the insurance became untenable) – and the numbers, which Harsimran just about registered, seemed to slow. His vision went watery and he felt faint. He was ambushed with fire extinguishers and lowered to the ground, needing the rest of the afternoon to feel any kind of return to normality. Amit waited with him in the trailer, trying to throw popcorn into his open mouth.

When the trailer for *Punisher* was released, Amit went viral.

If I speak, I'm in trouble.

Punish me, Daddy.

I'm just a hole.

His shirtless promotion photos were used on the covers of several magazines, and appeared in newspapers, too. For several days, he was trending on social media. He was filmed working with the Alpha Sculptor: 'The workouts were punishing.'

The film demolished box-office records for a non-musical. Harsimran's payment structure included no royalties. He brought Jasleen to the premiere, excited for her to meet Amit, but the red-carpet schedule was strict and they ended up sitting at different ends of the cinema.

'Oh, you know I don't like films,' Harsimran's mum said, when he and Jasleen went over for Saturday lunch.

'But it's your son—' Jasleen said.

Harsimran nudged her knee under the dining table.

'I'm happy you're doing well,' his mother said. 'It's just you always read about those actors. It doesn't seem like the best company to be in.'

'I'm thirty-three, Mum.'

'And still my son.'

Jasleen took the plates into the kitchen and started washing up. Harsimran wasn't sure what to say to his mum; she was getting even harder to talk to. He almost missed the way his father used to dominate conversations. Harsimran had always assumed it was his dad's talkativeness that silenced his mum, that she had a lot to say but wasn't given the space to speak. But, since his father's death, he'd come to realise that she was simply a person with little to add. Or she knew that, more often than not, her opinions would be contested. When Jasleen sat back down at the kitchen table, Harsimran's mum got up. She inspected one of the plates on the drying rack and turned the water back on to wash it again. Harsimran gave Jasleen the signal to breathe. She tapped the back of her wrist to say it was time to go.

'All right, Mum,' he said, getting up to leave.

'So soon?'

They stepped into the hall, which had turned into a kind of shrine to his father and grandfather. Their service medals were displayed next to photos of them in their uniforms. If she could have hung up their guns and badges, too, he was sure she would have.

'Do you wear one of those superhero suits?' his mum said, as they put their shoes on. 'With the underpants?'

Amit moved back to Mumbai to be closer to a new girlfriend, so they trained remotely for the sequel, *Punisher II: Discipline & Punish*. Harsimran received Amit's meal plan once a week, which had all macros measured to the gram, and his workout routine, with every set and rep laid out. Now that they were the same size and shape, their workouts were identical. The plan was to lift even heavier and stay in a surplus. Ordinarily this would have been music to Harsimran's ears, but Amit's meal plan was insane: half the ingredients he couldn't source at his local market, and, even if he could, he wouldn't have been able to afford them. He'd used up a large chunk of his relatively small payment from the first film in financing a hair regrowth programme, and the expense payments for the sequel wouldn't arrive for several months. But if Harsimran couldn't match Amit's physique, he was worthless. He put the programme on pause and ordered the moringa, cordyceps extracts and elk-antler velvet online.

When Amit returned for a weekend in Singapore, he invited Harsimran to a Halloween party. 'I thought it would be funny if we went as twins.'

Harsimran couldn't bring a plus-one, but Jasleen drove him to the party in Holland V before her evening shift at the hospital. Harsimran had looked at images of the mansion online – it had featured in several magazine shoots. He was very conscious that, without Amit, his costume didn't work, so he waited outside the house, walking up and down the road. They were supposed to arrive together, but Amit hadn't responded to his messages since yesterday. According to his Instagram Story, he was out somewhere else, at another party, and Harsimran decided to give up and walk home. Which was when the Benz drove by and his double stuck his head out the window.

'Brother, oh, brother!'

Harsimran wiped away the powder on Amit's moustache before they walked in. He followed Amit around, from Batman to the two girls from *The Shining* to a hot nun. The only time Amit introduced him by name was to Mario and Luigi, two producers, who were playing beer pong.

'Hey, I was thinking, wouldn't it be cool if we did a movie where me and Harsimran are cast as twins? Can't you just see that?'

Harsimran grinned, and tried to imitate Amit's accent: 'Let's do it!'

They drifted apart as the party went on and Harsimran finally met some relatively friendly people, Charlie Chaplin and Groucho Marx.

'Apparently, if the deal breaks down, we'll be shipping water in from other countries.'

Marx had brought up the water dispute between Singapore and Malaysia. All of Singapore's fresh water came from Malaysia, but Singapore owned the water-treatment facility that made it drinkable. Without Malaysia there was no water. Without Singapore there was no clean water. But the Malaysians were building their own treatment facilities, which meant the tap could be turned off, the whole city-state held at ransom.

'That's ridiculous.'

'Can you imagine how expensive that would be?'

'I don't see it happening.'

'You say that, but it's happening in Ethiopia. Any moment now, there'll be bombs. They have the faucet that controls the Nile. He who sits upstream wins.'

'Just like India.'

'Exactly.'

Harsimran's father had been particularly evangelical about what was happening in India. Even from his hospice bed, he'd update Harsimran and Jasleen about the Saraswati River.

'We're talking nuclear war,' he'd said, coughing. 'Nuclear war. The Indus Waters Treaty has been broken. That is an act of war.'

Harsimran was offering a less alarmist version of his father's view to Chaplin and Marx when Amit reappeared.

Chaplin agreed with Harsimran. He took off his hat, running his fingers through his hair as he spoke: 'I just don't understand how you can do that and not expect a reaction? They're saying the Indus might not reach the sea in a few years. Even without thinking of the international repercussions, the Saraswati is surely a drain on the national level—'

'I'll stop you right there, Asian Hitler,' Amit said. Chaplin quickly put his hat back on. 'I don't get riled up about much, but the way people talk about this really does get to me. I don't want to go all pandit pundit on you, but how is it a drain if unemployment is at an all-time low? It's providing farmland in places that haven't been farmed in hundreds of years, allowing the country to become more self-reliant, allowing a better spread of power across a wider range of the country. It's a new transport route which also reduces the flood risk every monsoon. You talk like it's some affront to nature, when it is nature itself. The water was already returning and running in the palaeochannels; all they're doing is bringing it to the surface, where it can be better used. It's a boost to GDP, a boost in terms of tourism. It's sparked regeneration. Hell, have you seen the cities being built? Have you seen what's happening at New Lothal? If this was happening in any other country in the world, it would be called an unparalleled feat of engineering, of technological prowess and good governance. But when it comes to us—'

Harsimran next saw Amit on set. After the unprecedented success of the first *Punisher* film, there were significant budget increases for the sequel. Most of the shooting would now take place in front of a blue screen, CGI doing much of Harsimran's work for him. The first half of shooting involved him jumping off things. But, in the second half of the film, Punisher is given a suit that allows him to fly. Rather than bothering with ropes, the director had Amit lie inside the suspended exoskeleton. All that was filmed was his face; everything else was arranged in post.

Their next joint role was playing a Hindu prisoner of war during the Mughal invasion. It was arguably an even bigger film – Arushi was set to feature on the soundtrack. To prepare for the role, Harsimran trained in sword combat; Amit's character organised a revolt, broke out of prison and killed dozens of Muslims, fighting every rank of the enemy until he reached the palace to save his sister from her forced marriage and conversion. It seemed a little questionable, plot-wise, Harsimran thought, but if that was indeed how the history had been, he reasoned, that was how the film would have to be. It was best he used his time going through his actions, rather than bothering about the dialogue.

At the wrap party, there was some gossip about *Bund*, the film that had rented the lot before Harsimran started *Punisher*. It turned out that the famine it depicted wasn't a historical one – the film took place in the present. The certification board had previously believed it to be set during the time of the British Raj, and seeing the modern-day setting had refused to certify it for release. The director was trying to stir up rage about this online, but people in the comments were laughing it off. 'If your movie isn't good enough to get into cinemas, how can you blame the government? It makes no sense. It's an *independent* body.'

Bund showed around the world, but not in India. Harsimran followed its rise as it gathered some awards at the smaller festivals; when he landed back in Singapore, he took Jasleen to see it.

'That's the scene I walked in on,' he whispered, when he saw the cow.

'This is so depressing.'

Amit picked his next role because he'd started dating someone in LA. *Forefather*, a short film about a Neolithic hunter, would be shot over a week in California, and would make it easy for him to spend the summer with his new girlfriend. There was no real script, and no dialogue at all. Harsimran didn't understand what it was or who it was for, and Jasleen did some research. It was being funded by a company called Primal Supplements, which was run by a popular YouTuber called the

Caveman. The company was disrupting the nutrient market, providing all the necessary pills to thrive on the increasingly popular Caveman Diet. The CDC had warned against the diet and you only had to search for the Caveman on YouTube to find endless 'Caveman EXPOSED' videos claiming that he was obviously juiced up on 'roids and that his abs were surgical implants. But this was by the by, at least to Amit, who claimed to be thrilled at the room the script would give him to flex his non-verbal chops. He spoke at length to Harsimran on the flight from LAX to the Californian ranch (Amit's new girlfriend had given them the use of her family's private jet), and Harsimran nodded along, practising his own non-verbal acting skills.

'It's about reflecting that interiority, right, a man who has access to no language, no language at all, conveying that humanity in what might otherwise be simply an animal ...'

Harsimran was trying not to think about food. The Caveman had imposed a two-day fast on them, which felt especially cruel considering what was available on the jet. If Harsimran had ever imagined himself on a private plane, it would have been sipping Dom Pérignon, not Primal Electrolytes.

'... It's not about cracking the US, or any of that. It's about finding scripts that feel new, you know? That have some stretch in them ...'

Perhaps Amit had broken the no-alcohol-and-drugs rule that had been part of the Caveman's paperwork. Not that he'd been taking his normal bathroom breaks. As Harsimran nodded, making the right sounds, he imagined questioning his friend: if the movie had no dialogue, and if stunt work was the majority of the script (wrestling a gazelle, catching a fish with a hand spear, punching a bear), then surely there was no need for Amit? He was a glorified face model. Harsimran flicked through the script, opening it on a scene in which he wrangled a wild horse. He was glad that he had triple-checked with the producers that there was no budget for live animals – 'The

soy-boy cucks would have our throats, those PETA betas' –
but still, to fall off even a CGI stallion at full gallop involved a
little more than reflecting a man's 'inner humanity'. Hard work
paid less.

When they landed, they were met by the Caveman himself,
shirtless, and his camerawoman, who had forgotten to press
record when Amit and Harsimran disembarked. They were
asked if they could go back inside and come down again. They
returned and re-emerged.

'It's gonna be a long weekend,' Amit said, as the Caveman
ran towards them.

'Brother,' the Caveman said, resting his forehead against Amit's.

'Brother,' he said, doing the same to Harsimran. The
Caveman's forehead left a patch of sweat on Harsimran's – he'd
already done his first Spartan workout of the day before they
landed, and he didn't believe in showering, for the damage it
did to the skin's natural microbiome.

When he'd first heard about the gig, Harsimran had
expressed his concerns to his wife.

'Why does he want an Indian as the Forefather and not a
gorah?'

Jasleen had found out that India was the world's largest and
fastest-growing market for Primal Supplements.

'He's appealing to his base,' Jasleen said. 'It's men like you
that like men like him.'

'Well, I'll never eat testicles,' Harsimran said, as they cued
up another Caveman video.

He'd spoken too soon.

When the four-by-four pulled in at the ranch, the food that
Harsimran had longed for on the plane was waiting for them
in the expansive lobby.

'Liver, kidney, testicles, penis,' the Caveman said. 'We do
top-to-tail here. Prime cuts. There's nothing better for breaking a fast.'

'Testicles of what?' Amit said. 'I don't eat beef.'

The Cavewoman let Amit know which cuts he could eat.

'Down the hatch!' the Caveman said, picking up a bite.

Amit ate a liver. It was true, he was a great actor. Not even his inner humanity was visible on his face.

Harsimran started with the bull testicle, figuring it was best to get it out of the way first.

'Fuck yeah, brother!'

When all the meat had been swallowed, they took a tour of the ranch. Everything was pre-industrial, save for one room where the laptops and phones were stored. They were connected to the internet via ethernet cables, to avoid Wi-Fi radiation, which the Caveman believed sapped the sperm count. 'If I had wireless, I wouldn't have my four cubs,' he said.

The only other things made after the 1800s were gym equipment, two bright blue jet skis out on the lake, and the guns. They would sleep on roll mats on a hardwood floor – mattresses were for pussies. There was no toothpaste.

Instead of freshening up with a shower – there really wasn't one – they went round the back to the plunge pool for an ice bath. The Caveman, already wearing nothing but trunks, entered the water. Amit yelped when he got in. Harsimran was proud of his own silence.

They dried off in the sun on the way to the simulated hunt and went through different primal movements – crab, ape, bear. At first, Harsimran felt a little ridiculous, but it really did get the blood flowing. There was no time to catch their breath, though – as soon as they were done crawling, the Caveman gave them weighted vests and ankle weights. Holding kettlebells in either hand and pulling weighted sleds tied to their waists, they walked towards their imaginary enemy, their invisible prey, grunting.

When Amit didn't turn up at breakfast, Harsimran thought the Caveman diet had given him stomach trouble. Or that he'd gone somewhere to have a line without being seen. They waited, and the Caveman used the time to go through some of the fight scenes with Harsimran, ensuring that Harsimran knew what he meant when he said 'Neolithic physicality'. Taking five for a quick fix of Primal Supplements, the Caveman left and Harsimran called Amit.

'I'm out, bro,' Amit said.

'You left?'

'It's a madhouse. The money doesn't matter.'

'What about me?'

'I just needed to breathe, man. It's not my scene.'

'You took the jet?'

The Caveman took only three days to release the videos about Amit.

'It's lactose-intolerant pronoun cucks like Amit Das, with man-titties pumped full of tofu oestrogen, that are exactly what's wrong with our society. Men used to be men. Hollywood was John Wayne. Now, it's Jon Whine. I wanted a He-Man and got a fucking He/Himbo.'

In those three days, Harsimran had tried to call Amit six times. The producers had offered Harsimran the role. Everything was in place for shooting to begin and to call in another actor now was impossible.

'The show must go on!'

Jasleen agreed that he'd be crazy not to take the opportunity; the rent was going to increase that autumn and this role paid more than all his stunt jobs combined. Harsimran signed the contract.

It was only when he returned to Changi that he and Jasleen figured out what was going on with Amit.

He had joined an ashram in Kashmir.

*

The ashram, officially the University of Spiritual & Universal Studies, was run by the Laal Guru Foundation. It was located on the grounds of Sharada Peeth, 'the oldest university in the world', near the Kashmiri Line of Control. Laal Guru wanted to reconnect the place of ancient learning with its roots as a temple dedicated to the goddess Saraswati.

Amit wasn't the first celebrity who'd visited USUS, and so Harsimran and Jasleen could read about it on tabloid sites. Students were given a strict rota of study: scripture, yoga, Ayurveda. Cut off from the outside world, they would be able to re-centre themselves. In keeping with Sharada Peeth's history as a place to worship the goddess Saraswati, music and poetry were performed each evening. There were no phones, no meat, no alcohol, no drugs.

'It doesn't sound like Amit,' Harsimran said.

'Does this mean you now need to do yoga twice a day to stay in the same shape as him?' Jasleen said. 'It just sounds like a fancy way to say "rehab".'

'He doesn't need rehab.'

'Well, if he's not working, what happens to you?'

There was no signal in the free-weights room, so Harsimran began to train cardio. He couldn't miss the call from his agent, whenever it came. He spent most of his time on the stair machine, his heart rate quickening when he heard his ring-tone, but often it was someone else's iPhone, or else Jasleen calling on her break at the hospital.

'Done any looking?' she asked.

'Done looking,' he said.

'I'm sure they'd take you back at the water park.'

The days were long and empty. Sitting in bed, Harsimran opened incognito mode on his browser and searched for

Forefather, to watch it again. He scrolled down as it played and read the comments. All these people – real people – loved his performance, but there'd been nothing but silence from his agent.

He heard the front door and quickly muted the film, closing the tab as Jasleen came in. She took off her scrubs and lay down next to him. Without saying a word, her eyes shut.

'Tough day?'

'Did you find anything?'

'I'll tell you if I do.'

'I can't have a husband who does nothing. The bills, the water—'

'Can you at least say hello first? You're sounding like my mother.'

It wasn't just water that was getting more expensive.

In the Red Sea, an oil tanker that had been dead for decades had finally sunk. It had been used by the Yemeni government as an off-shore store for oil. But, since it had fallen under rebel control, the maintenance fund had been cut. The steel hull began to erode and water seeped in. Four hundred thousand deadweight tons of ship sinking into one of the world's busiest shipping lanes was one thing, and two million barrels' worth of oil spill was another, but the situation had been compounded by the fact that the rebels had surrounded the tanker with mines to protect it from thieves. The men who had laid the secret mines had all been killed since, and no one knew exactly where the explosives were. The oil spread, reaching Hodeidah Port, where all Yemeni aid arrived, stopping all traffic coming in and out of the Red Sea. Which was about 10 per cent of world trade. Stocks were falling around the globe and the price of oil was soaring. 'We saw it coming,' one analyst said. 'We were watching it happening and we knew what it would mean, and now it's happened.'

The price of a bus ticket had gone up, so Harsimran walked to Wild Wild Wet, the water park where he had been working before meeting Amit. He stopped before he made the turning towards Pasir Ris, seeing the sign for Coney Island. He thought of Jasleen. On one of their early dates, he'd taken her there to search for the Coney Island Cow.

'I can't believe you've never seen it,' he'd said as they crossed the bridge that he decided to cross now.

The Coney Island Cow was the only cow in Singapore. There was no space to raise livestock in the country, and, even after all these years, the origins of the bull remained a mystery. At some point the animal had wandered on to the island and stayed there, wild and untamed.

His father had taken him to see the cow when Harsimran was a child. There was a gentleness about his father that day; he'd packed sandwiches and cookies for the beach. They walked the length of the small island more than once without finding the bull. It was getting dark. 'Perhaps he's at the vet's,' his father had said. He used the time for a 'teaching moment', telling Harsimran how, in the Sikh Empire, cow slaughter was punishable by death. 'And it was us Namdharis who were the ones who upheld that. You see in the news sometimes,' his father had said, 'these Hindus attacking Muslims in India for killing cows. Taking the law into their own hands. But it was *us* who started that, it was Ram Singh Ji.' Fed up with cow slaughter, the Namdhari faction of Sikhs turned violent, killing Muslim butchers in Amritsar and Ludhiana in the 1870s. 'The Brits were so scared of *us*, they executed the Namdharis with cannons. It was Ram Singh who invented boycotting, he who started non-cooperation, who would fight for the rights of animals.'

'So, you wouldn't have arrested him?'

They both stopped. Standing a few metres away was the Coney Island Cow. He was larger than Harsimran had imagined, and didn't moo. The signs had said not to approach him or to take photographs of him, and they just stood still, transfixed as the bull calmly returned their gaze.

The same signs were still up when he'd taken Jasleen to the island on their date. They spotted the bull early on during their walk. He held Jasleen's hand, and she leant on his shoulder. The bull ate grass, uninterested in them.

'Do you eat beef?' Jasleen asked.

Harsimran had given up on the Namdhari vegetarian diet he'd been raised on for the sake of gains, and once he'd tried chicken, eating pork or lamb didn't seem like a big deal, and, after that, why not beef?

Jasleen ate everything and anything, which was a relief – he'd packed chicken sandwiches. She told him about an American academic who'd written about how the Hindus of Rigvedic times used to eat beef. Apparently, activists had gone through the monograph's acknowledgements section and found the names and addresses of any Indians the American had thanked. 'They turned up at their houses!'

'Should we find the beach?'

They sat on the sand, facing the Johor Strait. Pulau Ubin was in front of them, Malaysia to the left. Harsimran thought about mentioning his memory of the beach, coming here with his father as a child, the cookies and their drawings in the sand. But he didn't want to look soft.

'I can do a handstand,' he said, instead.

When they got married, a few years later, the news broke that the Coney Island Cow had died.

'It's actually made me sad,' Jasleen said.

'It's just a cow,' he said. 'We had McDonald's yesterday!'

'But it's part of our story,' she said.

'Do you think they'll bring in another one?'

'That's where it all started for me.'

'Or they could switch it up. Coney Island Chicken. The Pulau Pig ...'

'Stop,' she said, smiling.

265

Now, as he crossed over the bridge for the third time in his life, the park was empty. He walked through the woods to the beach.

When he and Jasleen had travelled to India to visit her family's palatial mansion in Punjab, he'd met their prized murrah buffalo, Kismat. Her uncle boasted that the bull produced the most sought-after liquid in Punjab. Because of its impressive size, the bull's seed had become something of a sensation, with prices rising to thousands of rupees per frozen batch. 'You want to see?'

Jasleen had been busy with her old aunts, and Harsimran felt he had no option other than to follow her uncle to the business end of the operation. They pulled Kismat along and, with what might have been Pavlovian anticipation, the animal sped up, growing agitated.

'See, buffalo doesn't count as beef. So we can export it at good prices. His female offspring? They make twenty litres of milk a day.'

In a large barn stood the teaser cow and an apparatus that Harsimran could best describe as a synthetic vagina, a receptacle into which the extracted product would be shot. Music played from a Bluetooth speaker: Lata Mangeshkar, Asha Bhosle, Arushi. It was relatively straightforward getting the bull involved with the teaser; what was tricky was moving him towards the apparatus, and doing so with the right timing. The horrorshow that ensued had paid for the house and the land, had paid for Jasleen's study at nursing school, had allowed her to launch her life in Singapore. The two of them owed their relationship to the apparatus, to the brave farmhands.

He had to be better for Jasleen, he knew that. He sat and watched the barges move up and down the strait. He would work again at the water park and provide a stable income until his stunt work picked up. Sometimes you have to step back to step forward, he reasoned. Life was like salsa.

He was crossing back over the bridge when his agent called.

Her timing was impeccable. He took a deep breath before answering. She had an update about Amit.

'He's taking a break from film. He's going to do Chekhov.'

'Chekhov?'

'Theatre.'

'*Theatre?* Is he OK?'

'In any case, I'm not calling about him. I have a rather exciting proposition for *you*. I think you'll be perfect. It's a slightly strange one. But you've got an angle: famous actor's double. That's a hook. You're in great shape. They want some diaspora rep, for global appeal. I'll email you the details?'

Ever wondered how your ancient ancestors lived? Find out now in *The Old Way*, streaming soon.

More and more, our youth are sleepwalking into an easy life, looking down at their phones, with little appreciation for where they are from or who brought them here. The truth is, our lives are built on the backs of those before us and those before them. And now, with unrivalled scientific research, we are able to understand the lives and hardships of our original ancestors, those of the Saraswati Civilisation! But could you live life like a Saraswatian? Find out in *The Old Way*.

Ten contestants, with access to only the tools and amenities that their ancestors would have had thousands of years ago, will spend the summer bonding in the face of adversity and competing to prove which among them is most in touch with their roots. Applications are now open.

Harsimran was the final contestant to arrive at the cast meet. Shooting took place in the Punjabi countryside, near the Kali Bein River. The cast and crew were gathered in a large tent. They were introduced to each other, and while Harsimran would have considered himself to be the least famous person on the show, he wasn't exactly a million miles away. They weren't out-and-out celebs: a yoga-content creator, a soap actor, a retired politician, an athlete who'd won bronze at the Olympics, an Instagram priest, a hockey player, a cricketer, a glamour model and Arushi's vocal coach.

'Does she still need a coach?' Harsimran asked, as he was being miked up.

'Does Arsh, here, have to practise cricket?'

The tech guy finished with Harsimran's set-up. 'To remind you, anything you say now has the potential to end up in the final cut.'

After they handed in their phones, the cast were told to pack suitcases with everything they'd want to take on an exotic holiday. One of the producers checked Harsimran's bag and then radioed a colleague.

'What's wrong?' Harsimran said.

The producer's colleague came armed with more clothes to stuff in, as well as a large bag of protein powder and a laptop. He paused and then started unbuttoning Harsimran's shirt.

'Excuse me?' Harsimran said.

'The vest,' he said. 'It will look better.'

'Right, we're running behind schedule,' the producer said, ushering Harsimran towards one of the trucks.

They were filmed being driven through the green landscape, and were given prompts with which to talk to each other. When they arrived at the site, a model village of simple huts, they met the show's hosts, a former Miss India and a musical-talent-show presenter. Their reactions were filmed.

'You're at a six. Give us a ten. Eleven!'

Their reactions were filmed again.

They were instructed to open up their suitcases and then ridiculed for packing so much. 'Protein powder, bro?' the male host said. 'You think they had this, all those years ago? Your muscle gain will have to be natural, now! And so many clothes?' He turned to the cameraman. 'This kind of over-consumption would not have existed. It is time to go "back to basics".'

They were given simple hemp clothing, approximations of Saraswatian style, which were based, as the show's hosts were keen to emphasise, on real-world archaeological evidence and scientific research. 'Everything is from reality,' Miss India said. 'We are drawing on the way things have always been.'

They were encouraged to save meaningful conversations for when the cameras were rolling. Because of this, it was three days before Harsimran realised he hadn't told anyone he had a wife, and, when the time came, it seemed like that moment had passed. He continued to laugh and chat with the fellow contestants and, judging by how much the roving cameras seemed to gravitate towards him, sensed that things were going well.

They learnt to capture rainwater and divert it in irrigation canals, to build clay pots and to pave roads with stones. They cooked ancient vegetarian food, largely grains, and went out into the forests to pick berries, learning which plants were poisonous. Since the Saraswati script had been cracked, it had become 'clear that the ancients practised Ayurveda', and one challenge involved Harsimran and his opponents creating different Ayurvedic remedies. They had to solve clues written in the Saraswati script, to climb trees, to fashion children's toys. Whenever you won a challenge, you were given a replica Saraswatian seal. Within a week, Harsimran had three: a donkey, a lion and an elephant.

Harsimran saved the yoga YouTuber from falling from a floating pontoon bridge they were creating and was encouraged by the producers to spend more time with her. He did as he was told and found himself in the line of the roving cameras more often. He wasn't proud of the thoughts he had. He was conscious, at all times, of being watched. Conscious of Jasleen. He just needed to focus on the prize money.

He won the well-digging challenge, in which he used the

type of spade the ancients would have owned, lining the pit he dug with broken branches so that it wouldn't cave in as he progressed, inch by inch, towards imaginary water (the producers tipped a bucket of water in when they deemed he'd gone far enough). The challenge wiped out another wave of the contestants, and for the first time, Harsimran felt like he might just win. He climbed the rope ladder up to the cameras.

They learnt how to speak certain Saraswatian phrases at pre-Vedic ceremonies. They dug holes and wiped with leaves. Fashioned rafts and simple boats, carved oars. Traded goods, used weights and counters to perform complex maths. They set fires, cleaned their teeth with burnt bread. Planted vegetables, milked cows, made yoghurt. After three and a half weeks, Harsimran, the cricket player and the yoga influencer were the only contestants remaining. When the cameras were off, they removed their microphone packs. The cricket player asked if there was any good gossip about Amit.

'I wish I had something to say,' Harsimran said. 'But, with him, what you see is what you get.'

'But I heard he had problems with drugs, no? There was something about a wild night in Vegas. Those dynasty kids are all the same.'

The final challenge, they were told, wasn't a physical test, but a mental one. Apparently, it was a practice of Saraswatian mystics to leave their settlements for days at a time to meditate. They'd retreat from society and camp on the banks of the river.

Though ideally the challenge would have taken place next to the Saraswati River, the stretches of the route which had filled now with seasonal rainfall couldn't be cleared for filming, so they stuck with the Kali Bein. But, because the show would be released in time for the planned 'opening' of the new river, Harsimran was told to refer to the river as the Saraswati. They would splice in establishing shots of the real Saraswati and no one would know the difference.

The yoga teacher told Harsimran that it used to be toxic, the stream, until Eco Baba had restored it, gathering hundreds of volunteers to remove silt and hyacinth from the water, and building sewers to divert waste.

'It's a holy river all the same,' she said.

He'd never heard of it. Apparently, Guru Nanak had disappeared from his disciples to meditate on its banks and, bathing in the water, came to the realisation that there was only one God. It seemed that, to understand the world and have some kind of epiphany, you had to get out to its periphery. Perhaps that was why Amit had gone to the meditation retreat.

The three of them said their goodbyes and were dropped off at distant sections of the riverbank.

'Just don't drink from the river. We'll drop off bottles whenever we see you're anywhere near running out. If you want to tap out, you just have to say it twice to one of the cameras and we'll pick you up. Last one standing wins.'

Harsimran worked out, the first morning. He stripped to his shorts and did pull-ups on a tree branch, supersetted with push-ups and pistol squats on the muddy ground. A sound he mistook for a dragonfly turned out to be a drone. He made eye contact with a future viewer and smiled. He finished with burpees and dived into the river to swim. Perhaps the skills from the cadet corps and national service were finally going to come in useful, after all.

When Harsimran joined the National Police Cadet Corps at thirteen, his grandfather told him the family story. Their oldest known ancestor was a man called Jhelum, who was drafted by the British to fight in the First World War. Before that, he

271

had worked in the Punjab Irregular Force as a specialist fighter in the North-West Frontier. There, he fought tribal Afghan rebels under the command of General Blood. A loyal servant, he eagerly travelled from India to the Suez Canal to fight the Ottomans when he was called up, and then moved north, to Gaza. The family legend had it that he and his captain had been marooned alone in a trench for two days, waiting for backup. The close bond they developed there was the reason that, when the war was over and the captain was sent to Singapore, he asked Jhelum to come along with him and serve as his private bodyguard. There was a photo somewhere at Harsimran's mum's house, of the old Sikh man, standing sentry at the gates of the grand mansion. His son had been a guard, too, and his grandson a police officer. Of the daughters and wives, Harsimran learnt nothing. The family legend meant a lot to his father; he would carry his inherited patch of red fabric that had passed through the hands of countless generations in the breast pocket of his uniform.

Harsimran made a small boat out of twigs and leaves, and let it go in the slow current, wondering if it would come into his opponents' view downstream, or were they upstream? He went searching for berries. He made some dough and baked it over a fire that took him an hour to build. He ate his bread. Washed himself, careful not to take in any water. When night fell and the embers died, he briefly considered masturbating, but reckoned the producers would have night vision installed. He thought of Jasleen. He thought of Miss India, and then the yoga teacher.

He attempted to imagine what life would have been like for someone living by this river, thousands of years ago. He could see them working, eating, having sex, fighting, but what did they think about? There was little to do but think, but nothing for one's thoughts to bounce off. No wonder they started having visions of gods.

He climbed a tree and jumped into the water, spinning twice in the air like the Brute and causing a huge splash. Water entered his mouth, his nose. He smiled at the cameras, hoping the stunt would get him some added screen time. He lay out to dry and woke in the dark. It felt like much of the day was passing out of focus – like, when reading a book, you find yourself going several pages without taking any of the words in, your eyes glancing off the shapes, lost in a kind of accidental meditation until something catches you out, a sound, an odd word, and you realise that, if you were asked to talk about what you had read, you would have no idea what to say, flicking back a few pages to start again, or ignoring them and forging on, or perhaps closing the book and moving on to something else, the phone vibrating in your pocket, the phantom vibration that Harsimran kept feeling, where his right trouser pocket would have been, where his phone should have been, wherever it was, locked in some box in the producer's mobile office. He missed Jasleen, missed Amit. How rare it was to make a friend as an adult! It was day, it was night, all slippery; everything that flowed, time, water, it was all passing through his fingers. He stripped down and got in the water and thought of the contestants downstream. He thought of the woman in the water. He thought of her perfect body in the river.

He made another fire. Burned the bread. Slept, didn't sleep. There were berries in the woods. He found a mushroom, but, when he poked it, a green gas spurted out. 'Spores,' he said, 'sponge, spork.'

He started carving a pattern into a tree trunk with his knife and lost steam. It dawned on him that perhaps the producers, the crew and the other contestants had left, that he was still here, alone, continuing a challenge that no longer existed, like that Japanese soldier they mentioned in national service. He stepped into the river; he drank the water, peed.

He vomited. Using his hands, he dug up dirt to bury the sick.

'Don't film me! Privacy, lah!'

He was swimming the next time he vomited, and felt bad for the others downstream, if they were still there. The drone hovered above, its alien light blinking.

'Can you see me?' he said. 'Can you really see me?'

In the final cut of the show that aired over a year later, which I binged in three days, Harsimran had been completely edited out.

There was no mention at all of his ever being involved in the show, but, if you knew to look, you could spot a few brief instances where the ghost of Harsimran was present. A slice of his shoulder in frame, his voice shouting 'Go on!' in one of the group exercises, a third water bottle in the last episode, with his name on it. His twelve-day stint by the river, in which he had outlasted the cricketer, would only be known to the cast, crew and those close to him.

The yoga teacher won the show, and used the prize money to set up her own yoga institute, having undergone a spiritual transformation by the water. She was proof that the way of the ancients could help others, especially the manic youth, achieve inner peace.

Before the decision to wipe Harsimran from *The Old Way* was made, one teaser trailer of the show had been released, in which he figured prominently. Once he'd recovered from his stomach bug at a local hospital, he was sent to join the others to film it. A partnership had been agreed between the show and the new theme park: Saraswati Land. The whole cast of the show were driven together on a coach, which was held up for several minutes, a mile outside the park's entrance, as a stray heifer had decided to stop in the middle of the road. It had walked out of the local cow sanctuary and backed up traffic until the next turning.

Saraswati Land was a replica Saraswati Civilisation settlement on the banks of the new river. From his vantage in the coach, Harsimran could see stagnant pools of water in the riverbed. Before they reached the theme park, they were brought to a stop again. Men without uniforms had blockaded the road and were talking to the television crew in the truck in front. One of the producers got out and was followed round to the back of the truck. He opened the doors and the men quickly checked inside, before clearing them to move on.

'Beef exports,' the cricketer explained. Cow vigilantes had set up checkpoints on the main roads. 'Why pay tax when the country governs itself?'

The cast were shot doing a tour of the park.

'Children don't respond or relate to ruins,' their guide said. 'You only have to look at Pompeii, a marvel of the ancient world which is utterly boring. Our mission is to enliven the old world for future generations. To let them know their origins.'

They entered through a stone archway and walked up a street paved with large, uneven slabs. Small houses lined the streets, with verandas that would have been used by merchants as shopfronts.

'You've heard, I'm sure, about the super sewer that will run below parts of the Saraswati? That's ancient knowledge. Note, here, the gutters on each side of the street. Here, rainwater is led towards the irrigation systems. That large expanse near the car park? That's a replica reservoir; it'll be filled in soon. Our forefathers were experts at manipulating water, with truly the most efficient irrigation and sewage systems in the entire ancient world. Here, there is little rainfall, and it fluctuates greatly depending on the season. But their ingenious systems allowed them to store water when there was too much rain, preventing floods, and to use water when there wasn't enough rain, avoiding droughts. They saw the chaos of nature and created order, took control.'

Harsimran zoned out, kicking a pebble down the paved road. They stopped outside the bathhouse, which was an impressively large structure. Bathing, the guide said, was thought to be a key ritual, with social and religious significance.

The cast were asked to bathe, and stripped down to their swimming costumes. Harsimran chatted to the cricketer, who told him about his new deal as brand ambassador for an Ayurvedic laxative.

'It's a pill, but the ingredients are all traditional. From what I've heard, you could have used it the other week!'

'It was the water,' Harsimran said. 'So, they pay well?'

The cricketer winked.

Perhaps a similar deal might come Harsimran's way. He'd be the face of anything for the right price.

Once they'd dried off, they were shot marvelling at the translations of replica inscriptions, and then they split up to deliver their lines.

'Give me wonder,' the camerawoman said.

'Saraswati Land,' Harsimran said. 'Where the ancient and the future combine. Catch me in *The Old Way*, streaming now, for more.'

'Could we try that again, but brighter?'

The shooting coincided with Saraswati Land's launch party, which was being held at the bathhouse, hosted by the butter mogul who'd funded the park. The cast were all invited.

'Apparently, there will be A-listers,' the vocal coach said, as they walked up the paved street towards the party. '*A-list* A-list.'

'Isn't that us, now?' the yoga teacher said, to no reply. It had been remarked upon in the coach that winning might have gone to her head.

The bathhouse was filled with light. Politicians circulated in the room as quickly as the waiters with the canapés. Everyone that Harsimran talked to – a lobbyist, a culture reporter, the secretary to a local politician – looked past him as he spoke, scanning the room for people 'they really did have to say hello to'. They'd apologise and walk on, and Harsimran would reach out for another flute of champagne, searching for another friendly face. Which was when he saw him. Leaning against what some historians contested was an altar, dressed, not in black tie like everyone else, but in a simple kurta pyjama.

Amit.

Harsimran felt his pulse in his gums. He looked away, took another pakora – he needed to regain his lost mass – and then turned back to the altar, allowing his eyes to pass over Amit once more. He looked lean. He was talking, and a large circle of people were listening, and then – as one – laughing. Harsimran could hear them over the general din.

Harsimran headed to the luxury Portaloos that had been set up outside, and buried his washed face in a lavender-scented towel. When he opened the door, Amit was there. Of course he was.

'Bro!'

'Amit?'

'Bloody hell – now, how long has it been?'

'Not since America—'

'Do you mind if I ... ? I really need to go.'

Harsimran stood by the sinks while Amit peed.

'So, I hear you've undergone a transformation,' Harsimran said.

'You could say that.'

'You seem born again.'

'I went from Vegas to the Vedas,' Amit said, finishing up. He checked the stalls were empty and then shut the front door.

'Well, it was a bit of a ruse, if I'm honest. I had this very big project coming up and was advised it would be good to clean up my image.'

'What role?'

'The creator.' He laughed. 'Brahma.'

Amit took two bottles of champagne from one of the servers and they walked on through the park.

'I thought you were doing theatre?' Harsimran asked.

'Yeah, I was restless. I had to pull out of the action-movie stuff. But I was just fucking around with theatre. That's all anyone in theatre is ever doing. Me playing Caliban is basically you being the Brute. Theatre isn't acting. It's all pantomime.'

There was a relief in knowing that he was still the same person. They popped both bottles open, and Harsimran felt he had to keep pace with his old friend.

'Quite the bouquet on this one,' Amit said, taking another swig straight from the bottle. 'If the ashram had blanc de blancs, I'd probably go back, you know. But, yes, they're doing a big biopic about Saraswati. There's already talk about a Tridevi trilogy. They had Kishan Dhayal pegged for Brahma, but then there was that whole thing with the underage sugar baby. Which only surfaced after they'd already filmed his parts.'

'They reshot?'

'What they did was have me act out the scenes solo. A capella. And they're going to edit my face on to his body, so it all fits with the scene. Shame, really, not to be acting opposite Arushi. I mean – *God!*'

'They stuck your head on his body?'

'Clever, right? Didn't have to work out!'

'I can tell.'

'Easiest money I ever made. The scale is totally different, they want it international.'

'And you're here because ... ?'

'Didn't read my contract properly; they'd baked in all this political bakwas. Mindy told me about your little reality-show thing – maybe we should toast with something stronger?'

They hid inside one of the market stalls for over an hour.

'You know, I heard that Yankee Neanderthal's been done for tax fraud. I can't believe you actually did that film.'

'I needed the money, bro.'

'You never *need* money. People *want* money. People *need* water, shelter.'

'And how do you think they're going to get water or shelter?'

'Maybe we should go to my hotel. They've got a great bar.'

They stumbled towards the car park. Amit couldn't find his chauffeur, but he could find his Bentley.

'It's only a short drive,' Amit said. 'I clear right up, when it's time.'

'I don't think—'

'I can do my own stunts!'

It took Amit a few moments to figure out how to turn the engine on, and then they were off. He was a surprisingly competent drunk driver.

'Thing with me is I sober right up. When it's time, I'm all clear. You know what I mean? And it'll go on auto once we hit the main road.'

'This is James Bond, this car.'

'There's no way of buying a car these days without looking new money. Even classic is gauche. And if you buy something cheap – like, ordinary – you look like a Silicon Valley prick.'

'Are the seats heated?'

'It's like having a giant fucking TV. The real rich don't have big TVs. Shit ain't chic.'

'Why would you get heated seats in India?'

They sped through the new housing development near the theme park.

'Plus, no average viewer should have that kind of definition – they can see everything, man. People posting photos of my make-up from *Punisher*.'

'You can't even hear the engine, it's—'

Turning a corner fast, the Bentley hit a stray bull, who'd stepped out into the road from the cow sanctuary.

The bull bounced up on to the windscreen and crashed clean through the glass, his horns making the first contact. Amit's head was thrown forward by the impact, his airbag quickly pierced by the bull. His forehead landed on the steering wheel, sounding the car horn.

The animal groaned. His eyes, clouded by rheumatism, bulged with confusion. Amit was unconscious. The horn was still blaring. Lights turned on in houses up and down the street, the glass sparkling. Shards covered everything. Harsimran grabbed Amit's hair and pulled him off the wheel to stop the noise. It wasn't clear whether he was breathing. Harsimran slapped him, and glass dust showered off him.

'Amit. Amit.'

He felt around for his friend's pulse. He could hear a door being opened. Voices, footsteps. Harsimran reached over Amit's body, pulled the lever and pushed the seat flat. He straddled Amit's waist and put his lips to his mouth, breathing into it. He pumped his chest, trying to kick-start his heart, and the cow's groans intensified behind him.

'Come on, penchoot, come on.'

Harsimran repeated the procedure again and, the third time, Amit came to.

The voices were closer. People were shouting.

Harsimran opened the door and got out, trying to pull the bull off the hood of the car. Its body was lighter than he'd expected, probably malnourished, and it landed with a sad thud on the tarmac. If it wasn't dead, it was dying.

'What are you doing?' someone shouted in Hindi. 'What have you done?'

There was no time to think.

Harsimran pushed Amit over to the passenger seat and got in the driver's side. The people were almost upon them, filming. They were shouting. They were running. Harsimran got the car going just as someone jumped on to the bonnet.

'Scum!' the man shouted, holding on as Harsimran reversed. 'Stop the car!'

He took a swipe at Amit through the hole in the windscreen. The punch brought Amit back into the present, and he tried to push the man off the bonnet, but the man grabbed on to the steering wheel, yanking it to the left. They almost crashed.

Harsimran punched his hand, bone on bone, and when the man wouldn't let go, decked him in the face. The hit was clean, but the man still held fast on the bonnet, managing to get his legs over the dashboard. He was about to climb into the car fully when Amit kicked his crotch. The man fell back on to the bonnet and Harsimran swerved, turning round, and then veered violently left and right until the man's body fell off to one side of the road. He checked the rear-view to see if he was moving, but got distracted by the sight of motorbikes. Wind rushed into the car as they accelerated.

'Seat belt.'

'They've got cricket bats.'

'Do we call the police? Will they know who you are?'

'Oh, man. Oh, fuck.'

Amit's hair was thrown back dramatically. Harsimran yanked off his bow tie and undid his top button.

'Where do we go? Where are we going? I don't know these streets.' Harsimran glanced back again and wished he hadn't.

'We're going to run out of road eventually.'

'They can't chase us forever.'

'We're better off hiding—'

Amit took out his phone to film the people chasing them

and then turned the camera towards Harsimran. Two men on one motorbike came speeding on to the road from a side street, drawing level with them. The motorcyclist pulled close to the car and the man sitting behind him lashed out with a hammer, hitting the roof of the vehicle. Harsimran retaliated, veering towards the right and knocking into the bike. As the bike lost control, the hammer flew through the air, coming in through Amit's passenger window and landing in the back seat. Amit reached back to grab it.

They sped towards a bridge, the headlights behind them getting fainter.

'Someone's looking out for us.'

'I wouldn't say that.'

A truck coming from the opposite direction pulled across in front of them, blocking the other end of the bridge. The words 'HORN OK PLEASE' were painted in orange, green and white on the back. A group of vigilantes scrambled out.

They were surrounded. There was no way forward and no way back. Harsimran stepped on the accelerator and then turned sharply to the left, breaking through the fencing on the side of the bridge and falling through the air, down into what he thought would be the river below. But there was hardly any water. It was the Saraswati construction site. The engine burst into flames under the crumpled bonnet. Harsimran couldn't move his head.

He heard Amit struggle with the car door. When it finally gave way, he ran around the car to open Harsimran's side. The men on the bridge were shouting. Feeling returned to Harsimran's legs and feet, in the form of pain. He coughed as Amit pulled him out and dragged him through the mud.

'Come on. Up, up!'

The shock wave of heat provided some clarity. As did Amit slapping him.

'We need to run,' he said, hammer in his hand.

Harsimran managed to get up. He staggered behind Amit,

his resolve returning. Despite the pain in his left ankle, he ran. There were no bearings in the dark, he couldn't have said if they were running up- or downstream. He heard the disquieting sound of a motorbike revving.

'We're sitting ducks.'

They climbed out of the riverbed, up on to one of the concrete banks. 'Wait a second,' Harsimran said, stopping to take off his shoes, which he was struggling to run in.

'Are you kidding me?'

'They're pinching.'

They ran on, quicker now that they were out of the mud. Surely the motorbike would struggle in the riverbed. If only there had been woods or hills behind which to hide. But the land here was flat and featureless. If the harvest hadn't just happened, there might have been fields of crops they could have hidden in. Suddenly, he felt the coolness of metal underneath one of his soles. He stopped and turned.

'Amit!'

It was some sort of service hatch, covered by a metal grate. Harsimran gripped the metal bars and pulled. He strained with all his strength. Amit crouched in front of him and pulled, too. The sound of engines intensified. They pulled and pulled, and Harsimran used the back of Amit's hammer to pry the fucker loose. They both fell back, and then climbed down the ladder into the hole.

Harsimran pulled the grate back into place on top of them. Descending felt like entering a well – Harsimran almost expected water at the bottom. The air got thicker as they stepped down each rung, the smell unbearable. Harsimran could taste it at the back of his mouth. Shit.

It was the new super sewer.

They watched the steady stream of waste flow by in the light of Amit's phone torch.

'Turn it off,' Harsimran whispered. He could hear voices. The vigilantes were arguing.

'I need to get out,' Amit said under his breath. 'I can't handle this.'

'Don't be stupid.'

'I'll actually throw up.'

They couldn't exit the way they'd come in. The vigilantes were within earshot.

'There should be other service hatches, right?' Amit said.

'Shh.'

Amit projectile-vomited into the sewer channel.

'Stop.'

'I can't—'

'Did you hear that?' someone said above.

Amit retched again.

A beam of light, likely from one of the motorbikes, hit the metal grate and split into ten perfect lines. The shadows broke as a person stepped towards the hatch.

Harsimran looked at Amit and put a finger to his lips. Amit heaved again, but caught it in his mouth, trying not to make a sound.

'Swallow,' Harsimran mouthed.

Torchlight shined down on them, casting prison bars across their faces as they looked up at the vigilantes looking down.

They ran.

Harsimran lagged behind Amit and looked back. No one had come down the ladder; maybe they were unable to shift the grate. Not looking where he was going, he stepped in something wet. Oh, how he regretted taking off his shoes.

It was several minutes until they reached the next service hatch. Harsimran's lungs burned. He attempted to catch his breath, which involved taking in more of the smell. Then came the footsteps.

The judge walked into the courtroom, and everybody rose.

When Amit was called up to make his statement to the

court, he muttered a prayer under his breath before delivering what Harsimran considered his greatest performance yet.

'It was all a horrible mistake. I shouldn't have agreed for Harsimran to drive me home. We had been drinking, yes – celebrating the launch of a brilliant initiative – and I couldn't find my driver. He was very persuasive and took the wheel, and I allowed him. That is a great regret.'

He didn't look in Harsimran's direction.

'I suppose I was a helpless passenger. And because we had been co-workers in another life, I trusted him. I will never know if he hit the cow on purpose. I'd like to believe it truly was an accident. But whatever his intentions, he hit the poor animal. The windscreen smashed. I was in utter shock. People approached, no doubt to help, but Harsimran, perhaps seeing the trouble he might be in, decided to run. He reversed the car and drove away. I was essentially a hostage. I couldn't leave, for those pursuing us would have assumed me guilty and may have attacked me. And I felt I couldn't stay either, for I was being made an accomplice in his heinous crime.'

Amit's lawyer, a bit of a celebrity herself, called up the video footage from Amit's phone, which placed Harsimran in the driver's seat. It was surreal, after so many months, for Harsimran to see his face up on the court TV, the fear in his eyes. Then she played clips that the vigilantes had filmed as they ran towards the car: Harsimran pulling the bull off the bonnet and getting into the driver's side.

Amit's lawyer made sure to mention the fact that Amit had never eaten beef in his life, that he'd taken time from his busy schedule to study at Laal Guru's Sharada Peeth retreat, and that, at the time of the incident, he had just finished filming a role in a movie about Ma Saraswati.

In contrast, she called up unreleased footage from *The Old Way*, in which Harsimran claimed the water, ostensibly from the Saraswati River, was poisonous. She brought out Harsimran's bulking diet plans as evidence for his long history of eating beef. And then she showed the jury the video from the Caveman's YouTube channel, in which Harsimran could be seen eating the testicles of a bull.

Because of his size, Harsimran wasn't bothered by the other inmates. Jasleen visited as often as she could, but then had to return to work. They spoke on the phone every day.

'Amit didn't win everything,' she said. 'They pulled him from that movie about the goddess. They're going to sub in another actor's face.'

Most of the prisoners Harsimran spoke to in his first months knew of Amit Das. One, who had a smartphone, kept Harsimran up to date about Amit, often against his will.

'He's in *Architectural Digest*,' he said. 'You can swim through his house. Look. In the Neelum Valley. The ground-floor rooms are connected by water.'

His mother flew out to visit him. When he'd first seen her during visiting hours, he was sure she would chastise him, like she had when she heard of the conviction. He was supposed to have been a police officer and now he was a prisoner. But something in his mother had softened.

'Jasleen has been taking good care of me,' she said.

'That's great.'

'Do they feed you OK? I asked about bringing food, but they wouldn't let me.'

'I eat well, Mum. I've put on weight, actually.'

'Yes. When we get you out, anything you want. We'll feast.'

'That'd be great.'

'Masaran di dal is still your favourite?'

'Always.'

'Your father used to hate lentils, you know. Upset his stomach. But I'd make it anyhow. You'd wipe the plate clean.'

Jasleen kept him up to date on the news. 'Wild Wild Wet closed down. There were all these photographs online. They shut off the water and it looked completely haunted.'

His mother mentioned the water blackouts, too. 'For a week, you could see houseplants lining the streets, by the bins. Everyone was giving them away.'

In the newspapers at the prison library, Harsimran pieced together a similar picture in Egypt. Rockets were being fired into Ethiopia. Conflict was increasing in the fertile crescent, too, as the Turkish, Syrian and Iraqi governments raced to pump the groundwater from the Tigris–Euphrates Basin. The more that fresh water was removed from the river system, the more salt water emerged, ruining crops in all three countries. Afghanistan and Iran were both attempting to divert the waters of the shared Helmand into their territories. New dams upstream on the Mekong threatened Myanmar, Laos, Thailand, Cambodia and Vietnam. There was an increased threat of clashes over the flow of the Imjin. When plans for a potential dam of the Indus in Tibet were discovered, Indra carried out a nuclear test on the salt flats of the Great Rann of Kutch. Another clash broke out in the Galwan Valley, over a tributary of the Indus, causing the deaths of thirteen Chinese soldiers and twenty-four Indian soldiers.

The idea of water scarcity being a problem in India seemed ridiculous to Harsimran. His ground-floor cell turned damp with every downpour. It had flooded every year for three monsoons, leaving him ankle-deep in water. For those few weeks, he'd be moved up a floor to a communal cell, doing his best to avoid eye contact with anyone.

The fourth time his cell flooded, a few months after Indra's crackdown on dissent, the water reached almost a metre high. The entire ground floor was ruined. The upper floors were already at capacity. There was no budget to arrange for the prisoners to be transferred to other facilities while the essential works took place, and, in any case, the other prisons didn't have space for them. Cases were reviewed. It was agreed that Harsimran would be released after four years. If he'd committed the crime twenty miles to the south, in a different state, he would have been stuck with a life sentence. But now he had his freedom.

He'd think back, over the years, to that water, his saviour, appearing seemingly from nowhere, as it does at a spring, and then rising. It came through the window, through the door. It came up out of the toilet. He waded through it, along with the others on the ground floor, all stopping, guards and prisoners alike, to glimpse the flash of colour as the scales of a fish glimmered beneath the hip-level murk, before struggling on towards the stairs.

POORAN BHAGAT
1896

The day before Ravi and Beas left, the family gathered by the well. It was hard to come to terms with the fact that two of their children were leaving not just Hakra, but the country, even if both Sejal and Jugaad had abandoned their own parents, all those years ago.

In Ravi, it wasn't just a son Jugaad was losing, but his strongest field hand. Now that the kids were old enough to take on much of the work on the farm, Jugaad had been earning extra money at the Hawthorn site. He dug, along with hundreds of other men, to try to flatten the valley for the eccentric Englishman. And, with Beas going to the Caribbean, who would help Sejal with the dairy, with the cooking? Little Chenab? How would his wife have time for her sewing? And, if they lost the income from all her dupattas, how would they afford the animal feed? The oil? Life would get a little tougher before it got better. But the world was larger now than it had been when Jugaad was growing up; who was he to stop them wanting to venture out into it?

'How about a story?' Jugaad said. 'For old time's sake.'

Putting the finishing touches to the large red blanket she'd been sewing, Sejal shook her head. 'I'm in no mood.' She was out of gold thread; the design only showed red on red.

'I'll tell it, don't you worry.'

'Dad's stories are always the strange ones,' Jhelum said.

'And this one is the strangest! Have I ever told you the tale of Pooran Bhagat?'

'Yes.'

'A thousand times,' Sutlej said.

'Then let it be a thousand and one,' Jugaad said, clapping his hands together. 'A long time ago, our hero, Pooran, the son of King Salwan and Queen Ichhran, was born under an auspicious star. The king's adviser, Gorakh Nath, told them to raise Pooran as a spiritual man. That meant being trained in spiritual ways for the first twelve years of his life. You kids think you have it hard – imagine nothing but study and prayer for twelve years!'

'Jugaad—'

'Well, the king agreed, and Pooran was sent off to be raised by Gorakh Nath and his disciples. And while his son was gone, the old king grew restless and took on another wife. He married his low-caste servant, Loona, a great beauty many years younger than he was!

'The twelve years passed quickly alongside his new wife, and soon enough his son Pooran returned to the royal palace, a very handsome young man. When Loona, the new wife, first set eyes upon him, she was overcome with ... She fell for him. But then he was introduced as the child of her husband ...

'Loona was driven crazy with desire. When she was with the king, she was thinking of the prince—'

'Jugaad—'

'She tried to sedu— to win over Pooran's heart, entering the prince's quarters. Pooran turned away from her advances. He would not waver from the righteous holy path. Especially with one of his father's wives!

'Feeling rejected, the beautiful Loona lashed out. She lied to the king, telling him that his son had made advances on *her*. Servants working that night had indeed seen her running through the halls, away from Pooran's quarters, and confirmed the story.

'Ignoring the pleas of Pooran's mother, the king summoned Pooran to his court. The young man was restrained and the king's trusted servant sharpened his axe ...

'First, the left hand. Chop!

'It dropped to the floor and blood spurted over the priceless upholstery.

'Next, the left foot. Chop!

'The right foot. Oop!

'And then, the right hand! And then ...'

'The willy!' Jhelum shouted out.

'Exactly! Pooran's dismembered body was dragged out of the court and down the great steps, leaving a trail of blood. He was pulled down the main road to the city's central well. The king followed, walking the red path. And it was the king himself who lifted up his son by his long hair and dropped him down into the dry well.'

Jugaad tossed a stone over his shoulder into their own well for dramatic effect. There was a moment's pause before the splash.

'The body landed with a thud. Everything was drying up in the kingdom. It had been weeks and weeks since the last rain. It was said some peasants attempted to lick the blood from the flagstones, such was their thirst.

'Gorakh Nath, the king's spiritual adviser, watched on in despair. He stayed by the well, long after the crowds eventually dispersed. His disciples, who had helped to raise Pooran, gathered around him.

'They hatched a plan to retrieve the body. Each night, the disciples would fetch water from the nearby sea and pour it into the well, along with extra salt. Slowly, bucketful by bucketful, the body rose to a height from which they could pull it out. Gorakh Nath had collected Pooran's hands and feet from the court, and he sewed them back to the rotting stumps of Pooran's dead body. Then, using his great spiritual powers, Gorakh Nath infused the body with magic.

'Pooran came back to life!

'He rejoined his religious brothers, and they wandered through the lands, begging for alms. He arrived in the city of Queen Sundaran. Like Loona before her, she fell for Pooran instantly.'

'She fell in love with a dead, rotting man?'

'Could you see where his hands had been sewn on?'

'And his—'

'No, no, for Gorakh Nath's magic was so powerful. Pooran was as beautiful as he'd ever been. And Queen Sundaran was so taken by him that she asked Gorakh Nath if Pooran could come to her palace to bless her ... privately. The holy men obeyed her wishes, and Pooran accompanied the queen.

'Sundaran led Pooran directly to her private chambers, where she attempted, like Loona had, to win him over. But Pooran wouldn't go along with it. Instead of spending the night in bed with the beautiful queen, he meditated. Madness!'

'Jugaad—'

'Word spread throughout the land about Pooran, the religious saint with great willpower, the man who lived beyond the material world. Stories about him reached King Salwan and his second wife, Loona. In the years since Pooran's death, Loona was overcome by guilt. She had been unable to give the king an heir, no matter the advice of the spirituals, no matter the diet. She called for this mysterious saint to be brought to them, thinking he might fix their problems and give them a son.

'When Pooran entered the great hall, the king and queen were stunned. He'd come back to life? Once they began to believe their eyes, they panicked. Surely, Pooran would be intent on revenge.

'But the young mystic told his father and stepmother that he forgave them. And that act of forgiveness freed Loona from her vices and her sins. She led the rest of her life following a spiritual path ...'

'I will miss all your stories, Dad,' Beas said.

'You make sure to carry on telling them!' Jugaad said. 'And if you hear any good ones out there, you make sure you remember them for me.'

Sejal began to cry. The girls consoled her. The boys started up a game of cricket. If the ball hit the well, you were out. Jugaad joined in, picking up little Indus. He wasn't as mobile as he'd been, the work at Hawthorn's ruining his back, but he could still put a mean spin on a bowl. One ball had so much backspin it ended up falling into the well.

They ate a simple meal, and the night was so temperate that they slept together in the courtyard, one family, under the red blanket.

In the morning, Sejal gave Beas a set of phulkari dupattas she'd made for her. Then she took the red blanket and cut it with a knife, making an equal section of the cloth for each of the six children. It was only when she'd handed them all out and saw that there was a spare that she realised she'd accidentally cut seven pieces, not six.

When Ravi and Beas were ready to leave, Sejal handed them each a section of the cloth and said, 'Wherever you end up, you bring this back to me and I'll stitch it together. And if you can't, you pass them down, and you tell your children to return.'

And, as she had divided the cloth between them, they too would divide what they were given between their own children.

INDUS

The river pays no attention to Partition – the Indus, she 'just keeps running along'

David E. Lilienthal, on the Indus Basin Dispute

1

Mussafir shifted into the highest gear and pedalled towards the tracks. The freight train, which had come from Istanbul via Tehran, and was heading north now to Islamabad, took several minutes to pass in its entirety – enough time for the thieves to run alongside it and jump in. Mussafir waited until the last carriage had gone before he turned and cycled on in pursuit.

The men would pass from car to car, rifling through packages in search of valuables – electronics, designer clothes, shoes – before leaping out, leaving the doors open. As the train continued on, packages would fall out of the open cars and land next to the tracks, where they would stay unless someone was there to take them. Mussafir didn't steal things: he found them.

His most prized finds included leather belts, luxury chocolates and toy cars, all of which he'd managed to sell on the streets of Larkana for good change. But he'd cycled here this afternoon not just for stock, but for a sign. If he found anything of real worth, he would go ahead with his plan and leave. If he didn't, he would stay.

The odds seemed to be on his side: the wind was strong, blowing his long hair back, and at a bend in the tracks, the lighter packages floated out into the air, the brown cubes drifting and falling like exploding blocks of Minecraft grass.

A box was perfect before it was opened. Closed, it might contain anything. Apple Watches, Air Jordans, VR headsets. But a box only ever contained what it contained, and, more often than not, that was some form of disappointment. Fake Al-Nassr shirts – Mussafir was Messi, not Ronaldo – enema pumps. But, today, each box contained his fate. Would he, at fifteen, accept his cursed lot, or risk it all for something better? When he opened the first of the fallen boxes, he was certain he would do the latter. The package contained a hundred portable phone chargers. What could be an easier sell? Loading them into his bike's pannier, he cycled on, finding a box of Power Horse energy drinks and some packs of broken biscuits. With his new loot, he might be able to fund his way to the border without further depleting what little his grandmother had left him.

He played his favourite Arushi album, the soundtrack to *Dil ya Dimaag*, on full volume as he cycled back to the village, taking the road not to his empty home, but to Tarfaan's.

It was a long way, and he stopped in the shade of a petrol station, where he got three bars of connection. The first thing he did with the data was search for Arushi.

No posts on main, no Stories. Her lack of engagement simultaneously worried him (What was she up to?) and pleased him (She was a person out in the world, living every moment!). He read through Arushi's mentions, which took a while, and found little of note. His Google Alert on her name had come up with nothing since his last check, a few hours earlier.

He refreshed Arushi's timeline just in case, and then looked at his own feed, @Daily_Arushi, to check the engagement on his most recent post, a photo that she'd put up on her Story, a chia pudding she'd eaten before a recording session, spoon balanced between her thumb and finger, which showed her new nails. Her boyfriend, a film producer, had treated her to a manicure – people in the comments were taking this as a sign that a proposal was imminent. It was not.

His feed was not its usual mix of film clips, business tips and cat pics. Instead, he noticed a video of Indra, India's prime minister, appearing repeatedly. He played the clip, which took an age to load. Slowly, Indra's mouth began to move.

'All through history,' he said, 'we have been a persecuted minority, attacked for our unwavering belief. Time and again, oppressors have sought to rid Bharat of its indigenous religion. They came in from the west, from the north, ransacked villages, murdered men and children, raped women, whom they forced to convert. They sought to bend our way to their will. But we would not bend, and we would not break.

'We understand how our mother river disappeared, yes? An earthquake sent her underground. Now think of the Mughal invasion as that quake. Causing the true identity of this country to disappear, forced underground under the Muslims, under the British, under the secularists. But we are bringing that river to the surface. She is our ecological answer to centuries of foreign rule. Of India becoming Bharat again! So fight, my great players, as if Saraswati herself flows through your veins. Fight and show on the cricket field what your forefathers would have shown on the battlefield! We will win this tournament together and—'

Someone had overlaid parts of the speech on to footage of Pakistan beating India in the match. The Shaheens hitting sixes, bowling wickets, running and cheering as the final score is confirmed, lifting the trophy. They had sped Indra's voice up, so that it came out squeaky and high-pitched. '*Fight and show on the cricket field what your forefathers would have shown on the battlefield!*'

Mussafir knew Arushi followed cricket, and often hosted Twenty20 parties, but there was nothing at all on her feed about the match, or about Indra. She was admirably apolitical. To quote one of her favourite sayings: *Life is for living.* If Mussafir ever got a tattoo, that would be his first. His second? *The present is pre-sent.*

His phone died, and he cycled on. Tarfaan was the only person who knew Mussafir was behind the Arushi stan account. He was the son of the village lender and lived in one of the few houses that still had stable internet connection, up on higher ground.

Most of the villagers worked on farms in the Indus floodplain. Now, the earth was cracked like old leather, ashen as dry elbows. Mussafir's grandmother had said it was India turning off the tap. Mussafir welcomed the dryness, at first. He was born into water, his grandmother often said – his mother had gone into labour at the height of a flood, the doctors coming on a boat, arriving too late – which was why he was a good swimmer. He remembered doing breaststroke laps over their land, his legs occasionally grazing soil beneath the surface, ploughed field, broken bund. When the water drained away, it revealed all sorts of objects: empty petrol canisters, plastic bags, action figures. Mussafir collected the finds and tried to sell them on at school. His friendship with Tarfaan began when he'd found an unopened pack of football cards. Tarfaan bought them off him but kept them sealed. The pack might have contained an Mbappé or a Lamal and so needed to stay in mint condition.

In the dry times, the two of them would pan for gold on the banks of the Indus. It had been in the news that a single Alexandrian coin had been sold for millions of American dollars. And one time, sifting through the muck not far from where he was cycling now, they'd spotted a strange shape on the red banks, making pained noises.

'A dolphin.'

Beached in the low-running river, the blind river dolphin was dying, but not dead.

'We should put it out of its pain.'

'I'm not touching it,' Tarfaan said.

Mussafir steeled himself and picked up a rock. He hammered its skull. But it continued to make noises.

'You have to do it harder.'

He hit it again, and again, and the dolphin was dead.

'It must be a kid,' Mussafir said. 'We'll be able to drag it.'

'No way.'

Tarfaan didn't know hunger like Mussafir did.

'Come on, help.'

They dragged it along the dirt road until they reached Mussafir's house. He thought that his grandmother would want to cook it, to preserve its meat, but she was adamant it be sold.

'Hunger is temporary; money is forever.'

They transported the body in a tarp to a fish market. A trader paid cash and took the body in an ice cooler to Karachi, where it was sold to a dealer from Dubai who sourced ingredients for an elite supper club. In the Gulf, the body was sliced for omakase, one piece of endangered blind river-dolphin sashimi costing more than the lump sum Mussafir's grandmother had received for the whole body. She used the money to buy an old cow, and Mussafir was forced to get over his dislike of milk.

'I knew you weren't actually going,' Tarfaan said, when he saw Mussafir parking his bike in the gully.

'Can I use your plug?'

They sat in Tarfaan's room and Mussafir methodically charged up the battery packs.

'I know it's hard with your grandmother,' Tarfaan said, attempting serious conversation. 'But you can't actually—'

'We're not doing that,' Mussafir said.

'But leaving, Messi – it's so extreme.'

'When you've got nothing to leave behind, it's not leaving.'

Tarfaan sighed. 'Can you stop, for once, with the lyrics?'

'If I don't post for more than a few days, then you can tell people, but otherwise, I need you to keep it all between us. If you see me posting, then you know that everything turned out OK.'

He unplugged a charger and put another one in. Tarfaan sighed again, opening a lukewarm Power Horse. It was unlike them to be silent.

'What do you think, fifteen hundred rupees, fully charged?' Mussafir eventually said.

'A thousand, dead?'

'Yeah. And maybe a hundred rupees for five minutes' rent.'

'I'll tell my children I once knew Jaffar Bezos.' Tarfaan put on his American accent: 'Pakistan's Elon Mosque.' Another long pause. 'I don't want you to go. It's such a stupid reason to leave.'

In what might have been the most exciting news of her career, Arushi had been cast to play and voice a literal goddess in the biopic *SARASWATI*.

She had now moved beyond the realm of the playback singer and was an actor in her own right, fronting what would be the cinematic event of the decade. Mussafir had posted the news on @Daily_Arushi before finding out who Saraswati was. Goddess of music, voice, speech. Arushi was born for the role! The film would release to coincide with the official opening of the Saraswati River, in a matter of months.

As part of her extensive promotion for the film, Arushi had posted about a competition. The winner would get VIP tickets to an exclusive preview screening of the film, and the chance to meet Arushi herself at any one of several stops on her All-India Tour: Mumbai, New Delhi, Bengaluru, Kolkata and New Lothal – a brand-new city that had been built at the mouth of the Saraswati River. Inspired by the literary goddess she was playing, she asked her followers to reply with a quote from their favourite book. A handful of comments had already appeared by the time Mussafir saw the post. He acted swiftly.

Knowing that Arushi liked poetry, he scrolled through her feed until he found a selfie she'd taken with one collection: *The world is full of such beauty. Notice it. Be present. Simply look around ... it's everywhere ...*

He found the book online and opened a preview to copy a quote. He sent a reply from his stan account and his personal account. But that was only two shots at the prize, among thousands. He knew he should have shared the details of her competition with his followers – of which there were almost ten thousand – but that would have only helped decrease his odds of winning.

He googled 'impressive authors', 'classic literature quotes', 'smart book lines', and set up new fake accounts from which to send them. It was slow work and, with the competition's deadline coming up fast, he dipped into the savings his grandmother had left him to pay a click farm to set up more bot accounts. The bots posted Goodreads quotes on an industrial scale and liked each other's comments to increase their visibility in the thread.

It was only after he'd won the ticket to the New Lothal screening that he learnt India and Pakistan had cut off all diplomatic relations and the border between the two countries was completely shut. Like his grandmother always said, short-sightedness ran in the family.

Mussafir cycled downstream and set up shop outside Mohenjo-Daro, the ancient centre of the Indus Valley Civilisation. He walked up to the tourists, offering a Power Horse in one hand and a phone charger in the other. The biscuits he kept for himself.

He'd come to Mohenjo-Daro before on a school trip and had visited again with Tarfaan to get ideas for one of their get-rich-quick plans. Back then, the government had announced a financial reward for any ancient artefacts found in Pakistan.

Even their history teacher, normally so strict, encouraged them to search their gardens.

'Our country is too wedded to the idea of itself as a Muslim homeland. This is true, but it neglects all that happened on this land before 1947. While we ignore our ancient history, the Indians are inventing their own. "Saraswati" Civilisation, that is fake news. It has and always will be the *Indus Valley* Civilisation, based around the basin of *our* river, a river that actually exists.'

They started digging around the river.

'A quarter of a million rupees for one find,' Tarfaan had said. 'I think I'd move to UAE.'

'No, bro, you have to invest. You put money in and get more money out.'

All they found in the dirt was more dirt. But then Mussafir had an idea. They sketched glyphs of the Indus script from the Mohenjo-Daro museum and then attempted to carve them into rocks.

After half an hour, they tossed their failed attempts into the river. They'd make their fortune some other way. Tarfaan would learn to code, and Mussafir would run the business side of things. He'd taken YouTube courses in management and finance, and listened to every episode of the *123 CEO* podcast.

In the first episode, the host said, 'Supply and demand is the highest truth,' and Mussafir couldn't agree more, as several tourists, low on battery after long coach journeys, formed a queue in front of him.

At Dokri station he sold five more chargers, enough for a ticket to Hyderabad Junction. He sat on his bicycle seat in the train's unreserved section, refusing to sleep in case anyone tried to steal from him. When he arrived, he sold a few more energy drinks and chargers, and boarded the train south-east to Badin.

Out on the platform at Badin, he took the Power Horses

and chargers from his bike basket to try to trade something for tea and lunch. He ran through his plan as he waited in line for his food, and checked the map again. He would cycle down towards Seerani and Bhugra Memon, crossing the border to the east of Nareri Lake and Zero Point, where there was no physical fence between Pakistan and India. Whether he was caught would simply be a roll of the dice. He was barely fifteen and an orphan; he could always plead ignorance.

The vendor handed the food to Mussafir, who, looking around while he waited for the tea, noticed something was wrong.

His bike wasn't where he'd left it.

It was gone.

His father's bike.

He started to stride towards the exit. But he knew within three steps that it was no use. Whoever had taken it was already out of reach.

He sat down and finished his lunch, trying to keep things in perspective: he had his money, he had his goods. The map said it would be an eight-hour walk to the border, which was doable, plus however many hours on the other side to a road where he might get a bus.

No one ever wins with the odds stacked in their favour.

You can't spell Success without the three S's. Struggle. Hustle. Strength.

It took longer than the map said it would to get to the next town over. Mussafir tried to ration himself to only one energy drink. Of the few cars that passed, no one was willing to offer him a lift. Rather than listen to it on his phone, he hummed the songs off of Arushi's latest album. When he made it to her, all this would have been worth it. He reached a village shop and bought a bottle of water. He sat down in the shade behind the small building, which was when he heard the voices.

'I suppose this is our last stop before the border, old man.'

The border?

'That'd be right.'

'You need anything else?'

'It would be good to give them something to eat. I'm fine.'

'There are carrots, I think.'

'Get the lot.'

Mussafir peered around the corner and saw an old man leaning against a large lorry. A middle-aged man disappeared into the shop. Mussafir could hear creaking, what sounded like an animal inside. The old man walked slowly around the lorry and opened the back door. There were the groans of several cows. One stepped towards the opening.

The younger man emerged holding a sack of carrots. He threw them into the back and then took two cigarettes out of his pocket. The cows shuffled about inside the lorry. There must have been about half a dozen of them. The men smoked towards the front of the vehicle.

Surely this was another sign from above.

While their backs were turned, Mussafir stalked forward to the lorry. He could just about hear the younger man. 'God willing, they'll be OK to you.'

'They wouldn't beat an old man.'

Mussafir quickened his pace and then stepped into the back of the lorry, squeezing in between two agitated cows. He pushed his way through to the other end and ducked down, out of sight. He held his breath and pinched his nose. The animals were packed in so tightly that they couldn't really react to his presence. Their eyes were covered with blinders, even in the dark of the lorry.

After two long minutes, the younger man slammed the doors shut. Mussafir couldn't see a thing in the dark. The lorry lurched forward and turned. He stood up, holding on to two cows for support. He took out his phone and put on the torch light. It was like a scene from a horror movie, the groaning of the cows, the dark.

On the map, he could see they were travelling the right way. Relieved, he opened up his socials and searched for Arushi.

He watched the blue dot approach the border on the map on his phone. Almost two hours passed before the lorry came to an abrupt stop. The cows moaned. There was more road left on the map. Mussafir ducked back down.

He listened, failing to make sense of what was happening outside. After several minutes, the doors opened. It was dark outside, and he thought he might go unnoticed. But then the old man beckoned the cows out. One by one, they started to move. Mussafir had no other option than to come forward, too. It had been another short-sighted plan.

'Moswin!' the old man shouted. 'Moswin, come here! What are you doing, kid? Who are you working with?'

'Don't hurt me, please,' Mussafir said. 'I swear, I'm no one. I just needed to get to—'

'FAO huh? WOAH? CIA?'

The younger man came to the door holding a knife.

'Everything OK, Attaf?'

The old man, Attaf, shone the torch on Mussafir's face and stepped into the lorry.

'Moswin, you watch the cows,' he said to the younger man, before turning to Mussafir. 'Who are you? Why are you here?'

'It's like I was saying, Moswin,' Attaf said, ten minutes later, after hearing Mussafir's reason for crossing the border, 'the education system never fully recovered.'

It was decided that Mussafir would wait with Moswin for the repairman to come and fix the lorry's engine. Then Moswin would drop him off at the nearest train station. Attaf would continue on foot with his cows.

'So, he's going to the border,' Mussafir said, as he and Moswin looked out at Attaf walking away. 'He's going into India.'

Moswin said nothing.

'Do you like music?' Mussafir asked.

'No.'

'Really?'

'I like silence.'

As soon as Moswin fell asleep, Mussafir stepped out to pee and headed on into the night, attempting to follow the old cowpoke. He caught up with him at dawn, towards the end of the road.

'Leave me alone, kid, honestly. Go back.'

'I have drinks,' he said, holding up the Power Horses. 'And free charge.'

'You can't be with me.'

'I just need to know where to cross.'

'I told you, I'm not going to the border.'

'But that's a lie.'

'How so?'

'Because I overheard you and Moswin.'

The old man squinted. 'What did you hear?'

'As soon as we get to the crossing point, we can go our different ways. I won't bother you at all.'

'That'd be the day.' Attaf sighed. 'It's that way,' he said, pointing back the way they'd come. The old man stepped off the road, followed by his obedient cows.

Mussafir waited a minute, and then continued on behind him.

Whenever the old man paused to let the cows eat or drink, Mussafir stopped. Attaf never looked back, but there was no way he hadn't noticed Mussafir. After a day's walking, Attaf and the cows crossed a canal, and Mussafir tried to enter and exit the water at the same point. He struggled to get out on the other bank, which was steeper than it looked, and the old man stretched out his hand to lift him up.

'All right, kid, my battery is low.'

They made camp together without a fire.

'So, why are you crossing?'

'After tonight, you'll turn around.'

'But where are you going?'

'It's in your interest not to know.'

Attaf took some milk from the cows and offered some to Mussafir. The teenager tried a different tack. He sat in silence, while the old man looked out at the dark. Eventually, Attaf spoke.

Despite his appearance, Attaf was not a farmer. He had worked for years as an administrator of the polio vaccine, travelling through the border districts. A few years ago, when the floods were at their worst and the Right Bank Outfall Drain was at capacity, the government had planned to intentionally flood a village to reduce the risk further downstream. In retaliation, thousands in the area refused the polio vaccine. If polio broke out, it would spread among the population, crippling crucial services. Attaf knew right away that the strike would force the government's hand. 'I don't think I've ever seen change happen so quickly. And that idea stuck with me.'

Mussafir stayed silent and let the old man meander on.

Now that water was being diverted into the Saraswati, Attaf told him, the Ravi, Beas, Sutlej, Chenab and Jhelum were dying, and the Indus was dead. Prime Minister Indra's party had effectively torn up the Indus Waters Treaty, an agreement that had been written to stop the hot war at the border. And if the making of the agreement had stopped a war, the break-ing of the agreement should have meant the resumption of fighting. But Pakistan, brought to its knees by several years of disastrous floods, had few resources to launch a counteroffensive of note. Any true escalation introduced a nuclear threat.

There were skirmishes in Kashmir and in the mountains, car bombs in a few cities, but deaths were in the dozens, not the hundreds. There were even some in the cities who thought the diverted water might be good for Pakistan: there would certainly be no risk of further floods.

Attaf was too young to take part in the last war, and too old to fight in this one. But he joined a guerrilla group, who would retaliate at a level their government wasn't ready to reach. With the looming possibility of things going nuclear, they couldn't do anything that might be mistaken as originating from the actual army. Bombs would have to be home-made. 'But a bomb has only a small blast radius. What we're attempting here is more widespread.'

'Worse than a bomb?'

Attaf paused. 'Towards the end of the Second World War, there was a mission called Operation Cherry Blossoms at Night.' The Japanese plan had involved flying seaplanes over California and dropping ceramic pots which contained a mix of flour and bubonic plague. The flour attracted rats, who would spread the plague.

But then the atom bomb dropped a few weeks before it was due to take place. At that point, the mission had already changed. It was decided soldiers would infect themselves in their submarines and then run ashore. When they were apprehended, the black death would spread.

'So, you have … bubonic plague in there?' Mussafir pointed at Attaf's small cooler bag.

'Not exactly.'

'Not *exactly*?'

'Rather than people,' Attaf said, 'we're going to strike cattle. Start a chain reaction.'

'Cows?'

Cattle – from catel, from capitale – never quite reached the social heights of other domesticated animals – horses, say, or dogs. Respect for cows, and the subsequent stigma around killing them, might have been financial: a cow was worth more alive, through its dairy products, than it was dead, as meat.

To protect their assets, humans started living in close proximity with their livestock, sometimes keeping them inside their homes. Close enough that, one day, a morbillivirus jumped from a human to a cow, or vice versa, and began to duplicate and mutate. In humans, this became measles. In cows, rinderpest.

A cow who was infected with rinderpest would experience high fever and loss of appetite, followed a few days later by a foetid ooze originating from the eyes and nose, unstoppable salivation and mouth ulcers, which were mirrored on the exterior in the form of skin eruptions on the flank. They would feel extreme abdominal pain and show difficulty breathing as the virus breached the inner organs, at which point, discharges would increase, with diarrhoea causing further dehydration. Too exhausted to stand, they would go comatose and die within six to twelve days of infection.

Cattle dropped dead across India, across the steppe. The Huns and Mongols, riding through Asia with great spoils of looted livestock, spread the virus from region to region. It arrived in Europe through cattle trading in Russia and by the eighteenth century, it represented such a threat to capital that the king of France invested in the world's first ever veterinary school, with the specific task of putting an end to the 'Russian Disease'.

But it was at the end of the nineteenth century that the truly devastating capabilities of rinderpest became clear. In 1887, Italian forces in Ethiopia had a hankering for beef. European cows were imported, and rinderpest arrived in sub-Saharan Africa. The virus maintained a 90 per cent kill rate across the continent for the next decade. It jumped between cloven-hoofed species – buffalo, antelope, gazelles, camels, giraffes, goats, okapi, pigs and sheep – silencing large swathes of the savanna. The first photographs of the continent were taken at the height of the epidemic, and Europeans saw the distant land for the first time on postcards showing wide open, empty plains. Rinderpest wiped out entire species, destroyed count-less livelihoods, caused widespread famine, broke the food chain and reshaped the landscape. 'Growth without end is a sign of disease,' Mussafir remembered from *123 CEO*. 'Viruses, colonists. Good businesses strive for controlled growth.'

The 10 per cent of cows who survived rinderpest would not be infected again, which allowed scientists to develop vac-cines using small doses of the virus. In a global vaccine effort, rinderpest was completely eradicated. And since the vaccine contained active rinderpest, its production was strictly pro-hibited once the last ever case was logged.

'So, in a sense, full eradication never happened,' Attaf said. 'Twenty-seven facilities around the world have safe stores of rinderpest in high-security research labs right now. Well – twenty-six.'

Attaf took a six-month plan to the organisation. If they'd had the resources, they could have birthed the virus just from its sequence. Instead, they would need to infiltrate the high-security lab in Lahore and steal a sample of rinderpest. 'But things didn't go to plan.'

After years of lobbying governments to destroy their stores of rinderpest once and for all, the World Organisation for Animal Health, WOAH, allocated funding to increase the financial incentive of its sequence-and-destroy programme. Finding the terms agreeable, the Lahori lab arranged for WOAH officials to come and kill their stock.

'That gave us a weekend to carry out a plan we'd envisioned would take several months.'

They paid off a cleaner to give them her pass and uniform.

Their hackers attacked the security system, corrupting all the footage captured while their plant went about the mission. The plant lit a cigarette in the bathroom, and, as all the scientists hurried out to the street for the fire drill, she entered the high-security lab.

'Getting it was the easy part,' Attaf said. Mussafir couldn't see his face at all now in the dark. 'The hard part would be getting it over the border.'

Their first plan had been to drive to the Wagah–Attari checkpoint and sneak the vial into India among a shipment of medicine. But imports and exports across the land border had just stopped; diplomacy had reached an impasse. Pakistan was joined by China in trying to isolate India's economy.

'The stock market is no way for men to fight.'

They tried their luck driving north to Kartarpur, following the Ravi against its current, the river weaving in and out of Pakistan, a loose stitch. A rendezvous was arranged in the Kartarpur gurdwara, built in the location where Guru Nanak Dev Ji had died. After his death, Hindus and Muslims alike claimed the Sikh guru as their own. They created two mausoleums in his honour, both structures sharing a common wall. But, as the flow of the Ravi shifted, the joint shrine washed away, and the gurdwara, one of the holiest pilgrim sites in Sikhism, was built on the left bank.

A few hundred years later, the Radcliffe Line was drawn along the river, and the left bank became Pakistan and the right India. Indian Sikhs wouldn't access the gurdwara until the Kartarpur Corridor was opened in 2019. It allowed Sikhs to visit the holy site through a liminal space that was simultaneously beyond the border and within it. One such Sikh agreed to pick up the vial in the gurdwara. But he pulled out at the last minute, the lives of thousands of cows on his conscience.

Attaf had been furious. The longer they held on to the vial, the more dangerous it became. With each failed crossing, the likelihood that it might spread on the wrong side of the border increased.

'So, the cows are infected?' Mussafir said, eying the water bottle that Attaf had filled with milk.

'Not yet. I'll do that at sunrise.'

'And you're going to cross the whole desert?'

'The Rann of Kutch? No. This was why I didn't want you following me. My plan isn't to make it across. My plan is to get *caught*.'

'Like the soldiers on the beach.'

'In Gujarat –' Attaf pointed into the distance – 'when a cow dies, it is almost worthless because no one eats the meat.'

The heat was worsening and record numbers of cows were dying. And, as more cows died, farmers grew increasingly desperate. They had turned to a border trade, attempting to sneak their cattle across the great salt plains of the Rann of Kutch to sell them on to Pakistani cowboys. 'The rate is much cheaper for buyers here than it is elsewhere in Sindh,' Attaf explained. 'So it works out for both sides.'

Border guards would either miss the traders or get paid off enough to turn a blind eye, or they would seize the livestock and arrest those attempting the crossing. The seized cattle would then be taken to vast, densely packed trading centres, where they'd be auctioned off.

'I'll infect them tomorrow morning and get caught in the afternoon, acting like I've just bought the cows. By the time the cows show symptoms, they'll already be at the auction lot, where they'll have been in contact with hundreds of others. Those others will be transported to different areas, and it will spread.'

'But what if you're caught by the Pakistani guards instead of the Indian ones?'

They were interrupted by the distant sound of gunfire. In the flat darkness, there were some lights. 'They use the salt flats for their military practice,' Attaf said. 'Tomorrow morning, you turn around. You need to go back to your parents. It's a disgrace you would run from them. From your community.'

'My mother died in childbirth. My father left soon after. And my grandmother, she passed, too, a few months ago.'

In the distance there was more faint light.

'It's young people like you I'm doing this for,' Attaf said, finally. 'It'll have been for nothing if you're not around to see things get better.'

When Mussafir woke, the old man was gone. He'd left a bottle of milk and some white clothes, and had drawn an arrow in the sand. Mussafir assumed it pointed back to the road and the route home. But, when he checked the map on his phone, he realised it pointed towards the border, towards the Allah Bund and the great white Rann of Kutch.

He changed into the white clothes and blended in with the landscape. There were Indian rupees in one of the pockets.

'Thanks, old man,' he said, finishing off a can of Power Horse. He checked in on @Daily_Arushi. Overnight, he'd passed 10,000 followers! He had a thank-you message prepared already in his drafts. He checked it over and pressed the 'share' button. While the app buffered, he took in the landscape. He had always thought of borders as dramatic. Tall mountains, wide rivers, barbed-wire fences. But everything here was flat, one country bleeding into the other like one colour into another in the dawn sky.

The post wouldn't go through; the connection was too poor. Rather than wait, Mussafir pocketed his phone and walked on.

2

Mouth coarse with thirst, Mussafir sang, hummed, rubbed salt from his lashes like sleep, as he walked, eyes shut, due east. His eyelids glowed red from the glare, amber auras floating as if in viscous liquid. All this was underwater once, Attaf had said two days ago, pointing towards the border – the salt flats sea. With the afternoon heat on his back, Mussafir allowed himself to squint, to drift. He saw Arushi running through the woods in her first perfume ad, turning into a tree as the rain fell on her, her skin hardening into bark, her arms into branches, sprouting leaves, casting him in shade. He could see her in a music video, imagine it, make it real on the plains, surrounded by backing dancers moving in unison as she sang, and from her mouth came his grandmother's voice and the song from which he was named, 'Wahan Kaun hai tera', on repeat until he unwound the cassette of *Guide*, tossed it into the river, the unspooled tape rising to the surface, glinting, like a dead black eel. 'Mussafir, jaayegaa kahaan,' Arushi sang, as his grandmother picked the lice from his hair up on the roof, that summer when the Indus burst its banks and the frying pan floated out of the kitchen window. 'Dam lele ghadi bhar, ye chhaiyyaan, payega kahaan.'

He opened his eyes, followed his own shadow. He would have liked to send a photo to Tarfaan: the setting sun, the lunar plains, the wind sweeping from one country to the next. In a parallel universe, they were planning their first start-up. *Your network is your net worth.* 'Duniyaa hai faani, paani pe likhi likhaayi,' he sang in the dark, and, appearing and disappearing like a stray thought, he saw a light. Flashing blue, red and yellow, it burned like mercury, shooting across Mussafir's field of vision. It flashed again, a pear-shaped droplet – closer, this time – a few feet from the ground. He blinked and it appeared towards the left, moving as if it had a mind of its own, red now, now blue. He took a step towards it and it seemed to jump, which Mussafir took to be a kind of encouragement. It seemed alive, seemed to move with purpose, direction. Unsure what to do, Mussafir followed it.

His grandmother had told him about ghost lights, but he hadn't believed they were real. She'd seen them on a trip through the marshes to visit her uncle, after her mother had died. It was only then, as a middle-aged woman, that she'd learnt of her adoption. Her uncle told her that he and his sister had found her, a toddler, next to the corpse of an old man outside a train station in Lahore. 'It was '48,' he said. There was a letter from Singapore in the old man's pocket, addressed to 'Indus Singh'. 'We'd only just arrived from Amritsar,' her uncle said. 'We waited, but nobody else came for you.' Mussafir could see it, make it real, the smoke in the air, the packed train, the girl in the arms of a new mother.

It was hard to know how long he chased the ghost light. At times, it would appear larger, closer, and then it would vanish, and he'd give up, his bearings lost, only for it to reappear in a different spot. To Mussafir, the ghost light was as alive as the few animals that walked across the Rann of Kutch – as alive, in other words, as he was, though he felt sure he was dying. After a while, the ghost light vanished. Mussafir awaited its return but for hours there was only the moon.

He woke to the sounds of gunfire, shivering. Impossible to know if the shots were louder or quieter than they had been before. He tried in vain to pee and thought of Arushi's face, saw it in the stars, her face superimposed on to the naked body in the deepfake. He'd known it wasn't her: her birthmark was missing. But he did watch the video – twice; heard the sound of another woman's scream.

If Mussafir was dead and this was the afterlife, then the Grim Reaper was an Indian wild ass. He licked Mussafir's lips, and the boy sucked in the dripping saliva. The wild ass's body cast Mussafir in blissful shade, and he grunted, moving again to lick Mussafir's face, his saliva a salve. The teenager felt some form of strength return and managed to sit up. He stroked the ass's face and summoned the will to stand. Eventually, he made it on to the animal's light brown back, gripping on to the hair on his neck as the ass walked. *Life is for living. Confidence comes from success, knowledge from failure.*

The sound of the ass's footsteps changed as its hooves touched the road. Mussafir dropped off its back and prayed. He kissed the tarmac, stood up and kissed the top of the ass's head. He felt strength in his legs for the first time in days. 'You saved my life,' he said to the ass. 'I love you. I will always love you.'

The animal seemed to take this as a goodbye, and walked away from the road.

'No,' Mussafir said. 'Stay. Please, don't leave.'

The donkey went on, in search of what, Mussafir couldn't know. He plugged in his final battery pack and checked the date on his phone: the screening of *SARASWATI* was tomorrow. He looked up and down the single-lane road. Left or right? He stood still as a shape approached, distorted by the hot horizon. The figure took half a minute to come into proper sight, and then it sped right past him – a motorbike. He decided to walk in the direction the motorcyclist was going, knocking the salt from his clothes, licking his lips.

Three more motorcycles and two trucks passed by before a small hatchback screeched to a halt several metres in front of him. He ran up to the car and, through the open passenger window, heard a whispered argument in English.

'Well, I stopped, didn't I? You asked me to stop, and I stopped.'

The woman in the passenger seat looked out the window. 'You need a lift?' she said.

He had practised Hindi for a moment like this – all those hours watching his mum's Hindi DVDs as a child, listening to her cassettes – but he was glad to be able to use his school English.

'Yes, please.'

'Where are you going?'

Uncertain, he pointed down the road.

'Dholavira? Us too!'

The driver said something he couldn't make out. But the woman turned and said, 'He's just a kid.'

She turned back to Mussafir. 'Well, in you get.'

The car was brand new. It had been a wedding present; the couple were newlyweds on their honeymoon. 'We were in a tent hotel,' the man said. 'Totally magical, this place.'

'We've been arguing for miles,' the woman said, 'about what music to put on. I mean, we'll only drive down the "road of heaven" once. Do you have any requests?'

Mussafir paused. 'I like Arushi.'

'Ha!' the man said.

'Now, that's a choice.'

'"Dil ya dimaag"?'

'Let's gooo!'

'Turn it up.'

The woman rolled all the windows down. The man stepped on the accelerator and they sped on, down the single-lane black road. The drums kicked in, then the violins. After ten minutes, the salt plains on either side of the road gave way to water, a shallow inland sea that surrounded Dholavira. The sky was perfectly replicated on the still surface.

'Flamingoes!' the woman said.

The birds were doubled in the shallow water. To share the world with flamingoes! As the man accelerated, Mussafir stuck one hand out of the window, feeling the rush of air on his palm. The album's third song came on, and they were all singing along.

3

In Dholavira, Mussafir used the cash that Attaf had given him for food, water and bus tickets. There were no checks. As the conductor came up and down the narrow aisle on the night bus, he expected to be singled out, but nothing happened. He slept the length of the journey, and woke as the coach pulled into the city of New Lothal. It was that easy. When he stepped off the bus, he could have been anyone. He could have been Indian.

The sun began to rise, and he aimlessly wandered down-hill, watching the city turn itself inside out. New Lothal was nothing like the towns he'd known; the streets were wide and straight, every turning a right angle. It looked more like a set than a city, a backdrop in a movie, glass buildings that could have been anywhere. He stumbled on to a main road, where he found a twenty-four-hour supermarket. Inside, he bought an Indian SIM and asked the cashier if he might be able to use the back of her earring to open up his phone.

She looked at him, sighed, and then took out her stud.

'Thank you, thank you,' he said, popping out the old SIM. He tipped her and turned off flight mode. At long last: data!

He sat down on the pavement and cycled through his socials. His thank-you message to his ten thousand followers finally went through and his phone buzzed with likes.

If only I could express this incredible journey in the right words. This community we have built together means the world to me. There is so much hate out there, so why shouldn't we be passionate about what we love? Even if all we have is music. Why not follow role models who make the world better? Thank you to every single one of you! Here's to the next milestone!

By the time he looked up from his screen, the commuters had vanished. He slept on the side of the road and, when he woke, there were five hours until the screening. He couldn't meet Arushi in his current state.

317

It was time to shop.

He found a mall, but, as he walked around, it quickly became apparent he didn't have enough money. He stopped to stare at a mannequin in one shopfront. A red jacket with golden zips, an intricate pattern on the sleeves. He loved it but could not buy it. There was no justice.

He left and found a small stall on one of the roads opposite. He could afford a shirt, but would need to make do with the white trousers he had on. He haggled with the seller, using the only money he had left to buy a blue dress shirt. He held it in a carrier bag, and then asked for directions to the river.

He stepped down on to the concrete ghats of the Saraswati River. Where the Indus had been wide, at certain points near his house looking more like a series of lakes than a river, the Saraswati was narrow and straight. It looked like one of the New Lothal roads; he almost expected its bends to be at ninety degrees. The water was a similar colour to the roads, too, but that might have been the darkening sky it was reflecting.

Further along the banks, workers were setting up temporary fencing. There were several signs advertising the Saraswati Puja, on Vasant Panchami: the official opening of the river. People conducted different prayers along the waterfront. On the opposite bank, smoke rose from a pyre. Mussafir was grateful to see others bathing. He stripped down, leaving his clothes and his phone on the bottom step to keep them out of sight of people walking above. Then, he entered the river.

The current was stronger than he'd expected, but it felt so good to be under the water, to feel clean. He opened his eyes and could see the edge of the banks as they sloped down towards the riverbed. It was all concrete. He felt the current change as he held his breath, with the water seeming to move upstream rather than down. He resurfaced, and all seemed to be well. The children were still playing, the women still singing.

He swam back to the steps, which was when he realised the water level had risen. The tide. The plastic bag containing his clothes and his phone was half underwater.

'Shit. Shit,' he said, as he ripped the bag open and the water poured out. His phone turned on, and he thought it had been spared, but then it instantly turned off. Water dripped out of the charging port. Without his phone, he had no means of navigating and no access to his grandmother's savings. Without his phone, he had no ticket or proof that he had won Arushi's competition.

Struggle. Hustle. Strength.

Without pressure, we wouldn't have diamonds.

The clouds cleared and he laid his clothes out in the sunshine.

The water evaporated out of his clothes and into the air. He watched the river roll on. Forward, forward. To have made it so far and fail? To have made it so far and give up? He would go on. He got dressed and retraced his route to the mall. The workers in the phone shop said that it would take several days and thousands of rupees to try to fix.

'Do you know where the Grand Mandir Theatre is?' Mussafir asked in English. They didn't. He went into the department store and asked the cashier there, too.

'I'm new here, sorry,' she said.

He stopped on his way out to spray himself with three different samples of aftershave. He used the display cream to moisturise his elbows. In an optician's, he fixed his hair. The workers there didn't know where the theatre was, either.

The mall's security guards suggested he head towards the culture district, and the taxi driver, smoking and leaning against his car, said the same. He pointed up the main road.

Mussafir walked as fast as he could. He checked the time at a bus stop and broke into a run. Eventually, he saw signs for the culture district, in the same direction as the New Lothal

Free Port, which was in the opposite direction to both the sea and the river. The sun was beginning to set. He was tired, so ridiculously tired.

The crowds led to the Grand Mandir Theatre. He pushed his way through the bodies, sweating. A fence separated the normal people from the red carpet, the photographers, the stars.

'I have a ticket!' he shouted at the guards. 'I have a ticket!'

But they couldn't hear him. He pushed his way up to the fence.

'I have a ticket!' he said.

The guard nodded to his left, and Mussafir started to push his way around to what must have been a side entrance. He'd made it out of the heart of the crowd by the time everybody screamed.

Arushi.

She stepped out on to the red carpet and smiled. Her body glittered with paparazzi flashes. She wore a sari, modest jewellery. Mussafir instinctively reached for his phone. But he couldn't photograph her, he couldn't record. He would have this moment solely in the present. He didn't blink. She stood, smiled, and turned. Then, she walked away. He finally opened his mouth to breathe.

'If I could just log in on your phone, I'll show you. I swear. Mine stopped working, but I won, I won the competition. I've come so far. If I can just log in. Or my name might be on the list. It should be on the list. Mussafir Mirza.'

'OK, OK. OK.'

When he made it into the theatre, the speeches had already finished. His seat was near the middle of a long aisle at the back, and he had to squeeze past dozens of people who refused to get up for him. By the time he sat down, the curtains had opened and the credits had begun. It was the largest screen he'd ever seen, and as it turned from black to brilliant white, the cavernous theatre filled with light and he could see the silhouettes of hundreds of people, all looking one way at one thing: *SARASWATI*. There was silence, and then the music began.

SEJAL JUGAAD
1898

Sejal sang as she took their last water buffalo down to the lake to drink. When they'd first arrived in Hakra, the oxbow lake had been part of the river. But, during a heavy monsoon, the river had burst its banks and changed course, leaving behind the crescent-shaped lake at what had once been a meandering bend. This year, the monsoon had failed to arrive and the lake shrank a little more each day, approaching new moon.

To get to the water, she had to walk through Gurdial's farm. Gurdial's son, like her Jhelum, was en route to the North-West Frontier. They'd been recruited by the Punjab Irregular Force, working together under General Blood. Neither she nor Gurdial had heard from their sons.

'Those tribals,' Gurdial had said. '*Animals*.'

It was hard to think of that distant border war, with all their quiet problems on their own plots – bouts of root rot, the hardened earth blunting spades. Times were tough, that was true. But still, she thought, they could carry themselves with dignity. They were not yet beasts.

She walked down the side of Gurdial's field and waved at him as he dug a trench. His pagh was tied loosely, revealing his bald head. She noticed every man's turban now that she tied Jugaad's for him. Her husband couldn't lift up his left arm like he used to. She'd been experimenting with different styles.

Gurdial came over to greet her. For a brief moment, Sejal wondered if he'd heard news from his son, if he'd found any mail at the general store. The shopkeeper had known her well; for a while, Sejal had been checking in once a month, hoping for word from Trinidad, Kenya, from America. But, by the time Jhelum left, she'd given up.

'Any news?' she said to Gurdial.

'I can feel the rains are coming. It's in the air.'

He was always talking about the weather – the weather and his yield. *The world to Gurdial is as large as his plot*, Jugaad used to say, back when the men had been drinking buddies.

Sejal nodded. 'I hope you're right.'

A pleasant enough encounter, she thought, before smiling and carrying on her way. She took a few steps forward, and that's when it happened. Her water buffalo did a poo. It landed with a soft thud on the dirt, drier than usual. Sejal turned and looked at it. They were running low on their winter fuel store. Normally, they had four water buffaloes' worth of dung-cakes to burn, but since the others had died, they had to rely on just the one to provide their cooking fuel. Sometimes, she'd walk out to look for firewood, but she didn't like cooking over wood; it burned too hot and too fast. Her favourite dishes needed time to gently simmer. In recent days, they'd had to eat their vegetables raw. In her old age, she'd finally become a person who pickled. If only her sister could have seen her now!

She crouched to the ground to knock dirt on to the shit to make it easier to carry. But when she stood up, holding the dung-cake, Gurdial was looming over her.

'Hand it over.'

'What are you talking about?'

'That happened on my land, so it belongs to me.'

'Don't be ridiculous, it's my animal.'

'Hand it over.'

'You can't claim somebody else's dung.'

'I'm kind enough to let you pass through here.'

323

He grabbed at the poo, but Sejal moved too quickly. His hand grasped her shoulder and knocked her back, and she fell. He picked up the dung-cake and walked on towards his house. What had happened to the world? To people? How many clothes had she given to his wife and daughter? At such low prices.

She stood up, glad to have left the baby at home, and marched on to the crescent lake.

Taking the long way home, she decided not to tell Sutlej or Indus, who would just make a fuss about it. She decided, too, not to tell Jugaad. It would be cruel to anger him when he wasn't able to respond. She saw it in his left eye, which drooped down with the rest of the left side of his face: the words were all in him, he just couldn't get them out.

Soon, their newest child, Saraswati, would start talking. But she would never be able to speak to her own father.

Sejal considered Saraswati a miracle. Her seventh child. She had feared labour in a way she hadn't before. She didn't know her own birthdate, but by Jugaad's guess she was thirty-six, which was a ridiculous age to have a child. She'd heard stories about older women. But then, a few days before the birth, it happened: Jugaad, already house-bound by a recent injury at the Hawthorn site, lost the ability to speak. His mouth drooped on one side.

If Sejal had died in childbirth, the child would have had no mother and a father incapable of caring for her. Could she really entrust a child to Sutlej and Indus, who were both yet to marry? When the girl was born, Sejal inspected her for defects. She had a small mole on her chin and weighed very little, but she was beautiful.

She wanted to talk to Jugaad about her name. If only the two of them could read or write! They had run out of major rivers in Punjab, and to name such a beauty after a stream felt wrong. She tried different options, but none of them fitted: Ganga, Yamuna, Sabarmati. The girl remained nameless for almost two weeks, until Joravar, the village elder, came to visit.

'I have just the name,' he said. 'They say there used to be a seventh river in these parts. Bigger even than the Indus. *Saraswati.*'

'Saraswati,' she said, tickling the mole.

Sejal felt guilty having brought such a perfect little thing into such a hardened, cruel world. A world where she might not always get the food she needed. This world, where a neighbour could push a mother to the ground to steal a dung-cake! Sejal was unable to nurse the child and fed her on the milk of the water buffalo. No matter their dire circumstances, her capacity for love for the child continued to surprise her. Her seventh child, and still the heart had room. She held her close when she arrived home from the lake. She sniffed her head. Another chance. Another chance at trying to get parenting right.

'Our own Sapta Sindhu,' she joked with Jugaad.

He smiled with half his mouth.

Sejal had to ration the atta. Both Indus and Sutlej asked for more roti. They'd been working out in the field all day.

'That's all there is,' Sejal said. 'I'm sorry.'

'We gave you money for atta.'

'I had to buy milk for your sister. This last week, the buffalo has been giving nothing.'

They looked down at their plates, and then at each other.

The Sunday after that, old Joravar arrived unannounced, along with Munshi and Renu Sanghera, a couple who lived a mile east. Sejal only knew Renu because she'd sold her a few of her dupattas. In fact, Renu was wearing one now. She'd lost count of how many women wore her patterns. In another life, Sejal's sewing would have made the family rich. But no one around Hakra had money to buy fine clothes. She had to sell anything she made so cheap that she barely covered the costs of her materials, ending the day not much further along than where she'd started it. But she couldn't bear to let her standards slip, to use cheaper fabrics or to stop buying her favourite golden thread.

She was embarrassed not to have food to offer her guests. With Saraswati in one arm, she put on some tea, using up the leaves she'd been saving for a special occasion and burning one of their last dung-cakes.

Joravar took a seat and cleared his throat. 'You have had seven children,' he said, slowly.

'Yes,' Sejal said, 'we've been blessed.'

Joravar indicated the Sangheras. 'Poor Munshi, here, and his wife, they have no children. No matter what they do, a child will not come.'

Sejal looked at Renu Sanghera, whose eyes were watering. Munshi stared at the floor.

'I'm sorry,' Sejal said.

'It is only fair,' Joravar said. 'You have too much. They have too little.'

Sejal tightened her grip on Saraswati.

'You will both prosper,' Joravar said. 'I hope you can understand.'

Sejal shook her head. The baby started to cry.

'Sejal,' Joravar said.

'No.'

'It is only what is right.'

'I don't understand.'

'You cannot feed another mouth.'

'Yes, I can. How can you say such a thing? You know nothing of our yield, or what we have in our store. This is my house. This is my—'

'The good of the village is the good of the family. And the good of the family is the good of the individual. This will only help you. You're getting old.'

'Get away from here. Go away.'

The water in the pot was beginning to boil. The spices and tea leaves rose to the surface and danced.

'We'd like this to happen amicably. It has always happened, and it will always happen. Many centuries. It's what keeps society going, no? Those who have too much give to those who don't have enough. It happened to my uncle; he came to our family and had a much better life than he otherwise would have.'

'*I* will give my child the best life.'

'You'll starve your little girl, Sejal. Is that what you want? She already has no milk to drink.'

'How dare you?' she said to Joravar. She turned to Sutlej and Indus for support. Their faces were grave. 'Tell him. Tell him to stop, boys. Get these people out of our house.'

'Ma.'

Sutlej sighed. 'It would benefit everyone. For us and the girl and them.'

'*Benefit?*'

'Mother.'

'Get out of my house! It was you? You called them here? If your father …'

She turned to Jugaad, who was sitting on the cot, and started pleading with him. She knew he would never agree to such an arrangement. But he could not speak. And whatever it was she said, no one would listen.

'It won't help getting hysterical, my dear,' Joravar said. 'This is already difficult. Don't make it harder than it needs to be.'

Renu continued crying. Munshi hadn't raised his gaze from the floor. Joravar prodded him with his walking stick, and eventually Munshi spoke.

'We'd give her the best life, pen ji. You have to know that. We have so much to give, but no one to give it to.'

'This is how it has always been,' Joravar said.

'Hush,' Sejal said, kissing Saraswati's head. She took a deep breath and looked around her. Joravar's face softened. She paused. 'OK,' she said.

'OK!' Joravar said, clapping his hands together.

Then Sejal kicked the big pot of boiling tea over, the scalding water hitting the old man's feet. He yelled, and Saraswati cried, as Sejal bent down and picked up the burning dung-cake from beneath the pot. She threw it at Munshi, and she ran.

She ran across the farm, ran past the well. She ran through Gurdial's field, up past the lake and carried on, trying to get to the river. Her sons caught up with her. Indus took hold of the baby, and Sejal collapsed, heaving. Sutlej picked her up and hugged her, muffling her screams.

After a month, Sejal was allowed to visit Saraswati. But when she returned to Munshi's house the day after that, he met her outside, closing the door behind him.

'I'm not sure it's a good idea so soon, pen ji. She's settling.'

'She's OK? I'd just like to see her. Her fever's gone down?'

'Uncle said that separation was important. We're trying to do right by you all.'

'You can't just show her to me? I've started sewing her some clothes – you'll take them when they're finished? And I've got her phulkari to make, for when she's older—'

'Time will help, I promise.'

'I forgot to give this to you yesterday,' she said, handing Munshi the seventh square of red fabric that she had kept safe since Beas and Ravi left. 'All my children have one. It's all part of one pattern. Promise you'll give it to her and explain. That you'll tell her.'

The Sangheras moved before Sejal could bring the clothes she'd made for Saraswati. Where, Sejal didn't know. She stopped cleaning the house. She stopped cooking. Indus and Sutlej had to attempt to make food for themselves and their dad. They walked down to the village and put out word that they were now both looking for wives. Sejal refused to eat. She sat in the courtyard, pricking her fingers with a needle. She tested how far she could spit.

'I wish you had been drafted instead,' Sejal said, looking at the pathetic meal her boys had made. 'It should be you two at war. In some ditch. Not Jhelum.'

The men ate in silence. Jugaad didn't touch his plate.

'They took my son from me,' Sejal said. 'They took my daughter. And I'm left with you.'

Sutlej sighed.

'You know, there's a curse on your father and me,' Sejal said. 'My aunt always said, "Those who turn from their parents are cursed to see their own children turn from them." *All* of you have been taken from me. Beas, Ravi, Chenab, Jhelum ... Saraswati. If she's not mine anymore, neither are you.'

Sutlej and Indus married in one ceremony. The girls' mothers didn't even bother making phulkari. Probably didn't even know how. Sejal thought of the intricate works Chenab and Beas had left with. Her needlework, thousands of miles away, her golden threads. She wanted to go to them. To be free of this place. Surely things were better where they were.

Sejal had taught both of her older daughters to sew. But her Saraswati, wherever she was, would never learn her mother's techniques. Who knew what Renu would teach her? Renu, whose roti were always misshapen, whose tadhka was often bland, who didn't know the words to most giddeh, who probably didn't know any qisse, Renu, who didn't dance at weddings and didn't cry at funerals. What would she teach her child? What woman would Saraswati become?

Her new daughters-in-law were fine enough. They helped

on the farm, they cleaned, they cooked. No longer needing to do so many chores, Sejal's routine relaxed. She woke, swept the courtyard, milked the buffalo. She spent the afternoons sewing. She wanted to make new patterns. She practised for hours, experimenting with new designs. She had all these ideas for what she could render in cloth: patterns that showed the crops on the square plot of the farm, that showed dreamed-up places, the places her children had fled to. She could stitch the ocean, the island where Beas lived. She could stitch people dancing, playing music, could create mountains, forests, invent a whole new world. She swept again. What was it her mother used to say? *No matter what happens, there's always more dust to sweep.*

Slowly, she grew accustomed to her routine, sitting in the shade with Jugaad, feeding him, sewing as she talked to him. 'I have many regrets,' she said, 'but risking it all for you – that I'll never regret. We had so much fun, didn't we? Yes, we did.'

She showed him her works in progress. 'You remember that cornfield? The one on the way here? And the stalks were taller than you? I've tried to make it look like that.'

There was a set routine in the village, too. Jugaad's old friends still gathered to drink. The women still gossiped as they washed clothes and filled their pitchers. The kids still jumped from the bunds. They played the same games Sejal once had, probably had similar conversations, too. Life for them now was unimaginably different from what it had been like in her time, but really, how much did the life of a little girl change from generation to generation, age to age? The patterns changed, but the threads were all the same. If not this war, then some other one.

But both her routine and that of the village were disturbed by the arrival of the travelling story-wallah. He shouted as he cycled up to the central street, 'Gather, gather! Qisse, qisse! Brand new and age old! Hear it here!'

How long it had been!

'Jugaad,' Sejal said. 'Do you think you could make it into Hakra? The story-wallah's here! And he might have our post!'

Her husband slowly shook his head. He pointed at Sejal, and then pointed to the door, and nodded.

Sejal walked down to the village's central courtyard with her two daughters-in-law. Children ran from roof to roof above, and then rushed downstairs to get good seats. Some climbed the tree in the courtyard, and Sejal looked up at their dangling legs as she sat down. The storyteller had collected the post for the village on his cycle in and was handing out letters to those who came up to him. Many of the women were wearing Sejal's patterns. People gave the story-wallah food and fresh tea, as a vote for the stories they wanted, and others shouted their requests from the small crowd. Sejal hoped he would ignore them. She wanted to hear something new.

He began his opening speech, about the world as he saw it from his bicycle – villages like this one, dotted across the land. 'Without stories,' he said, 'we would not know where we're from. How things were, back then. How different, how similar! While we might not know great kings and beautiful princesses now, our hearts beat with the same rhythm as theirs did, do they not? Put your fingers to your neck – that pulse, that's the same as it is for a person in the Himalayas, in the Andes, in the Alps! The same as the first men and women to walk this fine world, the same as those who will live here hundreds of years from now. I have travelled far and wide, and no one story has affected me like the one I am about to tell. One that is sure to quicken the beating in your chests!

'Now, let's begin.

'Seven generations ago, in a land not so far from here ...'

*

After the performance, Sejal waited in line to speak to the storyteller. She told her daughters-in-law to go on home without her. When she finally got to speak to him, they were the last people in the courtyard. 'My husband, he's always loved qisse. All these years, when he hears one, he's like a child. But he's not mobile anymore and he couldn't come tonight. I'd pay whatever you want if you could come and just do one for him. Just one. Before you leave in the morning for wherever it is you're going next.'

'Of course, if you tell me the way, I can be there for breakfast,' he said. He asked her name. 'And I think this is for you, then,' he said, giving her a letter.

Right in front of him, Sejal ripped the thing open. 'Can you read it for me?'

The letter looked to Sejal to be quite lengthy, but, after a pause to read it in his head, the storyteller only spoke a few sentences out loud.

'"Mother, Father – all is well. As I dictate this to a friend who can write, I am sitting in a motor vehicle! Some days are hard ... but others are good. And all of them are an adventure. I can't wait to tell you all about it, but until that day, I hope these few words will suffice. With much love, Jhelum."'

Sejal neatly folded the letter. 'I can pay.'

'No, no,' he said. 'I'll be around in the morning, don't worry. I'll tell you what, I'll trade you a story for a story. I'm not often in these parts; you must know ones I've never heard of.'

'Oh,' she said, 'I only know the same old few.'

'But what about your own?'

When the storyteller left Sejal and Jugaad's house late the next morning, Sejal's words turned around in his head: *We've been cursed, my husband and I, because we fell for one another across a divide.*

It was good material, he thought, as he cycled, usable material, and he couldn't help but translate the real history of their lives into a story that would engage an audience. A couple defying the wills of their parents and eloping, only to raise children who'd grow up not just to defy them, but to leave them. Their love posed in opposition to the world. Their seven children bound for far-off lands – that was current, he thought, that was new. He did feel bad for not reading out her son's letter in its entirety. But what good would it do a mother to know her son was writing from a hospital bed?

He worked on the couple's narrative in his head, as he cycled on from village to village, but it took a few months before he began to tell the qissa of 'Sejal Jugaad' in his shows.

Whenever he told it, the crowd responded well, thinking he was speaking of characters from a distant time, not of a couple who were alive now. Still, it took him several years to feel he had fully got the thing right. At that point, he cycled into a city and recited the story to the printer who provided him with paper copies of other qisse, from 'Heer Ranjha' to 'Pooran Bhagat'. Whenever he visited places where people could read, he could make extra money from selling the leaflets.

'"Sejal Jugaad"?' the printer said. 'Never heard of this one.'

Often 'Sejal Jugaad' was the booklet that sold the most copies. People seemed to want something new. But, even with it set in ink, every word fixed in place, he couldn't help but think of the ways in which he might change it. The words on the page were dead, unable to move, but the ones that came from his mouth during his different performances were alive. He slightly altered the ending, for example, while up in the hill states, in his first performance of spring.

'... and Sejal and Jugaad, they lived happily on the farm, content in the knowledge that, wherever their children went, they would find a love like theirs, too. Confident that one love story led to another.

'They drank from their well and looked down at their view of the great Saraswati River, the river upon which they had met, the river along which they'd fled. And, while their story is ancient, the oldest of those I've recounted tonight, and though that river no longer exists today, and that tribe has long since vanished, the children of their children's children? They continue on. Everywhere that water goes, it's already been.'

SARASWATI

Ih phulkari meri maan ne kadhi
is noo ghut japhiyan paawan

My dear mother embroidered this phulkari
I embrace it again and again with affection

In the beginning, rain fell like smashed glass. Cloud-seeding planes that had flown the length of the Saraswati River, from Kailash to Kutch, put in their final shift, lacing the sky with silver and salt, forming crystals. By the time Prime Minister Indra's fleet passed through New Lothal and reached the coast, there would be nothing but clear skies above.

The official viewing areas along the concrete ghats of New Lothal, already full, were still somehow filling, as people pushed through the narrow security gates. Those who had camped out for the best views were steadily pressed into the temporary fencing as the crowd edged towards the water. The new skyscrapers shimmered, balcony parties in full swing now, a few hours from the scheduled passing, the penthouse floors dark, commandeered by sniper units. A Mexican wave took over both banks, having started at the river's mouth a few miles west to arrive here at what could be called its throat.

Drummers played at different rhythms up and down the

banks, forming less a beat than a constant thrum. Drones drifted above the crowds, filming people chanting and praying, capturing the hands of children squeezing through the metal fencing at the lowest steps of the ghats to touch the water, to feel the current of the river, which, despite the fanfare and furore, all this fervour, flowed on unaware.

By the time I stepped down on to the ghats, followed by Katrina and your father, it was really coming down. According to the British inquest, there were four people per square metre then, which meant we could move with relative freedom and make our own decisions. I thought of you as the people around us started to push, though I wasn't yet showing – you were more an idea than anything else, known only to your father and me, a hope.

The loose chorus of chants was pierced by a cry and then a laugh, someone spilling a berry blast on their yellow chunni. We were all in yellows and whites; it was Vasant Panchami, the fifth day of spring, the day of the Saraswati Puja, though spring didn't mean what it used to, even then. It occurred to me that you'd never experience a spring of my childhood, that the seasons you would know wouldn't feature the same unfurling of petals, the rush of an animal's birth, fallen blossoms in eddies of warming wind. Our memories would appear to you as fictions, with your springs revolving around the floodings, the coastline edging in. The river rose with the rain, the lowest step of the ghat disappearing entirely.

'Poncho?' Katrina said. 'We could be poncho people.'

'OK, but you two stay here and hold our spot,' your father said. Though Katrina liked to claim she was perfectly mobile, her left leg had never fully recovered from her fall in the mountains.

I felt uneasy about your father leaving us. So many more people were flooding in, there were so many men around, and the rain was only worsening. Within moments, he was beyond my sight, gone.

'Feels like we're in one of your crazy colonies,' I said to Katrina.

'Awaiting our queen,' she said.

I received a message from Nathu: a photo from Radha Johns' balcony, in one of the buildings on the opposite bank.

'Our favourite archaeologist has got in touch,' I said, showing Katrina the photo. 'He's learnt how to take a selfie.'

At the exhibition launch over the weekend, he had invited the three of us to Johns' viewing party. But we said we'd prefer to experience such a historic event at ground level, among the people. In any case, it sounded like the party would double as a memorial for her son, and we didn't want to intrude. How differently things might have turned out if we had accepted his invitation. If I had been up there, looking down, I would be another person now.

'Jealous!' Katrina said, handing my phone back to me. 'Is that Moët?'

We took a photo together, but it wouldn't go through to Nathu – my connection was failing. If your father needed to message or call, I wouldn't know. I felt contact in my lower back, a hand or an elbow. Everywhere I looked, there were men. Young men laughing, others staring. I held on to Katrina's hand and my breath quickened as someone lit a flare. It burned into my retinas, an after-image floating over the red scene, briefly obscuring the sight of your father, grinning, as he struggled towards us, prized ponchos held aloft. He stuck out his tongue.

I hope you'll inherit your father's calm nature – I was panicking already, fearing the damage that the growing crowd could do to me, to you, but there was no exit. We were approaching five bodies per square metre, I would find out, and the crowd behind us was as dense as it was in front. At that point, security had been overwhelmed and people were streaming in freely. Five people per square metre, almost six.

If it hadn't been for the exhibition launch, your father and I might not have been in New Lothal that night. Our original plan was to escape the noise and rent out our place during the Saraswati Puja. The paper had folded, and I was out of work. I liked the idea of not having to report on the event, of not having to be on. But Katrina had flown in for the launch party and was sleeping on our sofa. To be in the city and not see Indra's procession felt like turning our backs on history.

Much of the talk at the launch was about the Saraswati. The name of the goddess repeated in the echoey din, as if the whole room were partaking in an arrhythmic prayer. The curator clapped her hands; it was time for my speech. I thanked the people without whom the exhibition would have been impossible to bring together; first of all your father, whose work in the records helped me to trace the movements of the seven children of Sejal and Jugaad, and then Katrina, whom I had come to consider not just a distant cousin, but a new sister. And there were the other descendants who had come: Nathu – who introduced me to your father at the archive – Gyan and Harsimran, with whom I had conducted lengthy interviews; there was the curator who had brought all the pieces together; and, above all, there was my half-sister, your masi in Shimla, who had provided me with the files our late father had collected about Sejal and Jugaad, without which there would have been no exhibition at all, none of these people gathered together – Harsimran on the online stream and Katrina, Nathu and Gyan standing in front of the fabrics.

I was about to pass the microphone over to the curator, when I noticed a thin man with a slight limp walk into the room: Satnam.

After my first visit to the Hakra farm proved to be a failure, and the email I'd sent to the address on Satnam's seed bank website went without a reply, I assumed that I would never hear from him. But because I had included a description of the farm in my piece, 'Sejal, Jugaad & Me: A Family History', I sent a copy of the draft to the same address. Satnam was the first of anyone I'd mentioned in the essay to respond to me. In his short email, he said that he had information I might like to include in the piece and attached a document he'd translated from his bibi ji's diary. I was shopping in the market when the file came through, and when I saw the first words I abandoned my basket: *Heer Ranjha.*

The document included several qisse that his grandmother remembered hearing when she was growing up, along with early memories of Hakra. As a child, she said, she had been fascinated by the stories of distant relatives in far-off places. Africa, the Caribbean, the names themselves made her jealous. All she'd ever known was Hakra. When her marriage was arranged to a man who lived in England, there was no place on earth that seemed as exciting and as exotic as Wolverhampton.

The text included no mention of her life after she turned seventeen and left Punjab. I knew all the qisse she recounted already, but there was one story that immediately led me to start redrafting my piece. According to her mother, Satnam's bibi had a cousin who was born in the same week as her. As toddlers, the two girls were inseparable. Her cousin had accompanied her mother and grandfather, Indus, to Lahore, to pick up some money sent by an uncle out in Singapore. Not long after they left, Lahore became part of Pakistan. It took everyone a different amount of time to believe that Indus, his daughter and his only grandchild weren't returning. They were likely dead.

I was ecstatic. Up to that point, I'd understood my inability to find anyone from Indus's strand of the family as a flaw in my project. But now, I was more certain about it than ever. I took up the invitation in Satnam's email, and drove to his farm to meet him.

After passing miles of uniform green and yellow fields, I pulled up outside Satarupa Park to ask for directions. I could see kites flying above the treeline. The security guard standing in the shade of a sign – 'established with the generous support of Mr Kush Bhatt and the Hawthorn Trust' – pointed me in the right direction. The reason I was lost was that the dirt road I remembered taking last time had since been paved. I followed the new road only to find that the tarmac stopped abruptly part way along the route.

The building projects on either side of Satnam's farm appeared to have been abandoned, metal rods jutting out of the unfinished concrete. A group of boys were sitting on the third floor of one of the windowless buildings, taking turns trying to throw pebbles into a bin placed on the other side of the road. When I got out of my car, they stopped talking and watched me approach Satnam's gate.

A woman opened it, Reha. At first I assumed she was Satnam's wife, but as we walked around the house towards the field, she told me she was only visiting. She and her son lived in Chandigarh; she taught English.

'It's changed so much,' she said. 'He's turned it into something else entirely.'

When we emerged at the back of the house, I could see what she meant. There was an abundance of colour in what had been a drab field. All sorts of vegetables were growing alongside herbs and trees. The idyllic scene was disrupted by a man shouting in English, 'Go on, square it, square it!' A pair of water buffalo looked lazily over at the noise. A thin man with a long beard was watching what sounded like a football match on a laptop propped on a crate in the shade. We walked over.

'Satnam,' Reha said, introducing me.

'You brought good luck with you,' he said in English. 'We've just taken the lead at Villa Park.' He grinned at me, his hands busy stirring a mixture inside a large clay pot. 'I'd shake your hand but I don't think you'd want me to.'

'What is it?' I asked, looking into the pot.

'Cow dung, cow urine and ghee,' he said. 'Mother Nature's pesticide.'

Reha made us tea in the courtyard, which was lined with rows of dried gourds, hollowed out and filled with heirloom seeds. A water buffalo calf walked unsteadily up to me, curious, and lay down. After washing his hands, Satnam returned with a piece of cloth.

It was a phulkari dupatta, unlike anything I'd seen before. 'Like in your story,' he said. 'My bibi's story. The woman stitching all those pieces. There were others but my parents sold them.'

The piece showed seven streams diverging from one source. The detail on the water was masterful, the depth and the highlights, the gold.

'Do you know who made it?' I asked.

He shook his head, finishing his tea.

The buffalo calf followed Satnam and me across the field. The peepal trees, which had looked brand new when I'd last seen the farm, were establishing themselves along the edge of the land.

'They hold the soil together,' Satnam said, as we reached the corner of the square plot.

There was no water in the well, having been long diverted. At the bottom, glinting in the sun, were a few coins. I took a photo, zoomed in. A key, an orange bouncy ball, a leather cricket ball, several cigarette butts.

'It's beginning to flow, see,' Satnam said, pointing beyond the peepal trees. Sure enough, there was water in the trench, wind passing over its surface. That was the first time I believed the Saraswati project would actually materialise, rather than being just a talking point in the news, a topic to debate. Here, there was water where there had been nothing. And in the water there would one day be fish and birds, and, upstream, women washing their clothes, filling pots, and boats passing through the young reeds, their paddles forming ripples, music, as they had done before. I thought of the ending of the qissa – Sejal and Jugaad looking out at the water – and I turned to Satnam as he spoke of the first appearance of the water, the beginning of it all.

'Seeing people come together like that,' he said, 'you know, for this common cause. It was quite something.'

'Surely everyone didn't agree?' I said. 'Weren't there those stories?'

Satnam looked at me and then back at the river.

'I have this memory,' he said. 'I have no idea if it's real or not – you know those early memories where everything takes on the dimensions of a dream – but I was on the bus with my bibi ji, I think we were going to the supermarket or something, and I'd agreed to go because if I went there'd be chocolate, or doughnuts, or whatever, and we're on the bus and I'm old enough to realise the driver's gone past our stop, and then the stop after that and Bibi is pressing the button, and it's ringing out, but on he goes, and soon he turns left where he should have gone right and the other passengers on the bus, there were only a few, they're calling out, starting to panic. My bibi didn't say anything to me – we couldn't really speak – but she did hand me my DS from her handbag. I didn't even want to play, it was all too exciting, turning on to an A-road, on to the motorway. A man behind me was hyperventilating, the woman next to him was on the phone to the police. We're heading south of Wolverhampton, and within minutes, there's a police car riding alongside us, its sirens flashing but emitting no noise – that was a new concept to me – and we're going so fast and you can hear the bus straining at the speed, it felt like all the screws were slightly loose, everything rattling, this horrible noise, and Bibi is just doing simran, over and over, and two men are arguing with the driver, but he's behind that protective glass they have, that plastic. The police car pulls out ahead, I suppose to try to slow him down, eventually forcing

342

him to stop, but he pulls off to the left, on to the hard shoulder, and everything's really shaking, and at that point I'm scared, genuinely scared, and he takes the exit on to another A-road. He's bombing it and we can hear sirens now, and he turns, turns again and comes out into all this traffic, a total gridlock. The woman behind me runs to the doors and presses the emergency button and we all get off, my bibi holding my hand, and there's this relief.' He paused. 'This total relief.' He stared at me. 'I did enjoy your piece. I do want to help with it. But the reason I asked you to come, the real reason, well – you're a journalist, right? I read some of your articles. Say I was able to tell you who was driving that bus, you could get that news out there without naming the passengers?'

Satnam had screenshots of a SpeakFree chat that proved that Kush Bhatt – a local politician who was running in the upcoming election as part of Indra's party – had directly ordered the violence carried out by the Saraswati Six. Satnam came to New Lothal to meet me and a journalist friend a month later.

The city was the largest part of Indra's Saraswati Greenfield Development Policy, one of seven new settlements, from Mool Sarovara at the new source of the river, to New Lothal at the river's mouth. The first plans said the city would be built in the original location of Lothal, an ancient Saraswatian town and the site of the world's first ever port, from which Saraswatian traders sailed out into the Gulf of Khambhat. But the city was relocated several miles west, at the point where the new Saraswati met the Gulf of Kutch, almost equidistant from Jamnagar and Bhuj. New Lothal was designated as a special economic zone, with its own tax rates and free port, to help attract foreign businesses. It wasn't a place I'd ever imagined visiting, let alone moving to, but with the state of journalism as it was and jobs increasingly hard to find, I couldn't argue against relocating to the city when your father was offered such a strong salary. He would be working at the newly established Pre-Vedic Archive, in New Lothal's culture district, as part of a team creating a catalogue raisonné for ancient Saraswatian finds.

A large market had emerged around the buying and selling of ancient artefacts, and it was his team's job to date and register each find, determining its authenticity and, where possible, its providence, before it was sold on. The work meant that our apartment building was supplied with extra security: many traders would stand to lose a lot of money if your father's team deemed their finds inauthentic. Others were angry that the team was authenticating too many items, driving the market price down. I got a call from our guard when Satnam arrived.

'I have news,' he said, as we walked over to the restaurant. 'I've found them.' He gave me his phone. 'The phulkari. The ones my parents sold, they must have been traded and traded again.' The six pieces were available on a London art collector's website for thousands of pounds each. 'Scroll down,' he said.

The collector had carbon-dated the pieces. 'Late 1800s. Unknown providence.'

'Sejal,' I said. 'That could really have been her!'

We entered the restaurant, and he quietly told my friend about his involvement with Kush Bhatt and Pala Chauhan, who was currently serving time for drug possession. I struggled to concentrate, unable to stop thinking about the phulkari, about Sejal. In the toilet, I looked at the different pictures on the site, zooming in. It was then that I noticed one throughline across each of the pieces, including the one that Satnam still had in Hakra. A golden thread. In every dupatta a single golden thread ran across the entire length of the piece in some form, so that if they were correctly aligned, they might be connected, pulled together. It was a signature. Her signature.

I stepped out to call Nathu, who called Radha Johns, who called an art dealer in Mumbai. The dealer asked his contacts in Indian folk art if they knew of any phulkari dupattas in their collections bearing the same trademark golden thread.

The first pieces were found in Canada.

Gyan agreed to go and see them for me, video-calling me as she walked through the rooms of antiques at the collector's house in Vancouver, and then turning the camera around when she came to the phulkari dupattas.

'It looks like a match, hey?'

'Can you put me closer?'

She put the camera up to the cloth and followed a golden thread across a vividly detailed abstract work with her finger.

I knew that Gyan had rejoined her old band, Tansen, and was working on new music, but it was only after she left the collector's house that she told me she'd ended up getting together with one of her old bandmates, Clem. 'I always told myself I'd never go there,' she said. 'Which I don't regret, the way we both were in our twenties. But now we're in our forties, and we don't have the energy to mess each other about. If these last few years have taught me anything ...' she said, without finishing her sentence.

The Canadian collector gave us the details of other dealers, and I found two more pieces in England, along with Satnam's. I was walking around New Lothal, viewing apartments with your father, when I saw the plans for the Folk Museum and got the idea about the exhibition.

We had spent the morning hunting in the city's cheaper east side and had gone on to the culture district to test out your father's future commute. Next to his new office building was the Museum of Bharat and the Museum of Indian Technology. Opposite that was the National Library and the Grand Mandir Theatre, which was already open and functioning.

It was surreal to think that these wide, straight streets would one day be ours. Everything here was flat and square, completely different from the steep, winding roads I'd previously called home in Dharamshala and McLeod Ganj. But all this would be normal to you. In no other place I'd known had the border between inside and out been so strictly delineated, the constant cool of the climate-controlled buildings belonging to a different world entirely from the hot streets outside. Here, people moved from their air-conditioned apartments into their air-conditioned cars via cooled underground car parks, never having to interact with the reality of the weather. Architecture was what separated us from nature, and there was nothing natural about the city at all; your father said the whole place felt like an airport duty-free shop. In several of the apartments we viewed, you couldn't even open the windows. The one marvel was New Lothal's western district, photos of which were printed all over the city on the temporary walls around the construction sites. The closer to the coast you got, the more expensive the housing was – despite the flood risk.

For thousands of years, I told your father, nobody ever built by the sea. Every culture knew it was safest to settle inland. It wasn't until the colonists that this changed: port cities sprang up, cutting shipping times, bettering profit lines. There was no practical reason for New Lothal to be built by the sea, I said. 'It's so stupid.'

'It does look cool, though.'

The city planning commission had hired a Dutch architectural firm that specialised in floating architecture to help design the western district's waterfront. There, buildings, roads and parks would all be built upon hollow concrete platforms, which were attached to the seabed by steel beams. The foundations would rise and fall depending on sea level, reducing the risk of flooding. The artist's rendition of the western-district plans looked something like a spider's web: buildings sticking out into the sea, roads surrounded by water. Apparently, they would be transporting desert sand from the Thar down to the coast to build a series of new beaches.

We turned on to Netaji Street to see the largest building in the culture district: the Museum of Military Conquest. The Monument to Freedom was being erected in front of it. At that time, only a few of the buildings were fully completed, and when we walked past the Folk Museum, the smallest in the culture district, it seemed less a site where something was being constructed than a place where something was being destroyed. Your father suggested I google them and get in touch.

The curator was as enthused as I was about the discovery of the phulkari. She took the project off my hands and put out a call for more pieces online. In the end, over forty works were brought together from North America, Europe, East Africa, South and Southeast Asia and Australia. By the time plans for the exhibition were coming together, I was ready to publish 'Sejal, Jugaad & Me'. My agent sent it out: some magazines were interested but a much larger offer came from a podcast producer who wanted me to expand and serialise the story.

I told the curator about the podcast at one of our meetings. She had finalised the plan for the show, approximating a chronology based on the development of technique and style. About thirty of the forty-four pieces would have 'connection points' where the golden thread that passed through one piece would join up with the next. We had reason to believe that every single piece was connected in some way to this larger pattern, but some of the pieces of this enormous puzzle were missing. I was amazed, watching it all come together on the curator's computer screen, but that was nothing compared to seeing all the pieces in one room at the finished museum.

Your father and I were the first people to view the exhibition. *The Endless Thread: Phulkari of Sejal Kaur of Hakra* began with the copies of 'Sejal Jugaad' that your masi had given to me. Saraswati Kaur Sanghera, our shared ancestor, had collected several copies of the qissa. The earliest leaflet was published in 1903, and they continued on until the 1930s. It was in her letters, which had been preserved in the family house in Shimla, that my father had learnt that Saraswati had been adopted, and that the names of her birth parents were Sejal and Jugaad. The different Punjabi editions were displayed in a glass case, along with photographs Satnam had sent me of the Hakra farm. In one picture, seven of the phulkari are pinned to a clothesline, the farm beyond visible in the gaps between them. Above the display, my shortened version of the qissa was written in Hindi and English on the wall. I wasn't quite happy with my rendering of it, and, looking up at the printed words, I couldn't help but notice things I might change.

After the story, exhibition visitors moved into the second and largest of the three rooms. The first piece was a red phulkari with a traditional wedding pattern, dated to the 1870s. Slowly, as visitors walked around the room, they could see Sejal's confidence in experimentation beginning to grow. After three pieces, she turned from abstraction towards the figurative: people, animals, plants.

If someone didn't know the exhibition's conceit to start with, they might have thought the arrangement of the pieces a bit erratic, with the garments hung at varying heights. But the first page of the exhibition leaflet encouraged people to look for the golden thread. Sometimes the thread went horizontally across a piece, and other times it was vertical or diagonal, and where there were gaps between the pieces, to signify the dupattas that were missing, the curator had paid an artist to continue the golden line in paint on the wall, and that one continuous line spanned the entire two-room display.

At the end of the collection was a wall dedicated to the red cloth referenced in the qissa of 'Sejal Jugaad'. An estimation of the cloth's original size was projected on to the wall, as well as an idea of how it had been divided into seven sections, and divided again and again. At the bottom of the wall were the few scraps of the cloth we had managed to bring together from Gyan, Harsimran and your Shimla masi.

Your father and I stood before the red wall for several moments before the interns arrived with drinks and snacks, and the business of the launch got under way. We were now living in the dry state of Gujarat, so I didn't have to explain why I wasn't drinking. But, without alcohol, the evening lacked the party atmosphere I had envisioned. The talk was not just sober, but often sobering. Perhaps that was to be expected from the museum's guest list: financiers, art historians, folklorists. I was stuck in a conversation with a corporate anthropologist about the worsening rinderpest epidemic when I spotted Gyan.

'... if they can't get the vaccine out into the backwaters soon, we're talking economic breakdown—'

'I'm really sorry,' I said. 'But my friend has just—'

'Of course.'

I hurried over to Gyan to give her a hug.

'In the flesh!' she said. 'You're shorter than I imagined. We must be the same height.'

'I guess you've only seen me from the shoulders up,' I said. She'd changed her hair. It had been long on our calls, but was now close-cropped. 'I'm flattered I give off tall energy.'

I took her round to look for the phulkari which featured on Tansen's new album cover. It was the one she'd seen in Vancouver.

When she spotted it and pointed, I realised I'd missed the more exciting news. She was engaged.

'It's for tax, don't get too excited,' she said. 'Tax and citizenship.'

'Romantic.'

She was showing me a photo of Clem when Katrina arrived. 'Who's the hottie?' she said, instead of hello.

'Gyan's hubbie.'

'Fiancé,' she said, smiling.

I introduced the two women. They had briefly lived in New York at the same time, and they started listing different areas

349

and street names, trying to discern their exact proximity, if they might have ever crossed paths before.

'Fifty-first, that Afghan place? Next to the bagels,' Katrina said. Nathu tapped my shoulder. 'Can I steal you?' I hadn't seen him in months.

'Everything's still in boxes,' I said, 'but we really do have to have you over for dinner.'

'It'll have to be soon,' he said. 'I'm returning.'

'To Delhi?'

'To Kenya. I'm planning to retire, to *properly* retire, in a small town. A quiet little place.'

'Quiet doesn't sound very you.'

We stopped to sit on a bench in front of a phulkari that was worn through, with a burn mark running the length of one side.

'Let's just say that my services are no longer required here.'

'They're pushing you out?'

'There are only so many times one man can disagree with the group. They see me as trying to put brakes on it all. As if brakes are a bad thing.'

He'd publicly criticised the Archaeological Survey's position that there was evidence of a continuous culture and religion from the time of the Saraswatians to us now in modern-day Bharat.

'It's like if I said there was a continuity between the person who sat on this bench before me and the person who will sit on it after me.'

I opened my diary app to find a date for Nathu to come over for dinner, where we might speak more openly. While I was on my phone, Harsimran called.

'I'll go and find your husband,' Nathu said, showing me a metal flask he had in his blazer's inside pocket. 'Sure he'll be excited to see me.'

On FaceTime, I showed Harsimran and Jasleen the exhibition. It was late in Singapore.

'Where's our one?' Harsimran said. His family had donated one of the first pieces in the collection. It had been kept in a bank deposit box along with their gold.

'Pride of place,' I said, showing them the piece.

'You should start sewing, Jas,' he said to his wife.

'Didn't you learn to make clothes on your TV show?' she said.

'I lost that challenge.' Harsimran turned suddenly serious for a moment, looking at me. 'Whatever happens, though,' he said, 'if they do make a movie about all this, you'll make sure they cast me? I want to be Jugaad.'

'You don't want to play yourself?'

'Maybe Amit Das can have that part,' he joked.

The curator tapped her glass with a knife.

'Too soon,' Jasleen said. 'We'll leave you to your party, pen ji.'

After my speech I found Satnam out on the balcony, smoking.

'I didn't expect to see you again,' I said. 'Are you still going through with it? The leak?'

'They think it's best to press print closer to the election, for the impact. In any case, the extra time is good.'

'Yeah?'

'I've been trying – failing – to find a buyer for the farm.'

'You're selling it?'

'You interested?'

'I'm not a nature person.'

There was a slice of noise as the door opened and closed, your father joining us.

'They want you for a photo,' he said.

The rest of our group was standing by the red fabric.

'Where will you go?' I asked Satnam, as we walked over.

'My parents are getting on,' he said. 'It'll be somewhere near them. The Black Country.'

I introduced him to Katrina, Nathu and Gyan, and your masi. After the photos, Nathu topped up people's orange juice.

I covered my cup with my hand. I was quiet while the others talked, tuning into their different conversations: Katrina recounted our trip to Kailash to your masi, Gyan and Nathu were discussing Tansen's tour – she'd be flying to Jakarta the next day for a flood-relief benefit – and Satnam was telling your father that we should come round, he had an abundance of saag.

A plan was made: Katrina, Nathu, your father and I would visit the farm a week later, after the Saraswati Puja in New Lothal.

We were at six people per square metre, according to the British report, when the first of the boats emerged from the darkness and entered our floodlit stretch of the river. I was forced forward on the concrete step, the front half of my shoe hanging over the edge. I tensed, aware I was now invading the personal space of the woman in front of me, because of the man behind me. Many put their phones in the air to record, cheering as the small figures on the boat were shown on the large screens. They were children, part of the leading party's youth programme. In white shirts and brown shorts, they uniformly saluted and waved their flags. As the crowd raised its voice, I could hear your father or Katrina only when they shouted.

Katrina repeated herself: 'Look! They think it's Arushi!' We'd been placing bets on which celebrity might be accompanying Indra – there was a different figure for each stretch of the river. Katrina showed me a post from @Daily_Arushi on her phone: *Arushi will appear in Saraswati Puja procession in NL – confirmed!*

Katrina and I had seen the actress in *SARASWATI* the night before, and now we would see her in real life. The movie had been as terrible as your father warned us it would be. He was fed up with lazy reimaginings of old myths, but we went for the atmosphere as much as anything else. The theatre was so full, several people were sharing seats. There was a comfort in crowds, I'd always thought, a group of people looking forward at the same thing. To think there were so many people upon the earth, and all their lives were as vivid as mine! Whenever I had ventured beyond Himachal Pradesh to places like Delhi or Mumbai, I'd find some kind of joy in being on those busy streets, all those faces on the metro – that is, when your father or some other friend was by my side.

Of course, among all those faces were those with darkness in their gazes. I had thought that the danger of the men was that they might act individually within the crowd, parasites upon the general body. While we spent our lives seeking out different forms of proximity with friends, lovers and family, it was also proximity that we most feared. While I'd heard the stories of men in crowds groping and assaulting women, I'd never before experienced the horror, not of the individual within the crowd, but of the crowd itself – not until the night of the Saraswati Puja.

If it was true that there were plain-clothes police officers along the banks, they did nothing to stop the pushing. Steadily, we were being forced towards the temporary fencing that had been put up at the water's edge. We were shouting at those behind us to stop, but the music coming from the loudspeakers drowned us out as the next boat appeared.

On this one there were dozens of priests conducting a prayer. A statue of Saraswati was held up, tinsel garlands and fairy lights dangling from her four outstretched arms. Standing at the boat's rear was a man with a loose turban and a white beard: Laal Guru. He had recently been appointed minister of education. By the time you would be in school, his new textbooks might already be tattered and defaced by students, and the version of history your father and I had once studied would be history itself.

I gestured for Katrina to look up at the big screens to see him, but advertisements were playing. Your father was saying

353

something I couldn't hear. Another flare went off – closer to us, this time.

'We should leave,' I said. 'Can we leave?'

'I love you, too,' I think he said.

I was being pushed enough that I should have slipped on to the next step down, but there was no space in front of me into which I could fall. Your father reached out to me, and again I thought of you. His mouth was moving, but I heard nothing.

After the priests came the drummers, and then the dancers and the acrobats. Several military boats let off fireworks as they passed. Somehow, more people were pushing through the thin bottleneck of the security gates. Some were letting off fireworks of their own, sparklers and small rockets, sending further panic through the crowd. Drones took to the sky, flashing different coloured lights. They moved around in formation to create shapes, pictures and words. I recognised some Saraswatian symbols through the smoke: the snake, the boat, the horns of the bull. They reconfigured again as the song changed, shifting from Saraswatian to Brahmi to Sanskrit, and then to English and Hindi: *A new beginning for Bharat.*

When Arushi's voice came through the loudspeakers, the density of the crowd officially reached seven people per square metre. That density threshold is the point at which humans in a crowd behave like a liquid, where no single person can move of their own volition or make any kind of decision. We were no longer individuals with agency, but part of a whole. Some attempted to fight against the flow, but they were crushed just like those of us who succumbed to the power of the crowd, the feeling of someone behind you, beside you, a mother, a father, a brother, a sister, forcing you forward until there was no space at all ahead. I fell two steps towards the river's edge and was pulled away from your father and from Katrina in an eddy of limbs. People were screaming, pressed up into the fence, and it was me and all the people behind me forcing them further into it. The crowd kept reconfiguring around me,

I couldn't see the people I loved anywhere, every face was that of a stranger. Arushi was singing the main theme from the film we'd just seen, and, because of the echo between the different loudspeakers, her voice seemed to elongate and warp, the song splitting into two and three and four. It was then that I saw Indra.

When the prime minister spoke, there was a delay before any noise came out of the loudspeakers. Another wave of people rushed forward behind me and something hit my head and my shoulder; I covered my stomach with my hands, as if that might help protect you. But this meant I lost what little balance I had as they pushed, and I fell forward another step, though my feet were no longer touching the ground. I was being suspended between the bodies in front, behind and on either side of me, which were all crushing in, the bodies of strangers. Still I could not see Katrina or your father. Indra's voice echoed across the different loudspeakers along the brand-new ghats, and was therefore unintelligible to me; it was as if he were speaking complete nonsense, some made-up language.

'Run!' someone shouted. Or: 'Bomb!'

Perhaps the terror, in retrospect, was the fact that there was no actual attack, that it was simply the crowd, its sheer size and density, that caused all that chaos and damage. People were trying to climb up the floodlights, they were crawling up the fencing. The voices that I could hear were begging for an end, but we could not stop – it was not me pushing into them but all the people pushing into me. I could not control what was already happening, what my body was being forced to do. It was and was not my fault that, at a certain point, the fencing before us broke and several people fell into the water, and the people behind them, too, for the pressure of the crowd persisted, and people had to push back and fight, they had to kick and punch for some of the pressure to cease, and some attempted to pull others out of the water, but not everyone could be reached, not everyone saved. More fireworks were going off, or was that gunfire? And Indra was as close to us now as he would be, waving and smiling as his boat progressed from our right to our left, west towards the river's mouth and the sea. The crowd swelled again, to get closer to him, and more shots were fired and another flare, compounding the panic. Quickly, the tide turned and the current flowed back away from the river towards the narrow exits. I didn't have the time or the space to turn to face the direction of travel, and, as I was pulled with the people, I looked out at the river, at Indra disappearing beyond the reach of the floodlights and back into the darkness.

We were one body moving with the properties of liquid overspilling its container, water with nowhere to go but forward, away from its source, though we were moving uphill then, up towards the gates. We were eight people per square metre, we were nine, we were choking on our own breath, words lodged in our throats, and I was fighting to breathe, turning up to the sky to gasp. At the front of the crowd, up against the heavy-duty security fencing, broken ribs were piercing lung sacs, people who had nowhere else to go but forward into the metal were imprinted with the pattern of the grating, their skin gashed in perfectly straight lines, and they were dead, had been dead for minutes, and the people being forced into them were dying and those who were pushing into them could not know what lay ahead, and kept on towards the gates. They had to get out, they couldn't possibly stay among the threat of a bomb or a knife, some other attack, and I looked towards the screens, the celebrations continuing downstream, Indra smiling and bringing his two palms together in greeting.

I managed to scream your father's name and I was not looking, was unable to look where I was stepping as I heard a cracking underfoot, or rather I felt it, and I managed to glance down as I was forced forward to step again and I saw that I had stood on somebody's face, somebody who had fallen, and

I had crushed her nose and the person behind me was now stepping on her too, and the person behind her, for there was nowhere else to put one's feet, and no option but to move, to move forward, to be moved.

It became clear that we had to stop, that we had to struggle to turn the current, but when I pushed back, I was one body against the whole, I was nothing. I couldn't continue without resisting, I had to push back, even when it was futile, when all action was useless. As I struggled against the people screaming, gasping, I was hit – hit in the throat, and then in the ear – and I was kept upright by the crowd, I did not fall, I couldn't. As the fight broke out around me, one pure soul, some saint, helped to lift me up as the crowd started to slacken a touch, and, instead of being crushed, my body rose, floating upon the surface of the crowd, and drifted.

I woke up in an empty hospital room. There was a TV and a view of the New Lothal skyline: it must have been expensive. Different tubes sprouted out of me, connecting me to a range of apparatus. There was a tube in my mouth, bending down into my throat. I could not speak.

The next time I was conscious, a nurse was present; seeing me blink, she rushed out of the room. The doctor appeared and, when she spoke, I heard her voice as if in slow motion: 'You can hear me?'

It hurt to nod.

'OK,' she said. 'This will be a lot to process. Several days ago, you suffered a blunt trauma to the larynx. We conducted an emergency laryngectomy and have removed your voice box. All points towards a good recovery.' I pointed to the pen in her top pocket. She gave me a pad of paper and, with great effort, I wrote your father's name.

'He's fine. He's always here, and your friends. They've been by your side. We'll put out a call.'

It's a point of shame, thinking back, that it wasn't the first thing I did, but when she said that, I touched my stomach. The slight bump was still there.

'And baby is good and well,' the doctor said. 'We've been doing tests.'

When I came to, the television was on and I could see footage of people queuing for polling stations. The news channel showed the Saraswati festivities, crowds cheering and people dancing. I was not surprised, noting the specific channel that had been put on, that there was no footage of the crowd crush. To anyone who was not there, who was tuning into channels like this, the day would have been simply yet another success. Indra bringing people together, delivering on campaign promises. They played a clip of the speech that Indra had been delivering from his boat as he approached the end of his journey in west New Lothal, and I turned up the volume with the remote.

'The man who can see the future is he who has a full understanding of the past. He can see that history is not a line like a road, but a circle. Where there has been darkness, there will once again be light. The rain will fall on the parched fields. The water will flow again!

'In the coming weeks, we have the chance to return our country to its former glory, once and for all, in a record term. What have I promised that has not yet been delivered? I promise only that which is foreseen. I vowed that we would reshape our country to fit what had once been, and we have redrawn the maps the way they used to be. I promised that this great river would be returned to you all, and look where I am now! I promised to turn the desert green and to build towns where villages once stood. And now, look around at this city, inspired by one that has not existed for thousands of years! No matter the evils that come our way, no one can rid this great land of its indigenous people, of its culture that stretches back continuously, further than any other on the planet. It is from our way that all others are descended. Let us not be ashamed or afraid to celebrate that. Let us not hold back in our affirmations. I have sailed the length of this mighty river and I have seen many thousands of great people. I see now before me not a unity among different people, but *one people*. Not a collection of states, but *one country*. Not a list of possibilities, but *one future*. Stay—'

I pressed mute.

I could hear somebody breathing. I slowly turned to my left and saw Katrina next to me, sleeping. I couldn't make a noise with which to rouse her – the pipe was still down my throat. I tried to touch her but couldn't reach. I knocked on the side of my bed, louder, louder.

'Oh my God!' she said. She took out her phone and made a call. 'She's awake,' she said. 'Yes, now!' She turned to me. 'I'm so glad you're OK. Can you hear me?'

I gave her a thumbs up.

She held my hand. 'It's all going to be OK. And the baby – I can't believe you didn't tell me! We've been so worried, but it's turning around!' She sighed. 'We've spent too long visiting each other in hospitals, you and I.'

I had all these things I wanted to say back to her. She kept talking. She and your father had managed to stay together in the crush, and had come out relatively unscathed. There were dozens of missing people, probably more – outside the country, it was being reported on as one of the worst crowd-crush disasters in modern times.

Your father burst through the door. He kissed my forehead, and my hand.

'I'd just left,' he said. 'Why do you always wake up once I've left? Every time I'm here, you're sleeping ...' He took a long breath. He tried to force a smile, and then stopped.

I squeezed his hand. His forefinger was dyed violet by an electoral stain.

Often, your father would read to me – books he was enjoying, or that he remembered I liked, or the news. Rinderpest had been eradicated, he said, there were no new cases. *Varuna III* had reached the International Space Station. There was mounting pressure for Kush Bhatt to be dropped by Indra's party.

Satnam, I thought, eyes widening. Unable to interrupt him, I listened to your father move on to the cricket.

Sometimes, he'd read messages that had been sent to me – 'Your producer is calling this the most impressive reason for a writer missing a deadline. She sends her best' – and once, when he came with his family, he spoke into a special microphone his sister and brother-in-law had bought him. The speaker – which his sister had pre-loaded with recordings of prayers – attached to my stomach, so that you could listen. Your father overwrote one of the tracks and introduced himself to you.

'Earth to baby,' he said. 'Do you copy?'

I could direct his conversation by writing questions on a pad of paper. When I was finally discharged from the hospital and returned to our apartment, I found that he'd kept all those little scraps, all those questions.

Still?
How are we paying for all this?
Election?

Your parents?
Can you ask for the nurse? Toilet

360

How long will Katrina be gone?
Can you change the channel pls?
Is something up? How was your day?
Sure?
I like your new hair
Stop! Ticklish
What would your first real meal be if you were in my shoes?
Seriously? Can you change the channel – something funny?
Itch! Left leg
Lower
Work's OK?
Can you turn the volume up when you leave?
So, no landslide?
The lengths I would go to to eat some momos
Seriously, it suits you
How many dead?
Curtains?

Eventually, I'd been given a whiteboard and an eraser, and there was no more record of what had been said beyond that. And now I can remember only those conversations I wrote down on paper. It was like your father said: we didn't study the cultures who wrote on slate.

I wasn't out of the hospital that long before I was readmitted. Your father and I were walking along the river path when my waters broke. It was hot, and I was incredibly uncomfortable. My sweat stank in a way it never had before, and I was conscious of being in public. Conscious of people looking at my throat. But, after being stuck inside for so long, I wanted to get out as much as possible. The liquid ran down my leg. Again, your father didn't panic, even though you were early.

I endured the entire labour without the ability to cry out. Perhaps it was my silence that meant the midwives worked quietly. It felt like it was happening to somebody else's body, even if the pain was only mine to bear. And when I first saw you, you could have been somebody else's baby, any child, but then they lifted you above me, and it felt like you held my gaze, son, however briefly, before slowly opening your mouth to make a sound.

The first human words were sounds we made in shocked response to natural events, I read in the taxi as you slept. You were nine months old and I was finally getting round to the parenting books. I was taking you to see the phulkari exhibition at the Folk Museum before it closed.

The first people mimicked clapping thunder, crashing waves – first in wonder, perhaps, and then in warning. We shaped our mouths to form the sounds of animals, faking their calls to lure them in our hunts.

We read the language of their trails, runes of broken twigs and paw prints. We drew the shapes of our prey in our dwellings, as if making them abundant on the walls of the caves would make them abundant on the plains.

After the first stories, we began to pray. Those first cave drawings became ideograms, and then rebuses, which evolved into syllabaries, and then, around four thousand years ago, in the fertile crescent, the phonetic aleph-beth. And when the East/West stone was discovered, the first Saraswatian glyph in the sentence was the cow. Its shape was not too dissimilar from the ox of the Egyptian hieroglyph that became the aleph in Hebrew – the face of the bull and its horns still seen in the upturned A. The first symbol of the first alphabet, which spread from Sumeria to Greece and Rome and the rest of the world, the aleph was not a sound itself but its absence, a glottal stop. But when the symbols travelled west and became the alphabet, the alpha bore no links to cattle, it was just a shape, a letter abstracted from the world, a uniquely human invention.

Language was thenceforth what separated us from the world, allowing us to imagine things beyond what we sensed, giving us dominance over all we named, the fish of the sea, the birds of the sky, and all the living beings that crept on the earth—

You woke up crying. I'd have to change you as soon as we arrived.

I sat on a bench and observed members of the public interacting with the work that meant so much to me. They paused briefly to read snippets of the text before wandering on, scanning a few pieces, very occasionally stepping forward for a closer look at the stitching.

Often, they skipped the final room.

There were several moments when the gallery was completely empty save for you and me, and I got a glimpse of what it must look like each night at closing time, the works hanging in the silence after the cleaners had been through.

A young man, maybe sixteen, with long, thick hair, spent much longer inspecting the pieces. He was wearing a bright red jacket with golden zips, and brand-new sneakers which squeaked with each step on the polished concrete floor. He stopped to take some photos of the pieces on the opposite wall, and then joined us on the bench. He busied himself on his phone, and I took mine out, too. I went on to my feed and was instantly shocked. The first thing on my timeline, posted forty-five seconds ago, was a picture of the opposite wall. The teenager was the only other person in the gallery; it had to be him. I looked across at him. He was gaunt, with sharp cheekbones and the feeble beginnings of a teenage moustache. He had strong, thick eyebrows, like you, and he subtly smiled as he scrolled. I looked down at my phone. The image had been posted by @Daily_Arushi, with the caption: *Always take Arushi's recs seriously. This exhibition is a wonder. Perfect ending to my year in NL!*

I didn't follow the account personally, or Arushi's, but I suppose the algorithm knew I was a fan. I clicked on to the profile. One hundred thousand followers. The pinned post, from a year ago, included a screenshot of a notification: *@Arushi_official is now following you!*

In another life, I would have started a conversation with him. Maybe I would have explained my involvement in the exhibition. But I didn't want to have to go through the pained effort of speech. My new approximation of it. We sat in silence, and then he received a phone call.

'... Yes, bro. Abu Dhabi, I don't know, this time tomorrow. I think Zayed International. Yeah, they sorted me out.'

I liked the teenager's post and picked you up.

In the museum cafe, I met the curator. The phulkari craft workshops had been a success, she said. 'Even I started to get the hang of it.'

A select few pieces would tour together, she said, to some small galleries in Europe, and the rest of the works would be returned to their owners. Now that they had all come together, I could see a kind of beauty in the dupattas being spread back out across the world, as if the little golden lines connecting them in the gallery would now stretch across the continents. The curator held you and you gripped her finger, making nonsense sounds. 'How old is he now?'

I paused, and pressed down on the stoma at the base of my throat before replying.

I had to vibrate my food pipe to generate sound through the stoma. My voice appeared foreign to me, coming from some other animal. It was low and coarse, and it saddened me to think this would be the only sound you would associate with me, that you would never truly know what I had once sounded like.

'Nine months.'

The oesophageal speech sounded a little more human than it had when I'd first left the hospital. At that point, I was

364

only using the electrolarynx. I'd put the vibrating device to my neck, above the point where I normally felt for my pulse, and when I pressed the button and moved my mouth, I could speak in a robotic tone.

Your father liked to mess around with the electrolarynx, putting it to his own throat and saying to you, 'I am your father,' like Darth Vader. How we laughed whenever he put it to your little neck and you giggled! My new laughter meant breathing heavily in and out of my nose.

I had all these things to say to you, but to speak took such effort. It would take me an age to push out a full sentence. And in that lag I grew endlessly frustrated – disgusted, even – opting instead to type.

Already you were babbling, making sounds that meant something to you. Our first language is our own. You would grow frustrated that I couldn't comprehend whatever it was you were trying to communicate. At which point you'd revert to our shared language: crying. A cry could mean food, sleep, poo. An animal sound, for animal things.

Whenever I tried to cry, I had to force myself to press on my stoma to achieve some semblance of catharsis. It was as much about the release of air as it was sound.

I should have been speaking to you, I knew that. I was being a terrible mother. I should have been singing nursery rhymes to you, I should have been telling you I loved you. I was jealous of your father, how he talked to you. Jealous of him describing his day. I hated the baby sounds he made with you, those pathetic noises, and how warmly you responded to them.

I was glad that my work was solitary, that the only professional relationships I still had, with my agent and my editors, could be maintained solely over email. A few foreign papers wanted me to write about my experience of the Saraswati Puja, but I didn't know how to turn it into anything. The podcast had been put on hold for obvious reasons. While I was fine for it to be read by someone else, the producer felt that only my 'authentic voice' would connect with listeners. Your father agreed.

Many of the friendships I had made over the course of the research could survive with just the written word. Katrina and I kept up our correspondence over lengthy text chains as she travelled around Chagos with her new team, quelling the spread of the ants. They were now able to work on all the islands apart from Diego Garcia. Nathu emailed from his new home in the Great Rift Valley. He often went up to Lake Turkana. The lake, which had been larger every time he'd seen it over the past few years, had finally begun to shrink back down to what had once been its normal size. He sent me pictures of the tops of old buildings re-emerging above the surface. He was enjoying the slower speed of things, he said, and had begun to attempt to grow vegetables. *Making use of my trusty spade.*

Gyan and I occasionally messaged, but she was often busy with the band. *The world feels larger and smaller,* she said, midway through the tour. *Each place is unimaginably different, but everywhere has a McDonald's. We spend so much time in hotel rooms that the most noticeable change is the plug sockets.*

Harsimran had become quite the poster on social media. He'd set up his own business as a personal trainer and put out home workout videos on YouTube, which your father and I tried and failed to follow along with.

I received one letter from Satnam and never heard from him again. The envelope was full of seeds. The note read: 'Indirect sunlight, water weekly – SSH.'

The one person who refused to communicate with me using the written word was your father. Probably at the instruction of my speech therapist, he always encouraged me to use my new voice. Even if he had some small message that could have been a text while he was out – doing the groceries, say, or taking you to his mother's – he still called, forcing me to speak. If I was silent while we were together at home, he might even press my stoma himself.

'You can't just turn me on,' I said.

'I sure can,' he said.

If I laughed silently, through my nose, he might tap his neck, signalling for me to be vocal.

'Your laughter is my favourite sound,' he'd say. 'I want the little one to hear it, too.'

Having worked as a freelancer for so long, I'd grown accustomed to the day's quiet sprawl. But caring for you often made me want to escape the apartment while your father was at work. Outside the apartment, I could break up the rhythm of chores, washing your clothes yet again, rinsing the bottles, dusting surfaces. Out in the world, it might seem like I was a person on the way to or from somewhere. But I was only ever leaving and returning to the house, to the to-do list. I'd take turns at random, trying to get a better sense of this city to which I felt little connection. The only way to know a place, your father would often say, was to get lost. But, try as I might, I always ended up circling back to a familiar road, or path, down into the same park, the same yoga instructors conducting lessons on its gentle slopes. At the top of the hill, I could see the river bisecting the city: the residential streets on this side, and the offices on the other. Rush hour every morning and evening generally meant a crossing of the river. In the distance, I could make out the city gradually merging with the sea, in the western district. I pushed you on, walking from the park's heat into the cool shaded streets. I was outside the guarded perimeter of the free port when I received the text from your father. It was unlike him not to call.

Are you OK? Tell me now.

Then: *Is this real?*

I replied: *On walk. What's up?*

He phoned me a few seconds later.

'You're there. You're OK? Tell me. Just tell me!' I'd never heard such panic in his voice.

'Yes! What is this?'

'Everything's OK? The baby?'

'Yes,' I said.

'Tell me what we did on our first date.'

'What's got into you?'

'Tell me.'

'We went for brunch. Then you took me on a boat ride. Canned G & Ts. The boat rocked and you spilt your drink all over yourself. And, from the bridge, we rented e-scooters, went around in the rain.'

He let out a deep breath. 'You won't believe what's happened.'

He'd received a call from an unknown number while at work. On the other side of the line, he'd heard me screaming. Then a man's voice, saying he'd broken into our apartment, listing the exact address. The man said that he had me at knife point. And that your father would need to make a bank transfer for him to leave us alone.

'What was wild,' he said now, on the phone, 'was that it was your voice. It was really you. But, obviously, you before the surgery. You sounded exactly how you used to.'

The scammers had cloned my voice, likely using clips from the audio recordings of my articles that were published online and the podcasts I'd appeared on.

Your father started to cry. 'It sounded so real.'

'Where are you? I'll come to you.'

'If it hadn't been for the surgery, I wouldn't have known it wasn't real.'

'Take deep breaths,' I said. My throat was hurting. But I couldn't cut the conversation short.

After that, we changed our passwords and froze our cards. I started to plan my daytime walks so that I would end up at your father's metro exit in time for his commute home. To see your father's face materialise from a crowd of faces, my one person, that still held its magic. To see him briefly as a person in the world before he saw me, that subtle shift in his eyes right before the smile of recognition – that could turn a day around.

I am still, after so long, fascinated by the person your father was before me, and sometimes I'm even jealous of those who've known him longer than I have. The person you love is a stranger before you meet – they've lived a whole life before you arrive that you'll never quite be able to access, and so they will never be fully knowable to you. And, holding you, waiting for him to come up those stairs, I realised that this relationship is reversed between a parent and a child: the person you know so well, who you see for almost every single minute of the day, begins, gradually, to fade from you, in snatches at first, going to nursery for the first time, and then school, and then they begin to live a portion of their life purposefully hidden from you in their teenage years, and will, inevitably, one day, live an entire part of their lives beyond your view. The person you become after I die will be a stranger I won't ever know.

Standing with you in my arms, waiting for your father, as the rush-hour crowds streamed out of the station, I felt over-come by the fact that there were all these thousands of people inaccessible to me, all our lives rubbing up against each other's without ever crossing, and I felt that the love I had for your father and for you could have been so easily missed, if I hadn't met Nathu, or hadn't received a call about the death of my father, if I hadn't heard about Sejal and Jugaad, if a thousand things hadn't happened in the very sequence they had. He might have been nothing to me, any one of these blurring faces, and it might have been some other man I was seeking out now, some other child against my chest. And, by that notion, I no longer felt afraid of all these people, but experi-enced a kind of diffuse love. Men like your father were among these faces, women like Katrina and Gyan, people who had been strangers to me, who I had come to trust, and as long as that were true, I should love these people, unknown to me, as if I might one day know them. I pressed on my stoma to cry, and let my harsh sobs sound out, and it felt good to shape the air. Then, suddenly, miraculously, your father's face appeared, coming up the stairs. He was listening to music and nodding his head as he walked. I decided right then that I must begin to speak to you, son, in whatever voice I could muster.

I'd sing to you, awfully, and would read to you, more often than not from a book of origin myths I had once bought for your father – we had both agreed not to bother with children's books until you really asked for them. As I spoke, you would reply in your private language. It took me a while to build the strength in my voice to last an entire story. With each word requiring such effort and force, I would often edit down the stories in my mind as I spoke them, or else would stop when my throat began to hurt or when I had to clean the mucus from my stoma.

'Kintu, the first man, in the time before time, wandered the empty earth with nothing but his cow. He walked across the land until Nambi and her younger sister fell from the heavens ...'

'And after the rime dripped, there sprang from it the cow called Audhumla; four streams of milk ran from her udders, and she nourished Ymir.'

'But the Emperor was furious and he called the Mountain God to trap the dragons beneath a mountain. But they managed to escape as rivers, bringing water to the people.'

'... If you take a stick a foot long and every day half it, in a myriad ages it will not be exhausted. A single grain of millet makes no sound upon falling, but a thousand grains make a sound. A thousand nothings can become something. And the rain fell, forming an audible chorus as ...'

'Roog created the world by speaking: "Water! Air! Earth!"'

'Mangala made four pairs of seeds for the four winds, and from the seeds came an egg, and in the egg were the first people.

But Pemba, determined to dominate the world, broke free from the egg early, and he ripped out a piece of his placenta and that became the earth ...'

'Viracocha breathed into stones and made the first people, giants with no brains, whom he destroyed in a flood ...'

'The first people were a brother and a sister, and the brother hit the sister with a fish and ordered her to multiply, and she gave birth to a child every seven days ...'

'In the beginning, the world was a vast swamp, home to a giant trout, and the world was placed upon the trout, the movements of the trout, the movements of our waves ...'

'And Guthi-guthi put one foot on Gundabooka Mountain and another one on Mount Grenfell and looked out at the land which was bare and dry. He called to Weowie, a water-serpent who was trapped in Mount Minara, but there was no response.'

'And Saraswati did not like the advances of her father, Brahma, and ran from him, and Shiva didn't like it either, and beheaded Brahma so he couldn't look upon her, but Brahma sprouted another head and another, so that he could look both heavenward and in every direction of the wind, and so Saraswati went to the one place where she couldn't be seen, down to the earth, where she became a river, the greatest of rivers, bringer of floods, and Brahma, turning earthwards, found her once more, and so Saraswati disappeared beneath the ground, running all this time beneath the earth, waiting until it was the right time to reappear, which was now, right here,' I said, as we walked towards the river's mouth.

Your father and I had taken you on a day trip to the coast on the western fringes of New Lothal. We pushed you along the river path, and it was unclear whether we were walking upon solid ground or floating above the surface of the sea. We headed towards the largest of the artificial beaches. It was a hot day, and the wind off the water was strong and welcome. While your father went off in search of food, we watched the world pass from a bench. I wasn't sure how far you could see by then, what shapes you might have been making out. I spotted a spider on your arm and flicked it away.

There was a border between the dark fresh water of the Saraswati and the greyish salt water of the sea. People were swimming, venturing towards the line, and tentatively crossing from the sea into the river and back. Some teenagers were diving off the pier, daring each other to attempt flips. You would never have known, looking out at the bright scene, that miles north a war was beginning. Somewhere, not far from here, soldiers were stepping into their uniforms, tightening their belts. They were putting keys in ignitions, checking directions.

I wished I could have brought you into a better world. But was that not a sentiment expressed by every generation of mothers? Right back unto the first people of the plains, there must have been mothers who wished that things were better, as they ran from known dangers to unknown hopes. I removed your dummy, tickled your chin.

Your father returned with two paper plates of steamed momos from a nearby vendor, and some tea. I cut one of the dumplings open to let out its hot air. Now that you were a year old and my throat had recovered, the two of us were officially on solid foods.

'Yes,' I said.

'Yes,' your father said.

While he and I ate, you became restless, and I gave you my empty paper cup to play with. You fidgeted, and then fell back on to my lap. I lifted my finger to my stoma, but before I could say anything, you opened your mouth to form what was, for the first time, not a noise or a sound, but a word.

Acknowledgements

I might not have started writing this novel, and likely wouldn't have got it to this stage, were it not for the initial vote of confidence from and the continued support of my editor, Luke Brown. Thank you.

Thanks, too, to Mehar Anaokar for the detailed edits, and to Laurie Robertson for the advice. I'm grateful to everyone at Serpent's Tail who helped turn my manuscript into a book, and to those who worked to get it into your hands. Thank you, Rowan Cope, Steve Coventry-Panton, Jonathan Harley, Sarah Kennedy, Robert Loyko-Greer, Rosie Parnham, Penelope Price and Sharona Selby.

I am grateful for the wealth of research I could turn to after I started writing this book, particularly about the Saraswati river. For readers looking to find out more, I'd recommend Shirley Abraham and Amit Madheshiya's *Searching for Saraswati* and Michel Danino's *The Lost River: On the Trail of the Saraswati*.

Much of the book was written before and after work, in cafes and tube carriages, and I'm thankful to Helen and John Stott for providing me somewhere quiet to work when I needed to finish my edits.

In one sense this is a book about searching for family and community, and I'm very lucky to be as close as I am to mine. Thank you to my parents, Jasvinder and Kulwinder, and to my brother, Haraman, for your patience and encouragement.

And for the invaluable motivation, the infallible support and for all our energising conversations, thank you, Holly Stott.